JUST LIKE ANIMALS

———— WERELOCK EVOLUTION ————

HETTIE IVERS

Just Like Animals
Copyright © 2018 Hettie Ivers www.hettieivers.com

Cover: Najla Qamber Designs www.najlaqamberdesigns.com
Photo: Wong Sim
Model: Mitchell Wick

Please be advised that this book contains sexually explicit scenes and graphic language. If such content offends you, please do not read.

ISBN: 978-0-9994405-2-0

Join my newsletter mailing list to hear about new releases, author giveaways, and ARC opportunities!

http://bit.ly/HettieNews

ABOUT THIS BOOK

Although *Just Like Animals* is Book 5 in the Werelock Evolution Series, it may be enjoyed as a first read or standalone within the series. It is not essential to have read *Werelock Evolution: The Complete Trilogy* or *No Light* prior to reading *Just Like Animals*. That said, having read the books that precede this one may enhance your enjoyment, as those who are familiar with the earlier books in the timeline will pick up on a few jokes and references that will be lost on new readers. This book also continues the broader overarching storyline of the series.

Please be advised that Hettie Ivers has a tendency to see satire and irony everywhere, and she has never met a foul word or raunchy euphemism she didn't like. *(With the exception of "baby batter"—which remains a hard limit for her.)* This book contains violence, foul language, adult content, and a lot of over-the-top werelock characters. If such material offends you, please do not read. *(Or read it and be offended, if that's your bag.)*

CHAPTER 1

Raul

"**S**IR, CAR'S OUT FRONT."
I nodded in acknowledgement, but my feet were rooted to the cement floor of the club, my eyes transfixed by the gyrating blonde as I tried to determine if I was seeing things.

Nope. It was definitely *her*. And she was drunk off her ass. Of that there was little doubt. Yet she still displayed an enviable natural rhythm out on the dance floor—with that barely clothed, to-die-for body that I had found myself jerking off to in memory on more than one occasion over the past ten years. More times than was probably healthy, given the fact she was strictly off-limits.

More than off-limits. She might as well have been taboo. Maybe that's what made her so attractive? Or maybe I was just a masochist.

Her girlfriends appeared equally inebriated. Men surrounded her like vultures. Two of them were putting their hands on her. I took a step closer without thinking. Then another.

"Sir?"

I rationalized that I just wanted to confirm it was really her, to see her up close … make certain she was okay and that she had a safe ride home. I told myself I had only pure intentions *this time*.

I'd checked up on her over the years and knew that she'd completed medical school and was now finishing her residency at UCSF Hospital. And that she was engaged. A fact that came back to me in a blinding flash when she flung her arm up in the air and the enormous rock on her finger caught the flare of the strobe light.

She was engaged to some big-deal society schmuck. Silicon Valley trust fund baby trash. I'd seen their cheesy engagement photo spread all over social media seven months ago and had pegged the guy a class A douchebag at first sight.

She'd looked radiant in the photos. Better than I'd even remembered. And happy. So fucking happy. A fact I'd had conflicting feelings about at the time.

She didn't look happy now, though. And once again, I felt conflicted over this observation.

Sure, she was grinning as if having the time of her life, throwing flirty bedroom eyes at the men dancing with her as if she hadn't a care in the world. *As if she wasn't engaged to be married.* But those eyes were red-rimmed and puffy beneath their well-applied makeup, and lined by dark circles. They looked more green than blue. She'd been crying hours earlier. I was sure of it.

My inner animal took over. Before I knew it, I'd nudged the guy at her back out of my way, my hands had encircled her tiny waist, and I was yanking her lush, round ass into the swiftly growing ache in my groin. *Definitely a masochist.* I delivered a mental push accompanied by a flash of yellow eyes to the asshole in front of her when he looked up to glare at me in protest. He did a double take and nearly tripped over his own feet trying to back away as quickly as possible.

I felt her body stiffen against me, a trickle of alarm tightening her muscles, a sliver of fear tainting her perfect scent. It only made her smell more edible. I groaned as my jean-encased cock swelled and lengthened against her ass, along with my canines. She attempted to pull away from me. And though it irritated me, at the same time I was quietly pleased. Impressed that even drunk she possessed strong survival instincts.

When I failed to release her, she tried to crane her head back to see who had taken hold of her and had scared off her dance partners, but I hauled her little body tighter in against mine to prevent it, my forearm crossing her chest, my palm caging her throat. I didn't want her to recognize me.

Not yet. I wanted a moment between us where there was no history to get in the way. Where we could be two strangers dancing in a club, and I could pretend that I had a chance with her.

"Relax." My thumb stroked back and forth over the rapid pulse beating in her neck. "One dance and I'll let you go. Promise."

I'd weighted my words with Alpha energy, and yet they sounded half-command, half-plea to my own ears. Regardless, they seemed to reassure her enough that the tension in her body dissipated. And soon that delicious body all but melted into mine as our hips began to move as one and my roaming hands took liberties they shouldn't have. I couldn't stop though. Not when I scented what it was doing to her. How wet she was getting beneath the scrap of material she was wearing.

She had one of those flimsy, strappy dresses on that looked and felt more like a form-fitting slip. Silvery pale grey in color and barely long enough to hit her upper thighs. My hands slid over the silky smooth material like they had every right to, feeling every hard ridge of muscle and soft mound of flesh that lay beneath. She wasn't wearing a bra, and the temptation to explore her breasts— to feel those diamond-hard nipples through the thin fabric of her dress right there on the dance floor—was more than I had strength of will to resist in the moment. Not when all the blood in my brain had already rushed to my cock.

She was tall for a woman. Lean and fit but still curvy where it mattered most. And my God, those fuck-me legs! I remembered the first time I'd really noticed them. She had been fifteen and wearing a cheerleading uniform. And I'd never been able to look at her the same way since.

Those lean, muscular limbs looked about a mile long now in six-inch designer heels that she wore as comfortably as if she'd strutted out of the womb wearing them. I wanted to lick the length of those legs. I wanted to feel those toned thighs locked around my waist.

Clenching around my face.

Christ, I was a liar. There was no way I was letting her go after one dance.

She'd begun making those beautiful moan-y, breathy, I-need-to-come noises that only a woman can make, and I was close to losing my shit, debating whether to teleport us to privacy or sink my dick into her right there on the dance floor and worry about erasing the minds of onlookers later.

I looked down and saw that one of my hands was rubbing her upper thigh.

And it was wet.

Her thigh. Was. Wet.

I told myself it was only sweat from all of the dancing she'd done. And if I'd been human and unable to smell the difference, I might've convinced myself. But my other hand had wandered up under her dress from behind and was rhythmically squeezing and exploring the flesh of her thong-clad ass cheek, rubbing its way toward her hot, needy center—where she was *dripping wet.*

Fuck me, I needed to stop.

We needed to stop.

But instead, I brushed her hair aside with my chin until my mouth found her neck, kissing and sucking her perfect skin. She moaned and arched into me, and then she rubbed her ass up and down along the length of my erection.

Once.

Twice.

I'd been so wrong before. The girl possessed no survival instincts whatsoever.

None at all.

Because she drew my hand that was on the front of her thigh straight up under her dress to her soaked pussy, and she came against my fingers before I had time to register what was even happening.

My mind blanked, retreating to a dark, desperate, possessive place where there was only the sound of her erratic, panting breaths, her frantic heartbeat, and the sensation of her fluttering, wet clit pressed against my fingers, her cum soaking my palm as I sank my canines into her neck.

CHAPTER 2

Raul

Bloody hell, I'd bitten her!

She spun around to face me, her hand clutching the side of her neck. Pink hit her cheeks the moment her startled eyes met mine, and she gasped. "Holy baby Jesus in a filthy fucking manger."

Despite the seriousness of the situation, my lips twitched helplessly at her outburst. "I'm so sorry." I cleared my throat to keep from laughing. "I don't know what came over me, Bethany."

"Raul. *Wow.* Wow, oh, wow." She shook her head continuously, staring as if she couldn't fathom that it was me. "Holy shit. Oh, my God. Oh, my Gawwwd. Wow. I didn't know you were *you* … and you … didn't know that I was *me*." She explained it aloud to herself. "I mean—obviously. Because I never would've—and you never would've—I mean—we, *we* never would've …"

Damn. She was cute all flustered, gesturing wildly with her hands as she rambled on.

"I'm sure what you experienced was a moment of shock. Panic? Exactly," she confirmed to herself. "Panic.

It was reflexive. Instinctual. A PTSD response. Yes." She snapped her fingers as if she'd found the explanation for it all. "I read about how this happens to individuals who are orally fixated. I read it in a medical journal somewhere. I think. God, I don't normally get myself off on strangers' hands ... in uh ... ahhm ... pub"—she trailed off as she watched me suck my fingers into my mouth, tasting her—"lic."

Fuck me. That taste. Definitely not letting her go. I hummed and nodded. Her jaw fell open. I took advantage of the opportunity, pulling my fingers from my mouth and slipping them into hers before she could object. I used her moment of stunned inaction to lower my head closer to her shoulder and assess the damage I'd done to her neck, whispering, "You taste fucking delicious, Bethy," next to her ear on the way down.

I was no expert in mating bond bites by any stretch, but her neck didn't appear to be as bad off as I'd initially feared when I'd tasted her blood in my mouth. Certainly not the way I imagined a mating bond bite would look.

Huh. Maybe it hadn't been deep enough to be damaging or significant? Somehow I felt disappointment at this rather than relief. I was sick.

I licked over her broken skin a few times, partially healing it with my saliva. Then I kissed the spot. "Didn't mean to hurt you." I pulled back to look at her. "You were just so hot. I got carried away."

Her eyes were dazed, her pupils wide. Her lips had closed over my fingers. When her tongue moved tentatively against them, I feared I might bust a nut in my pants. I vowed that I would come in her mouth before the night was through.

"I'm afraid you're going to have a hickey for a few days," I advised. *Or a few weeks.* Or maybe a lifetime? Best guess was one of the three.

Her hand reached up and lightly grasped my wrist. Slowly, she pulled my fingers from her mouth, giving them a timid, parting suck as they passed between her plump lips. I was absolutely coming in her mouth before the night was through.

"It's late. I should go."

Hell to the no. "Of course. I understand. But maybe you could buy me a drink first? So I don't go home feeling cheap and used."

Her eyes widened and she turned so red I feared she might pass out.

"Kidding, Bethy." I held up both palms. "A joke to lighten the mood. But I am serious that we should have a drink and catch up a bit."

She looked unsure. And entirely too sober all of a sudden. I couldn't have her overthinking this.

"Look, if we try and ignore what just happened, it'll only be more awkward the next time we run into each other, don't you think?" I reasoned. "C'mon, we're old friends. We can handle this like two responsible adults, can't we?"

"Hi, Bethany's friend," a slurred female voice broke in, bringing too much perfume with her into our personal space.

I endured introductions to several tipsy girlfriends. To my annoyance, Bethany introduced me as her "best friend's brother." It shouldn't have bothered me. It's what I was to her. It's what I would always be to her.

Unless I'd bitten her too hard.

We got drinks and found a quieter spot tucked away from the dance floor. She was still flustered, but she put up a good front, plastered on a bright smile, and proceeded to catch me up on her life, confirming mostly facts that I already knew.

"So I'm finishing my residency, and I'll be opening my own gynecology practice next year."

"That's amazing. Congratulations." The reminder that she stuck her fingers inside of other women's pussies for a living wasn't helpful when I was still struggling to get my mind off of hers.

"I adopted a rescue puppy last week, I'm getting married in three months, and I just couldn't be happier," she concluded.

"Wonderful. Where's the fiancé tonight?"

"Who?"

"Your fiancé." My eyes slid to the giant princess cut diamond on her finger in indication.

"Oh." Her eyes lit with understanding. "Oh, you mean Gregg? That fiancé?"

I frowned. Nodded. "There more than one?"

She broke into high-pitched, nervous laughter. "No, no, it's just the one," she confirmed, punching me playfully in the arm. "You were always so funny." She sighed and took a sip of her drink. Then she took another sip that turned into a chug as she downed the remains of the glass.

"Gregg's cheating on me," she announced with the next release of air that escaped her. "Not that it's an excuse for me to use your hand to masturbate myself on a dance floor or anything."

"I see." They were the only words I managed as conflicting emotions and a million thoughts jumbled through me. How hard had I really bitten her? Could I get away with killing Gregg without upsetting her? Would I be able to resist biting her again if she continued to make reference to coming on my hand?

"It's just—you were touching my breasts," she continued in a rush. "And I'm really into nipple play. And then you were rubbing my thigh … and your hands felt so good everywhere on me that I had this mad impulse to come on them. I always preach that women should follow their sexual instincts. So I did. Would you excuse me a moment?" She didn't wait for my reply before jumping up from her seat and bolting in the direction of the bathroom.

Jesus. She was the same Bethany I remembered. Adorably quirky. Strong-willed. Unconventional. Sexy as hell.

And I was fucking her tonight. Off-limits be damned.

CHAPTER 3

Bethany

"IT'S NOT OKAY TO SHAG YOUR BEST FRIEND'S BROTHER."

"What?" Jessie's petite, freckle-dusted nose wrinkled up in the bathroom mirror to my right. "You don't have a brother."

Ugh, she was too blitzed to be helpful. "No, Jessie, that's what you're supposed to say to me right now." I snatched the lip balm out of her hand. Lip balm was always helpful.

"You mean that big hot guy?" Kylie squawked in the mirror to my left. "Raul? Mr. orgasm on the dance floor? Of course you're going to fuck him. Who gives a shit who his sister is?"

The three of us were holed up inside the one large handicap-accessible stall within the women's bathroom that contained its own sink and mirror, steadfastly ignoring the irritated remarks about us hogging the "good stall" that were coming from ladies who were waiting in line for an open one.

"You both suck. How about you remind me that I'm *engaged*, huh?"

Kylie snorted. "Bitch, remind yourself. You just ate an

entire PocketPak of Listerine strips. If that's not a commitment to fuck someone who isn't your fiancé tonight, then I don't know what is."

"If I had a brother that sexy, I'd totally let him fuck you," Jessie interjected.

"Okay, not helpful. That just came out creepy, Jess. You got any cheek stain or cream blush in your bag?"

"You're as pink as a vagina already." Kylie shook her head, studying my face in the mirror. "You don't need cheek stain. You need to get revenge-laid tonight by a sex god and then call off your engagement tomorrow morning."

"I am not calling off the wedding."

"Then I'm wearing a slutty red dress, raising my hand, and objecting."

"You will not. Marchesa doesn't make a slutty red bridesmaid dress."

"I can't wear red," Jessie spoke up. "It clashes with my skin tone."

"No one in the bridal party is wearing red."

"I will," Kylie insisted, reapplying her eyeliner in the mirror. "And the minister will agree with me when I show him photos of the groom's dick on my cell phone."

Jessie gasped, and the mass of red hair she'd been working into a French knot fell to her shoulders. "Gregg sent you photos of his dick, too?"

Kylie groaned.

It took effort not to roll my eyes. "Jess, *I* sent the photos of his dick this afternoon to you both from the texts I found on his phone that he'd sent to another woman." She still looked confused. Jessie was a genius medical researcher when sober and a complete moron after a few cocktails. "Never mind. I'll tell you tomorrow."

"It won't sound any better then," Kylie told her.

"Gregg and I will work through this."

"Mm, I dunno …" Jessie gave me an uncertain look in the mirror. "There's really no good medical fix yet for a small penis."

Kylie narrowly avoided stabbing herself in the eye with pencil liner when she burst out laughing.

"His penis isn't small," I said in defense of my cheating fiancé. "That was a bad photo. It wasn't quite … to scale."

"No? I thought his hand provided just the right scale, actually," Kylie snarked.

"Couples get cold feet and have flings before they tie the knot. It happens all the time," I argued.

"Keep telling yourself that." Kylie swept her shoulder-length dark hair back into an oversized clip and zipped up her wristlet. "Come on, Jess, let's dance." To me, she said, "I better receive a high-res photo text from you of the best friend's brother's dick by zero eight hundred hours."

"Ha! Right. Because that's happening. There an 'or else' you were going to tack onto that ultimatum?"

"Yeah." Her sly smile spread into a wicked grin. "Or else maybe I'll be the one taking photos of his penis." She wagged her brows at me in the mirror and ushered a confused Jessie out of the stall.

"Oh, come on," a female voice complained with a noisy rap on the stall door when I remained inside, closing and locking the stall after Jessie and Kylie had departed. "I'm supposed to piss myself out here while you're busy make-up-ing and debating whether to cheat on your cheating, small-penis-having fiancé?"

"Holding it in is great exercise for your Kegel muscles," I responded absently, drawing closer to the sink mirror than I'd had the ability to do before when Jessie and Kylie had been sharing it with me. "Trust me, I'm a gynecologist," I mumbled as I drew my long blonde hair to the side and inspected the fresh love bite on my neck.

It didn't look like more than a really serious hickey, but I could've sworn I'd felt a strange throbbing sensation deep beneath the surface of the wounded skin when Kylie had joked about being the one to hook up with Raul. I made a mental note to inject a little antibiotic in a few days if it continued to feel tender.

"So, what are we going to do about your cheating ex?"

We? Cute. "I don't see why my problems need be your problems, Raul. Appreciate the big brotherly concern on my behalf, though."

"There's nothing brotherly about it, I assure you."

The way his eyes ran over me made my mouth run dry, even as I swallowed the burning whisky from my glass. He didn't look like he'd aged a day, and yet he was so much hotter than he'd been the last time I'd seen him. There was a certain calmness and maturity to him now—an air of authority that hadn't been there before.

Ten years. It'd been ten years since he had shown up out of nowhere at my parents' front door in Santa Cruz, flanked by two equally tall, well-built hotties. They had invited me to come with them to Argentina to attend a surprise party they were throwing for my best friend Milena—Raul's little sister. It seemed like yesterday, and yet so very long ago.

My memories of that day were still mystifying. And not simply because of how odd and abrupt Raul's appearance and invitation had been, or even because of the bizarre and shockingly uncharacteristic way that my mother had immediately consented and even *encouraged* me to go with Raul and his friends to South America, of all insane motherly reactions.

No, it was the way Raul had first looked at me standing out there on my front porch that day: Like a drowning man looks at a lifeline. Like my aunt looked at limited-edition Louboutins. *Like my dad still looked at my mom when she wasn't paying attention.*

In hindsight, I often wondered if I'd only imagined it.

Raul had gone on to flirt with me, gifting me with that self-assured, dashing smile that I'd seen cause dignified, married female members of the PTA to blush clear down to their toes back when he was in high school and I was still in elementary school. I knew that smile had melted the panties off of countless girls before me. But even as his mouth had casually flirted, going on about how well I looked all grown up and saying how much fun we would have in Argentina, his eyes had reflected something else. Something dark. *Fearful.* Some kind of desperate, internal struggle. He'd stood there with his hunky Argentinian friends and said everything he could to entice me to go with them. But his eyes had warned me not to come. Pleaded with me to say no. It hadn't made sense.

And of course, it had only made me more determined to go. To show him what a truly great time we'd have together and erase that strange fearfulness lurking behind his imploring brown eyes. To this day, I still couldn't reconcile how in the world my eighteen-year-old self had ultimately found the strength of will to choose the more mature, sensible course of action and decline his most exciting international party invitation. I'd often wondered (and fantasized) over the years about what might've happened between us if I had gone with him that day instead.

"How's your mom?" Raul's deep voice and change of topic pulled me back to the present.

I'd been staring at him. And it would appear that he'd been studying me right back. But while I was certain I'd been gawking at him with an empty, glassy-eyed look—*and maybe drooling on myself*—Raul's brow was pinched in concentration. He seemed to be considering me as if I were a brain-bender puzzle that he was working to decipher. A complex combination lock whose code he was determined to crack. Weird.

"She's good," I answered automatically. "Thanks for asking."

"Your parents still live in the same house in Santa Cruz?"

"Yep. Same one." Oh, God. We'd regressed to polite catch-up conversation already. This was depressing.

"They're still together then?"

"Uh-huh." Don't remind me. Why would he even ask that? "They just celebrated their thirty-third wedding anniversary." I smiled brightly, like it was a wonderful thing.

He gave me a sympathetic smile in return, nodding his head. "I'm sorry. Bearing witness to unrequited love is almost as painful as engaging in it."

Fuck. And there went my heart.

I felt it. As sure as I felt the growing chasm splitting my loyalty.

How could Milena claim that her brother was perpetually clueless, insensitive, and inherently selfish when Raul was capable of noticing something so personal about my parents' relationship—*her* best friend's parents—that no one else ever picked up on? *Not even Milena.*

How had Raul known? He'd never even spent much time with them that I could recall. Or *any* time with the two of them together, actually, now that I thought about it. Had he picked up on it solely based on my reaction? On something I'd said to him in the past?

"Shit, I'm sorry, Bethany." He pressed a hankie into my hand just as I felt a tear escape my right eye.

What the hell, I was crying now? I quickly dabbed my eyes and pulled it together. Brilliant, Bethany. I'd steered us from boring catch-up sesh into awkward maudlin territory.

"I shouldn't have pried. That was wrong. You're entitled to your privacy. I'll stop. I won't try it again."

What was he talking about? Why was he so apologetic? "No, no," I assured him with a laugh, "it's just the whisky, see? It burns my throat and then my eyes have this reaction." I took another big gulp to further support my stupid explanation, making a show of squeezing my eyes shut and wincing as I swallowed. Oh, my God, I was acting like an ass.

I opened my eyes to catch him draining the contents of his own glass.

"Cheers to fucking emotional shields," he muttered under his breath as he brought his empty glass down onto the tiny café-style table between us with a clatter.

Emotional shields? "What's an emotional shield? That a new psych term?"

At first he seemed taken aback. Then he answered simply, "Yes." His expression was hard and impassive, despite the polite smile he forced. "It's a new theory related to protective instincts where one's emotions are concerned," he expounded. "It's a good thing for a person to have strong emotional shields."

He'd totally just made that shit up. I went along with it anyhow. "If it's such a good thing, then why'd you toast-slash-curse emotional shields just now?"

His eyes held mine, but he didn't answer. And behind his shuttered features I sensed that same desperate internal struggle playing out—warning me to run while begging me to come closer.

"What are we going to do about your cheating ex?" he repeated his earlier question. But this time he spoke the words slowly. Carefully. And their meaning seemed to have changed entirely. Because the question sounded sensual now. Sexual. And I knew that he was really asking what we were going to do about *us.*

There could never be an "us."

Raul's sister had been my best friend since kindergarten. Sleeping with her only brother would be in poor taste. Particularly when I knew how strained things had been between them for more than a decade.

The sad truth was things had been strained between Milena and me for nearly as long. Just not in the same way. Raul and Milena's kind of strain was the overt, bitter Cold War kind, whereas mine and Milena's was more the tragic growing apart, slow-death-of-a-childhood-friendship kind.

The last time I'd seen Milena, her husband Alex had given me a warmer reception than she had. As the years had passed, she and I had spoken on the phone less frequently. Half the time when I called I ended up talking to

Alex longer than I did my best friend. I often felt like I was bothering her, or that she didn't want to hear from me. She never opened up to me anymore, and I couldn't seem to get straight answers out of her whenever I questioned her about her life.

Sometimes I got this niggling sense in the pit of my gut that Milena was mad at me for some reason. That she resented me for something that I had done. But for the life of me I couldn't figure out what it might be. She was the one who had left *me*. If anything, I should've been resentful that she'd gotten engaged at eighteen after a whirlwind romance with an older Brazilian guy—a multi-bajillionaire businessman who had swept her off her feet in record time, prompting her to move to São Paulo and alter all of her plans for college and her future in the blink of an eye.

But I couldn't blame her. And I would never resent her. Alex was near perfection in human form. He was everything Milena had ever needed in a partner and male figure in her life. More importantly, he adored her. *Worshipped her.* Hung on every word that came out of her mouth and fretted over every frown that wrinkled her brow. It would've been disgusting were it not so damned cute.

I was happy for her. For both of them. And because of that, I overlooked the fact that Milena's husband Alex was probably most definitely for sure a Brazilian mob boss. *Who had once been Raul's boss,* I reminded myself. Which meant that Raul might also be mixed up in the Brazilian mafia. And everyone knew it was bad form to sleep with a Brazilian mobster who was also your best friend's brother.

I cleared my throat. "I never said Gregg was my ex."

"Excuse me?" Raul's eyes narrowed. His voice had dropped an octave.

Whoa. *Hot when angry.*

"Look, Raul, I haven't even given Gregg a chance to explain himself yet."

"Explain himself?" Raul's nostrils flared, and I could've sworn that his irises lightened for a split second. Then a phone went off. "What's there to explain?" He retrieved a phone from his pocket. Without so much as checking to see who was calling, he pressed a button to silence it and set the phone on the table. "He cheated. He's fucking history."

Protective much? God, he was getting me wet all over again. He was only Milena's half-brother. Did sleeping with half-sibs really count?

"It's more complicated than that," I said, squeezing my thighs together to tamp down the pulsing in my sex.

"No, it's not, Bethy."

I got distracted staring at the angry line of his luscious mouth and momentarily forgot what we were talking about, because I blurted, "I like it when you call me Bethy."

I liked it when he got all angry and protective, too.

His phone vibrated against the table. I glanced down to see a FaceTime request from "Princess Elsa" flash across the screen. He quickly declined it and flipped the phone over, screen side down to the table. He ran a hand through his hair. "Bethy, I—"

It buzzed again.

"Did you want to get that?"

He sighed and shook his head, looking annoyed. "It's just work. It can wait."

He had programmed his work in as *Princess Elsa?* "That was work? At this hour?"

"How long has he been cheating on you?"

Five months at least. "I'm not sure."

"How many?"

"Times?"

"No. Women."

Ouch. "Can we talk about something else?"

"Fine. Let's start with his address."

I groaned and downed the remains of my Johnnie Walker. "How about we start with another drink?"

"Deal," he agreed as a man in a suit was approaching our table. "Stephen, I'm busy," Raul said, not bothering to turn and look at him. "Go order us another round, and then go back and wait with the car."

The man stepped forward nonetheless, extending a phone.

Raul's jaw tightened. Slowly, he turned and leveled the man he'd addressed as Stephen with a look so cold it made me want to recoil.

"Sir, I apologize for the interruption."

Sir?

"But she's threatening to blow cities up unless you sing the *Frozen* song with her. Chaos wants to talk to you about it."

Huh?

With an infuriated eye-roll, Raul stood and yanked the phone from Stephen's hand. To me, he said, "Please don't go anywhere. I'll only be a minute." I got the impression, based on the weighted glance he threw at Stephen, that it was now also this man's job to make certain I didn't go anywhere.

Which might've explained the weird manner in which Stephen just stood there watching over me after Raul was gone, like he was guarding my person.

"Hi, Stephen. I'm Bethany." I extended my hand to him in greeting. He nodded once in acknowledgement but didn't take my hand. "Please, have a seat," I offered, gesturing to Raul's vacated chair with my awkwardly outstretched hand. He kept standing. *O-kay* then. I gave him my biggest, brightest I-can-win-you-over smile. "How do you and Raul know each other?"

It was clear the man worked for Raul in some capacity, but I wanted him to confirm it. He didn't. *Fine then.* New tactic.

"So what's with the 'Sir' business?" I asked, raising my volume to a level that ensured I would be heard by as many people as possible around us. "Are you Raul's sub? It's all good with me if you are," I told him when he looked momentarily stricken by my public outing. That's right, buddy, this girl is not so easily deterred. *And never ignored.* "You can be his full-time bitch. I'm only planning to use him for revenge sex tonight. Possibly tomorrow morning, too, if he's as good with his cock in reality as he is in my imagination."

"I'm better," Raul's voice startled me as he abruptly returned and reclaimed the seat across from mine, passing the phone back to Stephen, *his rankled sub.*

Stephen walked away, leaving me alone with Raul: my best friend's super-hot, totally off-limits older brother whose cock I'd just admitted to fantasizing about. And who was now assessing me with an intensity that made my clitoris hum. I knew I needed to stop this flirtation and steer him back into the best friend's brother safety zone fast. But instead, I quipped, "I have a fantastically pornographic imagination."

The corner of his mouth lifted, but the intensity of his gaze didn't falter. His face was directly in front of mine now, although I wasn't sure how that had happened. Nor was I certain how or at what point his hand had wedged itself between my thighs underneath the table. Yet there it was. Inching ever closer to my soaked panties. "I'm counting on it, Bethy. Why don't we fuck all weekend and see whose imagination is dirtier?"

"I—I'm on call this weekend."

"I'm happy to pay by the hour."

"Being on call at the hospital doesn't work like that. I'm in medicine, not prostitution."

He laughed. It was a beautiful, throaty sound that somehow made me feel like whatever we were about to do was okay. Made everything that was wrong with my life and this entire situation feel less overwhelming and scary.

But God, I really didn't want him to be in the Brazilian mafia. My hand shot down to halt his between my legs.

"I don't like violence," I told him. "I can't sleep with a mobster."

He pulled back to look at me but didn't withdraw his hand. I couldn't read his expression. At first it looked like confusion. Maybe regret. But then he reassured me by saying, "I'm not a mobster, Bethy."

"Really?" It came out overly eager. Hopeful. "So what do you do for work?"

He frowned. "Lately, I ah …" His eyes flitted about, scanning the club. "Well, I guess you could say I work as a teacher." His brows drew together. "But I'm more like a friend and mentor," he clarified, his free hand scrubbing over his jaw. "For a special-needs child. She's ah … a prodigy. Highly intelligent. Super-talented. But she has difficulty with … social interaction."

Oh, fuck, there went my heart again. And my grip on the wrist of his hand between my thighs. "Wow. That's such important, commendable work, Raul. I never even knew you'd studied special education. Is it normal for you to get calls from your students on weekends and late at night?"

"Mmmm … no, it's a unique situation in that I more or less mentor my current student full-time." He grimaced slightly. "I'm more like … a manny."

"Come again?"

"A *manny*. You know, as in a male nanny?"

"Oh. That's so … progressive of you." I sounded out of breath. It was both the shock and relief of his revelation and the fact that his fingertips had just grazed my outer pussy lips through the thin fabric of my thong underwear. *I could do this.* I could have revenge sex on my cheating fiancé with my best friend's half-sib who was employed as a manny. "So sensitive of you …"

I gasped as his fingers yanked the strip of silk fabric aside to skim along my naked, drenched slit.

"That's right, Bethy." His breath was warm against my ear. "I'm still the same sweet, progressive, male-feminist surfer who grew up down the street from you in Santa Cruz."

"You were never that sweet." I was panting. "You fucked most of my babysitters."

I felt his laughter against my neck as one of his fingers entered me.

Oh, yes.

"Caught you making out with one when I got up to get a drink of water once." Why was I still talking? *How* was I still talking?

"And now you *are* a babysitter," I pointed out, unable to resist taunting him over the irony. *Because I loved to hear him laugh.*

He didn't disappoint. He chuckled over my earlobe caught between his teeth. The sound made me feel warm all over. Safe.

His thumb found my clit. Another finger was working its way inside me to join the first, and suddenly I felt so hot and needy. *Full inside.* And yet so greedy for more as he began to work his fingers. *Exploring.* Stretching. Moving smoothly in and out.

"And now *you're* the one I'm going to fuck, Bethy." He said it like it had already happened. "Here. Now. In the middle of this club."

CHAPTER 4

Raul

SHE CLENCHED WILDLY AROUND MY FINGERS THE moment I said it, confirming what I already suspected: *Bethy was a closet exhibitionist.*

Fuck.

I pressed down hard on her fluttering clit and smothered my growl against her neck.

I couldn't pull her into my lap fast enough as she proceeded to moan-squeal and fall apart, squirming against my palm, scrabbling blindly for any piece of me that she could get her hands on.

Damn. The girl knew how to orgasm.

She soaked my hand riding out her bliss. Her fingers wound around my neck and her mouth crashed into mine, initiating our first kiss—*for the second time.*

I took what she offered like it was my last fleeting chance at salvation. Consumed her lips as if they were the one truth left in the world that could expunge the bottomless void of pretense, regret, and disappointment that permeated my existence.

She had no memory of the first time we had kissed

My sister Milena's pack had seen to that. Bethany's memories of the forty-six hours she and I had spent together in Argentina and Brazil ten years ago had been wiped out almost as soon as our time together had ended. A fact that I was both resentful of and eternally grateful for.

They were some of my worst life memories. Also my best.

And this—our *second* first kiss—was every bit as soul-shattering as the one we'd shared those many years ago.

Not simply because she tasted better than any woman I'd ever known. Or because having her mouth fused with mine had the bizarre effect of making me feel like I was breathing for the first time in my life. It was the utter lack of artifice in the way her tongue laid waste to mine, sucking it into her own mouth and devouring it on an unladylike moan.

What made Bethany so great—what had separated her from all other girls in my mind since that first kiss we'd shared on a dance floor in Argentina—was the same thing that still set her apart from all others: *She was real.* She wore her heart on her sleeve and waved it at the world. When she kissed me she threw every emotion she had into it.

I felt it. And it felt more genuine and pure than anything I'd experienced before or since that first time she'd kissed me.

My wolf felt it, too.

The urge to bite Bethany again grew stronger the more she clung to me, her soft body melding into mine, rubbing against me where I was most vulnerable … and hard as a fucking boulder. I fought the urge, asserting authority over my wolf each time her perfect scent caused my eyes to shift and my mouth to water, each time the bold thrust of her tongue against mine taunted my canines to breach the surface of my gums. She was kissing me now as if she couldn't wait another second to have all of me inside her. Still, somehow I managed to keep my wolf's darker, more possessive urges at bay.

Until my little exhibitionist wedged her hand down the front of my jeans and wrapped her slim fingers around my cock.

"*Fuck.*" I said it aloud that time as I felt my balls draw up and my canines extend down. I swiftly broke our kiss and angled my face away from hers, pressing down on her head and her shoulder with a disjointed, "In your mouth. Now."

My words came out gruff and demanding, like a command, and I wanted to flay myself. I'd just ordered sweet, totally off-limits Bethy to get on her knees and suck my cock in a crowded dance club.

Squeezing my eyes shut, I prayed enough blood supply would make its way to my brain that I might formulate the right words of apology—the means to salvage this blessed insanity unfolding between us.

But then I heard her murmur, "Yes, *Sir*," with a playful giggle, and I felt her slink down the front of my body to her knees on the floor between my thighs.

There was a God after all. And miracle of all miracles, he didn't completely hate me.

I lost more blood supply to my giddy brain as Bethany made quick work of the button and zipper of my fly, allowing my grasp on my wolf to slip even further as more of my pack members on guard throughout the club drew stealthily closer, surrounding us. I sensed uneasiness emanating from some of them, along with the scent of Stephen's blatant disapproval. I directed a low growl of warning at the backs of several heads—a reminder to check their opinions and keep their feelings to themselves.

I was Alpha, whether my perpetually disapproving head Beta Alcaeus thought me worthy of the title or not.

Alcaeus had likely tipped Stephen off to the danger of who Bethany was after our phone call. If he hadn't, then Mike had surely said something to Stephen and the rest of them. I'd scented Mike's anxiety the moment I'd stepped onto the dance floor. None of my men had any objection to public copulation, so it could only be an objection to my choice of partner.

It didn't matter. I wasn't stopping this.

Even though a nagging voice in my head insisted that they were right: I shouldn't be doing this. That Bethany could never be mine … *that she would hate me if she ever learned the truth of what I now was—not to mention what I had done ten years ago.*

Nothing else mattered as Bethany's perfect pink lips wrapped around the head of my cock.

Not Sloane's tantrums. Not Alcaeus's dire warnings. Not the fact that we were in a crowded, noisy club where someone might catch us, or the reality that I was now set on a path that would no doubt lead to the motherload of all fucking disasters.

As she swirled her tongue and moaned around my shaft, sucking me farther into my mouth, I gave in to my wolf's fantasies, reveled in his visions of biting her repeatedly as I indulged in my own fantasies of fucking her senseless, claiming her in every way, again and again. By some miracle, I managed to keep my hold gentle on her head, willing my fingers wrapped around her blonde hair not to squeeze too tightly as she bobbed up and down, bathing me in her saliva.

When her mouth came off my dick with a pop and she babbled something or other about my "beautiful penis" before lowering her head to suck one of my balls into her mouth, I knew I'd commit murder to keep her. Go to war with my sister's pack if they tried to take Bethany away from me.

She was mine.

And I may have growled it aloud as I pulled her by the hair from my exploding balls and back onto my cock, forcing myself between her parted lips and clear to the back of her throat as I erupted with a sudden violence.

Gentle! Be gentle, I reminded myself too late.

It registered that I had her nose pressed up against my groin, my fist locked in a death grip at the back of her head, and I'd pushed myself partway into her throat.

She needs to breathe, I reminded myself. She's *human. Fragile.*

I was still coming, but I told myself I had to let go and pull away. That it was too much; I was scaring her. I might hurt her.

Then I felt her swallowing, her throat pulsing around my spurting head, milking my cum while working my cock farther down into her throat like a goddamned porn star, and I nearly lost all semblance of self-control, my hips lifting off the seat to thrust fully into her mouth to fuck her throat. "Ah, yes … fuck yes! Fuck … fuck … *fuck* …"

That's it. I was marrying her.

She was perfect. We were meant to be. Amid a moment of blinding euphoria, it hit me that this was what true love must feel like.

And I might've said some of those things out loud, because a few of my men actually broke form to turn around and look at me.

I barked at them in Portuguese and they quickly recovered, righting themselves. But the intrusion into my blissed-out Bethany bubble served to jolt me back to reality, helping me to regain my eroding self-control.

Pulling my still mostly rigid cock from the heaven of Bethany's throat, I swept her off the cold floor and into my arms, kissing everywhere but her mouth while she panted for air. And the moment she'd filled her lungs with sufficient oxygen, my mouth was stealing it back again until she was breathless once more.

"Your turn," I told her.

Setting her ass down on the edge of our small café table, I eased her onto her back, keeping her spread legs hooked over my forearms to hold her up and open for me as the scrap of silk she called a dress pooled at her waist, leaving her exposed—in nothing but a thin, soaked-through thong that I was seconds away from ripping apart with my teeth.

Her glassy sky-blue eyes fluttered open, and as her dreamy, dilated pupils focused on me, a surprisingly shy smile kicked up the corners of her swollen lips. But then some sort of comprehension passed over her features, as if she was just now remembering where we were, and her eyes skated about, dazedly taking in the broad backs of my security detail surrounding us on all sides, forming a tight superhuman wall that shielded us from prying eyes.

Confused, slightly guarded blue eyes returned to me. I saw fear there. And a whisper of accusation.

Aw, hell.

I swallowed. "Friends of mine," I reassured her. Not a complete lie.

Her brow furrowed. She glanced from the huge men encircling us back to me with a look that called bullshit. I saw the wheels turning. She was thinking they were mafia.

"It's the truth," I insisted. There was no way we were stopping now. "We're all in town for an international … manny … convention …"

Eh, fuck it. I dove for her pussy.

CHAPTER 5

Bethany

I HEARD THE SOUND OF FABRIC RENDING. HOT BREATH fanned my bare sex, and an even hotter tongue licked up the length of my slit before ever so lightly circling my throbbing bean—like a predator toying with its prey.

Heaven have mercy.

My pelvis arched off the table and I grabbed fistfuls of Raul's hair with both hands as his soft lips closed over my detonation button.

He sucked it into his mouth, and my whole upper body practically shot up off the table. When my shoulders crashed back down again, he was eating me in earnest, making rumbling, growling noises against my center as he rhythmically sucked at my clitoris.

Oh, God …

It sounded like a wild animal was feasting between my thighs. And somehow something about that was so hot and dirty. *So utterly delicious.*

I was strung so tightly already from the experience of swallowing his huge, gorgeous cock in public—surrounded by his super-built "manny convention" friends, no less—that my orgasm hit me hard and fast the moment he began fucking me with his fingers.

My head flew back over the edge of the small table, putting the taut, well-formed ass of a manny directly in my line of upside-down sight, just as the sounds of a woman screaming for her life assailed my ears.

Upside-down forms moved closer in a blur of motion. A large, masculine hand clamped over my mouth.

It wasn't Raul's.

When the woman's screaming abruptly stopped, but the animalistic growling between my thighs vibrated to new heights against my overly sensitized clit, it clicked that *I* had been the one screaming.

I started coming all over again as more unfamiliar male hands fastened onto each of my biceps, securing my flailing upper body to the table. The stranger covering my mouth spoke hoarsely in my ear, telling me to be quiet and calm down.

Calm down?

Mid-orgasm?

Panic set in. At the same time … my arousal skyrocketed.

Raul was definitely in the mafia. They all were. These big, built "friends" of Raul's weren't international mannies at all.

And they were holding me down because all my squealing and freaking out was clearly causing Raul to wig out, I realized. The growling near my nether region had grown louder. *Angrier*.

Yet it also seemed as if Raul was freaking out because his men were touching me—judging by the harsh-sounding words now being exchanged in Portuguese over my head and vagina. His mouth had relinquished my nub to the cool club air; his fingers had ceased pumping. And despite everything else going on around me that I should've been more panicked over, a sad, involuntary whimper escaped the back of my throat at the loss.

"Ah, fuck, no—"

The stranger covering my mouth had an accent, I noted, seconds before I was stabbed in the inner thigh and his words faded to white noise amid the deafening ringing sound that permeated my ears.

My vision went black and my body completely rigid.

I'd been stabbed! And the pain was blinding.

How had I been stabbed? My brain function grew foggy as I attempted to process it, and my body quickly followed suit—a sense of lethargy pervading my system.

I'd been roofied *and* stabbed?

But ... Raul had been right there—between my thighs. His huge manny-slash-mafia men had been surrounding me. How had they all failed to prevent me from getting stabbed and roofied right in front of them? It didn't make sense.

Faintly, I heard the accented man talking in my ear. Saying nice things. Comforting things about me being fine. Safe. He was no longer covering my mouth but stroking my cheek, and my head was cradled against his shoulder.

I couldn't get my eyes open; they were too heavy. I was too relaxed. But I told him I'd been stabbed and drugged, and that I needed to get to a hospital. My voice was so quiet I couldn't hear it over the loud music of the club. He heard me, though, because he reassured me that I hadn't been stabbed. "Just a love bite," he said. "No drugs. No hospital. All better now."

My thigh did feel better. Raul was sucking on it now. Healing the knife wound. Or ... love bite. *Whichever.* He was making a satisfied groaning noise as he did it that was really sexy, too. The more I focused on it, the more turned on I became.

"Raul won't hurt you," the foreign manny-mafia-man holding my head said. "He just needed to calm down."

Oh.

Right. That made perfect sense. Raul liked to bite people when he got anxious. I remembered it now—how he was orally fixated and that I'd decided earlier it must be his go-to PTSD response to bite people.

I'd overreacted. It was just a love bite.

A love bite on the thigh was hot.

As was the sensation of Raul's fingers as they resumed moving inside of me, and the scent of so many big, powerful men surrounding me—the notion that multiple pairs of male eyes were possibly about to watch me orgasm again on a little metal table in a crowded nightclub.

It all felt so dangerous. Yet at the same time, the unseen men around me made me feel safe. I could pretend they really were international mannies entrusted with the care of special-needs children.

Or vicious criminals entrenched in the Brazilian mafia.

Either way, I'd later claim to have been suffering bite-induced PTSD hysteria myself for taking up a breathy chant of "fuck me, Raul" when his thumb began flicking my slippery clit.

Accent-manny groaned in my ear as my dress was shredded straight down the middle. And then I was wrenched away from his hold on my head altogether as my body slid forward, my hips were lifted off the table, and my spread legs were pulled up around Raul's waist. The fat head of his cock pushed into me without further preamble, and as slick and turned on as I was, it was still an uncomfortably tight fit.

Hallelujah!

I always told my female patients that size didn't matter, that it all came down to skill and the right chemistry. But it did. It so fucking did.

Raul's fingers dug into my ass cheeks, raising me higher and holding me steady as he grunted and thrust forward, pushing deeper.

I gasped at the delicious burn, and my heavy eyelids flew open.

I might've been delirious with lust, and this public sex situation all kinds of twisted wrong, but I wasn't about to miss the sight of Raul Caro, my best friend's super-hot, totally off-limits older brother, former neighborhood man-whore, and despoiler of innocent babysitters—*who was presently either a really important manny or a dangerous mob boss*—as he rammed the length of that huge, infamous penis of his inside me for the first time.

I just didn't count on his eyes glowing a shade other than brown back at me when I gazed up at him. Or on seeing two long, sharp canines extend farther than the rest of his front teeth as his lips pulled back and he growled down at me.

And I definitely didn't expect him to sink those dagger teeth straight into my left tit as that legendary cock of his penetrated me to the hilt in one fast, fluid movement.

CHAPTER 6

Raul

Pure. Fucking. Heaven.

So tight. So wet.

That grip! Her pussy felt like a damn fist as it squeezed around me.

Devouring me. *Claiming me.*

I claimed her right back.

My canines had never known such bliss. If it were possible for canines to orgasm, then mine had just shot the load of the century into Bethany's perfect breast.

My cock had never felt so hard, so long and swollen. It was as if my wolf was aiming to root as deeply as inhumanly possible inside of our woman.

My woman. *My Bethy.*

Human Bethy.

Fragile Bethy!

Oh, fuck.

I caught the sound of a muffled whimper. Her heartbeat—it was so loud and fast. I could feel the pulse of it in my mouth. The smell of fear had mingled with the scent of her arousal.

I forced my canines to withdraw. I kept my feral eyes closed as my hands ran soothingly over her soft form—which had gone stiff beneath me.

Please be okay. Please be okay.

Gently, I sucked the bite wound on her breast to heal it, and a strange taste filled my mouth. I ran my tongue over my retracting canines and tasted the same.

Shit. Did that mean something?

What did that mean? I vaguely recalled tasting something similar after my wolf had bitten her thigh.

I kept sucking, trying to figure it out. And she started moaning again. *And clenching around my cock.* I really needed her to stop that while I was trying to restrain my inner beast—*and failing.*

My hips jerked forward. Then pulled back. I gripped her thighs and pressed forward again, forcing myself to go slower this time.

She arched her pelvis up to meet me, and I wanted to shout with happiness and relief. When she clenched around me once more, tighter than before, I was back to trying to restrain my beast nature as I thrust hard and fast into the cradle of her beautiful thighs.

Jesus H, the woman knew how to work her Kegels. Sweet, fragile Bethy was owning my dick, even as she was the one getting plowed by a powerful werelock. She was the sexiest woman I'd ever known.

And I was keeping her. I was killing her fiancé and I was keeping her.

I moved inside her like she was already mine, giving her everything I had. And she took it. *Like a boss.*

I shifted her leg higher, changing the angle of my entry. She bit her lip and moan-squealed. She was making her breathy, I-need-to-come noises again, only louder now.

I was ready to explode.

"Oh, yes … oh, God, Raul …" She gasped my name and started clenching around me like a fist again, staking her claim as her release was broadcast to everyone within supernatural hearing and scenting range.

And I lost it.

My canines fully extended. My feral eyes opened and held her bleary, euphoric gaze as I pounded into her tight, strangling channel, fucking her through her orgasm without pause or care for her human frailty—or the fact that I was baring my true animal nature to her—as I chased my own release.

I felt my balls tightening up. A tingling sensation that had nothing to do with werelock magic ran the length of my spine and a rush of semen shot through my shaft as I rode Bethany's writhing body toward a completion I realized in that moment I'd been searching for my whole adult life.

Yet as out of control as I felt, I wasn't so far gone that I actually allowed myself to seize that completion. Not fully. *Not yet.*

I wasn't wearing a condom. Despite the many promises to Mateus I'd broken, there was one rule instilled in me long ago by my biological father that I had yet to abandon—even though I knew it no longer made sense to hold onto it, given my werelock ability to avoid disease and thwart pregnancy.

Gritting my teeth and fighting against my wolf, I squeezed the base of my erection as I pulled from the wet, pulsating heaven of Bethany's velvet sheath and shot my load across her stomach and breasts.

The pounding bass of club music couldn't compete with the sound of my own heartbeat as I watched and awaited Bethy's reaction.

Her blue eyes reflected so many things as she stared up at me. Surprise. Recognition. And oddest of all: understanding. She looked more at peace than I'd ever seen her. So supremely sated. Yet I glimpsed confusion and fear rapidly brewing beneath the surface, battling with the resurgence of arousal I knew she felt as I watched her absently swirl her fingers through the cum coating her breasts, before sucking them into her mouth to taste me. Again.

This woman would be the death of me.

I leaned over her, covering her body from view while I used her torn dress to wipe off her abdomen. Though my men had kept their eyes averted, and most were giving us their backs as they shielded us from view of other club-goers, I felt increasingly anxious at having Bethany exposed like this. I needed to get her out of here, and quickly. That meant teleporting.

"You pulled out," she said quietly.

Not the first thing I expected her to comment on as she looked directly into my glowing yellow eyes. But that was Bethy: forever quirky and unpredictable. I nodded.

Without breaking eye contact, she reached up and touched my cheek. Her long, delicate fingers traced a line to my mouth, and I opened for her, resigned to what she was after. I barely breathed as, without fear or hesitation, she slipped a finger inside. But my lips peeled back out of reflex and I was unable to suppress a growl as the soft pad of her forefinger explored the razor-sharp tip of my upper left canine.

She paused but didn't flinch. And she never broke eye contact.

And I was hard as a fucking rock all over again.

"Is this why you and Milena … why you had a falling out?"

I nodded slowly, hyperaware of the delicate fingertip still pressed to my canine. It was the truth. *More or less.*

She swallowed and withdrew her hand. "What … um … ah …"

"Werelock. Subspecies of werewolf."

Her throat worked again, and I nearly lunged for it with the canines she'd just teased. From the corner of my eye, I could see the rapid pulse fluttering in her neck—so close to where I'd bitten her before. My cock jerked against her inner thigh.

"I adopted a rescue puppy last week," she told me dazedly, repeating what she'd said earlier. "I couldn't … couldn't be happier."

I nodded. She was going into shock. "It's okay, Bethy. I'm still the same boy who grew up down the street from you in Santa Cruz. Nothing's changed." Okay, so maybe that was a lie. "I'm going to get us out of here now." I cupped her cheek in my hand, and was elated when she leaned into my touch. "I'm going to use magic. You might feel a strange sensation, but it's perfectly safe."

She looked uncertain. Damn my sister and her pack for the impenetrable emotional shield they'd placed on Bethany's mind a decade ago. This would all be so much easier if I could access her mind to read her thoughts. *And conveniently erase her mind of experiences after the fact— such as seeing my wolf eyes and teleporting.*

"Put your arms around my neck," I instructed. She did

as asked without hesitation, but she still seemed lost.

"I'm getting married in three months," she announced shakily, once again repeating talking points from our previous conversation.

I knew that she was simply out of her depth and attempting to normalize the situation as her mind worked to process it all, but the mention of her douchebag fiancé did nothing to calm the possessive inclinations of my wolf. Or me.

I should have left it alone, but I couldn't. I took a breath and told her as gently as possible, "You're not marrying Gregg." My hips shifted as I said it, my cock instinctively seeking the notch between her spread thighs.

"But I—"

I pushed halfway into her before she could finish that thought. It wasn't up for debate. *She was mine.*

I let my animal nature take over, pushing the rest of the way inside as my mouth descended to her neck. As I tasted her blood on my tongue, I rationalized I was distracting her from the sensation of teleporting in order to make it less scary.

Deep inside, I knew it was wrong to subject her to my fucked-up world. I knew it was selfish to try and keep her. Worse still to try and force it. But my whole life I'd never gotten to have what I really wanted. I always lost everyone who was important to me.

I was keeping Bethy. *This time* I was keeping her.

CHAPTER 7

Bethany

At first, I thought I was dead. For a split second after Raul's teeth attacked my throat, I ceased to exist—my body literally fading into nothingness.

But then I felt Raul. *Everywhere.* Within me and surrounding me—his hard body pressing into my own, his thick cock sliding deep, his hand squeezing my ass, his fingers fisting my hair, his mouth sucking the sting from the side of my neck where he'd bitten me for the second time.

And Raul's overwhelming presence brought me back into awareness of my own physicality, making me feel more alive and present than I had in years—perhaps ever. There was probably a metaphor there for me to ponder. Later.

Beyond the overwhelming scent of Raul and sex, I smelled new leather. The loud music of the club had vanished, replaced by near silence save for the sound of flesh on flesh and our combined heavy breathing. The cushiony leather surface beneath me felt butter-soft against my back as Raul fucked into me.

I opened my eyes to find that he had somehow magically transported us from the club to the inside of a stretch

Hummer. This unexplainable phenomenon, combined with his werewolf confession a moment ago, combined with the fact that he had yellow eyes and had bitten me again, should have alarmed me enough to stop having sex with him.

Should have. But didn't.

I rationalized I was practicing what I preached to my female patients by following my sexual instincts. If anything, I was more turned on than ever.

Danger had always heightened arousal for me. And dangerous, forbidden sex with my best friend's off-limits dead-sexy older brother who was now a werewolf subspecies was hotter than anything I'd ever fantasized about.

So I went with it.

I got on all fours when Raul pulled out and told me to. And I was so blissed out on the sensation of him entering and filling me from behind that I didn't even question where we were going when the Hummer began to move. I didn't say anything when mid-moan, I glanced down at my hands braced against the plush carpeted floor and realized that my engagement ring was missing.

I couldn't bring myself to care about anything but what Raul was doing to me as he rocked in and out of my body from behind, moving slowly, deftly building a delicious, painstaking, coiling tension within me again as his fingers stroked my dripping slit, alternately avoiding and toying with my needy little pearl until my legs and arms shook from my extended state of arousal.

It was only one night. For one night I could let myself enjoy mind-blowing revenge sex. I might hate myself in the morning for this, but right now, it was beyond my ability to stop.

And I didn't want to stop.

Every little thing Raul did, everywhere he touched me, felt perfect. It was as if he could read my mind and knew exactly what I liked—where, when, and how to touch me. From my first orgasm on the dance floor with him, he had exceeded any experience I'd ever had before.

So I didn't say no when the long fingers of his free hand ventured between my ass cheeks to gently massage and probe my smaller hole, wordlessly seeking permission. Instead, I pushed back against those fingers, and I willed my tighter ring of muscle to relax as a single digit carefully entered me.

Raul groaned, his cock thickening inside me when my vaginal muscles jumped and seized around him in response. "Fuck. Ah, baby, yes. That's it."

His breath came faster, his next exhales sounding heavy and labored as slowly he began to work both my holes, all while maintaining a light, steady pressure on my clit. He seemed to understand without my saying so that I hadn't done this before, for which I was grateful.

"There we go … just like that. Stay nice and relaxed for me, Bethy. We'll take it slow. And only as far as you want to go."

A feeling of warmth and security flooded me at the sound of my name on Raul's lips, allowing me to further let go.

It was crazy—the fact I was able to trust him so readily. But in many ways, he *was* the same Raul who had grown up down the street from me. The same charismatic, mischievous, beautiful boy whose imploring brown eyes and sweet, flirtatious demeanor had always called to a special place in my heart. Even now, as he tempted me away from my comfort zone, leading me down a path that felt a little dark and scary, I couldn't help but feel safer knowing I was going there with Raul.

"Tell me if it's too much. I'll stop."

He had to be joking. It was almost embarrassing how well I was gushing onto the blunt fingertips softly stroking my clit now. I was tilting my ass up and back, trying to take more of him, faster.

I had never let Gregg or anyone else near my backdoor before. I'd only explored it on my own once or twice with a slim vibrator—*for research purposes.*

Clinically, I'd long understood that there were more nerve bundles in the rectum than the vaginal canal. And still, when I'd first gone into gynecology, never in my wildest imagination could I have guessed the number of women who would come in seeking medical assistance to remove sex toys and other objects they'd gotten lodged too far up their assholes. Eventually, I got curious enough to try and discover what the appeal was with this taboo erogenous zone. Yet nothing I'd tried on my own had ever come close to feeling like what Raul was doing to me now.

"Fuck, you're so sexy. So wet for me."

He made good use of the fluids rushing from me, spreading them where they would ease his entry as he began to work a second finger inside my virgin ass.

It burned a little, and my body resisted at first, a thin layer of sweat and goosebumps erupting over my skin. But the spike of arousal I felt at the sensation of Raul's cock expanding and twitching within me helped me to push past the small discomfort. As did the excitement I heard in his voice as he murmured words of encouragement, making me want to take more than just his two fingers.

"That's it. Nice and slow. Let yourself get used to the sensation. I'll make it feel so good for you, Bethy. Promise. Fill you up and make you come so hard—"

Oh, fuck. Without warning, my inner walls began fluttering like mad as a powerful orgasm overcame me. I teetered and nearly lost my balance when my right hand flew from the carpeted floor up to Raul's out of reflex to mash his too-gentle fingertips harder against my clit as I exploded, gasping and making little squealing noises as the muscles of my anus proceeded to pulse and clench spastically around the two fingers of his other hand still buried inside me.

"Oh, Jesus … oh, fuck," I babbled. "That's … oh, God, Raul … it feels so good … feels so—"

"Perfect," he growled through clenched teeth, his voice low and guttural. "Fucking perfect." His body had gone rigid behind me, his powerful thigh muscles taut and unmoving where they pressed up against the backs of mine. Only his stiff, engorged cock jerked and twitched involuntarily deep within me in response to the violent orgasm still rippling along my sensitized inner walls, gripping his cock as well as his fingers.

My vision narrowed and my one shaky arm still holding me up gave way amid the intensity of pleasure surging through my core. My forehead met the new-smelling carpet as I rode out the decadent sexual tremors that wracked my body.

I felt an unfamiliar pulling sensation in my womb as muscle tissue deep within my sex pulsated continuously. Every centimeter of the thin, fibrous tissue of my inner walls felt alive with awareness as Raul slowly removed his fingers from my ass, murmuring sweet words as he kissed my back and shoulder.

He reversed the positioning of our hands pressed to my sex, sliding his fingers from underneath mine and pressing my own against my sopping clit. "Keep touching yourself."

It was an order more so than a request. Although I didn't think there was another orgasm left in me, I obeyed. There was something in the way he said it that I was hard-pressed to resist.

"My wolf needs to fuck you now." His words came out soft and tender, belying the startling nature of his declaration. "I can't promise he'll be gentle. But you'll be safe."

I nodded into the carpet, not missing the way my pussy fluttered shamelessly around him—excited by the promise of a rough fucking. I knew he hadn't missed it either.

God, this was wrong.

And hot.

I braced my free hand against the carpeted floor next to my forehead as, true to his words of warning, something in Raul shifted, and a moment later he went from patient, cooing lover to an aroused beast pushed beyond the limits of his self-restraint.

He fucked me hard and fast, lifting my spread knees off the floor to deepen the angle of his penetration as he grunted and growled and drove into me with abandon.

Heaven help me, I was going to come again embarrassingly fast.

"You're not marrying Gregg," he decreed.

Who was Gregg?

"You're mine, Bethany."

I nodded again, his possessive shit-talking making me even hotter.

"You've *always* been mine."

His voice was gravelly, his words certain. They sent an unbidden shiver through me. *Not in a bad way, either.* As crazy as it was, his words rang with a truth that felt bone-deep. A truth I didn't care to analyze too closely in the moment.

My night had taken on a completely unreal quality somewhere between being eaten out in public while held down by international mannies and finding out that Raul was a werewolf subspecies.

"*Say it,*" he suddenly demanded, his grip tightening on my hips, his balls slapping my spread center. "Say you're mine."

"I'm … yours."

He growled and thrust harder. His hand fisted my hair, pulling my head up and forcing my back to arch. "Again."

"*Yours,*" I gasped, rubbing myself faster. I was right on the edge. "Always yours."

"*Mine,*" he proclaimed in a voice that sounded more animal than man. It scared and thrilled me.

"Ask permission to come," he commanded.

Dang. The kinky dom shtick was hot. And I did want to come again. Desperately. But there was something I wanted more, so I defied him and asked for it instead. "I want *your* cum," I told him, my voice breathless. "Filling me. Please, *Sir,*" I taunted.

He groaned and muttered to himself in another language before his hand smacked my rear. He yanked my hair and started pounding into me like the devil. I think I caught the words "dirty bitch" right as my orgasm hit, my pussy convulsing and squeezing around him, my frantic moans escalating, resonating through the cab.

He did come inside me then—partially, at least. He seemed to lose control of himself before realizing what he was doing and pulling out, the last of his hot cum spraying onto my ass and lower back.

He unleashed a string of angry-sounding foreign curse words right before I felt sharp teeth sink into my shoulder.

"*Ow.* No—ahh, *fuck,*" I stammered in genuine pain and panic—even as my orgasm continued—the animalistic violence of his unexpected attack shocking me.

That one had hurt.

And he wasn't letting go. He bit down harder as I tried to pull away, his body bearing down on top of mine, pinning me flush against the vibrating carpeted floor of the moving car.

"Raul? Please." My plaintive appeal seemed to have fallen on remorseless ears when he growled and his jaw clamped down more forcefully upon my shoulder. But as tears sprang to my eyes, his palm fell softly against the side of my head, his fingers curling around my ear in a calming caress. His other hand wedged itself in between my body and the floor to cup the tender flesh between my thighs.

As he sucked the bite wound on my shoulder, his fingers stroked my slippery folds, and I ceased struggling, stilling beneath him and succumbing to his ministrations. A similar sense of lethargy as the one I'd felt when he'd bitten my thigh and my breast in the club pervaded my system. Despite the throbbing sting in my shoulder, I began to feel high. Euphoric. A little dazed and delirious.

He had warned me about his wolf. *And he'd said that I would be safe.* My mind found twisted reassurance in that promise. And my body was finding relief in what Raul was doing to me—the pain and pleasure receptors within me blurring and blending.

By the time his canines withdrew, the pain I felt in my shoulder paled in comparison to the pleasure I was feeling as I came again—crying out as I squirmed against his palm and fingertips.

"That's it, sweetheart." His cock was still hard as the length of it pressed against my ass cheek, pushing me into his soaked hand. *Jesus, were werewolves perpetually erect?*

I was a mass of quivering jelly limbs by the time my tremors ceased, my body a useless, sprawled heap on the floor. I couldn't have gotten up if I'd tried. Raul seemed to anticipate this, because he wrapped a blanket around me and lifted me in his arms.

He deposited me onto the leather bench seat that stretched the length of our enormous ride. He sat next to me but placed enough space between us so that our bodies weren't touching.

He seemed nervous all of a sudden—or worried. But he asked without emotion, "You okay?"

I nodded faintly. I was at a loss. A part of me had expected him to apologize for biting me so hard that last time. When he didn't, I stated the obvious as I angled my upper body toward his. "You bit me again." Something stopped me from asking him why.

His brown eyes met mine: frank and unwavering. "I did." *No apology.* His posture turned guarded. His features followed suit.

"We didn't use protection," I pointed out, my cheeks flushing with guilt over my part in that. "It was irresponsible of me to ask you to come—"

"There's no need to worry." He reached out and tucked

my messy hair behind my ear. "I'm clean. As a werewolf, I can't catch diseases. I won't allow you to get pregnant, either."

I swallowed. "Won't allow?" I parroted with a nervous chuckle. "What, um, does that mean?"

"As a werelock, I can use magic to prevent pregnancy." He produced a fresh Johnnie Walker—that he'd very obviously just materialized out of thin air—and handed it to me, further illustrating his ability with magic.

My pulse spiked, and I released another anxious laugh, but I gratefully accepted the drink. I wasted no time in taking a large gulp before blurting, "What are we doing, Raul?"

His expression remained shuttered, but he gave me a lopsided smile as he continued to run his fingers through my hair, gently detangling the strands. "We're enjoying each other, Bethy. We're headed to your place now, where we'll continue to enjoy one another."

I took another liberal sip of strong alcohol, nearly finishing the glass as I digested his words. He wasn't asking permission. He was telling.

And he already knew where I lived, apparently.

"That okay?" he belatedly tacked on, adding the illusion of choice to my situation.

My childhood crush was now a powerful, magical werewolf creature. What would he do if I said no? Based on the way his men had responded to him back at the club, I suspected he was used to people doing whatever he told them.

Yet I couldn't bring myself to believe he'd ever force anything on me. Not when his touch felt so divine, his soft caress simultaneously soothing and exciting me as his eyes studied my face, patiently awaiting my response.

Ah, hell. Who was I kidding? What was there to force? As I let my eyes wander over the masculine beauty of Raul's extraordinary, naked physique, I knew I'd let him do just about anything he wanted to me.

I pretty well already had.

"Sure," I agreed with a shy smile. "That sounds like fun."

My heart melted all over again when Raul's smile blossomed into a wide, boyish grin, and he pulled me onto his lap and kissed me breathless.

His hand soon wandered beneath the blanket covering me, and other parts of me melted as his fingers began toying with me, pinching and playing with my nipples. He kept me right on the edge of orgasm for the rest of the drive to my place, stopping short every time I came close to coming, telling me I needed more practice controlling and withholding my release whenever I mewled in complaint.

By the time we arrived at my pretentious apartment building, I was too far gone and beyond ready to be fucked to care that I was still naked and wrapped in a blanket— while Raul was somehow magically dressed again—as he carried me through the lobby. I was barely lucid enough to mutter an acceptable greeting to my distraught-looking doormen as they took note of my disheveled, half-naked state and the hulking stranger carrying me.

I had the oddest sense Raul wanted my doormen to see me with him that way. But I never got the chance to question him about it, because his pants were down and he was inside me the moment the elevator doors shut, taking me hard and fast up against the rear wall.

"Let it out for me, Bethy," he egged me on as his hips hammered into me, his pelvis circling and hitting my clit with every thrust, his fingers digging into the flesh of my ass. "I want to hear you."

All the pent-up need from my delayed orgasms in the car ride exploded in me. I came quickly and with a blinding savagery, screeching Raul's name along with some other expletives.

"There's my dirty exhibitionist," he praised with a soft chuckle, kissing my sweaty temple.

When the elevator dinged open at my floor, Raul carried me to my front door—still hard inside of me. It was then that I noticed he was completely naked again. We both were. And I realized that I had no idea where my wristlet with my keys had ended up. It was probably still back at the club. *Shit.*

I winced up at him and mumbled, "Raul, I don't … don't have my purse. It had my phone … my keys …"

He smiled down at me like I'd said something cute. "I know. Stephen took them for safekeeping. They're in your apartment."

With that, he did that magic thing again where we ceased to exist for a split second, only to reappear inside my front door.

My muddled brain was still struggling to process the news that Stephen had already been inside my apartment—not to mention grasp how any of this crazy magic stuff was even possible—when Raul lifted me off his rigid cock and set me down on my knees in front of him on the tiled floor of my little foyer.

He didn't say anything, simply threaded his fingers through the hair at the back of my head and guided his wet erection to my lips. They parted to accept him without hesitation, and he proceeded to leisurely fuck my mouth, his thrusts slow and methodical.

It was clear he wanted to control the pace and depth of his movement, so I let him. I'd never been so turned on, so hot for anyone in my whole damn life.

"Touch yourself," he told me, his voice low and raspy, his heated gaze making the demand seem more like a plea.

Keeping one hand braced against his muscled thigh, I brought my other down between my legs.

"That's it, baby. Show me how you like it."

Show him I did. I was only too eager to please—to make him as hot for me as I was for him.

My efforts were rewarded each time Raul groaned and pulled on my hair, or grunted and thrust all the way to the back of my throat.

He continued to issue directives. "Spread your legs wider. Add another finger, Bethy."

He never had to tell me anything twice.

I was completely captivated, and so intent on timing my own orgasm to coincide with him spurting in my mouth that I didn't ever think to question why he hadn't just magically transported us from the Hummer to the inside of my apartment in the first place. Or to wonder why the ten-minute ride from the club to my apartment had taken us what had felt like well over an hour in his stretch Hummer.

I never thought once about the surveillance cameras that were in all my building's elevators, or the security sensors and the camera that Gregg had set up inside my foyer over nine months ago.

And despite my best intentions, my orgasm hit me several seconds before Raul erupted down the back of my throat when he started talking dirty, recounting how much he'd enjoyed fingering my ass in the Hummer, telling me how good it was going to feel for us both when I took his whole cock in my ass.

He carried me to my bedroom next. And I lost track of how many orgasms I had, or of how many more times he bit me. It hurt a little less each time. Either that or my body was becoming conditioned to welcome the initial sting of Raul's fangs, knowing the pleasure that would soon follow—because I also seemed to orgasm harder following each successive bite.

By the time he took me in the shower, it was past three a.m., and I was so exhausted afterward that I almost fell asleep standing as he supported my body weight and washed me from head to toe.

I could barely keep my eyes open as I sat on the bathroom countertop brushing my teeth. Raul stood in front of me, his hands braced against the quartz surface on either side of my hips, a goofy, enamored smile on his face as he watched me. I asked him if werewolves ever got sleepy. He laughed and answered with an evasive "Sometimes."

He made me drink a full glass of water before tucking me into bed. I was desperate to ask him if he'd be gone when I woke up. I had a sinking feeling that he would be. *Because he hadn't crawled into bed with me.* And because he seemed sad, or worried about something, as he sat on the edge of my bed, running his fingers over the damp hair at my crown.

I couldn't imagine going another ten years without seeing Raul. Not now. Not after tonight. But my heavy eyelids betrayed me, and I fell asleep before I could find the nerve to ask when—and *if*—I was ever going to see him again.

CHAPTER 8

Raul

"**T**IME!" MOM SHOUTED TO ME FROM THE KITCHEN.
Ugh. I hit the pause button on the Super Nintendo controller in my hand. I'd just beaten Japanese Mask Robot and was pumped to face off against Dr. Wily next, the final boss in the new Mega Man 7 game. I eyed the clock and scribbled the time down on the notepad on the floor next to me. "Got it," I called back before un-pausing the game.

Mom and I had been timing her contractions all day. I didn't know what exactly it was about them that we were timing or how it all worked; I just wrote down the time on the notepad she'd given me when prompted.

While we'd been out running Mom's "last-minute baby errands" that afternoon, the contractions had gotten so close together she'd said that she was certain today would be the day my sister Milena would be born. Mom was in such a great mood about it that she'd bought me the video game I'd been bugging her to get me for months. I was pretty sure she'd done it to keep me out of her hair.

She was busy in the kitchen now, making meat lasagnas and casseroles so I'd have something decent to eat while my

Aunt Aracely was here to help with the baby. Mom's twin sister, Cely, was arriving tomorrow to stay with us. Aunt Cely was pretty cool to have around—'cept for the fact she was a vegetarian who only prepared gross foods. I refused to eat that crap, and Mom knew it.

"Time." Mom's voice was notably weaker when she called out again. I paused my game and wrote down the time.

"Got it!"

I was in the middle of a boss rush in the game when I heard something clatter to the floor in the kitchen. Mom had gotten clumsier the bigger her belly had grown. It sounded like she'd dropped a dish or a cooking pan. Again.

Not wanting to pause the game, I hesitated before calling out, "You okay, Ma?"

She didn't respond right away. Then she said, "Fine. A plate … fell." She sounded strange. Winded.

Something told me I should go check on her, but I was already fighting Spring Man, and I didn't want to stop. I was dying to get to Dr. Wily. "Be there in a minute to help clean it up, 'kay?"

Kitsune's yapping pulled my mind back to the present. Bethany's rescue pup, a four-month-old Akita wolf, was running in circles around the redwood tree he'd pissed on. Dawn was over an hour away, the forest still dark beneath its canopy of giant redwoods. Poor little guy had probably never seen a real forest before.

I knelt down on my haunches and ordered, "Come." He scampered over. "Good boy." I patted his head and scratched behind his ears as I continued to praise him, welcoming the distraction from my own thoughts. My head was a fucking mess, and I needed to stay focused now more than ever.

I could tell Kitsune didn't like me yet. Teleporting him from Bethany's high-rise apartment to the redwood groves of Big Basin had unsettled him. He definitely didn't trust me. But he knew enough to listen to me. If he hadn't understood immediately that I was his new master, seeing me transform into an enormous wolf had cemented that fact.

Bethany had only had him a week, and it was clear she didn't have a lot of experience with puppies in general, much less an Akita wolf-dog hybrid.

The little beast seemed to have been partially potty-trained before Bethany had gotten him at least. But she'd mistakenly assumed that he was fully trained and had been leaving her balcony door ajar for him to go out there and do his business whenever she left the apartment. I smiled to myself as I imagined her trying to explain to the stubborn little mutt that he should use the patio when he had to go. I knew Stephen and Tiago had stumbled upon and cleaned up several of Kitsune's accidents earlier when they'd scouted out Bethany's apartment for me.

I sensed Mike trying to tap my mind to reach me. I allowed the connection, checked to make sure he was alone, and opened a link to my location.

When Mike teleported in, Kitsune began barking like mad. When he didn't obey my "quiet" command, I growled and flashed my wolf eyes at him before repeating it. He piped down. "Good boy."

I stood as Mike approached. Mike was head of my security detail, one of the highest-ranking Betas within my pack, and one of the first and only true friends I'd made when I'd joined our Salvatella pack over a decade ago. Although Mike shared a blood relation to our former Alpha, Gabriel Salvatella—the sadistic tyrant who'd been the bane of my existence for the past ten years—Mike was nothing like his late second cousin Gabriel.

"So ..." he dithered, biting his lip and cocking his head at me.

"So," I replied, ignoring his prompt.

"Things got a lot crazy a little quickly last night, don't you think?"

"I held my wolf back for ten years, Mike."

His wince was sympathetic. "I know, man. It's just—"

"I'll handle it. I won't let you and the others down."

He nodded, his gaze lowering to the ball of fluffy russet and white fur at my feet. "Her rescue pup's an Akita wolf," he observed with a wry half-smile. "Fitting."

I didn't disagree. "Name's Kitsune."

He chuckled. "Even better." He scrubbed a hand over his jaw. "You know you marked her, right? In addition to infecting her with werewolf venom multiple times." Mike always cut to the chase with me. It was one of his better qualities.

"Yeah. Probably."

"*Probably?* Raul, this is going to complicate—"

"It was already complicated."

"I know, but Alpha Milena—"

"I can handle my sister."

He nodded and dropped it. That was one of Mike's best qualities—knowing when to back off with me. "What about Bethany's mind?" he broached. "Any luck getting around that emotional shield yet?"

I shook my head. "I'll figure it out. If I can't, Alcaeus should know how to get past it." *I hoped.*

Mike gave me a questioning look, but then comprehension dawned on his features. "Right. We have a Reinoso insider now." He paused to watch Kitsune pawing at the leaf litter beneath his feet. "Alcaeus isn't going to be happy about this, though."

"Nope." Not happy was an understatement. He was going to be livid. But I couldn't waste time worrying about Alcaeus's reactions. Nothing I ever did was right as far as that guy was concerned.

"You suppose Alcaeus had a hand in placing that shield? That'd be a lucky break for us."

I shrugged. "Anything's possible." But not bloody likely.

Unfortunately, I feared Alcaeus hadn't had much of a hand in placing the shield on Bethany's mind. He was more of a give-orders-and-criticize-the-outcome type than a do-the-work type. I had a bad feeling that shield had been constructed entirely by Remy Bertrand—Alcaeus's stepbrother and Alex Reinoso's half-brother.

I'd spent enough years within the Reinoso pack as a human indentured servant to know that while on the surface Remy came across as the most harmless of Alex's powerful siblings, Remy's innate talent for emotional manipulation was far too similar to Gabe Salvatella's not to be taken seriously as a potential threat. Notwithstanding, Remy had long been the most overlooked and notably undervalued member of the Reinoso pack's reigning family.

I doubted any werelock in the Reinoso clan but Remy could've been capable of creating an emotional shield like the one on Bethany. Not even Gabe or his late brother, Nuriel, had been able to access Bethany's mind when they'd set out to kidnap her ten years ago. Their plan had been to use Bethany's life as a bargaining chip with Milena and Alex.

But when the mind compulsion tactics they normally employed with humans failed to work on Bethany, it had fallen to me—under Gabe's orders—to charm and persuade Bethany into coming with us to South America.

Just thinking back on the time my Bethy had spent in close company with Gabe and Nuriel made my stomach turn and my wolf anxious to teleport back to her side.

"Did you get everything in place for the asshole?"

Mike's face split into a broad grin at my inquiry. "I assume you mean the plan for Gregg? Oh, yeah," he said with a chuckle and a nod in the affirmative. "I'm rather looking forward to watching that play out."

"You and me both."

"Not to brag, but it might be some of my best work yet on short notice."

"Thanks for that, by the way." I meant it, too. Mike was a wiz when it came to hacking.

"My pleasure." He clapped me on the shoulder. "Always more fun to torment the deserving."

"Speaking of … what's going on up in Washington with Kai and the seer?"

"More of the same." Mike knelt to pet Kitsune. "You, my little friend, are going to love Argentina," he assured the puppy.

I felt myself frown. "What's happened? Did Kai see something in one of the seer's visions? Something about Marib—I mean Sloane?"

"You've got to stop slipping up like that around Avery, you know," Mike admonished, his eyes on Kitsune as he scratched behind the dog's ears. "No mother likes having her ten-year-old referred to as the reincarnation of a werelock renowned for harvesting souls as an undead being."

"Sloane is nine years old and eight months," I corrected him. "And I've only slipped up and referred to Sloane as Maribel once around Avery. Quit avoiding my questions about the seer."

"It was twice."

"Once. But it's been twice now that you've avoided my Washington question. What's happening with Kai and the seer?"

"Her name is Lauren."

I felt my jaw unhinge. "I—wait, are you serious right now? Please tell me you're not crushing on Kai's coed."

"Of course not," he huffed. "Since when does calling a person by her given name mean—"

"When you know we'll probably have to kill that person at some point, and yet you've started identifying her as a human being rather than the threat to Sloane's safety that she is."

"We don't know that she's a threat." He abandoned petting Kitsune and stood to face me. "Her abilities are novice, Raul. She's confused. She's had no guidance. Besides all of that, there's too much fear in Lauren's heart for her to be able to—"

"Did you sleep with her while Kai was on his pouting tour of Greenland?"

"No," he balked, his face flushing.

"Shit. You did. You slept with the seer."

"We kissed—by accident. It was one time."

"By accident? What, like you fell onto her and started making out?"

"I was in her dream, all right? She doesn't even think

that it was real. Besides, I made sure she wouldn't remember. And for the record, yes, Kai was away in Greenland when it happened."

"Jesus, Mike." I shook my head, cracking up. "What the fuck, man? C'mon, she's not *that* hot. You couldn't allow her even one week of peace from Kai invading her dreams and making creepy sexual advances on her? You had to take advantage, too? See what all the fuss—"

"I did not take advantage of Lauren. It was a lapse in judgment—a rash decision. I needed to come up with a distrac—oh, quit being such a dick. It's not that funny. And she *is* hot. Even Avery agrees."

"Please, you can't trust a woman's opinion on whether another woman is hot."

"Well, you certainly can't trust a mated man's opinion." He crossed his arms over his chest.

"Fair point. Guess it's settled then. You have a crush on the seer." I wiped the laughter from my face. "And I'm pulling you off seer watch and putting Avery on full-time."

"What? You can't—Raul, that'll never work. For one, Alcaeus will find out what we're up to if Avery is on the mission twenty-four-seven. And secondly, what if Avery sees something in Lauren's mind that connects Sloane and Maribel?"

"She'll find out sooner or later."

"Better if it's later."

"It's not going to change anything. You just admitted that your judgment's been compromised."

"Avery's still learning how to invade minds and cover her tracks. Kai will be onto her in no time."

"Kai already knows you're watching the seer. What's the difference?"

He groaned and yanked at the roots of his hair. "He doesn't know the extent."

"Mike, your emotions are involved. You know this is the right decision. You'd pull any one of our guys off a job for less."

"She had this crazy vivid vision, okay? But it ended too soon. I needed to try and keep her dreaming. I was trying to find a way to guide her back to the same vision."

"By tonguing her?"

"Fuck you. I'm calling the whole plan for Gregg off."

I busted out laughing. "Okay, okay, what was the vision that threw you so far off your game?"

He let out a sigh. "You and Kai were fighting."

"Really?"

"In wolf form."

Huh. "So I'm meant to kill Kai then," I processed out loud.

Mike cleared his throat. "Well, I didn't uh … didn't get to see the end of the fight."

"But I was winning. Right?"

He winced. "Mm—not exactly."

CHAPTER 9

Raul

I WAS GOING TO BURN IN HELL.

I'd always quietly anticipated it, but now it was for certain.

For over a decade, I'd stayed away to protect Bethany, living in constant fear that Gabe would find out about my innate mating bond connection to her and exploit it in order to gain absolute control over me. *Or worse: use it to kill me by murdering Bethany—just as Gabe's ancestors had done to my great-aunt Sofia and her mate, Joaquin Salvatella.*

I'd come so close to giving myself away when I'd stood on Bethany's parents' front porch in Santa Cruz ten years ago, gaping at Bethany in disbelief—my heart caught in a vise and my newly emerged wolf clawing me apart from the inside with his need to possess her.

Fortunately, I'd had Maribel inside my head at the time to guide me. She'd helped me conceal my initial connection to Bethany from Gabe and Nuriel. And she had ultimately set me on a path to believing that if I stayed away from Bethy and denied the mating bond connection long and hard enough, I could thwart it altogether.

But it had become harder and harder over the years, and Gabe had grown more suspicious over time as to what was always drawing me back to San Francisco. He'd been well on his way to figuring it all out, *and thus I'd been diligently plotting to kill him*, when little Sloane had done the job for me.

As I fingered the marks I'd left on Bethany's golden skin, I couldn't help but wonder if I'd made the mating bond pull worse—stronger somehow—through my efforts to reject it for so many years. The evidence of my wolf's desperation, his overriding need to irrevocably establish and reinforce a mating bond, was everywhere I looked as I canvassed what was visible to me of Bethy's gorgeous naked body. I itched to inspect every inch of her, but refrained, not wanting to risk disturbing her peaceful slumber by moving her.

What had I done?

Why hadn't I stopped after the first bite?

Or the fourth?

How was it I was only now noticing all the damage I'd inflicted? Purple bruises were beginning to form around the areas of broken skin.

I was a monster.

My brief trip to Big Basin with Kitsune had served to clear my lust-clouded vision. I felt sick as I took in the damning evidence of the aggressive, excessive manner in which I had gone about marking Bethany.

And yet … a deeper, darkly possessive part of me was rejoicing in what I was seeing. Judging by the size of my erection, my inner Neanderthal was positively reveling in it.

Yep. Hell it was. If they'd have me.

I was an asshole. I didn't deserve Bethany.

I forced myself to pull a sheet up over her. Then a blanket. She was passed out cold and didn't so much as stir.

God, she was beautiful. So sweet and perfect.

And a perfect fucking freak in the sheets.

But I couldn't keep her. I would only ruin her life and make her miserable. She was probably going to hate me as soon as she woke up and discovered all the bite marks I'd made.

I'd fucked up big time giving in to my suppressed desire last night. I had to find a way to reverse this for Bethany's sake.

And my own. I couldn't handle Bethany hating me forevermore. It would be better to give her up now and walk away than endure seeing her unhappy—watching her grow to despise me more with each passing day that she was tied to me.

I had to fix this.

I dialed Avery's number as I walked from the bedroom. Normally, I'd have simply tapped Avery's mind to reach her, but I knew how much that irritated Alcaeus. And I was going to need Alcaeus's help today.

"Really?" Avery answered on the fourth ring.

"Have you ever fucked up so badly with something that was critically important to you to the point that you felt driven to keep going with it? You know … like you wanted to be able to stop and fix it, but instead, something inside you compelled you to keep fucking it up more and more, and digging the hole you were already in deeper and deeper?"

There was dead silence on the other end of the line as I paced Bethany's living room. "Avery? You there?"

"Gimme a sec. It's barely eight a.m. My coffee hasn't fully kicked in."

"It's four in the morning here in San Francisco."

"And that's my fault? I didn't tell you to wake up early and dig yourself into a big hole."

"This is serious, Avery. I need your help. I feel out of control, and I don't know how to fix this."

"Ugh, don't pull that sad little brother shtick with me. Not when you're cutting in on my morning sex time."

"I'm not messing around. I need you to teleport to San Francisco. And I need you to bring Alcaeus with you."

"You need Chaos, too? Damn. That's some fuck-up."

"I can make it an order."

"You're so cute when you're needy and vulnerable."

"Avery."

"Okay, okay. Chill the Alpha vibe. What'd you do this time, Boss Man?"

The stunned look on Alcaeus's face when he turned to me wasn't reassuring. Neither was Avery's sharp intake of breath as she peeled the covers back.

"Are you kidding me?" Alcaeus shouted, stepping into my space. "What the hell do you think I can do about this?"

"I don't know. Just find a way to fix it," I ordered, waving a hand at the bed. "Undo it."

"Undo it? With *what*? A time machine? There's no undoing this, Raul. What the hell were you thinking? I told you last night to stay away from Bethany."

He looked dead serious. This couldn't be happening. There had to be a way to fix it. "Come on, man, you're centuries old. You have to have seen a fix for this kind of thing before."

His eyes shifted. A growl rolled up his chest. I got in his face and growled through my teeth, "You're supposed to be my head Beta. It's your job to fix this."

"And I live for the day when I get to kill you and call myself Alpha, you little shit."

"Chaos!" Avery spun around and stepped between us, pressing her palms to Alcaeus's chest. "Down, boy."

"Why are you taking his side in this? You're always taking his side," Alcaeus whined. "Why are you laughing? This isn't funny, Avery."

Christ, he really couldn't fix it. I was royally fucked.

And Avery really was laughing. Hysterically. She looked about ready to double over with laughter where she stood, wheezing and shaking, leaning into Alcaeus's chest.

"What the hell is so funny?" I snapped.

"Don't talk to her like that," Alcaeus fired back.

"You marked," Avery managed to get out amid wheezing laughter, "Alpha Milena's"—another wheeze—"childhood BFF." She turned away from Alcaeus and flung her arms around me, squeezing me in a hug. "You're so much more fun than I ever thought you'd be."

"Wait—" I pulled back to see a look of wicked triumph light her features. "No." I shook my head. "No, no, no, it wasn't like that. This wasn't about revenge against my sister. It was an accident. I never meant to mark Bethany. I just got carried away."

"Carried away?" Alcaeus balked, tugging Avery away from me. "You think?"

Avery snorted. "Whatever you say, Boss Man. But you should know, this kind of thing starts to look a lot less like a heat-o-the-moment mishap and more like a crime scene after about ... oh, the twelfth bite."

"I did not bite her twelve times." It was more like seven. Or ten.

"Well, I counted eight without checking her ass." Avery patted my shoulder. "And I don't have to look to know you marked her hiney. That's such a surfer-Alpha thing to do."

"I did *not* mark her ass," I denied.

Fuck, I definitely remembered biting her ass. More than once.

"I don't understand how any of this could have happened. How the hell did things get so far out of hand between you two last night in the first place?" Alcaeus's eyes cut to the bed where Bethany still lay unconscious despite our loud bickering. "Just how drunk was she? Last I heard, Bethany was engaged to some loser who was cheating on her."

"Whoa—wait, what did you say?" My inner animal stirred at the mention of my mate's cheating ex. "How did—you *knew* Gregg was cheating on Bethy? And you never told me? How long have you known?"

Alcaeus's eyes widened. *"Bethy?"* He looked from me to Avery and back again. "Please tell me this is all a bad joke."

Avery shrugged and said with a smile, "I'm as delightfully surprised as you are to learn about Raul's new girlfriend."

"Why didn't you tell me Gregg was cheating?" I repeated.

Alcaeus threw his hands up. "Why on earth would I think to tell you? I forgot about it almost as soon as Alex and Milena mentioned it to me. How was I supposed to know you were harboring some weird childhood crush on *Beth-y* that would result in you losing your damn mind and attacking her like a chew toy?"

"How long?" I pressed him through clenched teeth. "When did Alex and Miles mention to you that Gregg was cheating? And don't call her Bethy. Only I can call her that."

His eyes rolled. "Six months ago. Maybe seven? Yeah, more like seven. It was when I went back to Morumbi to visit them." His shoulders tensed. "Before all the shit went down between us over Sloane." Alcaeus's family's betrayal over Avery and her daughter, Sloane, remained a festering wound. "By the way, I'm pretty sure Alex calls her Bethy."

"How did they know about it? Bethany just found out about Gregg's cheating." Or at least it had seemed that way last night. Bethany had said that she hadn't even given Gregg a chance to explain himself yet. *I really needed to kill that guy.*

Alcaeus sighed and rubbed his temple. "Alex went snooping around in the fiancé's head and found out about it that way."

"And they didn't tell her?" They'd known for seven months? Maybe longer? My blood boiled at the knowledge that Miles had known about this and hadn't even thought to warn Bethany away from Gregg. Suddenly I felt less concerned about the flak I was going to catch from my sister for marking her best friend. "What kind of a best friend doesn't warn a person that their fiancé is cheating on them?"

"A shitty one," Avery inserted.

"Exactly," I agreed.

"Give your sister a break. What was Milena supposed to say? It's not like she could tell Bethany how Alex discovered Gregg was cheating."

Alcaeus was often quick to come to my little sister's defense—despite the fact that he wasn't on speaking terms with her at present. It was an annoying habit of his. And I wasn't the only one bothered by it. Avery and I shared a look as Alcaeus proceeded to justify Milena's actions.

"Bethany doesn't know about Milena and Alex being werelocks. She knows nothing of our world. And that's by Bethany's own choice," he said, giving me that pointed, know-it-all look of his that always made me want to smash his face in. "Milena was right to stay out of it. It's Bethany's business. Alex shouldn't have been snooping around in Gregg's head in the first place."

Squelching the impulse to lash out, I shook my head and argued, "Bethany doesn't know about Miles or any of us being werelocks because your former pack took the liberty of erasing from her mind all knowledge of what she learned and witnessed firsthand in South America ten years ago." *Along with the memory of our first kiss.*

"Right. And I'm telling you that Remy erased Bethany's memory at her own request," Alcaeus continued, his revelation prompting an unwelcome ache in my chest. "Bethany *chose* to have her mind erased. To forget that her best friend had become a powerful werewolf subspecies. She can't have it both ways. When you ask to be kept in the dark, that's what you get. Besides, you don't think Milena felt hurt by Bethany's choice? Abandoned?"

"You don't think that just once you could stop playing devil's fucking advocate for every situation I find myself in?"

"A good Alpha analyzes situations from all sides and remains flexible in his thinking."

"Boys," Avery cut in, "what does it matter who erased whose mind at whose request and who's still acting butthurt over it, hmm? The important thing here is that Raul has chosen a mate, and whether he did it by accident"—she gave me an exaggerated wink—"or to mess with his power-trippin' sister, the fact remains, this is fucking awesome news." She raised a hand in the air. "I call dibs on planning the engagement party. I'll just go send a save-the-date email invite right now to Milena to get the fun started, 'kay?"

"*No*," Alcaeus objected, wrapping an arm around Avery and pulling her into his side. "Honey, that's not the way to handle the Blind Warrior."

"Oh, c'mon, Raul started it. I'm just jumping in to support our Alpha."

"What happened last night had nothing to do with Miles," I insisted once more. "It was about me and Bethy."

Alcaeus pulled a face. "Can you please stop calling her that? It only makes this entire scenario sound that much more absurd."

"It does not. It's what Miles and I always called Bethany growing up."

"Omigod," Avery erupted, clasping her hands together in front of her heart as understanding lit her brown eyes. "Bethy's the hot blonde I caught you stalking on Facebook using your catfish profile, isn't she? She's the one Weenie Gabe was talking about—Milena's med student friend living in San Francisco."

I nodded.

Alcaeus's forehead crumpled. "Just how long has this been going on?"

"Long enough," Mike answered from the doorway.

"Mike," Alcaeus greeted with a sigh. "How could you let this happen? I specifically told Stephen to tell you to make sure—"

"I know, Chaos," Mike said, addressing Alcaeus by Avery's outrageous nickname for him—that had somehow caught on with my entire pack since Alcaeus and Avery had joined us seven months ago. "But you can only deny a true mate connection for so long. It's a wonder Raul managed to make it a whole decade with his sanity intact."

Avery let out a little gasp. "This explains so much."

"More than a decade," I corrected under my breath. "Not that I've been keeping track."

"Are you shitting me?" Alcaeus's scowl swung in my direction. "That's impossible. No one can avoid the mating pull for that long. I don't believe it."

"No?" I held my arms open. "Well, believe it, because you're looking at it."

"It's not possible." Alcaeus's eyes cut from me to Mike, who nodded soberly. "Jesus, Raul, every time I start to think you can't possibly be as much of an idiot Alpha as Alex was to mentor, you go and prove me wrong."

"Stop comparing me to—"

"There is no way," he insisted. "Bethany can't be your true mate. You kidnapped her ten years ago. You held her life over Milena's head—"

"I *had* to play along with Gabe and Nuriel's plan," I defended. "I had no choice back then. It would've been more dangerous for Bethany had I revealed my true intentions. But I was never going to let any harm come to her. Damnit, I even told Miles that after it was all over. Do you have any idea how sick I was over that entire situation?"

"No, Raul," Alcaeus said, his arm falling from around Avery's shoulder as he turned fully to face me, his volume rising along with his anger. "I honestly don't. Forgive me if I have a hard time keeping track of what lies you're spinning as half-truths from one week to the next to justify all the bullshit you've—"

"Hey, should we check Bethy's vitals, maybe?" Avery asked the room, her puzzled gaze fixed on my mate's unmoving form on the bed. "I mean her heart rate sounds fine from here, and I can hear her breathing, but that poor hickey-ridden girl is *seriously* zonked to be sleeping through all this."

Mike coughed behind his fist, and I couldn't help but crack a smile myself.

Alcaeus shook his head at the ceiling and complained, "You always do this."

It was true. Avery often managed to insert herself in order to diffuse the escalating tension between her mate and me.

"What?" Avery feigned innocence. "You mean play devil's advocate? Remain flexible in my thinking? I thought you liked—"

I let out a laugh as Alcaeus lunged for Avery, lifting her off the ground and into his arms as he growled against the crook of her neck, causing her to squeal and giggle. As much as Alcaeus was a thorn in my side, Avery was the balm. I loved that girl. She joked about it, but in many ways, she had assumed the role of surrogate big sister in my life since joining the pack.

Mike had once jokingly described Avery as a hotter, blacker version of J.Lo—all the poise, booty, and confidence of the megastar, but without the bling and diva-persona baggage. A fair surface-level assessment, I supposed.

In truth, Avery was a warrior. She could throw a punch better than most guys I knew. She'd grown up the hard and fast way—without much, if any, adult guidance, and having to figure out on her own how to survive whatever life had thrown at her. Then, ten years ago at the age of thirty-two, she'd been attacked and impregnated by a rogue werewolf, and she'd had to figure out how to navigate her new life as a lone werewolf on the run with her child—who was being hunted by powerful supernatural predators from around the globe.

Avery had put her trust in me and in my pack to protect her daughter, Sloane. It wasn't a responsibility I took lightly. Avery was someone I never wanted to let down.

"I'm planning to bring Bethy to Bariloche later today to have Rafe take a look at her," I assured Avery once Alcaeus stopped smooching on her and had set her back down on her feet.

"Well, in the meantime, you might wanna get inside her head and heal some of those bite marks and handprint bruises a little better before she wakes up, Romeo," she advised. "Lick them better at the very least. A girl can only do so much with concealer."

I cringed internally at the reminder of the greater obstacle and impending danger at hand where Bethany was concerned. "So … about that," I addressed Alcaeus directly, assuming an Alpha tone. "I need you to remove the block your former pack placed on Bethany's mind a decade ago. It's some sort of emotional shield, and I can't—"

"Wait—what?" he interrupted. A look of realization washed over his features, and then he confirmed my greatest fear. "Aw, fuck. That shield was Remy's work."

"You're blocked out?" Avery exclaimed, aghast. "But then Bethy's initial transformation—"

"Yes," I confirmed, not eager to hear her spell out aloud the harsh reality we were now facing—a reality that Avery herself was painfully familiar with.

If we couldn't find a way to get inside Bethany's mind, then I wouldn't be able to control her initial shift in seven days' time. And Avery was the only known human in werewolf history to have survived the initial werewolf transformation completely unassisted by one of our kind.

CHAPTER 10

Bethany

I DREAMT THAT RAUL WAS LICKING THE BACK OF MY thigh—sucking on a spot that felt tender. The tension was building in my lower abdomen the longer he did it, my sex buzzing and pulsing to life, prompting me to squirm and press my pelvis into the cushiony surface beneath me.

In my dream, he murmured softly in another language as his mouth traveled upward, licking the underside of my ass cheek before latching onto another sensitive expanse of skin on my backside. By the time he moved on to licking and sucking the opposite cheek, I was slowly circling and pressing my pelvis into the mattress.

When his hands began gently kneading my fleshy globes, my breathing grew shallow. His mouth trailed kisses up my spine before licking a path to my shoulder, where another wounded area captured his tongue's attention.

This time, a muffled whimper escaped me as his mouth latched onto that particularly raw spot. Raul paused to mumble something in English about being sorry and making it better, as the fingers massaging my ass rubbed lower, dipping between the cheeks to stroke and enter me where I was slippery wet and throbbing.

His masculine groan of approval reverberated against my shoulder as he sucked the smarting flesh in time with the movement of his fingers pumping in and out.

The sounds of my mewling and moaning became interspersed with my panted breaths as I was lost to the ever-tightening coiling sensation in my belly. But just as I strained for that precipice, rolling my pelvis faster and pressing my clit harder into the mattress with each successive rotation of my hips, the surface beneath me pulled away, leaving my body floating weightless in the air. Raul's mouth relinquished my shoulder. His fingers withdrew, reminding me that sex dreams were the cruelest of teases— never living up to the real thing, and hardly ever culminating in a release.

But then I felt hot breath moving *beneath* me—warm kisses trailing from my belly button to my sex as Raul's big hands ran up the back of my thighs, pulling them apart, squeezing my ass and drawing my weightless body downward until I felt the insides of my knees straddling his broad shoulders. Warm breath fanned my wet center; the tip of a tongue twirled and lashed at my clit. Fingers entered me and curled against my G-spot as Raul drew my fluttering little bud into his fevered mouth and sucked it like candy.

My upper body remained buoyant—suspended in midair somehow as if floating on water—as Raul's lips and tongue devoured me without mercy. *This was the best damn sex dream I'd ever had.*

My hands fell to his head below for balance, and my fingers wound through his hair, unconsciously clutching and pulling on it as sensations overwhelmed me. I'd always been too self-conscious to try this position with anyone I'd been with before. Because it was crazy intimate being eaten out this way—Raul's fingers making sloppy wet noises as they drove in and out, my juices gushing straight into his mouth and onto his stubble-roughened chin as he nursed my clit, humming against my sex in a way that stole my breath.

The pressure on my G-spot had me scared that I was going to soak his face when I came. Just when I thought I couldn't possibly feel more exposed and vulnerable and consumed with the need to come, he eased a finger inside my ass.

My whole body was soon shaking, my stomach muscles clenching spastically as the dual penetration and G-spot stimulation combined with his insistent sucking reduced me to frantic gasping and panted shouts of ecstasy. My orgasm hit like a freight train as it rolled over me, and I handled it with all the ladylike dignity that a woman robbed of breath yet still compulsively wailing obscenities could manage.

Raul's fingers withdrew, but he continued licking and sucking on my sensitive bits, grunting and growling as his shoulder muscles jumped and jerked with rapid, pulsing movements against the insides of my spread knees. I pictured him stroking his huge, beautiful erection, hard and fast, seeking his own relief. I wanted to tell him to put it inside me, despite how spent I was and how tender my insides felt, but he let out an extended groan and his shoulders ceased jerking a moment later, signaling his release.

I was lightheaded and dizzy and whimpering from

sensitivity by the time Raul finished lapping every last drop of my orgasm from between my spread folds. I felt my body tumble as gravity reclaimed me, the mattress rising up to meet my back, my head flopping down onto the soft surface of a pillow.

Fingers combed through the hair at my crown, smiling lips pressed to my forehead, and I heard Raul apologize for waking me up, saying that he couldn't rest without healing me first.

Waking me up?

Then he said something in an amused voice about making up for lost time, before murmuring, "You're in so much trouble now, Bethy," as exhaustion pulled me under into a peaceful state of sleep.

I was in the midst of another sex dream.

In this one, Raul's tongue was thoroughly laving a sore spot on my breast. When his mouth moved on to my nipple, nipping it between his teeth before sucking away the sting, my body came alive with need.

I ached for him to lick and suck lower—like he'd done in the last sex dream he'd starred in. This time, I wanted to feel his hard cock breaching me, stretching me wide and filling the pulsating void between my thighs.

Then my phone went off.

I tried to ignore it and remain in the hot dream, but it was too late because the sucking stopped, and I felt my covers against my breasts instead. I could see light behind my closed eyelids.

Ugh. I swung my arm out toward the nightstand, blindly reaching for my phone. As my fingers located it, a warm, masculine hand fell atop mine, halting me.

"I got it, Bethy," Raul's deep voice floated over me as gently he extracted the phone from my sleepy, uncoordinated fingertips, silencing the irritating noise.

My breath caught and my heart leapt into my throat.

Raul hadn't left. He'd actually spent the night!

I bolted upright in bed, rubbing the sleep from my eyes as they strained against the morning sunlight streaming in through my windows.

"You're here. I can't believe you stayed." I was so beyond thrilled to discover Raul hadn't left that I failed to filter myself—or restrain what was no doubt a freakishly dorky grin on my pillow-wrinkled face—as through squinted eyes I took in his gorgeous, tall presence standing beside my bed, dressed casually in jeans and a white T-shirt.

My grin broadened when I realized I could smell coffee. And pancakes. And eggs.

"I think I'm in love with you." The words flew from my mouth, and I belatedly slapped my hand over it.

My eyes went wide as mortification sank in.

"Does that mean I can stay for breakfast?"

That smile of his would be my undoing.

"No. I mean, of course. I mean—I didn't mean that last part like it came out. I just … really love eggs. And pancakes … and coffee." *Oh, shut up, Bethany.* "Would you excuse me, please?" I threw the covers aside and bolted for the bathroom, buck-naked.

I locked the door behind me and jumped in the shower, turning the water to its coldest setting.

I'd slept with Milena's brother!

Scratch that; I'd fucked my best friend's brother six ways from Sunday and back again, and I had loved every filthy second of it.

Shit, shit, shit.

I recalled having sex in the club. And then in Raul's stretch Hummer. And then—oh, sweet baby Jesus, in my building's elevator!

And he had bitten me—several times.

The memory of Raul's werewolf confession—along with the unexplainable magical abilities he'd displayed the night before—came rushing back to me. I reached up to finger the spot on the side of my throat where he'd bitten me. It still felt tender. I glanced down at my body beneath the freezing, sobering shower spray and found a crescent-shaped pink mark where he had bitten my left breast at the club. There was another one on my inner thigh.

It had all really happened. I'd fucked a werewolf subspecies last night.

I moved on autopilot, washing quickly as my teeth began to chatter.

Don't freak out. Keep it together. Everything's okay.

As I toweled off, I realized there was also a bite mark on my ankle, my shoulder, and the back of my arm. And two on my ass and yet another on the back of my thigh.

Grabbing iodine solution and swabs from beneath the sink, I stood in front of the full-length mirror hanging on the back of the bathroom door and methodically set to work assessing and disinfecting the affected areas, my brain switching into physician mode.

Oddly, most of the bites looked like they were several weeks old, rather than mere hours. The new skin covering and surrounding them was the bright pink shade you see when an initial scab falls away. But the bite on my shoulder was deeper and still healing. On my neck, it appeared he'd bitten nearly the same spot twice—the bite marks overlapping and, like my shoulder, penetrating far deeper into the tissue than the ones on my thighs, breast, arm, and ass.

"Bethy?" Raul wrapped lightly on the other side of the door.

I jolted and dropped the iodine solution.

"You okay?"

"Yeah," I responded a little too zealously as I bent to mop up the spill I'd made. "Fine. Be right out, okay? I'm just … doing my hair."

"Bethany, we need to talk."

"Okay!" *Why was I shouting?*

"I'm really sorry for biting you last night … so many times." He mumbled the last part.

"It's no big. These things happen." *Did they?* What was I even saying?

"I can explain everything."

"That's okay. I'm good." The notion that he might have an actual explanation for biting me so many times was somehow more terrifying.

"Most of the bite marks will be fully healed within a matter of days—I promise."

Most. Not all. "It's all good. My mom's a great derma-tologist. She's got advanced laser treatments for—for this exact um … sort of thing."

"Bethy, please? Just open the door."

Crap, the door! I was no safer behind it. Raul didn't even need for me to open it. I recalled the way he'd mag-ically transported us from the hallway to the inside of my apartment last night—not to mention how he'd magically transported us from the club to the car.

I felt my psyche going into fight-or-flight mode. I had to find a way to get past Raul and out of my apartment before a full-blown panic attack set in. *Think, Bethany, think.*

"Be out in a minute!" I hollered back, snagging my pajamas from their hook on the wall adjacent to the shower and yanking the bottoms on with clumsy fingers and trembling limbs.

"Honey, I can hear you just fine. There's no need to shout or panic. Everything's going to be okay—I promise."

"What? Who's panicking?" I returned with an exaggerated, ridiculous laugh, before checking my high volume. I often did shout whenever I panicked. It was a habit I'd picked up from my mom. "I'm just getting dressed."

"Baby, your heart rate's sprinting a mile a minute, and I can smell your fear from out here. Please believe me that there's nothing to be afraid of. I promise I won't bite you again."

I could've sworn I heard him append that promise with a quietly mumbled "today," but I couldn't be sure because I was already too busy trying to process his previous assertion that he could hear my heartbeat and smell my fear.

"I'm just anxious to get to work on time," I further dissembled as my shaking fingers struggled with the final button of my pajama shirt.

"Thought you were on call this weekend?"

"Would you just back off me for a minute?" I snapped, forgetting to be cautious as annoyance superseded my sense of fear. "I need to be at the hospital this morning no later than eleven and available to work through the night and most of tomorrow—*that's* what my on-call status means for this weekend."

"All right, all right. Got it." His heavy sigh carried through the door. "Relax. Take your time. I'll just ... be waiting for you."

I braced my hands against the sink counter and took slow, deep breaths, trying to calm myself and clear my head. Everything would be fine—he'd said so. And he had promised not to bite me again. *Today.*

Jesus Christ, he had canine senses and could hear my heartbeat and smell my fear. I needed to get a grip—and quickly—before he poofed himself through the bathroom door.

I turned the water on, grabbed my ultrasonic toothbrush, and went to work cleaning my teeth and swishing with mouthwash an excessive number of times in order to buy myself time, while hoping the noise would help mask the sounds of my internal organs going into panic mode.

I just had to go out there and act natural—like the werewolf thing was no big deal. Then I'd thank him for the super-hot sex last night and excuse myself, saying I had to get to work.

Right. And that would be that, I mentally assured myself with a nod to my reflection in the mirror. I rinsed one final time, smoothed the wrinkles from my pajamas, and opened the door.

Raul was standing there, waiting. Blocking my exit.

He was so tall and built he filled the entire doorway. And I was thrown off-kilter the moment I saw him—and the concern lining his handsome face. He reached for me, and I took several steps back, my bare feet nearly slipping on the damp tile floor in my haste to keep distance between us.

Hurt flashed in his eyes, but he raised both palms in the air in a nonthreatening gesture. "Hey—s'okay, Bethy." He backed up out of the doorway, allowing me space to pass. "I just want to talk to you. There's no reason to be afraid."

In truth, I was only partially concerned that he might hurt me because of the unknown factor his new species classification presented. I was more afraid that if he touched me, I was liable to shag him again, werewolf or not. There was a crazy animal magnetism thing happening between us that compelled me to toss sound judgment and sanity right out the window whenever I stared at his face for too long.

Or heard the sound of his voice. *Or got close enough to smell him.* Or touch him ...

I needed to keep my head on straight when I was around him.

When I still hesitated to move from the bathroom, he bit his lip and nodded solemnly at a spot on the floor. "Alright then. I'll just go to the other room and wait for you there." He turned and walked away without another word.

I stepped from the bathroom, my eyes following his retreating form—shamelessly eyeballing the way his fine ass filled his jeans and how the muscles of his broad back strained against the material of his T-shirt.

Closing my eyes and giving myself a mental shake, I counted to ten and followed after him, out of my bedroom and into the living room, where I found him standing next to my little dining table—that was dressed with a tablecloth and flowers and laden with delicious-looking food.

I stopped in my tracks. "Wow."

He winced and rubbed the back of his neck. "Too much?"

Dear Lord, grant me the strength not to drop to my knees and blow this werewolf right where he stands.

I looked from the serving dishes, which were piled with sliced fruits, pastries, pancakes, bacon, and eggs, to Raul's nervous yet hopeful brown eyes, and saw the neighborhood surfer boy I'd grown up with.

"Raul, I'm sorry. I overreacted. I'm still processing everything that's happened."

His smile was tentative as relief smoothed the worry lines on his face. "It's understandable."

"I really had a lot of fun … catching up with you last night."

"Catching up?" His smile broadened, reaching his eyes. "Is that what we're calling it?"

I felt my cheeks heat, and I couldn't help but crack a smile.

He took a small step toward me. Then another. "I had a lot of fun, too." He looked like he was about to say more, but then his demeanor shifted and he gestured to the table. "Could I interest you in some breakfast before it gets cold? I promise to sit on my side of the table and only bite the food."

I rolled my eyes. "Ha ha, you're *so* funny." I shook my head and walked to the table, allowing him to pull a chair out for me. "It's a little soon for biting jokes, don't you think?" But as I said it, I was already grinning from ear to ear.

"Agreed," he said with a chuckle, handing me a cloth napkin before setting to work piling food onto my plate. When he was done, he served and seated himself next to me at the table. "I really am sorry, Bethy." His eyes were sincere. "I didn't mean for things to happen the way they did last night."

"It's fine." I bit my lip and rolled one shoulder, suddenly feeling shy. "I can't believe you made all this," I said as I began to dig in, wanting to change the subject—and regain some level of normalcy. "I'm always either eating out or grabbing something from the hospital cafeteria. I don't even remember the last time I ate a home-cooked meal."

He sucked air through his teeth. "Ahhh—well, you see, the thing is …" He paused to clear his throat. "I don't get the opportunity to cook very much anymore, and since I feel so out of practice with it, I thought it'd be best this morning if—"

"This is all take-out?" I exclaimed in shock. "I mean, I figured the pastries probably were, but—"

"No. It's all home-cooked, even the pastries. Just not by me."

I took a bite of perfect scrambled eggs as I considered how best to decipher his words.

"I had a friend come over and cook while you were sleeping," he further confessed. His smile was sheepish—but not as much as I'd expect, given the circumstances.

"A friend?" I asked as nonchalantly as possible. A stranger had been in my apartment? *While I'd been asleep?*

"One of my chefs," he clarified after a beat, his posture and tone turning guarded.

Not a good sign. I took a sip of coffee and nearly choked on it as I realized he'd just said "chefs"—*plural*—and was reminded of my mafia suspicions. *Did werewolves have their own crime syndicate, I wondered?*

"Does this chef have a name?"

"Do you not like your food?" he evaded with a tight smile.

My pulse quickened despite my efforts to remain calm. "I love my food. I'd also love to know the name of the person who was in my home preparing it while I was unconscious."

He sighed. "Look, Bethy—"

The sound of someone outside my apartment door, inserting a key into the lock, interrupted us. And nearly stopped my heart.

Only two people had a key to my apartment, and today wasn't a cleaning day, which meant …

"Oh, good God." My fork slipped from my hand and clattered to the hardwood floor. "Gregg's at the door."

I sensed the blood draining from my face, making me feel faint as it occurred to me I hadn't thought of my fiancé even once since last night.

"Calm down." Raul took my hand in his, clasping it atop the table. "It's not Gregg. I promise. I had the locks changed last night."

And just like that, things went from bad to so much fucking worse.

CHAPTER 11

Bethany

"**U**M ... WHAT?"

The knob turned and the door pushed open.

"Not now, Mike," Raul said, right before a tall, handsome stranger entered my foyer and shut the door behind him like he'd done it a dozen times before.

"Right. I know you're busy, but I need a moment of your time, please," he addressed Raul directly. He seemed vaguely familiar to me. "Could we talk outside?" He gestured over his shoulder to my front door. "There's been a development. Time was of the essence, so I took the liberty of improvising."

Raul looked annoyed. "Improvising?"

"Fully deviating, actually," Mike replied before turning his attention to me. "Hi, Bethany. I'm Mike. My apologies for the interruption."

"Hi. Have we—"

"You two met last night," Raul supplied before I could ask, giving my hand a reassuring squeeze.

"Oh."

Mike laughed. "Well, I wouldn't say that we were properly introduced," he expounded, his grey eyes awash with humor. "But I helped hold you down once or twice while Raul—"

"Outside! Right now."

At Raul's sharp command, Mike turned and exited my apartment as quickly as he'd entered it a moment ago, chuckling and muttering, "You'd best be joining me."

Raul released my hand. "Please excuse me."

His chair scraped noisily against the floor as he scooted back from the table, and he arose so quickly and with such force that it toppled over behind him when he stood. He didn't bother to right it as he stormed out my front door after Mike.

I overheard them exchanging rapid words in Portuguese in the hallway a moment later. The arguing seemed to escalate quickly. Raul growled in anger, and I caught him tossing out the word "motherfucker" amid all the Portuguese. Mike said something in response, and then the hallway went completely silent—as if they'd done more than simply stop talking. It sounded as if they'd vanished from the hallway.

I sipped my coffee, contemplating whether they'd magically poofed somewhere. And then I began quietly giggling when I realized how insane it all was—the notion of people "poofing" places.

No, not people, I reminded myself. *Werewolves.* Because Raul was a werewolf. And he'd bitten me.

I was soon laughing so hard I had to set my coffee aside to wipe the tears of humor from my eyes.

Mike was probably a werewolf too. What if all the well-built "manny" friends of Raul's at the club last night had been werewolves? Should I ask? No, no, that might be rude. *Or dangerous.* Yes. I settled on dangerous, deciding it was best to know as little as possible.

I reined in my giggling fit when I heard a key being inserted into the lock of my front door, and the manny named Stephen, the one who had addressed Raul as "Sir" last night, entered.

Apparently, everyone but me had keys to the new locks on my apartment. Were they planning on giving me a set?

"Come, Kitsune," Stephen called into the hallway behind him, holding the door ajar for my Akita puppy, who ran in after him and headed straight for his water bowl in the kitchen.

"That—that's my dog." I stood, dumbfounded, as Stephen shut the door behind him. I was the worst new mommy ever. I hadn't even noticed my own puppy's absence this morning.

"Yes. I know," Stephen replied, his mouth set in a thin line. "I've been tasked with training him for you."

Tasked? "Excuse me? Why would you—?"

My front doorknob jiggled and opened yet again as Raul and Mike abruptly returned.

"You can go now, Stephen," Raul told him.

"No way," Mike objected. "Stephen stays. I am not handling you by myself."

"There's nothing to handle," Raul said through clenched teeth. "I'm fine."

"And your wolf?" Mike gave him a raised brow.

"Under control," Raul insisted.

O-*kay.* Yeah. Now was about the right time for a girl in a werewolf slasher flick to casually back her shit up out the door.

"I'm just gonna go get dressed for work now," I mumbled quietly, taking a step in the direction of the bedroom and hoping they would keep arguing and not notice me.

Raul's head whipped in my direction. His eyes took in the plate of food I'd barely touched, and he was at my side and steering me back into my seat at the table a second later.

"You need to eat more, sweetheart. Are you feeling okay?" Raul crouched next to my chair and placed a hand to my forehead. "You only got a few hours of decent sleep last night."

"I feel fine."

In the background, I overheard Mike and Stephen begin conversing in Spanish, and my ears pricked up. I was by no means fluent, but I understood a fair bit of Spanish. The dialect they were using sounded different from the Spanish I was familiar with, though.

"It's my fault." Raul's fingertips caressed my cheek before trailing down the side of my neck to the double mark he'd left there. Brushing my damp hair aside, he fingered the spot. "Still hurt a little?"

I shook my head. "I'm fine."

His frown indicated he wasn't convinced. His other hand fell to my lap, parting my knees as he palpated the bite mark on my upper thigh through the fabric of my pajama pants. "How about this one?"

I swallowed. "Also fine." His touch was examining, not sexual, yet my arousal kicked in nonetheless.

I had a feeling Raul knew it, too. He held my gaze as he continued to rub a larger circle around the mark on my inner thigh, his fingers inching ever higher. "Less tender than the bites on your neck?"

I nodded.

"Good." One corner of his mouth lifted. "Then I'm not sorry for waking you up last night to heal it."

My breath caught. "What?"

He leaned closer. His hand curled around the back of my neck, and he said in a low voice, "You looked beyond gorgeous straddling my shoulders." The tip of his tongue skimmed over his bottom lip. "I'm already dying for another taste of you."

It hadn't been a dream. I'd actually ridden Raul's face last night.

I was at once mortified and terribly turned on. I should've realized the sex was too good to have been a dream.

He drew closer, his nose touching mine, as he whispered, "The way you rode my fingers and squirmed against my mouth was the most beautiful thing I've ever seen."

I heard Stephen say in Spanish, "If they start fucking again, I'm out of here."

Raul's face pulled abruptly away from mine, his nostrils flaring, his irises swimming with gold.

I assumed his ire was for Stephen, but then his gaze turned sharply toward the front door, and I caught the sound of a key trying to force its way into the lock.

It didn't fit.

Shit. My heart began to pound, because I just knew. "I think that might be—"

A fist banged against my door. "Fucking bitch, you changed the locks on me?" Gregg yelled from the other side. "This is *my* building, Bethany. Open the damn door. I want my ring back."

My jaw unhinged. Gregg had never spoken to me like that before. Ever.

Clearly, either the doormen or one of my neighbors had tipped him off about Raul's overnight stay.

"Raul, no!"

I hardly had time to process that it was Mike who'd whisper-shouted before the table next to me flipped over, sending food and plates flying—and me ducking for cover—as Raul growled and lunged toward the door, transforming into an enormous black and white wolf in midair.

Oh.

My. God.

Mike and Stephen flew out of the kitchen and sprang into action, tackling Raul—as a wolf—to the tile floor of the foyer, knocking my entryway stand with fresh flowers over and smashing a sizeable hole into the wall that the foyer shared with my bedroom when all three of them crashed-stopped into it.

My brain was struggling to grasp what it was witnessing, when the three of them suddenly vanished—poofing into thin air.

Kitsune came running to me, barking up a storm. I scooped the little orange and white furball into my arms and cuddled him to my chest, babbling that everything was okay. The guy at the rescue shelter had told me Akitas only bark when something is wrong and they're unsettled.

"What the hell is going on in there?" Gregg pounded on the door again. "Bethany, let me in or I'll get security. Fuck that; I'll call the police."

Kitsune continued barking at the door. *Agreed. Something was definitely wrong all right.* I wasn't sure which of us I was hoping to convince otherwise as I continued to ramble soothing platitudes, carrying Kitsune past the wreckage in my living room and foyer to the front door.

I'd barely turned the knob and Gregg was forcing his way into my apartment, his eyes bloodshot and his skin ruddy with signs of another rosacea flare-up.

"Where is he?" he demanded, pushing past me. "I know he hasn't left yet. I want to meet the loser you threw our entire future away on. I cannot believe you—"

He stopped, his eyes blinking in shock when he saw the hole in the drywall and scanned the mess of food and dishes all over my living room floor.

"What the? Are you out of your mind? What have you done to my apartment? This is destruction of property."

I had no good answer for what had happened, so I assumed the offensive as he proceeded into my living room, stepping over a broken plate. "Stop calling it your apartment. My name's the only one on the lease, and last I checked, I'm the one paying rent and living here, not you." I kept my tone as steady and as calm as possible, hoping it would help to soothe Kitsune, who was now growling at Gregg.

"I own the building, Beth—"

"Your *parents* own this building. Along with other investors."

He had the gall to look affronted by that truth, the jackass. When I continued to stand there calmly holding Kitsune, providing no further explanation for the destruction Gregg was still taking in, he snapped, his face turning blotchy shades of red and purple as he blustered, "Seriously? You've got nothing to say to me? I've been texting and calling you all morning."

Crap. What had I done with my phone? I hadn't seen it since I'd woken up—when Raul had shut the ringer off for me.

"I show up here and find that you've blown apart not only our future but my whole damn apartment, and *nothing?*"

"*I've* destroyed our future?" I took a deep breath and set Kitsune down. "Go to the bedroom, Kitsune." I pointed to my open bedroom door, and I was shocked when the little mutt actually listened to my order and scampered off into the room instead of going straight for the food all over the floor like I'd expected.

"You've been fucking around on me for months, Gregg, so drop the self-righteous BS. It takes two people to ruin a relationship, and I'm not going to take all the blame for ours."

"*Me?* Who told you I was cheating?"

His green eyes lit with indignation, but I glimpsed the guilt behind them. He was furious that I knew. I could almost see his brain running over the possibilities as to which of his friends might have ratted him out. Yeah, he'd definitely been cheating for a while. Maybe more than the five months I'd estimated from the skanky texts I'd found.

"I've never cheated on you, Bethany. Don't try and blame your whorish behavior on—"

"I saw the texts on your phone, Gregg."

His mouth opened and shut several times. I crossed my arms over my chest and waited. The sound of a phone vibrating in his pocket filled the silence, reminding me that I still needed to locate my own phone.

"That's impossible. What texts? What were you doing going through my private texts? You had no business—"

"I needed a contact for the caterer."

"And I sent it to you the other day when you asked me for it."

"You sent me the wrong contact. When I called Brandi with an 'i,' she seemed unusually flustered when I gave her your name for the booking and the date of our reception."

His expression paled a fraction, but he shook his head in denial, nonetheless, as I continued.

"She rambled an apology, saying she wasn't the caterer and that she hadn't known you were engaged, before hanging up on me. I got curious and went through the texts on your phone after that."

He was still stubbornly shaking his head. And I couldn't help but note he seemed oddly reassured somehow by what I'd just told him—as if what I knew only scratched the surface, and he was relieved to hear how little I'd actually uncovered.

"You had no right," he lectured. "Whatever you *think* you found, you're mistaken. Do you have any idea how many women come on to me in a given week?"

A shout of laughter escaped me before I could restrain it. Gregg may have been tall and an attractive-for-a-corporate-guy type, but his inflated ego was so far out of sync with reality it was a joke.

"They do," he insisted. "I'm a broker, Bethany. I interact with a lot of people, and yes, sometimes that means flirting with potential female investors."

"Strippers are investing in multimillion-dollar Bay Area real estate now? Good to know. By the way, I went through your online credit card receipts, too."

His eyes flared and he sputtered, "Y—you have no proof of anything. You know damn well it's part of my job to sometimes take clients to gentlemen's clubs. So what if you found a few texts from random women on my phone? That doesn't make me guilty of cheat—"

"It does when you're texting them back photos of your dick, Gregg."

"Well, *you* had sex in a public elevator with some roided-out meathead you met at a dance club!" he exploded, talking loudly enough for the whole floor to hear him. "I had to wake up this morning to an email from security with a link to video footage of a stranger plowing my fiancé up against the wall of my own building's elevator, for fuck's sake."

My heart dropped into my stomach.

There was video footage?

Holy shit, I'd forgotten all about the surveillance cameras.

"You let him carry you through the lobby downstairs half-naked wrapped in a blanket for everyone to see," Gregg indicted. "And you couldn't even wait to get inside our apartment to spread your legs. No, you let him bang you in a public elevator like some desperate horny bitch in heat. You disgraced me in front of my own management staff, my own building security."

And that's what this was about: Gregg's ego. Not our relationship. Not me.

"Then I went online and checked the feed for the camera that I had installed months ago in this very foyer—*for your protection*," he emphasized, "and I had the joy of watching footage of you on your knees sucking that asshole's cock. What the hell were you thinking, Bethany? Was this your childish way of getting back at me for a few harmless flirty texts you found on my phone? You couldn't even come talk to me first? You just jumped on the first dick you could find?"

"First of all, fuck you for continuing to assume I'm an idiot. Secondly, I did not mean for things to happen the way they did last night. I was planning to confront you about the texts—"

"Well, it's too late now, because I've already forwarded your sex tapes to everyone on our guest list, letting them know that the wedding is off." He held his hand out. "I want my ring back."

"What did you say?"

"I said the wedding is off and I want my ring back."

"I meant the other part!" I screeched.

"I said I've already emailed your sex tapes to everyone you know, Bethany." His smirk was nasty as he watched that bomb settle.

CHAPTER 12

Bethany

MY LIFE WAS RUINED. MY CHARACTER ... MY
professional reputation ... everything I'd ever worked
for had just been blown to dust with one email.

"You did what?" I could barely get the words past the
tightness enveloping my throat.

"Sent it to *everyone*," he sneered. "Every friend, every
family member, every hospital and medical school associ-
ate you invited to our wedding. Your parents, your cousins,
your sweet grandma who adores me, your *pastor*—they
all got video footage of you getting fucked in an elevator,
Bethany. Followed by a clip of you on your knees masturbating and choking on some loser club rat's cock."

Oh, God, I was going to throw up.

My eyes filled with tears. My mind and emotions
reeled as I contemplated the horrified reactions of everyone I loved and respected most in life viewing such scan-
dalous, intimate video footage of me with Raul. I was going to have to relocate—to a remote village in Antarctica.
My parents would never recover from this. Granny Jean
might've already gone into cardiac arrest upon opening

that email. I needed to call her assisted living facility immediately—send a nurse to check on her.

Amid my sickening panic, self-righteous fury mushroomed within me, eclipsing every other pressing need and emotion assailing me, and I lashed out.

"His name is Raul, and he is *not* a loser club rat. He's a *manny*. He cares for a special-needs child, which is a more meaningful, commendable way to earn a living than any of the bullshit jobs your parents have ever handed to you on a platter. And—adore you? Ha! Granny Jean? She told me you were *basic*. The worst kind of basic nouveau riche. She's probably drinking a spiked Metamucil right now, toasting the fact that I finally found a man with enough cock for me to actually choke on."

"You told me size didn't matter, that it was all about skill and chemistry," Gregg balked, his shallow, narcissist brain latching onto my jab about his small penis rather than the one about how he didn't earn his living.

"It matters when you're also lacking in the skill and chemistry department!"

"Bethy, what's all this shouting about?"

Just when I thought things couldn't get any more crazy or tense, Mike walked out from my bedroom, wearing nothing but boxer briefs and a towel on his head, and talking with a British accent.

"Oh, hey, I'm Mike, Bethany's cousin." He held his hand out for Gregg to shake as he came to stand next to me, looking like a model—or an exotic male dancer—with his sculpted, tanned physique on display.

Gregg was so disoriented by Mike's half-naked arrival on the scene that he shook his hand, his eyes darting between the two of us. "Cousin?"

Mike shrugged. "Yeah, distant cousin—*step*-cousin, re-ally—through marriage. But still close family." He flashed me a cheesy smile before squinting one eye and pretending to connect the dots on an invisible family tree in the air with his pointer finger. "You see, I'm Bethany's mother's brother's wife's stepsister's kid." He dropped his hand and grinned at Gregg. "Bethy's always been the ultimate SCILF to me."

Dear God.

"SCILF?" Gregg took the bait.

"Uh-huh." Mike threw his arm around me, pulling me into his rock-solid bare chest. "You know ... step-cousin I'd like to fuck."

This day was not happening.

"So I flew out here early for the wedding."

Gregg's face looked to be permanently frozen in a frown of disbelief. "Three months early?"

"Well, yeah. I thought I might be able to sixty-nine some sense into Bethy. Tongue her out of making the biggest mistake of her life. But then *I* made the mistake of bringing my best friend along with me to go dancing last night. And he got his tongue in her first."

Of all the ...

"Hands off my girl, Mike." Raul strode out of my bed-room, dressed as he'd been five minutes ago—before he'd flipped out and turned into a wolf.

My stomach fell through the floor at the reminder of the recent episode I'd blocked out while preoccupied with Gregg's arrival. Mike released me, his arm lifting from around my shoulders as Raul came to stand on my oppo-site side.

"You know I don't share." Raul looked directly at Gregg rather than Mike as he said it.

Gregg's eyes narrowed, recognizing Raul from the surveillance videos no doubt. "You."

"Me," Raul confirmed. That one syllable somehow managed to sound like a promise of murder.

The momentary silence that fell upon my living room was disturbed only by the still-constant buzzing sound of Gregg's phone going off in his pocket.

"And you're a babysitter?" Gregg had the idiocy to ask.

When Raul didn't reply, but continued to stare Gregg down like he was contemplating which of his limbs to tear off first, Mike jumped in.

"Manny. We're both mannies, actually."

"I'm a manny as well," Stephen's deep voice proclaimed as he, too, emerged from my bedroom, wearing nothing but white grape-smuggler briefs that he filled out so surprisingly well I had to force my shocked eyes to look away from the disturbing size of his package.

I stole a glance at Raul and noted he'd ceased staring Gregg down long enough for his eyes to roll to the ceiling.

Mike coughed and covered his mouth with his hand when Stephen came to stand next to him, muttering, "I still don't get why I'm dressed like this."

Gregg's bloodshot green eyes swept over the three huge men flanking me, and while his ego had always been bigger than his dick, I could tell the moment my ex-fiancé's pea brain wisely deduced that he was outnumbered and outsized by built, hung "babysitters."

"I was just leaving," he announced, his gaze leveled on Raul. "You can keep her." His smile was ugly as he looked Raul up and down like he was trash. "Shacking up with a hot doctor is a boon for a nobody babysitter, I'm sure. Bet you think you've hit pay dirt. Well, don't get too comfortable here, because she's under eviction."

Turns out I'd given Gregg's pea brain too much credit.

"For what?" I challenged. "You have no cause to evict me." I was for sure moving out in order to relocate to a tiny cabin in the middle of nowhere, but I'd be damned if I'd admit to Gregg how much he'd just destroyed my life.

"Fornicating in public, indecent exposure, destruction of property—"

"Oh, fine, *fine,* I'm moving out. The hot water pressure in this building stinks anyway. Goodbye, Gregg. Try not to trip over your wounded ego on the way out."

He thrust his hand at me, palm up. "I want my ring back first, you cheating whore."

Mike whistled low, then murmured, "Hold it together, man."

I knew Mike's warning was for Raul, because a growling sound was emanating from Raul's chest, and I could've sworn I'd felt the energy shift around me like wind at the words "cheating whore."

Gregg didn't know when to shut up and save his own life. He looked from me to Raul. "What the hell was that?"

I patted my stomach. "You're giving me indigestion." I turned to Raul and placed a calming hand on his forearm. His skin was hot to the touch. I could feel the anger vibrating off him as his muscles twitched beneath my fingers. "You wouldn't happen to know where my engagement ring ended up last night, would you?"

He shook his head minutely, his deadened gaze fixed on Gregg. "Uh-uh. Haven't seen it." His voice was guttural, raspy, as he prompted, "Have you, Mike?"

"Nope," Mike readily replied. "Not since last night when I gave it to a homeless woman outside the club."

Oh, shit.

"You did what?" Gregg erupted, his face turning a brighter shade of blotchy red. "That was a forty-three-thousand-dollar rock."

Mike hunched one shoulder. "Well, I did apologize to the little old lady for the tackiness factor. Told her I'd give her something nicer the next time we came through town."

"You owe me fifty grand!" Gregg shouted at me.

Mike laughed. "You just said it was forty-three."

"I'm tacking on the cost of invitations and wedding deposits I can't recover."

Granny Jean had been right. Gregg was hopelessly basic.

"I'll mail you a check," I told him. "You need to leave." I gave him a pointed look, hoping that some self-preservation instinct within him would kick in. "Now."

He scowled and retrieved his still-buzzing phone from his pant pocket. "Fuck that. I'm calling the police and reporting the ring as stolen. As far as I'm concerned, all four of you are responsible for its loss."

There was no helping some people.

"Are you out of your mind? It was my ring to lose. You gave it to me."

"But you cheated on me."

"And you cheated on me for how many months, Gregg? With how many women?"

"Say, that's quite a lot of messages you're racking up there," Mike broke in with a nod at the phone in Gregg's hand that was continually going off. "Maybe you should check them," he suggested with a smile. "Make sure there's nothing important happening. Oh, that reminds me, Bethy. I think I heard your phone buzzing a few times back in the bedroom as well."

Mike pulled my phone from thin air—*literally*—and handed it to me. Gregg did a double take when he witnessed it. I felt a sense of impending dread in my gut, knowing it was time to face the music.

Too afraid to check my emails, I glanced over my many text messages first. After scrolling through count-less texts from Kylie from last night pleading for updates and demanding dick pics, I got to more serious ones from her from this morning where she was asking if I was okay, telling me that what had happened with Gregg was for the best and that she'd be over with wine and chocolate when my on-call shift was over. There were confused texts from Jessie and multiple frantic texts from my mom and my dad, saying that they would be by the hospital later to check on me. Stranger still, there were a handful of texts from my associates at the hospital telling me to take the day off, as-suring me that my shift would be covered. I even had a text from Granny Jean. It was a single eye-roll emoji with the hashtag #basic.

Not quite the horrified reactions I was anticipating from people who had been forwarded raunchy sex vids of me.

"What … the hell?" Gregg's voice was a breathless whis-per, as if the air had been knocked out of him.

I glanced up to find him shifting anxiously on his feet, his wide eyes focused on his phone screen.

"No, no, no. This can't be happening. This isn't real," he said a bit louder, before yelling, "What the fuck? This isn't real." He began turning in aimless circles. "That's not the email I sent. That's not the video I attached. This can't be happening to me."

His face had paled; even the blotchy parts were shades lighter. His hands were shaking as he clicked and scrolled frantically on his phone—that was still going off. "Who did this? I never sent this! Where the hell did that video come from?"

He'd sent the wrong video?

I went to my inbox and saw that I had hundreds of un-read messages—all of them replies to an original message with the subject line: *I regret to inform you the McIntyre - Garrett wedding has been cancelled.* I scrolled down un-til I found the original message sent by Gregg and opened it to find a video attachment with a freeze-frame image of Gregg putting bills in a stripper's thong.

Never would I have imagined I'd be overjoyed to see such an image of my ex-fiancé. But my heart felt lighter than it had since Gregg's arrival as I double-clicked on the video and a montage of Gregg cheating on me played out across my phone screen.

There were multiple video clips of Gregg getting lap dances, several of him making out in bars with different women, one of him having sex with someone else at his office, and another of him having sex inside his car in his office building's parking garage. Some of the images were grainy and hard to see, but they were clearly of Gregg and women who weren't me. The montage appeared to have been assembled from various surveillance videos.

In my elation, I emitted a watery giggle as I turned and beamed at Raul next to me, babbling, "It's not us. My life's not ruined. He didn't send out the elevator sex tape. Or the one of us in the foyer."

"He tried," was Raul's stony reply, his eyes on my un-raveling ex.

"I have to destroy those tapes," I processed aloud as the sobering reality that they were still out there hit me.

"Already done," Mike said with certainty.

Gregg's head jerked up from his phone at Mike's assertion. *"You,"* he accused, his wild eyes those of a trapped, desperate animal as they glared first at Mike, and then at Raul. "You guys did this. You ruined my life. Posing as a bunch of fucking babysitters!"

Mike and Stephen burst out laughing, and it occurred to me I hadn't seen Stephen crack a smile before now, much less laugh.

"This one's sharp, Bethy," Mike said, dropping both the British accent and the towel on his head at last. "Wherever did you find him?"

"Who are you?" Gregg demanded, his eyes darting back and forth between the three of them. "Who hired you to do this to me? Bethany, these guys set you up. This is a corporate sabotage scheme. And you fell for it."

My jaw dropped open. This was somehow *my* fault that he'd sent the wrong sex tapes to our entire guest list?

"Ah, Greggie with too many g's," Mike said with a sigh, "you're gonna wish we were only part of a corporate sabotage scheme."

"Now can I change my outfit?" Stephen asked on a whine.

I didn't hear Raul or Mike answer him, but Stephen snarled ferociously and transformed into a giant brown wolf.

Instinctively, I screamed and scrambled behind Raul's back.

Gregg tripped over his own feet and fell backward, landing on his ass. He quickly sprang back up again and darted for the door when the brown wolf snapped his mammoth jaws at him.

Before Gregg could reach the door, Mike was somehow standing in front of it, his yellow wolf eyes flashing menacingly. "Wolf got your tongue?" he taunted.

I didn't understand what Mike meant by that, but then Gregg's hands flew to his throat and he spun around, his jaw opening and shutting, his mouth moving to form words, yet failing to make a sound.

"No one objects to me disabling his vocal chords, right?" Mike looked to Raul for approval, commenting with disdain, "I can't stand the sound of a coward squealing. And I believe we've all heard enough bullshit out of this one that we can skip his final words. It's bad enough reading them from his mind."

The brown wolf growled at Gregg, causing him to jump and scream soundlessly. My ex-fiancé looked like he might cry as his head whipped back and forth between the giant wolf snarling at him from the living room floor and Mike—with his scary glowing wolf eyes—blocking the only exit.

Gregg's panic-stricken eyes cut to me, where I stood peeking out from behind Raul's back—and entering my own state of shock—as I watched the disturbing scene play out. Gregg mouthed, "Help."

"I'm afraid she can't help you," Mike told him. "And there's no need to mouth or pantomime; we can hear your thoughts loud and clear. We know exactly what a sorry sack you are."

They could hear thoughts?

They could disable a person's vocal chords.

The brown wolf transformed back into Stephen—dressed in the slacks and T-shirt he'd been wearing earlier when he'd come in with Kitsune.

"The truth is, we're not exactly mannies," Stephen revealed the obvious. "And now that you know about us, we can't let you live."

Slowly, my bloodless fingers released their grip on the back of Raul's T-shirt I'd unconsciously been clutching as it dawned on me the extent of danger Gregg and I were actually in.

Also, I realized Raul was growling—a lot.

He hadn't touched or so much as glanced at me since I'd ducked behind his back to get away from Stephen in wolf form. As I cautiously inched around from behind his broad shoulders to get a better view of him in profile, I saw that his eyes were as feral as Mike's and Stephen's, and his face was a mask of murderous rage—aimed squarely at Gregg.

"Sure, we do some babysitting here and there," Mike expounded, waving his hand about. "But we're more like an elite werewolf special-ops unit. Maybe think of us as a lethal, supernatural version of the Baby-Sitters Club. But instead of organizing daycare camps for kids, we spend our time warring with enemy packs and paving the way for a next-level breed of super-werewolves."

This was so much worse than Raul being part of the Brazilian mafia. He was in the *werewolf* mafia.

I still had my phone in my hand. Did 9-1-1 accept texts? What could the police possibly do against three huge werewolves with the ability to poof places and immobilize speech?

"But enough chitchat, eh?" Mike smirked at Gregg, who looked about ready to piss himself. "I think my boss wants a word with you."

Mike's attention transferred to Raul. "Think you can finish this without shifting and making a mess of his entrails all over my step-cousin's living room? If we don't wrap it up and get out of here in the next twenty-six minutes, we're going to have more minds on our hands to erase."

What?

"I won't need that long."

Faster than I could blink, Raul was in front of Gregg, his hand wrapped around his throat, choking him.

My own breath left me, and for a moment I froze—too petrified of what I was seeing to move a muscle.

"Let him talk," Raul said to Mike. "I've decided I do want to hear his final words after all."

Upon Raul's directive, Gregg began making terrible gurgling and choking sounds in the back of his throat, wheezing pitiably over what little air supply Raul's hand around his neck would allow.

"Stop it."

The words left me, but they were so faint and breathless in my paralyzed state that I barely heard them myself.

Gregg's tongue wagged aimlessly in his open mouth, his hands yanking desperately at Raul's wrist.

Holy shit. This was real. This was serious.

"What did you say?" Raul mocked him, tilting his ear toward Gregg's increasingly purple-red face. "Was there a final, burning question you had for me? Wait—did you just ask *why*? Are you serious? Nah, that wasn't it. *Who*? Really? That's what you're going to go with—still asking who I am?"

"Wow. I do believe that's what he's trying to say," Mike confirmed with a laugh.

Raul and Stephen started laughing as well as the three of them shared a look, and for the life of me, I couldn't figure out how any of this was funny.

"What a dumb final question," Stephen assessed. "How disappointing after so much set-up."

Mike gave a nod of agreement. "Even *why* would've been better."

Raul shook his head in amusement at my suffocating ex-fiancé in his unforgiving grasp. "Well, Gregg, *some* might say that I'm a nobody babysitter who has just hit pay dirt. A loser club rat who got lucky with your girl last night." Raul's laughing countenance abruptly fell away, and he leaned in to whisper, "But they're wrong. Know why? Because she was never your girl. *She was always mine*," he seethed. "You're the one who got lucky. And now that luck has run out."

What—what did he mean by that?

"Take a good look at *my* girl, Gregg, because it's the last time you'll ever see her."

Oh, God, he was going to kill him.

I had to do something.

Gregg's eyes bugged out as Raul raised him off the ground by his throat, growling, "Who am I? *I'm* the guy who worked his ass off his whole life, the one who earned every damn thing he has—the scrapper kid who had to claw his way up from the bottom of the food chain while watching assholes like you get handed everything you wanted in life."

CHAPTER 13

Raul

"**R**AUL, STOP! YOU'RE GOING TO KILL HIM. STOP!"

I heard her words, felt Bethany's fists pounding frantically against my back and shoulders. But it wasn't enough to dim the red haze enveloping me.

Ten years. For ten years I'd left her alone—the woman I wanted most—in order to protect her. I had thought that I was doing right by Bethany in doing so. And this asshole—the man she had chosen to be with and commit to for life—had taken her for granted. He had betrayed her trust. He'd attempted to shame her to all of her family and friends.

He'd made her cry.

He deserved to die. Painfully.

"He can't breathe, Raul. Stop it! You're going to crush his windpipe."

Arrogant prick had thought to claim the woman who was mine. And he'd hurt her—*my* Bethy.

"Stop him," she appealed to Mike and Stephen. "Raul, don't do this! Please let go of him. *Please*, I'm begging you."

The scent of Bethany's fear hit me. Along with that of her tears. She had moved to my side and was practically hanging from my bicep now, using all of her body weight in her attempt to get me to stop choking her worthless ex-fiancé—who had just lost consciousness.

Reluctantly, I forced myself to let him go. He dropped to the floor with a thud, collapsing in an unconscious heap.

Bethany released my bicep and dove to the floor after him.

I wasn't having it. I swung her back up again and into my arms despite her struggling.

"Let me go—I have to help him."

They were the wrong words for her to say to me. I was never letting her go again. And I was not letting her near that asshole to help him.

"He's fine." It was the truth. *More or less.* Gregg with too many g's would live. Not that he deserved to.

"He's unconscious!" She was still flailing and struggling in my arms. *And crying.* Her voice was shrill, hysterical. "He needs medical attention. Raul, you have to let me help him. *Please.*"

"I said he's fine," I snapped callously at the woman whose happiness and well-being I had sworn to myself ten years ago I would always place before my own.

Because as much as Bethany's tearful pleading gutted me, her loyalty and concern for a man who didn't deserve it from her awoke a dormant monster of bitterness within me that was as dark and ugly as it was childish and irrational.

Even my own fated mate chose another over me. A man who had cheated on her and lied to her.

She couldn't begin to understand what I had sacrificed for her safety over the past ten years—the ongoing pain my wolf had endured by staying away.

I could barely see straight as I carted her from the living room, barking orders in Portuguese over my shoulder so that Bethany wouldn't understand them as I told Mike to make sure the bastard lived, but to leave his mind to me.

I wasn't done with Gregg yet.

Be gentle! Be gentle, my wolf howled at me. The rage that had me in its grip thinned as I realized I'd carried Bethany into her bedroom and I was on top of her, pinning her to the mattress. And she was freaking out. Thrashing beneath me, she was babbling a mile a minute through her tears, alternating between berating and pleading with me.

My mate. Was. Terrified.

And it was all my fault. I'd fucked things up royally. *Again.*

"I won't tell anyone anything, I swear. You don't have to kill me. We can pretend this never happened. You and your men can walk away. I never saw any of you—I promise. Swear on my life. Please? Damnit, Raul, how can you do this?" she sobbed. "What's happened to you? How can you kill me like I mean nothing to you?"

I blinked. My brain struggled to process her words as my emotions fought to reset. Bethy thought I would kill her?

"Kill you?" My voice was soft. It felt even worse to say those words out loud. Like a knife in my throat. "How could—how can you even think that I—?"

I was acting like an asshole, that's how.

"I'd *never* harm you." I felt hollow inside as I said it. But I said it again and again, along with anything else I could think of to reassure her. "I promise you're safe with me." I kissed her tear-streaked face. "Always and forever safe."

I rolled us over so that she was on top. My fingers combed through her hair; my hands ran up and down her back and arms. But I felt helpless to soothe her as she continued to cry and blather more promises about not saying anything to anyone.

"S—swear I won't tell anyone you're a—a werewolf … subspecies," she said with a sniffle.

I wanted to flay myself.

She didn't understand. She wasn't getting it. And it was my fault. For waiting too long. For pushing things too fast.

For fucking it all up like I always did.

"Bethy, I'm sorry I scared you back there. I lost my temper. But you don't have to be afraid of me. I'm not going to hurt you. Not ever."

"What about Gregg?" she wailed.

"I won't hurt him, either. Anymore," I appended. Not physically, at least.

She let out a little gasp. "Because he's already dead?"

"No. No, he's not dead. I told you he wasn't dead." Didn't she believe me? *Eh, fuck, why would she?*

"You said he was fine. You never said he wasn't dead."

She was too smart to be mated to me. The fates had made a mistake. "Okay, you're right. But when I said he was fine, I meant that he was alive—that he would live." I was sick of discussing that S.O.B. "Listen, let's talk about this later. Right now we need to get you back to Argentina. I have a doctor there who—"

"Back?" Her brow pinched as she looked down at me, her glassy eyes red, her blonde hair in disarray. "I've never been." She paused, her frown intensifying the longer she stared at me. She seemed to be trying to gauge whether or not I was serious. I knew from her heart rate the moment she realized that I was. Dead serious. "I—I can't travel out of town, much less abroad, Raul. I'm on call this weekend. Besides, I'd have to get updated inoculations—"

"Sweetheart, I bit you a little harder than I meant to last night." Sometimes honesty was the best approach.

"You mean this bite?" Her fingers flew to the initial bite I'd made and had subsequently repeated on the side of her throat.

"Yes, that one." As well as the ones on her thigh, shoulder, and breast. *Often partial honesty was a better approach.* "I have the best doctor in the world in my employ at my home in Bariloche. I want Rafe to take a look at your neck for me, okay?"

"There's no need. It's totally fine." She'd begun shaking her head continuously. "I'll just inject some antibiotic if it's not better in a few days." Her wobbly smile was strained.

The scent of her fear permeated the air, and my stomach roiled as I realized Mike was right: I was going to have to take her to Bariloche by force. She was too confused. Too frightened of me to go willingly now.

And I wasn't leaving San Francisco without her.

I reached out to Mike through our mind connection, letting him know we were going to have to sedate Bethany after all. I'd been appalled at the idea when Mike had suggested that it might become necessary, but now I was grateful he'd had the foresight to think of it and to teleport back to Bariloche this morning to procure a safe sedative injection from Rafe.

I cursed my sister's pack. This situation would be so much simpler and safer if I had access to Bethany's mind and could render her unconscious that way. It made me sick to think of injecting synthetic drugs into her system. But we were running out of time.

Mike's guys had taken the precaution of setting up surveillance and tracking devices on Bethany's family and close friends overnight. While we'd been busy scaring the shit out of Gregg, the guys had sent word telepathically to Mike that Mrs. Garrett was already on her way over to check on Bethy.

We still needed to finish with Gregg and clean up the mess we'd made of Bethany's apartment. And now it seemed I would have to find a way to put Mrs. G off before we hopped a jet home.

Though Mike and I had teleported to San Francisco for our meeting yesterday, the rest of my men had flown in with Stephen on one of our private planes. In light of where things stood with Bethany, I'd decided it was best for us all to return to Bariloche via private jet. I needed more time to explain things to Bethany—to better prepare her for the supernatural world she was about to be thrust into.

And time to figure out how best to explain the way I felt about Bethany to Sloane. I doubted Sloane was going to be very happy about Bethy's arrival—or about the role of mate that Bethany would now occupy in my life.

"Antibiotics won't help, baby," I tried to reason with her. "I need my doctor—a werelock doctor—to look at your bite."

"But that's silly, Raul. I know tons of great doctors right here in San Francisco. Heck, *I'm* a doctor, remember?" Her laughter held a note of hysteria as she prattled, "My mom's a doctor, most of my closest friends are doctors, I spend my days and nights at a hospital surrounded by doctors ..."

As Mike entered the bedroom, I reversed our positions, flipping Bethany over so that she was once again on her back and I was above her.

The moment I did it, and she saw Mike coming toward us, her survival instincts kicked into full gear. She started squirming beneath me, then flailing like mad when she caught sight of the needle in Mike's hand.

"Raul, please don't do this. You don't have to do this. I swear I won't say anything."

"Bethany, there's nothing to be afraid of. No one's going to harm you. We're doing this to help you."

She began sobbing again. She wasn't hearing me.

She didn't trust me.

"Shh—everything's going to be okay, step-cuz," Mike tried to reassure her to no avail as he approached the bed. "It's only a mild sedative. It can't hurt you."

Her state of panic only escalated.

And I felt it as if it were my panic.

"Raul, you have to hold her still. Dragging this out will make it worse."

I couldn't do this. Her hysterical begging and thrashing was ripping my heart open. Calling forth memories and emotions I'd fought to block out over the years.

In my mind, she suddenly became my mother begging the paramedics not to take her to the hospital—struggling with them when they'd tried to move her onto a stretcher, pleading with them to let her deliver her baby right there on the kitchen floor instead.

For a moment, I felt utterly helpless. Powerless. Transported back in time to when I was the kid in the background repeatedly told to get out of the way; the little boy who'd had no control, no say in what happened next.

The idiot who'd simply stood there crying, watching his mom die.

Don't go there.

Can't afford to go there.

I was a man now. I was in control. I'd gone to great lengths and pushed extraordinary limits to ensure that I would always be the one in control—the one holding the power and calling the shots.

I got to say what happened next.

Taking Bethany was the right thing to do. She didn't understand the situation. Didn't know that her life was in danger and she needed to come with us in order to be safe. I couldn't give her a choice in this.

I wouldn't give her a choice.

A calm swept over me, shutting off my emotions and numbing the pain I'd felt in my heart at the sight of her tears. I sank my weight into her midsection, removed her hands that were clutching at me, and pinned them together at the wrist with one hand against the bed. My fingers that had been caressing her scalp in an attempt to soothe her fisted the roots of her hair to hold her head steady.

"Do it," I ordered Mike. "Put her under before we lose any more time."

Bethany's wet eyes flared at my command.

I knew I'd sounded cold. Callous.

The fear and horror I saw reflected in her blue-green eyes at my perceived betrayal would haunt me. But it didn't matter. I was saving Bethany.

I told myself she would understand later that this had been the right thing to do as Mike moved into position with the needle. I held her immobile as he pierced her jugular vein and depressed the syringe plunger, injecting Rafe's modified opioid directly into her bloodstream to put her out faster.

Fresh tears flooded her eyes, even as I felt the tension in her body settling, her muscles relaxing as her form went limp beneath my hold.

"*Slowly,*" I reminded Mike. "Not too much."

"I've got it. She'll be fine. Don't worry."

I tried to make my voice reassuring as I told Bethy again that everything was going to be okay, that she was safe with me, and that I was sorry.

I was—*so fucking sorry.*

Her glassy eyes were unfocused by the time Mike withdrew the needle. By the time he'd left the room, she was struggling to remain conscious as I stroked her hair and wiped her tears away.

I wasn't sure if she could still hear me as I pleaded softly, "Please forgive me for this, Bethy. Please understand. I promise everything's going to be okay."

"Hate you," she slurred in reply as her heavy eyelids finally gave in and lost the battle.

I sighed and kissed her sleeping forehead.

"I know. I hate me too."

CHAPTER 14

Raul

"**W**E HAVE TO SEPARATE THEM. I'LL TAKE THE BOY BACK to Brazil with me. You give the girl up for adoption here."

The screen in front of me blurred. My eyes stung as I blinked back tears. Mateus wasn't the kind of adult you could cry in front of. Although, there'd been a brief moment at the wake when I could have sworn I'd seen him crying by Mom's casket.

My sweaty fingers slipped over the controls as I pretended to still be engrossed in my game. I was getting my ass beat by Dr. Wily, and I didn't even care. I stole a glance at Aunt Cely. She looked like she was about to "go nuclear," as Mom would have said.

"If you think I'm going to give up custody of my nephew to the sperm donor who refers to him as 'the boy,' you're dumber than I always told Kamella you were."

"I can never offer you any support. Just like I couldn't Kamella. Sending money would've given us away. How will you support two kids on your own? Put your emotions aside and be rational about this."

"*Spoken like a true deadbeat. I don't want your money.*"

"*You don't understand. Kamella's death may have already given us away. I made up outlandish lies just to be able to come here. I'll have to invent more before this is through.*"

"*I want you to leave.*"

"*You're not listening to me. The girl's life can never be tied to mine. Do you understand? Her very existence will get us all killed.*"

"*The girl?*" Aunt Cely repeated, her blue eyes narrowing to slits as she puffed her chest out. "*By 'the girl,' I will assume you mean* Milena, *your newborn* daughter *and my sister's second child by your unfortunate participation. Let me assure you, I am one hundred percent on board with you never having anything to do with my niece.*"

"*You think this is my fault? That I wanted this?*" Mateus's face contorted and his voice rose in anger as he glared from Aunt Cely to my sleeping sister in her bassinet. "*That I wanted that—that—*"

"*Baby?*" Aunt Cely finished for him, her volume and exasperation level rising to match his anger.

"*Curse.*" He pointed a finger at my sister. "*That thing is a living, breathing curse.*"

"*Get out of this house!*" Cely screeched at him. Her head whipped in my direction. "*Raul, go to your room.*"

I jumped up from the couch, anxious to get away, but all the yelling had woken Milena up, and she started crying, her little wails adding to the tension consuming the house as Mateus continued to rage.

"*Kamella told me she was on the pill. That baby never should have happened to begin with. It sure as shit shouldn't have lived. Goddamn paramedics were supposed to save Kamella's life. I could sue them.*"

I went to the bassinet and bent over my crying sister. I felt stupid making the shushing noises like I'd seen Aunt Cely do before, so I reached in and touched the tip of my finger to the inside of Milena's little open palm when she waved it above her face. "Hey," I whispered. "It's okay."

She stopped wailing, and her blue eyes stared up at me like I was the coolest thing she'd ever seen. Her tiny fingers wrapped around the end of my forefinger, squeezing it tightly in her baby fist.

I felt myself smile, even as a tear rolled down my nose and fell on her little pink sheet, leaving a wet mark.

"She *is not an* it. *And you don't have a legal right to sue anyone, you selfish son of a bitch. You weren't Kamella's husband. You're not on either child's birth certificate."*

"Thank God for that." Mateus huffed. "If you do this, you're going to have to move away. You'll have to raise the girl to think she's your own. Best if she's surrounded by people who don't know." He was pacing now. "The boy complicates things unless I take him with me. He knows too much. Kamella told him things she shouldn't have. He could ruin everything if he doesn't play along."

"You're insane. I don't know what my sister ever saw in you, but you can leave this house now and go straight to hell for all I care, because I don't need your crazy advice or your help. And it'll be over my dead body that you ever take Raul to Brazil with you."

I lay in bed with Bethany after she fell asleep, listening to the sounds of her breathing and her steady heartbeat to make sure she was okay. In my head, I ran over all the ways that I would make this up to her.

I could make it up to her.

She would forgive me. She would understand.

Bethy was different. She'd always been unique in the way that she took people for who they were—even when they didn't fit into familiar societal categories or conform to acceptable standards of right and wrong. I'd noticed that about Bethy long before my wolf had identified her as our mate.

She would understand I'd done what was best for her— that I'd done this to protect her.

"Your future mother-in-law's here," Mike informed me from the doorway. "In the elevator on her way up."

Reluctantly, I extracted myself from my mate.

"Stephen and I'll take Gregg and check in with the guys. Reach out if you need help charming Marlee," Mike offered, lingering in the doorway. "I was thinking I could try my Russian accent on her."

Mike didn't hover unless he had something to tell me that I wouldn't like. But I ignored him while I rearranged Bethany into a more comfortable position on the bed— one that would also better conceal her bite marks.

"What?" I finally asked as I was tucking the covers around her.

"I've ordered Wyatt back from Puerto Iguazú."

My head came up. "Why? That wasn't your call. Why didn't you talk to me?"

"It'll be good for Bethany."

"Still not your call."

His back straightened. "Wyatt's a newly transformed wolf. He can provide a newcomer's perspective. Plus, he's mated, therefore completely safe to have around Bethany. He can help fill in history on Sloane, Avery trusts him implicitly, he's easily controlled, and he comes across as the least threatening member of our entire pack."

He had a point. Several good ones, in fact.

"Not to mention, he witnessed Avery's unassisted transformation, which may also prove useful in getting Bethany to understand the situation that—"

"You've sold me. Just keep him away from Alcaeus."

"Already planned for that."

Of course he had. Mike thought of everything. "You talk to Rafe about Bethany?" I knew he had, but I wanted to confirm that Rafe had agreed to behave.

"Yeah."

"And?"

"He said he'd try."

Motherfucker. "If he makes her uncomfortable, I'll take his other eye. Did you tell him that?"

"Come on, you know he's going to be rude and weird with her no matter what. The best we can hope for is that he behaves during her examination."

"He won't be examining her alone. Ever."

Mike laughed. "Then you've got it covered."

"Mrs. G, it's so great to see you," I greeted, giving Bethy's mom my best All-American quarterback smile.

"Raul?" Mrs. Garrett whipped her oversized designer sunglasses off. "Raul Caro?" Her eyes widened as she looked me up and down. "Oh, my stars, it is you. And you're huge! What on earth are you doing here? Where's my Bethany? I drove straight from Santa Cruz when I got the sex tapes and didn't hear back from her. I phoned the hospital, and they said they'd cancelled her on-call shift for the weekend."

"She's in her room." I leaned in and kissed Mrs. Garrett on both cheeks. "Sleeping."

"Sleeping?"

"Uh-huh."

"Wait, why're you—"

"Wow, Mrs. G, you look stunning—it's like you haven't aged a day," I told her as I ushered her over the threshold.

"Ah, stop it. You're crazy." She giggled and blushed. "Really? You think so? Because I feel so old. You have no idea. I mean the pressure nowadays to stay youthful-looking in my line of work is—"

She gasped as she entered and saw the mess we hadn't had time to fully clean up. "Oh, my sweet baby Jesus … what happened?"

I cleared my throat and decided to go with a half-truth. "Gregg."

Another gasp. "Gregg did all this?"

"Well … he came unannounced to confront Bethany and—"

"Ugh, that no-good cocksucker. I swear I'm gonna kick him in the nuts the next time I see him."

I coughed. "That'd be one way to handle it."

"I just can't believe him—cheating before the wedding like that. And sending out that disgusting tape? What was he thinking?"

"He wasn't. I'm afraid he was reacting more than anything."

"Reacting?" She cocked her head at me. "To what?" She may have also frowned, but it was difficult to tell with all the Botox and filler she had in her forehead. "Why did you say you were here again? Don't you live in South America now?"

"I do. I'm in town for a convention this week. Bethany and I ran into each other last night."

She took a step back, pursing her lips as she eyed me up and down again. "You fucked my daughter."

"I—what?"

"Don't bullshit me, Raul." She raised her pointer finger at me. "I know your type. And I know my daughter."

Damnit, we'd had to compel Mrs. G the last time I'd kidnapped Bethany. I was hoping to avoid it this time around.

"Look, the truth is Bethany found out Gregg was cheating a day or so ago. She went out last night with her girlfriends to blow off some steam. We happened to cross paths at a club and wound up having a bit of fun on the dance floor together." Not a lie.

"You're avoiding a straight answer."

"You'll have to ask your daughter. I don't kiss and tell, Mrs. G."

"Smooth. Very smooth."

I laughed. "It's the truth."

"It's a relative truth at best, Raul."

"There are no eternal facts, as there are no absolute truths."

Her lip curled in distaste. "I hope you didn't get into my daughter's pants throwing out sixth-grader Nietzsche quotes like that one. I spent a shit-ton of money on that girl's education."

"Ouch." I placed my hand over my heart. "I seem to remember you liking me more than this the last time we saw one another."

"Who says I don't like you? Were you here when Gregg came over?"

"I was."

"Good. Where's the body?"

"Bottom of the Bay, of course. Where else?"

She smirked. "Atta boy. Let me know if you need an alibi." The humor left her eyes. She leaned closer and asked, "Please tell me you terrified him just a tiny bit? Lie to me if you have to."

"Yes. I took care of it, Mrs. G." She had no idea how well I'd taken care of it.

"Well, that's something at least." She sighed; shook her head. "What a mess. I'm going to check on my daughter. Then I want words with you."

She said it like I was in trouble, and I couldn't contain my grin as I watched her disappear down the short hallway and into Bethany's room.

Marlee Garrett had balls. It was easy to see where Bethany got her spunk. I'd been impressed with the way Mrs. G had handled herself a decade ago in the face of Gabe and Nuriel Salvatella when we'd shown up at the Garrett's home to kidnap Bethany.

Of course, she hadn't lasted long against the power of Gabe's compulsion. With Bethany's mind blocked, Gabe had worked his powers of persuasion through Marlee by compelling her to play along, having her wholeheartedly encourage her eighteen-year-old daughter to go to Argentina with three older men, only one of whom Bethany had known and trusted: *me.*

It made me nauseous to think back on that day—how it had all gone down, and my part in it.

Mrs. G returned and reported with an attempted frown on her mostly immobile face, "She's really passed out cold back there. Do you know if she took something? Maybe an Ambien?"

"Hmm—don't think she took an Ambien." Not a complete lie.

"Must be all the stress. She's been killing herself between her hours at the hospital and planning this wedding." She shook her head. "When she wakes up, tell her I was here, and tell her that her dad and I are going to handle reaching out to guests and cancelling all the plans for the wedding, okay?"

"Will do."

"It's best if she doesn't respond to anyone on the guest list about Gregg's email just yet. She should let things settle first."

"Agreed." I smiled and nodded dutifully as she continued to issue directives for me to relay to Bethany as if I were her personal assistant.

She liked me for her daughter. I could tell. This was going so much better than I'd hoped. I wouldn't even have to invade my future mother-in-law's mind to steal Bethy away.

"I texted Lucas and told him not to swing by, given how wiped out she is. So let her know her father won't be over today, but do tell her I said she should call him tomorrow."

"'Course."

"You are planning on still being here when she wakes up?" she checked as an afterthought.

Enemy werelocks couldn't tear me away.

"I wouldn't dream of leaving her alone, Marlee."

Her mouth hitched on one side. "I didn't say you could call me Marlee."

I gave her a lopsided smile in return. "You don't mind, do you?"

"You're a little pushy, Raul." She tapped her manicured forefinger to her artificially plump lower lip, her blue eyes considering me. "And awfully cocky. I seem to remember other parents—moms in particular—saying that about you at some point, although I can't recall the exact circumstances. I'm sure it'll come to me." Her Botox-frozen brow managed to climb a fraction. "You know, you're setting yourself up to be the rebound guy with her."

"I don't think so, Marlee. I've never been the discardable rebound type."

"There's always a first time for everything, darling," she said, her tone droll as she bent her head and fished through her leather shoulder bag. "Here's my card. I expect you to update me."

"You're really good at giving marching orders."

"Thanks for noticing. Have to run—wedding to cancel and all." She went up on tiptoe, turning her cheek at a slight angle to me.

I bent and kissed her on both cheeks. "Pleasure reconnecting with you, Marlee."

"Always, Raul. Give my best to Milena and her husband, will you? I can't wait to see pictures of the little one. Did they find out the sex yet?"

"Huh?"

"The sex of the baby. Did they find out? Last I heard from Bethany, they hadn't."

Her words hit me like a punch to the solar plexus—with a rusty spike.

Miles was pregnant?

"Milena must be six months along by now, so surely they know."

Six months pregnant?

How had I not known about this? There was no way Mike didn't know already. The guy had a tight network of eyes in place across the globe—both real and digital. He had to know. *Which meant he just hadn't told me.*

"It's uh … a surprise." I forced myself to smile. "They decided to keep it a secret." From me.

"Oh, well, that's fun, too. I'll just pick out something unisex to send them."

"That's very kind of you. I'm sure they'll appreciate it."

I went through the motions of making polite chitchat as I saw Marlee out. She finally remembered to ask what I did for a living—to confirm I wasn't the unemployed loser surfer she'd probably always assumed I'd end up being. I was so distracted by the news I was going to be an uncle that I told her I worked in robotics—a ludicrous lie I'd never be able to fake, much less in any way substantiate.

We parted ways with her telling me not to fuck things up with her daughter.

Mike returned with all but three of the pack members who were in town with us and set them to work righting Bethy's apartment. Stephen and the others were with Gregg—implementing phase two of Mike's plan for ruining the entitled asshole's life.

I confronted Mike once we were alone in Bethany's room.

"You knew about Miles being pregnant, didn't you?"

He didn't need to answer. I felt it.

"Does Alcaeus know?"

"No."

I nodded. "Good. See that he doesn't find out."

"Of course. I'll do my best. No good can come of him knowing. It'd only complicate things. Confuse his loyalty." The column of Mike's throat bobbed with a swallow. His grey eyes on me were wary. "To be honest, I figured the same might be true of—"

"Does Avery know?"

"No."

"That's for the best as well."

"Agreed."

We lapsed into silence, listening to the music of Bethy's heartbeat.

"My loyalty won't waver, Mike," I broached at last. Because it needed to be said. "I wouldn't be here if it weren't for Maribel. Sloane is our future. Alpha Milena's child won't change that."

Not a complete lie.

CHAPTER 15

Bethany

MY HEAD WAS POUNDING. THERE WAS A BUZZING SOUND all around me—a deep, continuous humming noise—as if I was inside a vibrating cocoon.

Or an aircraft with large engines.

I swallowed against the dryness in my throat, and one of my ears popped, releasing the pressure and drawing my attention to the fact that my other ear still had air trapped in it—partially muting the low male voices I now heard talking as everything came back to me in a nauseating flash: I'd been drugged and kidnapped.

By Raul.

It seemed I was on a plane. I was stretched out on my side on a soft surface and covered with a blanket. And suffering the worst case of dry mouth I'd ever had. My eyes felt sore and swollen—a reminder of the fact I'd been crying when last I'd been conscious.

Oh, crap—where had Raul said that he was taking me? South America?

I kept my eyes shut, didn't move a muscle, and barely breathed as I tried to discern my surroundings and identify the men who were talking around me.

"I think we should attack their current weak link: Kai," a deep voice with a slight accent suggested. It sounded vaguely familiar, but I couldn't place it. "I say we go after Kai's little coed: the seer. She's low-hanging fruit, ripe for the picking."

A soft catcall and laughter ensued. "So ripe," an unknown male voice inserted.

"What are you suggesting?" Mike's voice broke in, sounding hard and defensive.

"Don't look at me," Raul responded with a laugh. "I didn't say it. Although … Kai and the seer might be our best angle. What would Gabe have done in this situation?"

"Kidnap, torture, and kill the seer," Stephen answered. "Possibly her family as well."

"No," Raul rejected.

My heart settled in relief. Raul wasn't a cold-blooded killer. He may have been the head of a werewolf mafia ring, but he wasn't a killer.

"I don't believe in torture," Raul appended. "And we'll only kill the seer if we have to. Mike's partial to her."

Several guys laughed.

Annnd he was a killer.

"She's awake, you know," Mike said.

Great. Stupid werewolves and their superman senses.

"I noticed. Grab her a water, will you?"

I'd been trying to keep my anger in check until I figured out exactly what I was dealing with, but the mention of water pushed my anger past my ability to contain. I flung the blanket covering me off and bolted upright— which was a bad move, because my head felt like a ton of bricks. I clutched it in both hands as it swam dizzyingly.

"Easy, Bethy." Raul was beside me—or in front of me, rather—in an instant, gripping my shoulders to steady me as I blinked the drug-induced sleep from my puffy eyes.

As my vision adjusted, and I began to make out the shape of Raul's form and the outline of his face in front of me in the dimly lit cabin, he pressed a cold glass bottle into my hand, his fingers wrapping overtop mine to help me hold it.

"Here. Drink some water, baby."

Fleetingly, I envisioned wresting the bottle from him and beating him over the head with it for daring to call me "baby" after he'd drugged and kidnapped me. If I hadn't felt on the verge of dying of thirst, I might've given in to that temptation. But I had to be smart about this, so I let him help me bring the bottle to my lips, and I chugged.

I couldn't swallow the contents fast enough, and half of it spilled down my chin and neck as I alternated between choking and swallowing. But when Raul tried to pull it away from me, I protested, my grip on the glass tightening, fighting against his pull as I shook my head and managed to cough-croak, "More."

"Easy there, step-cuz. You need to drink it slowly," Mike advised. "Try sipping it."

Mike was next on my list of werewolves to beat over the head.

"Fucking Rafe," Raul complained. "I thought he said it was a mild sedative, perfectly safe for humans and with no side effects?"

"No such thing," I sputtered in between fits of coughing and choking.

"Grab her another one," Raul ordered someone, before saying to me, "Bethy, I'm so sorry about this. You'll want to drink a lot of water in the next twenty-four hours to make sure it's all getting flushed from your system, okay?"

Really? Thanks for the tip!

I wanted to scream, but I was still coughing, and besides that, my throat felt like sandpaper. Screaming would hardly help.

I looked around me while I got my coughing under control. I truly was on a plane—a private, crazy-nice one. Bigger than a 747, I estimated. We were in a large lounge room furnished with leather chairs, chaises, and midcentury modern-looking daybeds like the one I was on. There were multiple flat-screen televisions on the walls and no visible windows, making it hard to guess what time it was.

Mike and Stephen were in the room, along with eight other hunky-looking guys who were surreptitiously scoping me out—while I sat there choking on nothing, dressed in my pj's. It was probably best to assume they were also werewolves—possibly the same group of "international mannies" who'd been at the club last night.

I couldn't help but note their interest in me seemed to be more related to the way Raul was poised on his knees at my feet, fussing over my well-being. I got the strangest impression they were somehow trying to evaluate whether I was a threat—although that made no sense. And it made me even more annoyed to think that the concern in the room appeared to be for Raul, the perpetrator of this situation, rather than for me, his victim.

"How long have I been out?" I asked, my voice raspy.

"Not that long," Raul evaded, taking the empty bottle from my grasp and pressing a fresh one into my hand. "You'll want to drink a lot of water for the next—"

"I know, I *know*." I yanked the full, uncapped bottle of water from his hand, causing some of it to slosh on my lap as I grumbled, "Doctor, remember?"

I tipped the bottle back and managed to get water down without choking this time. When I'd drunk my fill, I lowered the bottle and told him, "But thank you for the advice, and for confirming what I already suspected: this isn't the first time you've drugged and kidnapped someone, is it?"

Mike had the nerve to chuckle. "See? Told you guys she was fun," he boasted to the room.

I shook my head and told Raul directly, "Milena was right about you."

His nostrils flared, his brown eyes shadowed with hurt as they rolled away from mine.

But I refused to put his feelings above my own in this, and I proceeded to lash out. "Shame on me for ever doubting her reasons for not speaking to you anymore. What I really don't understand is how she neglected to warn *me* against speaking to you. That seems like something a best friend should remember to mention, right? Hey, my brother's a dangerous criminal now. You should probably avoid flirting and dancing with him if you ever run into him at a nightclub. Oh, and he's also a magical shape-shifting werewolf creature thing, by the way. Maybe steer clear of him if you don't want to be bitten a bajillion times."

"Guys." Mike jerked his head toward the door, and the bulky crew of werewolves exited the room. Only Mike remained with us.

Raul took the bottle from my hand and set it within reach on a side table. His voice was patient as he said, "Werelock. It's werelock. We're a more advanced breed of werewolf that evolved as a result of the union between warlocks and—"

"*Whatever.* I don't care what you call yourselves. I want to go home. I should be at the hospital right now—doing my job. You had no right to abduct me."

"Fine." He sighed. "Whatever, then." After a strained pause, he added, "I only thought you might want to learn a little more about the distinction between our species before you turn into one of us six days from now."

I felt the blood drain from my face. Great. And now I was gonna hurl. My only consolation was it would be all over Raul, since he was crouched directly in front of me.

My eyes cut to Mike, desperately seeking some sign of denial.

Mike nodded soberly. "I'm afraid it's true, step-cuz. You've been infected with werewolf venom. That's why we had to—"

"Stop it. I am not your *cuz.* Or your SCILF." And this could *not* be happening to me! I was in the prime of my life. I'd finished medical school. My career was just starting. No way could I be turning into a Halloween monster.

Mike's lips twitched faintly at my use of SCILF, but his eyes weren't quite as friendly as he said, "Apparently your sedative was a bit mild after all. Perhaps you'd like something stronger than water to drink to take the edge off this bout of hysteria? Or maybe another injection?" he threatened under his breath.

"Lay off," Raul warned. To me, he said, "Honey, I know it's a lot to digest, but I thought you'd appreciate me being honest about what's coming."

Christ, they were both completely serious about this. Still, I held out hope that somehow this wasn't really happening, that it was all a mistake. I could handle almost anything in life but turning into a scary giant dog.

"Well, thank you for your honesty with the doomsday warning," I said with a dry laugh. "It's right on schedule. I was just beginning to feel like my looming panic attack had waned."

"Bethy, there's nothing to panic about. You'll be perfectly safe." Raul's warm hands were sliding up and down my forearms in a soothing caress. "I'm going to take care of everything." It was unsettling just how well his touch could make me believe that was true.

"Spoken like a true sociopath who just drugged and kidnapped a woman. Stop that." I pulled my arms away, wrapping them around my midsection. "Does Milena know anything about this? I just cannot believe she didn't properly warn me about you."

His jaw stiffened. "My apologies on behalf of my dear sister. It seems she failed to warn you about a number of men who weren't any good for you."

"What's that supposed to mean?"

"Nothing. Look, I said I was sorry. I'm trying to explain the circumstances and why I did what I did. Why can't you try and understand that I had to—"

"Are you serious right now? Just so I'm clear, was that a *sorry* for sticking me with a hypodermic needle back in San Francisco? A *sorry* for almost killing my ex-fiancé in front of me? Or a *sorry* for kidnapping me?"

"I will not apologize for Gregg." His eyes shifted fully to their startling amber-gold color as he said it. "He deserved far worse than he got from me."

No. Not hot, Bethany. This was in no way hot. Pull your pussy together!

"I can handle myself, Raul. I don't need you to rescue me from my relationship mistakes."

"Wow, that hurts," Mike interjected. "So you didn't need our help intercepting the sex videos of you that Gregg tried to send out to your pastor and all your friends and relatives? Shall I let that email go out now as Gregg originally intended?"

My heart tripped a beat. "You said you destroyed those tapes."

"Don't threaten her." Raul's feral gaze shifted to Mike. "Not ever. Understand?"

"Threaten her? I would never," Mike denied with a laugh. "I was only teasing her. I told her before that I destroyed those tapes."

Right. And now I wasn't so sure it was the truth.

The door flew open and Stephen poked his head in. "Hey—"

"Not now," Mike and Raul responded in unison.

"Avery went off script and attacked Kai," Stephen reported nonetheless.

Mike sprang up from his chair. "Fuck. I'll handle it."

"You can't," Stephen told him. "Kai was with the seer girl when Avery attacked. The seer is witnessing their fight right now."

Raul swore and leapt smoothly to his feet. "I'll go."

"And you think my emotions are too involved," Mike complained to Raul. "That *my* judgment's compromised? You need to order Avery to stay away from Kai."

"Like that'd work," Raul grumbled. "Watch after Bethy."

In the next blink, Raul and Stephen were gone—vanished into thin air.

That left me alone with Mike: the werelock who'd just joked about sedating me again a moment ago.

I swallowed the ball of fear climbing my throat as Mike reclaimed his seat and turned to look at me. His expression was impassive, but his eyes had shifted to the golden color of his wolf.

Shit. I was pretty sure that meant something. Probably not anything good.

I stood. "Um … is there a bathroom on this plane I could use?"

He nodded slowly.

"Great. All that water …" I babbled.

After ten seconds passed and he made no move to show or tell me where the washroom was, I pressed, "Could—could you please tell me where—?"

"I'd prefer for us to be friends, Bethany."

The way he said it, his words felt more like a threat than an olive branch. He might as well have said he'd rather not have to torture and kill me.

"Do you understand?"

I nodded quickly.

When he still didn't tell me where the bathroom was, I blurted, "I have bladder control issues."

He canted his head to the side, his mouth curling with amusement. "I don't think so, cuz. In fact, I'm pretty sure most of the guys on this plane know how well you can control your Kegels at this point."

Oh.

My God.

There was so much that was so wrong with that.

"Raul's the Alpha of our pack. Do you understand what that means?"

I shook my head as my face heated over his Kegels remark. "Not … exactly." And I wasn't sure I wanted to know if it meant that Raul killed people or did other violent things.

"It means he's our leader, our shepherd. For better or worse, we all feel a certain level of connection to him—some to a higher degree than others. To an extent, Raul's will connects us all to one another as well." He leaned forward in his seat. "Can you imagine what that might be like?"

Again, I shook my head.

His lips twisted with a wry smile. "You'll know soon enough." He paused, and I was contemplating reminding him I had to pee, when he revealed, "Raul only became our Alpha seven months ago when Gabriel Salvatella, the former Alpha, died. Previously, Raul served as head Beta for nearly a decade under Gabe."

"Why are you telling me this?"

"You think Raul and I are monsters for what we've done to you today."

I didn't deny it. Nor did I risk his anger by confirming it.

"But you have no frame of reference for what a true monster is, Bethany."

"Some might consider that a blessing," I couldn't help but snark.

"Indeed." He chuckled. There was no humor to it, though, only sadness. "Let me put things into perspective for you then. Gabe and my mother were first cousins. When I was a boy, my mother defected with me, hoping to escape the ongoing violence and infighting that had become rampant within our Salvatella pack. We were gone for almost a week before Gabe hunted us down. He had my mother executed for her desertion. He wasn't gentle about it. And he made me watch."

I sucked in an uneasy breath. "I'm sorry." What else could I say? Why was he telling me this? Was he trying to tell me that's what Raul's job now entailed—killing defectors in front of their children? That this was my future as a hostage within their pack?

He shrugged. "There are worse stories than mine. I suspect you'll hear some of them soon enough. Make a right out the door. Your bedroom is at the very end of the hallway. You'll find a bathroom in there, along with clothes and other essentials we packed from your apartment."

I mumbled a bewildered "thanks" and bolted.

CHAPTER 16

Raul

As Stephen and I teleported to Avery's location, I tapped her mind and told her to knock it off with Kai. She responded back with a curt *"Don't distract me,"* along with an image of her repeatedly blasting Kai's body against a brick wall.

When we arrived at the crime scene—the dormitory courtyard of a small liberal arts school in Washington State—I took the liberty of searching Avery's most recent memories to see what had transpired. It seemed Avery had done a solid job of terrifying the seer by arriving out of nowhere to blast Kai's body up into the sky, then slam him against the side of a nearby building. Kai wasn't fighting back, or even doing much to defend himself.

Interesting. It was a fair guess Kai still felt guilty over betraying Alcaeus, his best friend of four centuries, to Alcaeus's own Reinoso pack. It was also no surprise Kai would be careful not to harm Avery, for fear of harming her mate Alcaeus in the process. But to not defend himself against Avery meant either Kai was seriously wallowing in self-loathing over his betrayal or he was hoping to placate

Avery and possibly distract her from harming his favorite coed.

I noted Kai's concern for the seer in Avery's memory of the attack. He'd told the seer to run the moment he'd spotted Avery. Naturally, the girl was still standing there looking horrified and panicked. Not surprising she'd have terrible survival instincts, given the fact she was apparently into Kai.

Well, we'd see how long Kai's passive tactic lasted the moment he saw me standing next to his little obsession.

Telepathically, I instructed Stephen to scan the perimeter and erase the minds of any onlookers, if necessary. Fortunately, it was nearly eight o'clock at night and cold as fuck outside—for humans, at least. Most students weren't likely to be out unless they had to be.

After conjuring two hot beverages, along with more appropriate cold weather attire for myself, I strode up to the infamous seer who Mike had "accidentally" made out with and who had managed to capture Kai's attention to the point that he was acting like a horny teenage idiot.

At first glance, standing in profile to me, the petite, long-haired brunette looked cute enough, but she was nothing spectacular. There was a crunchy, au naturel, Berkeley-esque vibe to her that reminded me of girls I'd gone to high school with back in Santa Cruz. She had a decent bumper on her, though; I'd give her that. I'd noticed it before the few times I'd seen her—both in Mike's mind and in person. But as far as the overall picture went, I'd seen better talent, and I knew Kai had, too. He'd once been mated to the late Maribel, after all.

So what was his fascination with this little seer about?

The sound of my boots crunching through the dirty snow and leaves startled her, and she yelped as she turned to find me approaching.

"Whoa. Easy, there," I greeted. "How's it going?"

Her mouth opened and shut. Her caramel-brown eyes were wide. She looked from me back to the spot in between the dormitory buildings where Kai was now getting his ass kicked supernatural-style, then back to me again.

"Don't worry." I gave her my most laid-back surfer smile. "I'm not gonna let her kill him." I extended a lidded, to-go coffee cup to her in offering. "Here, I got you that gingerbread chai stuff you like."

Her brows pulled together. She looked me up and down like I was completely mad. "I don't drink that crap."

Okay, so I could see why Mike liked her. I shrugged and vanished the chai.

She sidestep-stumbled several paces away from me when she witnessed it. I pretended not to notice as I sipped coffee from the remaining cup.

"Who're you?"

"I'm Raul." I held my hand out. She didn't take it. I withdrew it, saying, "It's nice to meet you, Lauren."

She only seemed mildly rattled by the fact I knew her name. "How do you know Kai?" she asked instead. "Why isn't he fighting back?"

Ignoring her first question, I told her, "He's not fighting back because he knows he deserves every bit of that beating she's giving him."

"Why? What'd he do?" Her tone was defensive.

"I'll level with you." I stepped closer. She fidgeted but didn't back away this time. "I'm not here to answer your questions." I tapped into her mind and said, "You feel unconditionally safe with me, Lauren."

She blinked. Then she nodded.

I'd had no experience entering the mind of a seer before, given that all the seers had been wiped out by Maribel shortly after I'd become a werelock. So it was shocking to me how effortless it was to enter Lauren's mind and compel her.

For some reason, I'd expected it to be harder than compelling a normal human, but it really was no different—perhaps easier. Mike had explained that it was like a two-way street kind of deal in that the same extrasensory sensitivity that gave seers, clairvoyants, necromancers, and the like their great ability to tap into otherworldly activity also left them open and vulnerable to paranormal influences.

Still, I'd half-expected Kai to have erected a shield of some sort at this point. After vowing to leave Lauren alone for good, he'd returned from his pouting sesh in Greenland to play even crazier head games with the attractive coed—and to end his renowned, over-a-century-long run of celibacy by having sex with the seer in an alley behind a campus bar, of all things.

Of course, casting a shield over the mind of a purported potential seer was only likely to draw more enemy werelock attention to her. Doing so would be like waving a flag that there was something important to hide. And Kai knew we were watching.

One thing was for certain, though: whatever this kinky dance was that Kai was doing with the seer, there was no way my sister, who was Kai's Alpha, knew about it. Miles would never have approved of all the mind entering and manipulation Kai was engaging in with Lauren. I knew for a fact Miles had put a stop to that behavior with humans after becoming Alpha of the Reinoso pack.

I flipped through Lauren's memories like she was an open book. Kai had clearly tampered with them, as had Mike. But Kai's tampering was easier to spot, which wasn't like him. Another indication Kai was unraveling—becoming sloppy and desperate. None of Kai's behavior lately where the seer was concerned was in keeping with his staid, stoic pack doctor personality as we knew it.

The question remained: Why? Mike wasn't convinced Lauren possessed sufficient innate ability to even be among the next generation of seers we were all searching for, much less a seer skilled enough to be considered a threat to Sloane.

Mike believed Kai's interest in Lauren to be more personal than anything else. It certainly seemed that way. But it was possible Mike was simply bitter over Kai getting the jump on him and having dirty alley sex with the coed before he'd had a chance to make a serious move on her.

I knew the exact moment Kai finally sensed my presence, because he ceased taking abuse from Avery and started defending himself, then resorted to giving Avery a gentle blast when she laid into him harder.

Quickly, I told Lauren, "You never met me tonight, and you never saw Kai get attacked. You parted ways with Kai after you … did whatever it was you two were doing tonight. And then you headed to the library to study. Got it?"

She nodded, and I waved her off. "To the library you go. Don't look back."

She was over twenty paces away by the time Kai managed to successfully subvert Avery without harming her and teleport over to me. At over four hundred years old, Kai looked only thirty-five in human years. Regardless, the guy was way too old and far too uptight to be hanging with a hip young coed.

"S'up, Doc?" I greeted him with a smile.

"What did you do to her?" he demanded, his bright blue wolf eyes flashing anxiously from me to Lauren's retreating form. He appeared torn—wanting to follow after the seer to make sure she was okay, while knowing that displaying too much concern for her well-being would give her importance away.

Oh, yeah, this looked very personal, all right.

Let the games begin.

"Nothing, man." I kept my tone casual as Avery teleported to my side. "Let's see … I introduced myself to her, offered her a gingerbread chai latte, told her she hadn't seen anything, and sent her on her way to the library to study. That pretty much covers it." I grinned at him. "For now."

"You weren't even trying back there," Avery broke in to accuse Kai. "Do you know how rude that is? How sexist?"

Kai ignored her, growling at me, "Stay away from Lauren and keep out of her head. She's not the next great seer. She's nobody."

"Yeah, yeah, heard you've been saying that. And yet …" I squinted one eye at him and sucked cold night air through my teeth. "Here you are, so …"

"I was checking on her. That's all. You need to call Mike and *all others* off watching her." He directed a stink eye at Avery at "all others," and I almost busted out laughing, knowing he was right to view Avery as more of a threat to Lauren than Mike was—at least from an immediate safety standpoint. "It's my fault for drawing undue attention to her when she doesn't have true ability. You're wasting your time by—"

"Wow, you really got it bad." I shook my head at him. "Avery, I need to talk to Kai alone a min—"

"I am not leaving."

I bit the inside of my cheek and gathered patience before shooting Avery my best covert "Please trust me" expression. One of the things I admired most about Avery was that she was hardwired to protect her daughter Sloane above all else. But the fact that Avery was immune to taking orders—particularly when she believed her child's safety was at stake—came with its share of challenges.

"How's that working out?" Kai asked, giving me a bland smile. "Being a new Alpha and having two higher-ranking Betas in your pack who won't take orders from you?"

I gave him a tight smile in return. He was referring to Alcaeus, who also couldn't be commanded. "About as well as it did for Alex when Alcaeus was in your pack and Alex was Alpha, I suspect." I should know, since Alcaeus was constantly drawing parallels and comparing my performance to Alex's as a young Alpha. Alex hadn't been able to command Alcaeus either.

"Well, it's good to hear there may be hope for your pack after all then."

"It's going great, Killjoy," Avery told Kai. "Thanks for asking. Chaos is doing quite well without your constant nagging, too, in case you were wondering. And he hasn't missed feeling beholden to Alpha Milena's emotional manipulation or being subjected to her ongoing PMS, either."

My lips curled with genuine amusement as Avery laid a supportive hand on the back of my shoulder.

"If you boys are going to compare dick sizes, I think I'll be on my way after all."

I exhaled and gave her a smile of gratitude. I wanted to see how serious Kai was about the seer. Also, to get a sense of where he stood with regard to viewing Sloane as the reincarnation of his deceased former mate, Maribel. I couldn't have Avery present for the latter.

"Until next time, Killjoy," she muttered before tele-porting out.

Once I was certain Avery was gone, I told Kai, "Congratulations on getting back in the game again after a hundred and eight years."

His nostrils flared. His jaw tightened. And his skin flushed. Wow. Was that embarrassment I scented rolling off him? Guilt even?

"Heard all about how you've been banging that 'no-body' coed who definitely is not the next great seer," I pro-ceeded to goad him. "Oh, and in case no one has given you sex pointers for this century yet, you should know that nowadays, most ladies prefer a bed over rutting in a dirty alley or on the frozen forest floor." I raised a concilia-tory hand when he began growling at me. "Just a friendly suggestion."

Internally, I was celebrating the brief indication of sur-prise that I had glimpsed behind Kai's angry blue irises. "I got eyes everywhere, Kai. How was Greenland, by the way?" I asked to further drive the message home. "Feeling better now that you got that emotional breakdown out of the way?"

He was silent, his facial muscles taut, his steely blue gaze leveled on me with disdain.

I tapped Stephen's mind and confirmed that he was done scanning the surrounding area and on his way over to us. I let him know to hustle, because I was nearly done with Kai, and I was anxious to get back to Bethany as quickly as possible.

"Say, how does my sister feel about you remaining in wolf form for longer than you do human form lately? Is Miles cool with that? Come to think of it, how does she feel about you mind-raping that poor human seer?" I winced. "Somehow I can't see her being okay with that. You know she only sees things in black and white, wrong and right, and all that."

His expression remained pinched, his eyes cold as they considered me. "It's a shame you've spent your whole life so blinded by jealousy and hurt, you've never gotten to know your own sister. Milena's always been either a threat or a commodity in your eyes, hasn't she, Raul?"

"You only think you know her," I snapped. "Wait until she finds out what you've been up to with the seer. You think she'll understand? Think again."

"Perhaps she won't," Kai responded calmly after a beat. "Can't say I'd fault her if she didn't." His gaze lowered to the ground before returning to me. "We all make choices we have to live with and be accountable for. The difference is you still blame Milena for things she had no control over— for the choices others made that you were forced to live with. Decisions that Mateus, your mother, and your aunt Aracely made that impacted both of you. If you're a victim of their choices, then Milena is too."

It was no wonder Kai and Alcaeus had been friends for four centuries. They were cut from the same old-guy know-it-all cloth.

Stephen strolled up to join us, and his intrusion helped me to calm my rattled emotions and regain focus. I decided to double-down and take aim below the belt.

"Hey, just out of curiosity, Kai, what bothers you more: that your lifelong friend works for me now and refuses even to speak to you, or the fact that your former mate was reincarnated as someone prophesied to be incapable of connection, and yet somehow she made a connection with me but doesn't remember you?"

"Sloane is not Maribel," he hissed.

I could almost see the explosion of emotions my taunt had ignited within him. Direct hit. And *score.*

"Right. Right." I couldn't help but chuckle in the face of his blossoming inner fury. "I agree it's definitely a toss-up. I know I'm still trying to decide which delights me more. So I suppose outright denial's probably the better option for a guy in your shoes."

Kai looked like he was on the verge of shifting and attacking me. But then he started laughing—so hard he ended up dabbing moisture from his eyes.

Clearing my throat, I gave Stephen a confused, annoyed side-eye glance. The wacky doctor was obviously unraveling if this was the best he had in his dated arsenal of werelock posturing and clever comebacks.

Finally, Kai stopped chuckling. His tone and expression turned dead serious as he said, "You're nothing but a wounded, overgrown child power-grabbing and lashing out at the world, seeking an emotional solace you're not smart enough to ever find—because its source has been right under your nose all along."

He shook his head at me in disgust. "But that's not your greatest folly. That's just the cancer that eats away at you, the abscess that erodes your heart, propelling you blindly in all the wrong directions in life. What will ultimately seal your destruction is your infantile arrogance—the way you underestimate your opponents every time. Never start a fight you aren't prepared to lose, Raul. Remember that."

His eyes swept over Stephen before returning to me. "Keep your pack away from Lauren. I won't warn you again."

With that, he was gone.

Stephen turned to me and asked, "Is it me or did Chaos give you almost that exact same speech a month ago?"

I hunched one shoulder and shook my head. "Could be. They all sound the same after a while."

"The topic was different, of course," Stephen clarified. "But something about it sounded so familiar."

I nodded. "It's their shared use of the word 'folly,' I believe."

"That's it." Stephen snapped his fingers. "And the part about infantile arrogance."

"Yup. Alcaeus does say that all the time. It's classic old-guy speak."

"Definitely," Stephen agreed. "So you want us to back off the seer?"

It was my turn to laugh. "Hell no. Let's turn up the pressure. We've found our Reinoso weak link."

As I was teleporting Stephen and myself back to the jet, I felt Sloane's fear tugging at me, her strong emotions pulling me into her subconscious—where she was in the midst of what felt like a really bad nightmare. She hadn't had one of those in weeks, and instantly I felt guilty for not singing the *Frozen* song with her the night before.

I kept my focus as we rematerialized aboard the plane. I tapped Mike's mind to check on how Bethany was doing, and to let him know I needed him to watch over her a while longer while I went to help Sloane navigate her nightmares, before teleporting to Sloane's side in Bariloche.

CHAPTER 17

Bethany

"**W**AIT ... BACK UP TWO SENTENCES." I SET MY WERELOCK cocktail—that smelled like straight-up gasoline—down and raised a skeptical, mildly unsteady palm at Tiago. "Did you say werelocks can heal from *anything?* Even cancer?"

He grinned, showing off his adorable dimples. "I did. In truth, Bethany, they can't get cancer to begin with. Not even werewolves can."

Werewolves were definitely the lesser species between the two, from what I'd learned. Yet even they were disease-proof it seemed—immune to more than merely STDs, as Raul had informed me the night before in the Hummer.

"Shut the door."

"No," he said with a laugh. "I won't shut it. It's true. Ask any of the guys. They'll tell you."

Tiago was the accented manny from the club the night before—the one who'd cradled my head against his shoulder and reassured me I hadn't been stabbed when Raul had bitten my thigh.

Tiago spoke fluent English, Spanish, Italian, and Portuguese, but Italian had been his first language. He'd confided in me earlier—with a sense of embarrassment about it that was even more endearing than his dimples—that he spoke with a slight Italian accent no matter what language he was conversing in.

Tiago was hands-down the sweetest of all the Salvatella pack killer mannies I'd met on the plane. I couldn't help but think he'd be perfect for Jessie. If he wasn't a killer and all. Or a werelock.

Ten more minutes of Tiago explaining how virtually impossible it was to kill a werelock unless you used serious magic or removed vital organs for an extended length of time had me picking my glass of gasoline back up again to take several burning gulps, despite the hideous smell and taste of it.

I was on a private plane with nearly two dozen indestructible beings who looked like exotic male dancers and models. Some of them—such as Tiago—were so sweet and polite I had to keep reminding myself they inevitably morphed into big scary dogs. Whereas others immediately gave off that natural-born predator vibe and seemed one shot of whisky or a single wrong glance away from sprouting full-on fur and fangs and attacking.

Although I'd been introduced to all of them, I could barely remember half their names now, distracted as I was trying to absorb everything else that I could about them as a species. The more I gleaned, the more unnerved I was becoming.

The alcohol, as awful as it tasted, was helping somewhat to keep my nerves in check. Goodness knows my emotions had been volleying all over the place.

Earlier, after locating the plane's master suite—which Mike had designated as my bedroom—I had been stunned to find half the clothes I owned neatly hung up in the walk-in closet. This had comforted me more than Raul's repeated assurances that no one would harm me. Because who would bother hanging someone's clothes up for a ten-hour flight if they planned on killing them, right? None of these guys wore my size.

So I'd changed out of my pj's, put my best big-girl game face on, and bravely sought out the party of supernaturals hanging out in the bar/dining area of the luxury aircraft. Mike had made initial introductions on my behalf. But then Stephen had returned—without Raul—and he'd pulled Mike away to discuss some sort of urgent "pack business." Mike had advised me to have a drink, socialize, and try and relax.

Easier said than done. I found my eyes constantly drifting toward the open-arched doorway to the dining area, hoping to see Raul appear. No explanation had been provided as to why Stephen had returned without him, and I was still too angry—*and too proud*—to inquire after his whereabouts.

I started taking more frequent sips of my petrol on ice as Tiago gave me the lowdown on werewolves mating for life.

"So it's kinda like penguins, only the 'awww' aspect is made morbid by the fact they die together? No matter what?"

"I know, right?" he agreed, showing me those dimples of his again. "I feel the same way about it. Of course, I haven't found my true mate yet, so it's hard to relate. Once you change into a wolf and your mating bond with Raul solidifies, I think you'll start to feel differently."

"Say what?"

"You and Raul." His dimples vanished at what could only have been a look of staggered confusion on my face. "He claimed you last night. You know—the biting? He marked you. You two are mated now. For eternity."

I'd always considered myself a serial monogamist, but eternity sounded like an awfully long time. Longer than a life sentence. "I'm mated? For eternity?"

He nodded.

Don't panic. Nothing good will come of freaking out in a roomful of wolves.

I went to take another sip and realized my glass held nothing but ice.

"May I freshen your drink?" Tiago offered.

"Yes, please."

"She's cut off, T." Mike intercepted my glass before I could pass it to Tiago. Then he made it vanish and handed me a glass of water instead.

"Aw—why you gonna regulate like that, cuz?" I whined. I needed that gasoline now more than ever.

"I said to have a drink to relax, not pass out," he lectured. To Tiago, Mike ordered, "Bring her something to eat."

Tiago left and Mike took his place next to me.

"I'm socializing, Mike. Becoming one with the pack connected by Raul's will … erm, whatever you said. Why're you sniffing at me?" *Why hasn't Raul come back?*

"What'd they give you to drink?"

"Unleaded gasoline, I think. But they pour it over ice, add a little sugar around the rim, and call it 'Nahuel's Blunder'—or something like that. They said it's a new drink the pack doctor Rafe came up with recently that's become all the rage in—"

"C'mon, guys!" Mike complained, his voice carrying above the noise in the crowded dining area as he aimed a glare around the room. "Who gave her the Nahuel special?"

Laughter and high-fives spread through the gathering of wolfmen.

Great. I was missing the joke—and likely the butt of it.

"Don't worry," Jorge called out to Mike. "I watered it down." Jorge gave me a smirk and a thumbs-up. "Just strong enough to take the edge off."

I finger-waved weakly back at him. Jorge was totally the natural-born predator-looking type. He'd probably just poisoned me. "Who's Nahuel?" I asked Mike.

"Nahuel Salvatella was the former Alpha's younger brother," Mike explained, scrubbing a hand over his eyes. "Over sixty years ago, his alleged true mate got him black-out drunk on moonshine and managed to chop his idiot supernatural head off."

Jesus. So Jorge was plotting to decapitate me then? I automatically took a sip from the glass of water Mike had given me and was disappointed to find that it was … water.

"Wait, wouldn't chopping his head off have gotten her killed, too? Tiago said when werewolves are joined with their true, predestined mate, a mated werewolf's death will trigger the death of his or her true mate as well."

"Yes, but she was still human." Mike raised his hand, signaling to Klaus, who was behind the bar pouring himself another drink.

So there was still an out for me while I remained human—*if I was willing to take Raul's head off.* I wondered if it required a special ornamental sword …

"Nahuel hadn't turned or marked her yet," Mike

continued as Klaus handed him a tall glass of diesel fuel on the rocks.

There went my out.

I smiled faintly back at Klaus when he flashed me a toothy grin. Klaus ranked right after Tiago in my book as the second sweetest werelock I'd encountered on the plane. *Or was Klaus only a werewolf?* I couldn't recall which exact species he'd been introduced to me as. Mike had said that as long as I was human and lacked the ability to scent the difference, it would be hard for me to distinguish between the two.

"The initial mating bond isn't felt as strongly for humans as it is for werewolves," Mike went on to say. "And human mates are supposed to be given a choice before they're claimed. In theory," he muttered under his breath.

"And Nahuel's mate wasn't given one?"

Mike raised a sardonic brow, his drink suspended on its way to his mouth. "She got him sauced and took his head off, Bethany."

"Right." I nodded. "Guess not." I hadn't been given a choice either. Clearly the choice part for humans was more in theory than practice around here.

Mike consumed half his drink before adding, "He had murdered her parents hours earlier. Probably didn't help him in winning her affection."

Tiago showed up with a plate of food then—an assortment of cured meats and cheeses. "Charcuterie?" he offered, setting it on the bar next to me. "Some nibbles to hold you over. Got a steak coming momentarily."

Great timing. I smiled politely as my stomach turned in protest.

I had no intention of eating anything now, and I pushed the plate aside once Tiago had walked off.

When my eyes returned to Mike, it was to find him giving me a hard look. "Don't make me force-feed you."

I bit the immediate retort on my tongue and calmly took another sip of water before reminding him, "Didn't Raul say not to threaten me?"

"He told me to look after you, Bethany. I choose my methods."

I kept my tone nonchalant, and hoped that he couldn't hear the pounding of my heart above the noisy banter around us as I challenged, "But isn't Raul your Alpha? Don't you have to listen to him?"

He smiled—barely—as he leaned closer. "Yes. And he never said I couldn't discipline you in the process of looking after you."

Nice. "So it's all a matter of clever wordplay and loopholes?"

"Not exactly. But I think you'll find that within our pack, intent carries more weight than words often do. Raul's primary intention is that I keep you safe. If I see you making choices that could harm you, your well-being takes precedence over his directive that I refrain from threatening you."

"That doesn't make sense."

"Sure it does." He shifted in his seat. "Think of it this way: if you were holding a gun to your own head and I had to threaten to kill your parents or blow up the hospital you work at in order to prevent you from harming yourself, don't you think Raul would be in full support of me threatening you in order to save your life?"

"I would never in a million years. Talk about an extreme, outrageous examp—"

"Just eat your fucking meats and cheeses, Bethany." He pushed the plate at me. "I don't feel like arguing right now."

Okay, then.

We sat in silence as I forced a few bites of meat down. Mike was definitely in a worse mood than he'd been in earlier, before he'd gone off to talk with Stephen.

"You seem upset about something," I broached after I'd muscled down a fourth bite of meat and had gotten my game face back in place. "Wanna talk about it?"

He huffed like I'd made a ludicrous suggestion.

I tried to remember his mother had been violently murdered in front of him as a child.

"Hey, what do you have to lose? You're stuck babysitting me anyhow." I lowered my volume and said, "And for the record, being bossy and dismissive with me will get you nowhere. I'm the impossible-to-ignore type who'll alternately nag and charm you to death until I get what I'm after."

"Right," he dismissed me. "I'm fine. A little tired is all. So, what have you learned thus far about our pack?"

Grateful for the change in conversation and the fact he was at least feigning civility with me again, I swiveled in my bar seat to face him. There were quite a few takeaways from the conversations I'd had with some of the twenty-two werelocks and werewolves I'd met aboard the Salvatella pack's tricked-out 747-8.

"Um, let's see … the last Alpha, Gabe, was pretty much universally hated, from what I've gathered."

"For the most part." Mike's eyes skated about the room. "We're still weeding out and killing off any quiet remaining supporters."

"Awesome." Just like a mafia family would do.

Mike pinched the bridge of his nose. "What else did the guys tell you?"

"Werewolf saliva has magical healing properties, were-wolves can't get cancer or other diseases, and they live longer than humans. But were*locks* live crazy long, are essentially ageless, and are virtually indestructible unless serious magic or vital organ removal is involved in killing them."

Mike nodded and prompted me to continue while he polished off the rest of his drink.

"Nobody will talk to me about the initial transition into a werewolf. They said Raul ordered them not to."

"That's correct," Mike confirmed. To my annoyance, he offered no further information either. "Anything else?"

I hesitated a moment before leaning in and whispering, "I think the guys see me as a threat." I pulled back to find Mike's brow crumpled. There was an awareness in his eyes, however, that belied his mask of confusion.

"How so?"

I rolled one shoulder. "Dunno, really. It doesn't make sense to me … it's just a feeling I get."

He looked away, crunching on one of the ice cubes from his otherwise empty glass as he stared through the crowd of werewolves and werelocks laughing and chatting around the bar.

"I'll let you in on a secret, Bethany." Turning back to me, he drew nearer and confessed, "*I* see you as a threat."

CHAPTER 18

Raul

"WHO AMONG US CAN DWELL WITH THE CONSUMING fire?" Father Salazar's booming voice echoed through the church rafters. "Who among us can dwell with everlasting burnings?"

Aunt Cely's bony elbow jabbed into my shoulder. "So help me, Raul," she hissed in a faint whisper.

I flicked the switch to turn Tetris off and tucked my Gameboy back inside my jacket.

Miles gave a quiet whimper of protest and squirmed in Cely's lap, craning her head back to look up at my aunt's face, which was swiftly growing pink with embarrassment. And anger.

My almost two-year-old sister disliked going to church as much as I did. Watching me play Tetris was the only thing that kept her quiet and occupied during Sunday sermons.

"On," Miles babbled. "Tetris on!"

It sounded more like "Dedriss" whenever my little sister said it, but the popular game's name was recognizable enough that people in our pew started to giggle behind their hands when Miles continued to whine, "Dedriss back on."

Aunt Cely tried to shush her to no avail, and I chewed the insides of my cheeks to keep from laughing myself.

Five minutes later, I was following behind Cely's stomping heels as we made our way through the packed church parking lot. I was making silly faces at Miles, who was perched over my aunt's shoulder and grinning excitedly down at me. I gave her a thumbs-up for her part in sparing us another hour of misery.

Cely's big push for us to become churchgoers was a joke anyhow. Back in Ohio, Mom had never made me go except for on holidays. By her own admission, Aunt Cely had never been much of a churchgoer herself. But when Cely had moved us to Santa Cruz, she'd insisted Miles and I grow up with religion. She'd even enrolled me in Vacation Bible School, ruining my first summer in our new town.

It took three tries, two swear words, and a lot of fist-pounding on the dashboard by my aunt for our car to start up, which did nothing to improve Cely's mood.

I sat in the back distracting Miles, who hated being strapped into her car seat when we weren't moving. I didn't blame her.

When Miles began to fuss, I smushed her chubby baby cheeks together between my palms, creating extra rolls of face fat, and causing her nose and lips to push out and her eyes to droop down in a way that looked completely ridiculous. It never failed to make me laugh. And whenever I laughed, Miles would start giggling like mad too.

"Here, now you give me a manatee face." I took her little hands in mine and helped her to smush my cheeks together. "Like this, see?"

"Man-tee!" She squealed and kicked her legs with delight at the comical sight my smushed face presented. "Man-tee!"

"Raul, stop getting her wound up," Cely scolded as we pulled out of the parking lot at last. "I'm trying to listen for engine noises, and I can't hear anything over all the giggling and shrieking back there."

"Pretty sure it's running," I sassed.

She threw her pointer finger straight at the ceiling. "You are on thin ice, mister!"

The car behind us honked twice, and I cracked up so hard that tears sprang to my eyes. Miles started laughing along with me, as she often did—even though she had no idea what was so funny. She was in good company, because neither did our Aunt Cely.

"What the—? Why'd that guy honk at me? What happened? What the hell's so hilarious now, Raul?"

"He thinks you gave him the finger, Cely."

"He does not think …" She let out a gasp as she looked in the rear view mirror. "Shit, he does. He just gave me the finger back, that jerk."

"Whoop, whoop!" I held my hand up for my sister to give me a high five. "That's four more quarters for the swear jar in just this drive home from church. Aunt Cely'll be taking us to Disneyland in no time."

Miles mimicked my "whoop" and wacked her little fist against my palm.

We drove another several blocks before Cely spoke again. When she did, her voice wasn't angry or indignant. It was simply sad. Resigned. "Raul, you have to stop calling me that around Milena. She's getting old enough that she might remember later on. Besides that, she mimics everything you do. She already calls me Ma-Cely. She's confused. We have to change that."

My gut wrenched. It felt like the time Billy Duncan had kicked me in the stomach on the football field.

"I'm sorry. I know you don't want to, but you need to call me Mom. You're the bee's knees to Milena … the pied piper …"

My eyes burned, despite how hard I fought not to get upset. And still I rolled those eyes at my aunt's idiotic choice of old-person expressions.

Mom never would've said anything so lame. How had they been related, let alone twins? Aunt Cely was constantly saying stupid, humiliating things that embarrassed me—in a new town where I didn't completely fit in and was trying to make friends.

It was bad enough I had to pretend she was my mom and call her that in front of my new teachers and the kids in the neighborhood. It already felt like a betrayal of my mom's memory. But calling her Mom in front of my sister?

"Man-tee!" Miles squealed and giggled. She was smushing her own cheeks together now, trying to get me to laugh.

Letting my sister think Cely was our mom felt wrong. It was too great a lie to tell.

Mom always said lies divided people. It was why she'd told me the truth about Mateus being my dad, even though he'd never wanted me to know.

But now that Mom was gone, all Mateus and Aunt Cely wanted me to do was lie—about everything.

And they wanted me to lie to my sister most of all.

"Raul?" Aunt Cely sighed. "Can we please talk about this?"

"I'm not doing it."

"Honey, I know I'll never be your mom. I'm not trying to replace her for you. I'm just trying to keep you and your sister safe."

"Father Salazar says it's a sin to lie."

She huffed out an embittered laugh and muttered something under her breath. But her tone was more playful than annoyed as she asked, "Since when do you pay attention at church?"

"I can play Tetris and listen to someone talk at the same time." Duh!

"Then what did Father Salazar mean about those who could dwell with the consuming fire? Did you hear that part today?"

I shrugged. "Yeah. I heard it."

"Do you understand what he was talking about? What it means?"

Another shrug. "It means that everyone's gonna burn in hell because nothing we ever do is good enough and God hates us all?"

Cely gasped, jerking the steering wheel to the right and nearly driving us off the road. "No! Raul, what on earth? Of course not. Where did you ever get such an idea?"

Was she kidding? "Church. The Bible. Stuff Father Salazar says all the time."

"Jesus, Raul," she swore, then caught herself with a groan. "Fine. That's another quarter for the swear jar." She shook her head at the road.

"Raul, that passage isn't about damnation. It's about redemption. It's about those who will be saved. He who is to 'dwell in the devouring fire' is the pure soul, Raul. He who is able to withstand 'everlasting burnings' is the righteous—the one who has known darkness, but can now walk with the light."

Every time I entered one of Sloane's recurring nightmares, I thought about what Aunt Cely had told me that day on our drive home from church. I wasn't sure why. It never once helped me to feel better about the horror I was about to witness a little girl face.

Fire surrounded me—as always—in Sloane's nightmare of her previous death *(as Maribel)* in Madrid. I'd missed the explosions, but the evidence of their impact was everywhere I turned. Unseen beings were screaming. Wailing.

The black cloud of smoke in the air was so thick as to partially obstruct my supernatural vision as the once-magnificent, castle-like structure in Madrid proceeded to crumble around me.

I found Sloane in the same place I always did: at the epicenter of the destruction—a lost beacon amid the madness—trapped in a ball of fire she couldn't escape from.

Dwelling with the consuming fire.

The little girl stood there calmly, her body aflame, her eyes fogged over with confusion. And pain.

Sloane may have been able to withstand "everlasting burnings," but the gruesome scene never looked anything like redemption to me.

CHAPTER 19

Bethany

"**R**EALLY?" I BLURTED. MIKE SAW *ME* AS A THREAT? "WHY?"
"Raul chose us over you for a decade. His decision
to claim you now could—*will*—change things. A lot."

"How so?" I eagerly pressed. What did he mean Raul
had chosen them over me for a decade?

"How *not* is more like it," he griped. "Women always
change everything."

"Uh … *yeah*—for the better."

Tiago showed up with a plate of vegetables and a steak
the size of my head.

"You can threaten to blow up all of San Francisco," I told
Mike, "but I'm not eating even half of that."

Mike chuckled. Tiago looked confused, but his dimples
came out nonetheless to share in the joke he didn't get before excusing himself again.

"Hey, I'm famished; where's *my* steak?" Jorge asked
from across the room, giving me a look that said he was
hungry for more than steak.

I angled my body toward Mike as Jorge sauntered over
to us. Jorge had made a point earlier of mentioning to me

how much he'd enjoyed holding me down at the club last night—and that he was looking forward to the next time. He was probably at least partially responsible for Raul freaking out and biting my thigh to stake his "claim." I'd barely refrained from making an immature gagging gesture in the face of Jorge's comment before. *Why wasn't Raul back yet?*

"May I be of assistance?" Jorge offered, looking from me to the steak. "I overheard something about a forced feeding."

Dick. "I'm good. Thanks." I had to wonder how many of the guys had overheard my conversation with Mike— on purpose or inadvertently—given their supernatural hearing abilities.

He grinned and pulled up a barstool. "Mind if I stay and watch how good?" Jorge spoke with a slight Spanish accent—which might've sounded sexy had it not been ruined by the fact he was obviously a complete pig.

"If you're that bored, who am I to stop you?"

Jorge laughed. "You're right, Mike. She is fun." His gaze roamed from my face to my chest. "And gorgeous."

"Back off, Jorge."

Jorge's grin didn't falter at Mike's sharp tone. "Just trying to get to know the pack's new queen, Mike." His eyes returned to my face as he said to Mike, "You and Tiago have been hogging her most of the evening. Why don't you go play with your seer for a while? You're running out of time to hit that before we have to kill her, you know."

Charming. Despite my aversion to violence, I really hoped Jorge was one of those quiet Gabe supporters on Mike's list to weed out and kill.

"That hasn't been determined." Mike's voice was cold.

Jorge's gaze shifted to Mike, affording me a much-needed reprieve from his lascivious staring. "Oh, no? Thought I heard Stephen say—"

"You heard wrong."

As much as I hated diverting Jorge's attention back to me, the rising tension between the two wolves had piqued my curiosity. Raul and the guys had been talking about killing a seer when I'd first awakened on the plane. Thinking back on it, I realized it had probably been Jorge's voice I'd heard suggesting the seer was "low-hanging fruit, ripe for the picking."

"Seer?" I asked. "As in a psychic?"

"There another kind?" Jorge's smirk shifted to me.

"Don't know, Jorge. They didn't cover the occult in med school. And my mom never let me call Miss Cleo's hotline like I wanted to for my seventh birthday."

Lance busted out laughing from the other side of the room. "Miss Cleo!" he exclaimed with a snort. *"Call me now."* He mimicked the late television psychic's phony Jamaican accent.

Grinning, I turned and gave Lance a nod of acknowledgement. I'd had a feeling that werewolf—or werelock, rather—was American. When I looked back to Jorge, I was even more delighted to note the smirk had been wiped from his face. He didn't like being left out of a joke, apparently.

"So, what's the reason you're lobbying to kill this seer woman?" I raised a brow at him. "Is she a fraud? Did she give you a bad tarot card reading?"

"No." His mouth twisted with disdain. "We need something from her werelock lover's pack. Something that involves you, if you want to know the—"

"*Enough,*" Stephen's irate voice cut Jorge off as he came through the arched doorway and into the dining area. Several more long strides brought him to the bar next to us, where I was most surprised to find Stephen's scowl of disapproval directed at Mike rather than at Jorge as he said, "What are you doing? Why would you let him sit here with Bethany and—"

"I was just about to stop him."

Stephen appeared unconvinced. "Bullshit. You wanted her to know—"

"She's going to know soon enough anyway. We've only a matter of days before—"

"I think it's time for Bethy to retire," Tiago interjected. His sweet voice suddenly sounded commanding—and he was pushing his way forward, shouldering Stephen out of his way, to get to me.

"Don't call her Bethy," Jorge scolded him. "Only Raul can call her that."

Tiago's fingers wrapped around my bicep, gentle but firm as he pulled me from my seat. "My apologies," he said to me, before saying to the others, "It's time for Bethany to retire."

"My steak," I mumbled in protest, not knowing what to think or say as Tiago began dragging me away. None of the others made a move to stop him.

What was going on? *Which one of them was in charge?* I had assumed that Mike was in command in Raul's absence based on how he'd been acting, but now that didn't seem to be the case.

"I'll send your food to your room," Tiago assured me as he led me from the bar and down the narrow hallway to the airplane's master suite that had been designated as my bedroom.

As the door clicked shut behind us, I took in Tiago's tall, broad frame blocking it, and my heart began to race.

Tiago probably heard it, too, because he said, "You know I won't harm you. Don't you?"

I didn't really know anything anymore, but I nodded in agreement to appease him just the same. "Of course." *Please let that be the case.*

"You're lying," he called me straight out. "We can scent lies, Bethany. So I wouldn't advise continuing to lie to any of us. Particularly Raul. Understood?"

Oh, my God. A rush of heat hit my cheeks. I suddenly felt dizzy; short of breath and claustrophobic trapped in this fancy bedroom suite with Tiago—whom I'd previously identified as the sweet, safe werelock aboard the plane. Where did that leave me now?

"Where's Raul?" I demanded. "I need to speak with him."

"Raul's been delayed."

"Why? Delayed where? Stephen's been back for over an hour." I had no idea what time it was or how long it'd actually been, but it felt like Stephen had been back for a while now, and I was anxious for Raul to return right this second. "When will Raul be back?"

"Calm down. Everything's going to be fine." He took several steps toward me, but stopped when I took retreating ones. "Raul is with Sloane. She had a nightmare."

"Who?"

"Sloane. The special-needs child Raul mannies for."

"Wait—he's really a manny?"

"Yes." Tiago's dimples returned momentarily. "In a way."

I rolled my eyes. "So I can't lie, but no one else is capable of a straight answer around here?"

"Bethany, I'd like you to get washed up and ready for bed." A directive, framed as a request, as he tilted his head in the direction of the suite's bathroom.

"Okay," I acquiesced. "I will. But I'd like for you to leave this room first."

He shook his head. "You have twenty minutes; then I wash you myself."

For a split second, I thought about screaming for help. But who on this jet did I really want rushing to my aid? Mike—the grouchy werelock dropping threats and talking about "disciplining" me? Creepy Jorge? Grape-smuggler Stephen? None of the monsters I'd met stood out as closet good guys.

New tactic. "You just got through explaining to me what it means to have a true mate. You told me Raul claimed me—*for eternity*. You really think your Alpha would be okay with you forcing yourself on me in the shower? That he wouldn't—"

"Whoa!" Tiago's eyes went wide. He held his hand up. "What are you talking about?"

"You just said you were going to wash me."

"Exactly. Wash you. Not rape you in the shower." His features screwed up, giving me a look like I was the demented one for jumping to unsavory assumptions amid my kidnapping predicament. "I was just going to clean your face with a warm cloth … make sure you brushed your teeth …"

A fresh wave of embarrassment overcame me. I refused to feel like the asshole about this. "Well, how am I supposed to know that? I've got wolves staring at my tits, commenting on my Kegel muscles, tossing around jokes about holding me down while their leader eats me out again. Pretty sure all the guys on this plane are convinced I'm an exhibitionist because they either witnessed firsthand or heard about my night of public club sex with Raul."

"You are an exhibitionist."

"Excuse me?"

"I didn't stutter."

"I am no—"

"And I'm gay, Bethany."

My open mouth shut.

His dimples reappeared. "You have sixteen minutes left."

CHAPTER 20

Raul

ALTHOUGH I COULDN'T GAIN ACCESS TO SLOANE'S MIND, she had somehow found a way to pull me into her subconscious when she needed me. She only did it when she was dreaming, so I didn't think she was entirely aware of what she was doing, much less in full control of it—which presented an inherent risk for me in allowing myself to be drawn into the depths of her mind.

Sloane may have been a child still, but she was extraordinarily powerful. Thus far, I'd been able to resist her call—to choose whether or not I allowed myself to be pulled into her subconscious. I'd also been able to hold onto my ability to withdraw from her nightmares when I needed to.

But that could quickly change after she shifted for the first time and inevitably became even more powerful.

As I got closer, I paused when I saw that she'd been crying—something Sloane didn't often do. Though I wasn't sure yet whether to view it as a bad sign or a positive development, it was an indication to proceed with caution. She was obviously more distraught than usual.

The flames consuming her never seemed to harm Sloane physically in her dreams, just as they didn't harm me. Within Sloane's subconscious, it was always the blistering agony of meeting a dark and ghastly eternity in which she would have no escape and little control that eroded her psyche without mercy.

Made sense. It was the inferno of loneliness, the blaze of confusion, and the raging pyre of a defeat she refused to accept that had swelled the storm of denial within Maribel's soul, twisting it beyond its breaking point.

"Sloane!" I called out to her, throwing up the shaka hand signal in greeting. "What gives, girl? You start partying without me again?"

Her tear-streaked face lit up when she saw me.

I jogged over and knelt beside her, making a quick study of the fireball encapsulating her. It hadn't changed at all since the last dream. Damn.

"You came."

"Of course I came. Are you kidding me? Hey, thanks for inviting me." I offered her my fist to bump. "I wouldn't miss your dream adventures for anything."

Her little pink lips tilted up. It was barely perceptible. And then it was gone.

"Hey, don't leave me hanging," I said, my eyes dropping meaningfully to my outstretched fist.

She still didn't bump it. It was outside her fireball. She stared longingly down at it. "There's no way out for me."

"Sure there is. C'mon, just try and bump it. The fire can't hold you forever."

She shook her head. Wisps of her long raven hair blew across her cheek. "I think it can, Raul." Her eyes lifted to mine. "I think it already has."

It was in moments like this, when I stared into little Sloane's wise violet eyes, that I'd swear she remembered me—remembered *everything*. It was as if she was Maribel again looking back at me. The same Maribel who had come to me in my own dreams years ago, when I'd been just as lost. When I'd felt hopeless. The same seemingly omniscient being who'd taken me under her wing and given me courage; helped me to shape my purpose.

But most of the time Sloane looked so much like her mom it was easy to pretend that she'd never been Maribel, that she was a fresh, untainted soul who didn't harbor the burden of guilt that came from killing and harvesting other souls for sustenance for a century in the ether.

"There *is* a way out, Sloane. We just have to find it. It's like a puzzle. A maze. There's a secret trap door somewhere. A cool hidden tunnel."

An unknown trigger point I needed to flip to help her let go and move on.

"I wasn't supposed to be born. It was a mistake." She said this the way she always did—as if stating facts. Facts that couldn't be altered or dismissed. "I can only do bad things … like before."

"No way was it a mistake. You and me"—I gestured between us with my thumb—"we're old pals. Remember? You helped me before. Saved me. You came back to hang with me. And now I'm here to help you."

I knew that she didn't remember, didn't recall anything of her former life as Maribel. Yet she clung to the certainty that she'd done bad things for which she could never be forgiven. She was right about the first part. I refused to accept the latter. Even though I had no authority to know such a thing.

"It's too late. I can't have friends. I can only do bad things now," she said, repeating the words that had become her familiar script. "The voices know. I was supposed to take the voices with me and stay dead." She paused; her forehead wrinkled. "You hear them, too, don't you? You must know."

I did hear them. They were all annoying bastards, those voices.

"They" were the angry, bitter accretion of bloodthirsty spirits. The dark, vengeful energy of greedy Salvatella ancestors attached to the faulty black heart that had once fueled Joaquin Salvatella's legendary blood curse. They lived on in symbiotic existence within the curse that was now a part of Sloane.

A curse Sloane had willingly sought and taken on when she'd been Maribel.

"Once I extract the black heart of the curse from your sister, Raul, I will bear the burden of keeping its darkness locked within what's left of my own damaged soul—for all eternity."

Maribel had absolutely known the danger. And Sloane was right: Maribel had definitely planned to drag "the voices"—the dark energy she'd absorbed within her soul—to the other side and remain dead.

Just because it hadn't worked out that way didn't make it a mistake.

But it did mean that I had to find a way to help Sloane manage those bastard voices she could now never escape. For in their symbiotic existence, "they" hoped to worm their way back into power through Sloane.

Using her.

"Yeah. I hear 'em." I scowled through the flames and billowing black smoke surrounding us at the continuous stream of disembodied, unwelcome editorializing. The judgments. The whispers and the hisses. The taunts. "And I'm gonna open a big can of shut-the-hell-up on them if they don't stop feeding you ridiculous lies."

She didn't crack a smile; not even a hint. "I was supposed to die, Raul. I was supposed to take the voices with me and stay dead. It was a mistake when I was born."

"Uh-uh. There are no mistakes, my friend. Tough times? Yeah. Dark moments? Sure. They can feel like mistakes when we're in them—feel like we made a wrong turn somewhere and got lost. But remember what we say?"

She stared stoically back at me before giving me a slow blink, followed by a delayed eye-roll. And I outright belly-laughed.

This was a good sign. A great fucking sign, in fact, as to how far Sloane had come in a short window of time.

I raised my "Aunt Cely" pointer finger at her, a shit-eating grin on my face that I refused to quell as I repeated the line Maribel used to say to me in my darker moments. "No one ever found daybreak by avoiding night, Sloane. Only by passing through it."

She exhaled—much like a normal ten-year-old might who was tired and grouchy and felt that an adult was asking something of her that required more effort than she cared to expend. Another positive sign.

"The darkness is your instrument, Sloane. It's your conduit to shepherd." *Make it your bitch,* I wanted to say to her, but I didn't think Avery would appreciate me teaching her daughter that.

"We're going to figure out a way to fist-bump our way through this together, 'kay? You and me."

We might not figure it out this time, in this dream, but I wasn't giving up.

Not because Sloane had been born the *Rogue* of rogues, prophesied to be an unstoppable supernatural powerhouse destined to alter our world forever. Or because of the loyalty and connection I'd once shared with her when I'd known her as Maribel. Or even because Sloane had taken on this curse (as Maribel) from my own sister—saving Miles from a burden of darkness that might've otherwise destroyed her over time.

I wasn't giving up because I liked her. Something in me related to her—both now as Sloane and before as Maribel.

I needed to see her figure this out. To see Sloane rise above the pull of darkness within herself and prove the whole world wrong meant more to me than I could ever express.

And I couldn't let it go. Wouldn't give up on her.

Maybe a part of me thought that if Maribel could be saved—if she could redeem herself as Sloane—that meant there was still hope for me.

That there was hope for all of us.

CHAPTER 21

Raul

I RETURNED TO THE PLANE TO FIND TIAGO STANDING watch outside Bethy's suite. He immediately tried to brief me on every detail that had happened with her during my absence, and while I appreciated his diligence, I'd no time for that. I only wanted highlights.

I didn't want to waste another minute away from my mate.

Though I'd been gone for less than two hours, I was beside myself with the need to see her. Smell her. Confirm that she was all right.

And that all of this was finally real.

She looked like a mirage lying passed out on my king-sized bed, sprawled overtop the covers rather than beneath them. Her hair, still damp from her shower, fanned out like spun gold against the black silk pillowcase beneath it, and she was wearing a little pink striped robe—one of her own that we'd packed from her apartment. It was short and clingy, leaving her long, sinewy tanned legs on display—and very little else to the imagination.

Yet imagine I did.

My mouth watered. My cock strained against the confines of my clothing.

And my hand reached out of its own volition to touch her, needing to confirm that she was real, that she was flesh and bone within my grasp.

After so many years of imagining and fantasizing about a moment like this, I almost feared she'd vanish like mist when my fingertips brushed against her thigh.

But she didn't.

She was real.

And I was a greedy, desperate bastard for her.

I reached for the belt of her robe, pulling the knot free and parting the material wrapped loosely around her. I told myself I just wanted a quick peek at her—to check her marks before I tucked her beneath the covers, where she'd be warmer and more comfortable.

But soon I was fingering those marks. Then my head bent to lick the ones I hadn't healed well enough that morning. She moaned my name in her sleep, and that was all it took to fully awaken the beast in me.

I was already painfully hard, so when her hand lifted off the mattress and fell between her thighs, it took all my willpower not to pin it above her head and slam my cock into her in its place.

Fuck it. I'd never claimed to be a saint. I definitely hadn't gotten where I was in life by always playing fair.

I vanished my clothing and climbed overtop her on the bed.

"Wake up, Bethy." I nudged her legs farther apart with my knees as I moved between them. She didn't stir.

Even in sleep, she was making those breathy noises I loved so much as her fingers groped clumsily between her wet folds. Her skin was flushed, her nipples diamond hard.

My canines extended and my eyes shifted as I scented how aroused she was. My inner wolf was clawing at me—demanding to fuck her.

As I watched her touch herself, I was close to losing it—overwhelmed with the need to take her.

But ramming into her like an animal would ruin my game. And Bethy was a prize worth any torture. I reminded myself that this was nothing compared to what I'd already endured for the past decade.

"Put them inside you, baby," I whispered, taking hold of her hand and control of her fingers, directing two of them inside her. They were so slim, and her pussy so soaked, that they glided in easily. "There you go."

I pumped them in and out, making sure the heel of her hand rubbed against her clit as I did so, working her up to a steady rhythm that had her panting and moaning continuously before I nudged her thighs wider apart and added a third finger.

Ignoring the fact I was leaking precum like a faucet and my balls felt so tight and heavy they might fall off, I focused on Bethy's breathing, on the cadence of her moans, and on the staccato of her heartbeat, as I spurred her to the brink of orgasm—and then stopped short, halting her hand.

She made a disgruntled noise in the back of her throat and grumbled something about "bullshit dream sex." Despite the agonizing pain in my balls, I found myself biting my lip to stifle laughter. If there'd been any remaining doubt, that was the moment I knew for certain I was irreversibly in love with Bethany Garrett.

Dipping my head, I kissed her cheek and murmured,

"You need me inside you, angel. Say it. You have to tell me to fuck you if you want to come."

I wanted to hear her panting, "Fuck me, Raul," over and over, like she'd done in the club last night. God, I'd all but lost my mind when she'd done that.

After two more whispered prompts, she said it. And I rewarded her by sucking her nipples and using her fingers to bring her to the brink of orgasm once more. Then I stopped and got her to say it again.

I did this two more times, until the scent of her disappointment nearly eclipsed that of her arousal, and the pattern of her breathing indicated she was finally waking up, while mindlessly, she still chanted, "Fuck me, Raul."

Quickly, I let go of her hand that was playing with her pussy and shifted into position, stretching out on my back on the side of the bed next to her free hand, which I then wrapped around my erection.

And, like a true gentleman, I pretended to be out cold as Bethany awoke to find that she'd been simultaneously fingering herself and stroking my dick in her sleep.

CHAPTER 22

Bethany

I WAS DREAMING ABOUT SEX WITH RAUL AGAIN. AND talking in my sleep. So much that I awoke to my own panted chant of *"Fuck me, Raul."*

I blinked my eyes open. The ceiling above me was unfamiliar. As was the humming noise of the plane engine in the background.

And the sound of Raul groaning in pain beside me.

"Don't," he grunted. "Fuck … please, don't stop … need you so bad, Bethy …"

Huh?

"Bethy … what are you doing to me? Fuck, that feels so good …"

Oh, shit—what *was* I doing?

I glance down at my body, then over at Raul's next to me. I'd been masturbating in my sleep—while giving a sleeping Raul a handjob!

I froze.

Oh, wow. His cock was enormous in my hand—wet from his precum and pointing straight to the ceiling.

I had three fingers buried between my thighs, and they

were soaking wet. My clit felt hard and swollen with the need to come as I rolled my thumb over it. Jesus, how long had I been masturbating?

Raul groaned again. I was still gripping his dick. I flexed my fingers experimentally.

He shifted, his hips lifting off the bed, causing my hand to slide down to the base of his erection. When he lowered his hips back to the mattress, my hand slid up his dick again. He groaned my name and repeated the action, rocking his hips up and down, fucking my hand in his sleep.

I tried to remember how mad I was at him—to remind myself that he was a scary werewolf creature who'd kidnapped me—but a rush of fluid coated the fingers between my thighs at the sight of Raul's powerful, naked body undulating next to me, his beautiful hard penis desperately seeking the touch of my hand wrapped around it.

Before I knew it, I was helping him—gliding my hand up and down his thick shaft while he continued to groan and say my name.

It made me feel powerful—knowing how much Raul wanted me. *Needed me.*

Mesmerized by the sight of him, of the sounds of him grunting and groaning and begging for more of my touch, I rolled onto my side, then shifted upon my knees, careful not to disturb his aroused slumber as I gained a closer view and a better grip on his dick while continuing to touch myself with my other hand.

"Yesss," he sighed. "Ah, please, Bethy ... *yesss* ... in your mouth, baby ... *please.*"

Like a woman possessed, somehow I found my head lowering over his midsection, my lips parting, my tongue extending to swirl over his salty, bulbous head, before taking him fully into my mouth. As soon as I tasted him—and heard his hiss of pleasure—I was lost.

I began sucking him in earnest while working what wasn't in my mouth with my hand. His hand fell atop my head, pressing down gently at first, then more forcefully, as he grunted and raised his hips, his cock seeking the back of my throat.

I didn't deny him.

"Ahhh, Bethy, feels so good … you're so beautiful … feels so perfect … fantasized about you for so long …"

His words were like crack. *And I was an addict.*

I ate his praise up like candy, along with his cock, until my clit was painfully swollen and my pussy throbbing—beyond dripping wet with the need to be filled.

So when Raul began mumbling, "Straddle me, Bethy" and "Ride my cock" in his sleep, I couldn't resist temptation.

I bobbed my head up and down twice more before pulling my mouth from him, shrugging my robe from my shoulders, and straddling his hips.

Taking him in hand, slowly I lowered myself onto his rock-hard length.

Drenched as I was, my insides felt swollen and tender as they stretched to accept his uncompromising girth. Not surprising—given how aggressively we'd gone at it the night before. Raul had been insatiable. *And I'd been right there with him.*

Yet after everything we'd done the night before, what I was doing now felt even more devious. *Dirty.* The fear that he might awaken at any moment to catch me fucking him in his sleep was a tremendous turn-on.

My head rolled back and I released a moan at the

sensation of his thick head pushing its way so deeply within me as I sank my weight onto him.

Fuck but he felt good—so perfect inside me.

I told myself I deserved to get off after everything I'd been through as I began to move over him, lifting and lowering myself, angling my body back and forth in order to catch all the right spots—my hips circling and rolling to the music of Raul's grunts and groans as his pelvis jerked and lifted beneath me.

I needed this.

He'd drugged me, the bastard.

He'd kidnapped me.

He'd left me alone aboard a private plane to South America with a gang of big horny monsters masquerading as the hottest male nannies on the planet.

My hips rolled faster the angrier I got, my movements more bold, the knot in my lower belly tightening, the pressure building.

"That's it—fuck me, baby," he directed in his sleep. "Faster. More. Want to feel you clenching around me … soaking my cock …"

He was suspiciously articulate for a guy who was sleeping.

But I was too close to the edge to analyze the obvious signs.

And then I was cartwheeling over it.

Holding my breath, I bit down on my lip to withhold the carnal, shamelessly unrefined noises threatening to escape as I did clench and gush all over him.

Spots were beginning to form in my vision from lack of oxygen as the tremors rolled through me. The metallic taste of blood seeped into my mouth from where I'd bitten my lip. And then my heart nearly burst from my chest when Raul's eyes abruptly opened, flashing feral yellow through the dimly lit bedroom to catch me in the act.

His hand shot out, his fingers wrapping around my throat.

CHAPTER 23

Bethany

I KNEW A MOMENT OF SHEER UNADULTERATED PANIC—fearing I'd awakened his angry inner beast rather than the man within. But his grip was careful as he pulled me down toward him, his upper body rising off the bed to meet me halfway as his mouth crashed into mine.

My lips parted for him, desperate for air, and his tongue slipped inside. Gentle. Exploring. Sweet.

Then consuming.

Oxygen was overrated.

My fingers dug into the muscles of his shoulders and back, clawing him nearer as I let myself get lost in the taste and smell and feel of him.

When he withdrew long enough to allow us both a breath, he murmured, "I'm sorry, Bethy."

The stress of the past twenty-four hours caught up with me then, and my eyes burned. Maybe it was the disturbingly overwhelming need I felt for him in that post-coital moment that prompted it. Or perhaps it was the sad sincerity I saw in his golden irises at his softly spoken apology that made me realize just how disappointed I was that he wasn't the person I'd wanted him to be.

"You drugged me." The first tears brimmed over.

"I know," he acknowledged with a remorseful sigh. "I'm sorry. I never wanted for things to happen this way. Never wanted to hurt you or disrupt your life." His lips brushed mine. His fingers tangled in my hair. "It's just that I've wanted you for so long." His tongue flicked out, licking the wobble in my lip. "Fantasized about you so damn much …"

He sucked my abused lower lip into his mouth, healing the bite I'd made.

God knows I loved the idea of being Raul's fantasy. But this whole situation had quickly become too dark of a fantasy for me.

"You kidnapped me," I stated the obvious as I pulled away—a reminder to myself as much as it was an indictment of him. "I trusted you. I used to play at your house all summer long when we were kids."

"Baby, I know this feels like a kidnapping right now, but it's really a rescue mission," he had the gall to say. And in spite of everything, I couldn't help but giggle at the absurdity as he brushed my tears away with the pads of his thumbs.

"Rescue mission?" I sniffed.

He nodded, the tip of his nose rubbing alongside mine. "You never wanted Gregg. You've been settling, honey. Playing it safe. You grew up so scared of ending up as the one fulfilling your dad's role in your own marriage one day that you settled for someone you weren't in love with."

My vision flooded with tears and I began crying anew. My therapist had said nearly the exact same thing.

"How can you know that?"

"Because you belong to me." He cupped my face in his hands, giving me a wistful smile. "You're my better half."

I'd always relished the idea of being someone's other half. But that was the stuff of Disney movies and fairy tales. The stark reality was I'd been kidnapped and was being held hostage by an aircraft full of horror-flick creatures.

I shook my head at him.

"I swear it's the truth," he professed, his eyes now brown and beseeching. "I stayed away from you for as long as I could. I've spent the past ten years worried that I would put you in danger if I ever allowed myself to be with you." He rubbed his cheek—slightly rough and scratchy with stubble—against my own, before kissing me again. "But I can't keep away anymore."

His words made no sense. Yet he sounded so earnest.

He's a con artist, Bethany. A criminal.

"I *won't* stay away anymore," he amended. "I need you too much."

He needed me. The crazy thing was I totally believed that part. Because he did need me—he was a fucking mess.

"And you need me, too. *Yes,* you do," he insisted when I started to shake my head in denial again. "Even if you're too angry right now to admit it. You know we're good for each other. Deep down, you know I'll make you happier than anyone else can—that what we feel when we're together is *right*. It's *real*."

I would've gone with "crazy." Or "scary."

Scary like the truth was scary.

Like vulnerability was scary …

He rolled me onto my back, stealing my breath when the full weight of his pelvis sank between my thighs, his rigid phallus bumping up against my cervix.

"I marked you, Bethy." A fact. Spoken with tenderness. And authority.

His arm hooked under my left thigh, drawing my knee up to his shoulder, deepening the angle of his penetration as he withdrew slightly, then pushed into me again. My eyes fluttered and rolled back at the sensation, even as more tears gathered on my lashes. "We're connected now."

God, we sure were.

He felt impossibly large inside me—our fit so tight as I took him at this angle, despite all my slick arousal fluid to ease his entry.

"For all eternity." He pulled out slowly, then shunted forward.

"You never"—gasp—"asked. Human mates are supposed to have a choice," I managed to get out between panted breaths.

His lips brushed my forehead. "I tried to give you a choice by staying away. I kept tabs on you from afar for a decade."

He had? What was he talking about?

"When I saw your engagement announcement online seven months ago, you can't imagine how sick with jealousy I was."

My foolish heart soared at his words.

He picked up the pace, rocking steadily in and out.

"And still I stayed away—because you looked so damn happy in your announcement photos. I left you alone because I thought your life was better off without me in it."

I felt the hurt in his words, saw the desolation in his soft brown gaze as slowly he fucked me, and it took my breath away.

"When I saw you last night on the dance floor … saw how sad and lonely you were behind the front you'd been putting on for the world … I lost control of my wolf. And myself."

His words rang with sincerity.

So did the possessive thrust of his hips.

And the casually demanding way he'd begun rolling and pinching my nipples.

He wasn't even hitting my clit at this angle, and I was ready to come again. Because I was mesmerized by him.

By us.

By the words pouring forth from his mouth that fulfilled every silly girlhood fantasy I'd ever secretly harbored.

"Now that I've had you, you're like a drug in my system. I want to taste every inch of you. Fill every part of you."

He was like the tide lapping over me—drawing me in. *Pulling me under.*

And in that moment, I wanted to drown.

"Do it," I heard myself pant. "Fill me." I wanted him to come with me this time. To *feel* him coming inside me. "I'm so close …"

"Can't baby," he said on a groan. I felt his smile, then his kiss of apology against my ear. "Not yet, okay? One day soon."

One day soon? What the everloving—?

Oh. I realized I'd just asked him to come inside me. Again. That's what he was saying no to. I'd gotten him to do it once already—*partially*—in the Hummer. And now I wanted the whole thing.

I wasn't sure why it was important to me. Probably because he was resisting it for reasons I failed to comprehend. What guy who possessed the magical power to prevent pregnancy and STDs would avoid coming inside a woman? *A woman he claimed was his better half.* It made zero sense.

"Please ... want to feel your release." I was intent on pressing the issue as I raised and circled my hips to meet his pelvis.

It struck me that his thrusts were too controlled—not nearly urgent enough considering the frenzied haze of lust that had enveloped me.

"How badly do you want it?"

His fingers swirled against my scalp and his mouth dipped to the hollow of my neck, finding his bite mark. He sucked on it, and my inner muscles began convulsing around his heated shaft in time with the pull of his lips and tongue—as if somehow his mark and my sex were connected now.

"Oh ... oh ... omigod ..." My eyes rolled back in my head. "Wha—what have you done?" I was instantly suspicious.

He hum-chuckled against my neck, then scraped his teeth over the mark. My core pulsed and seized around him again.

"Raul?" I gasped.

"It's only association, baby. Told you, we're connected now. I'll stop if you don't like it."

I didn't exactly hate it.

And I felt conflicted when he did stop—missing the sensation while at the same time reassured that he was being respectful of my boundaries.

Well ... some of them at least. I was still being held against my will.

Except it really didn't feel that way right now. Not at all, in fact. *It felt like there was no place else I'd rather be.*

He raised my left leg higher, hooking my knee all the way over his shoulder so that my ass cheek came fully off the mattress—further opening me up and changing the angle of his penetration. His big hand slid down the back of my thigh.

"Let me come in your ass, Bethy." His fingertips trailed along my cleft as he said it.

I didn't say no.

He hadn't actually asked. It was somewhere between telling and requesting.

He began lubricating my smaller hole with the slickness flowing freely between us as he churned in and out of my sex.

And I could do nothing but give him a glassy-eyed stare as he worked two fingers inside my ass, my mouth falling open to form a small "o" as my nails dug into his shoulder.

"That's it … stay relaxed. Feel good?"

I think I nodded.

"Good." The smile he gave me was so sweet, so … *Raul,* as he gazed down at me. It was hard to believe he'd changed at all. That he was a werelock now, and the Alpha of a pack of supernatural beasts.

His eyes remained intent on my face, cataloguing my every response as oh, so very slowly, he fucked me with his cock and fingers.

For better or worse, in this, I trusted Raul completely.

There were men who made women feel comfortable, confident, and proud exploring their sexuality, and there were those who didn't. Whatever his other flaws, Raul would always be the former.

"Breathe. Push out against my fingers," he instructed as he began to work a third one in.

"Oh … oh … fuck …" I winced and tightened up around him before his fingers were even halfway.

"Shh—it's okay." He held still and waited while I panted it out and tried to relax.

Two fingers had felt naughty—darkly erotic and arousing. Three fingers was a reality check at my back gate. *The reality that a huge cock would be breaching it next.*

When Raul shifted his hips, my abdominal muscles spasmed and cramped. I groaned. "I don't know if I can …"

I left that statement of doubt open-ended. I was not ready to give up. It had felt so good up until a moment ago when I'd started to panic.

"You haven't answered my question." Holding his fingers still inside my ass, he resumed the slow, gentle thrust of his hips, sliding his heavy cock in and out of me. "How badly do you want me to come inside you, Bethy?" His mouth dipped to the hollow of my neck to lick his double bite mark. *Once.*

Twice.

My clit pulsated in reaction, and kept going after he'd stopped. A rush of wetness seeped from me, and I arched up to meet his next thrust—inadvertently pushing his fingers in deeper.

"Oh … *oh, God …*"

The stretch felt uncomfortable for a moment, the unfamiliar pressure an awkward sensation to reconcile, making me feel lightheaded.

Then it began to change.

Raul's warm breath came faster against my ear as he spoke softly to me. "As life-altering as it would feel to sink balls deep in your beautiful tight ass and let you milk the cum out of me … I don't want to do it unless it's what you really want, okay?"

Dear Lord, he was good. *"Let" my ass milk the cum out of him.* He really had earned every bit of his reputation.

And it seemed that the praise lavished upon his sexual prowess was well deserved, too, because despite my mind wanting to snicker and cry bullshit, my sex throbbed with renewed need. My smaller ring of muscles tightened, then relaxed, pulsing in a way that sucked Raul's fingers in deeper.

It wasn't an entirely unpleasant sensation either.

My unattended clit was quivering so frantically that if he were to merely brush against it, I'd probably shoot off the bed in orgasm.

We groaned in unison as Raul's cock thickened and twitched within me. I squirmed and circled my hips, angling my pelvis up, trying to take in more of him.

His fingers sank a little farther, causing the uncomfortable stretching sensation to return. But this time, the burn made my belly flutter with excitement, my engorged pearl ache.

"There you go, sweetheart," he coaxed. "Push out and take it. As much as you want."

I wanted it all. But I was afraid of pushing against his fingers and taking it. Scared of the initial sear of pain and discomfort, while at the same time eager for it. Like last night when he'd bitten me, it was as if the pain and pleasure receptors within me were blurring—crossing and blending—one sensation heightening the other.

I licked my lips. "Need you to do it."

My fingers combed through his soft hair, gently

tugging him downward as I strained my neck to grant him better access.

His mouth found the bite mark again. As he latched on and sucked, my inner walls contracted, and he pressed his fingers as far as they would go inside my ass, setting off my orgasm as involuntary convulsions pulsed through both my holes. It felt like one giant, incredibly erotic muscle spasm originating in my pelvis and radiating throughout my entire body.

"Oh, fuck … holy shit …"

He growled and jerked his hips, pulled partway out, and rammed his cock hard and deep several times in controlled succession, changing the angle so that his groin connected with my clitoris at long last, thrusting my orgasm into violent Category 5 peel-me-off-the-ceiling territory.

I think I pulled most of his hair out as I wailed and babbled discordant pleas and expletives. It felt like it went on forever. My whole body was trembling from the tsunami that was still tearing through it when Raul growled and withdrew his fingers from me.

Then he pulled out, spurting on my stomach and breasts as he arose to his knees and quickly crawled over me, shooting more cum across my neck and chin as he straddled my face, pulled me up by my hair, and pushed inside my mouth, thrusting to the back of my throat as he unloaded everything he had left in me.

And it was *a lot.*

I couldn't swallow it fast enough and choked a few times before I managed to get it down, the heel of my palm pressing feverishly between my thighs all the while as I rode out the final tremors of my own release.

He muttered apologies as he withdrew from my mouth, and something along the lines of "That wasn't supposed to go like that," which caused me to giggle until my eyes watered with purely feminine glee.

I wasn't the only one who'd lost control.

He grabbed a warm, damp washcloth from the bathroom and cleaned me off.

"What happened to coming in my ass?" I teased when he was done.

He gave me a lopsided grin as he bent over me. "Next time, okay?" He kissed the tip of my nose. "I decided you weren't ready yet."

"Ha!" I snorted. "You decided you couldn't hold out."

He laughed. "Maybe." His cheeks flushed a little, making him look utterly adorable, and so nonthreateningly *human,* as he tossed the towel aside and stretched out next to me on his side.

But then his expression grew pensive and somber, killing the happy butterflies in my belly as reality crashed our sexy party.

"Look, I know I'm not the best guy in the world." His fingertips traced the lines of my ribs. "I know you deserve way better than me. But I promise I'm going to do whatever it takes to fix this. To make things right between us."

"Except turn this plane around and take me back to San Francisco?" I deadpanned.

He sighed. "Won't you please give me a chance? Give *us* a chance? Just spend some time in Bariloche with me. Try thinking of it as a vacation."

Pshh. I rolled my eyes. "Oh, well hey, why not? Someone already put me on a plane and packed half my possessions for me." I batted my eyes at him in my best imitation of an airhead. "As long as there's cable and access to reality TV where we're headed on this vacay, I'm in."

"Stop that." Smiling, he reached for my face, cupping the right side of my cheek in his hand and placing his thumb over my right eyelid to halt its fluttering. "You're gonna pull something."

Soon we were both giggling as he climbed over me and tried to do the same with my other eye, while I pretended to be an airhead fighting him off, protesting that he was going to mess my eye makeup.

Before long, we'd gone from laughing to kissing and rubbing up on one another again. But when I felt his erection digging into my thigh, I pushed against his chest.

"No. We can't keep connecting through sex, Raul. We need to talk."

"Okay, okay." He groaned and rolled off of me onto his back. "You're right." He wrapped his hand around the base of his enormous erection and muttered, "I guess this can wait."

CHAPTER 24

Raul

"Thank you." She bit her smiling lip and leaned up onto her elbow on her side, facing me.

When her blue eyes drifted over my erection and she unconsciously licked her lips, I began to have serious doubts about how well this "talk" was going to go.

Her skin was flushed, her nipples hard, and the aroma of her dripping pussy hung heavily in the air between us, too strong a scent to be ignored.

Fuck. I couldn't afford to screw this up, though. Not when I was making progress. She'd been laughing a moment ago, and now she was smiling at me.

"What'd you want to talk about?" I prompted, quietly praying she stuck to easy questions, because there wasn't enough blood supply flowing to my brain for it to handle much else.

"Are you really a manny?"

"Not in the traditional, professional sense, no. But yes, in the sense that I am committed to spending a good portion of my time mentoring a little werelock girl with special powers and special needs in an effort to help her work through her challenges."

Her eyes softened on me, and she gave me an adoring look.

This could work. If I steered the conversation right, I'd be fingering her ass and eating her out before we landed. We still had several hours left to go, given our delayed late-afternoon takeoff.

"And you went to see her tonight? Because she had a nightmare?"

"Yep."

I didn't elaborate. Because Bethy had rolled onto her stomach, crossing her legs at the ankles—putting her pert, beautiful hiney on display.

She frowned and asked, "But where are her parents? Shouldn't they be the ones to comfort her after she's had a nightmare?" Her hand flew up to her mouth. "Oh, no, is she an orphan?"

She was completely oblivious to the torment she was putting me through. My dick twitched and leaked precum when I failed to suppress fantasies of climbing on top of her and sliding between her plump cheeks to impale her pussy from behind—maybe with her thighs tied together just above the knees so she'd be crazy tight.

I shook myself internally. *Just answer the question.*

What was the question?

I swallowed. "No. Not an orphan. She has a mom and a … stepdad … of sorts."

"You don't like the stepdad?"

"Nah, I like Sloane's stepdad just fine." *Not a complete lie.* I liked the fact that Alcaeus was good at doing the shit that I didn't want to do when it came to running a pack. I liked that he made Avery happy, and that he would lay down his life to protect her and Sloane. *And I liked the leverage he afforded me with his former pack that my sister now headed.*

"His name's Alcaeus. I've known him for years. He's a great guy." I forced an agreeable expression. "He works for me, actually. He's my second in command." *Technically speaking.* "Sloane's mom, Avery, is a good friend of mine. You'll love her. Avery is also a higher-ranking member of my pack."

Bethany nodded absently, worrying her lip as she rocked her crossed ankles up and down, highlighting her toned hamstring and glute muscles in the process each time her legs curled back. I was going to come all over myself like a thirteen-year-old boy before this conversation was through.

"I look forward to meeting them. But why don't Sloane's parents take care of her when she has nightmares, Raul? Why do they call you?"

"It's complicated," I told her truthfully, then paused to consider my next words carefully. Where to start?

Mind off pussy. Mind off pussy.

"So, werelocks have the ability to enter a human's mind and um … well, read their thoughts. More or less." Damn, that could've been delivered better.

Way better, I realized, when Bethany's eyes widened in alarm and she sputtered, "Oh, my God. Please tell me you're not serious. Are you in my head right now? For how long?" She sat up and snatched a sheet, then proceeded to wrap it around her, covering her nakedness from me. "Shit, I remember Mike saying something about hearing Gregg's thoughts back at my apartment. I should've thought to question it sooner, but I just forgot with all the other information the guys were sharing—"

"Bethy, calm down. I am *not* in your head." Calm down and please take the sheet back off. "I have never even once been inside your head. I promise." *Not for lack of trying.* I held three fingers up. "Scout's honor."

Her throat bobbed. "Really? What about Mike? Or Tiago? Or—"

"None of my men have ever been inside your head either."

"Are you sure? Why not?"

Ah, fuck me. I was headed straight to hell already, so ...

"Because I respect your feelings and your right to privacy too much."

Her eyes shone with unshed tears. "You mean that?"

I nodded. I was the lowest form of human being.

"Thank you." She crawled over to me, dropping the sheet in the process, and kissed me sweetly on the mouth.

I'd already lost my erection though. Gently, I pressed against her shoulder, holding her back, then nudging her away from me. Scrubbing a hand over my face, I got up from the bed and conjured pants onto myself.

And I began pacing.

"Raul? Is something wrong?"

"No. I just don't want us to lose focus. We haven't finished talking about Sloane. Or mind-reading." I couldn't even look at her as I continued. "As I was saying, werelocks can read human minds and the minds of most common werewolves. To that end, werelocks can compel humans and werewolves to basically do their bidding as well. And they can sometimes alter memories and sway thoughts."

Geez, it sounded so insidious and dirty when I explained it out loud to Bethany like that. The gasp that came from the bed reinforced it.

"That's horrible!"

I nodded. "Mm-hmm." *Get to the important points.* Rip it off like a Band-Aid.

"Within a pack, werelocks will often access other werelocks' minds from time to time as a means of communication. The Alpha and higher-ranking werelocks within a pack typically have access to all lower-ranking werelocks' minds. But there are exceptions. For example, no one has access to Sloane's mind. However, Sloane has the ability to pull me into her mind when she needs me." I stopped pacing and looked over to gauge Bethy's reaction.

She looked completely spellbound. And shell-shocked.

"But she only does it when she's having nightmares. So I'm not sure she's entirely conscious of what she's doing. And she's only ever pulled *me* inside her mind like that. She's never done it with anyone else."

"Not even her mom?"

I shook my head.

"Why you?"

"Dunno. Sloane and I have just always had a really strong connection I guess." Not a complete lie. There was no way I was going into the whole Maribel reincarnation with Bethany. "And I like her." I shrugged. "She's a great kid. Her behavior can be pretty off sometimes, so people have a hard time understanding and accepting her. But she's amazing. Really funny, too." I couldn't help but crack a smile. "You'll see when you meet her."

"How old is she again?"

"Nine years and eight months."

A beatific grin broke out on Bethany's face. She looked like an angel with her halo of tangled, freshly fucked golden hair sticking out in all directions. Yet the expression on her face unsettled me. She was regarding me like I was some kind of a hero for my relationship with Sloane. I wasn't.

I felt my own smile fall away.

"That is so incredibly beautiful, Raul," she gushed.

I scrubbed a hand over my mouth. "Look, you should know, the werewolf world centers around a lot of belief in superstitions and prophecies, which often results in a good deal of paranoia. Pack life means everything to wolves. It's hard to fathom at first for those of us who were born human, but there's an immediate, instinctive pull to belong to a pack when you first become a werewolf."

"You felt like that? When you … became one?"

"Yeah. I did."

"When—how did—?"

"That's a conversation for another time." Hopefully not anytime soon. "In order for you to understand the situation with Sloane, you need to understand that in our society, rogue werewolves are considered an abomination of nature. Separation from pack life makes werewolves unstable, and ultimately, demented and violent. The threat of exposure their existence creates puts all other werewolves in danger." Here goes. "So in our world, the overarching rule of every pack is that all rogue werewolves must be exterminated."

She let out a gasp. The expression of horror that marred her face was every bit as bad as I'd suspected her reaction would be.

"To protect the greater good, of course," I appended.

Her pretty blue eyes shot fiery condemnation at me. "That is the most bigoted, intolerant, tyrannical—"

"You're absolutely right." I held my hand up. "I completely agree."

Not a complete lie. Not a complete truth either. But hers was exactly the reaction I'd been angling for to set up where I was taking this conversation next. And besides, the fastest way to appease any woman was to tell her she was one hundred percent correct, no matter what the argument was. It worked, because Bethany closed her mouth and allowed me to continue.

"So there's this centuries-old prophecy about a powerful *Rogue*-with-a-capital-*R* werewolf coming into existence who will usher forth the birth of a new breed of werewolf species: An aberrant rogue species completely unbeholden to the pack mentality and way of life to which all werewolves presently adhere. That prophesied werewolf—*werelock,* rather—is Sloane."

I didn't get to finger her ass again or eat her out before we landed. We ended up talking for most of the remainder of the flight, until Bethy's eyelids were blinking and drooping so much that I knew I had to stop and allow her to rest.

Her face had been a study in wonder and rapt concentration as I'd attempted to educate her on the werewolf world without completely overwhelming her. *Or revealing information I didn't want to share just yet.*

She'd tried to bring up Miles once, asking again how much my sister knew about my supernatural life, and again, I'd simply put her off—this time intentionally making her think that my estrangement from my sister was a sore topic for me that I couldn't bear to discuss.

In truth, it was a sore subject that I preferred to avoid.

But with Bethany, revealing that her childhood friend Miles was, in fact, a werelock herself, and currently Alpha of one of the oldest, largest, most powerful werewolf packs on the planet—*which also happened to be my Salvatella pack's longtime enemy and rival*—was a slippery road leading to any number of dangerous cliffsides.

CHAPTER 25

Bethany

I'D FALLEN ASLEEP SNUGGLED IN BED WITH RAUL ABOARD his plane. But I awoke in a strange new bed in a very nice but simply decorated room. Light was streaming in through the open shutters decorating the windows, and I could see glimpses of trees and greenery through the wide wooden slats.

I sat up and looked around me. Raul was nowhere in sight, and I felt a pang of disappointment at his absence—disappointment that swiftly morphed into annoyance as a beautiful woman with long ebony hair strolled through the open doorway of the bedroom.

Who the hell kidnapped someone—*professing to have been in agony with want for them for the past decade and vowing to never stay away from them again*—only to repeatedly duck out on them and leave them with strangers? It hadn't even been twenty-four hours since he'd kidnapped me, and already Raul had left me twice!

Damn. Was it normal to feel insulted when your werewolf abductor shirked on his obligation to be connected "for all eternity" to you?

"Morning," the woman greeted me, an inscrutably bright, Cheshire-like grin overtaking her exquisite, make-up-free face. "I'm Avery. Also known as Sloane's mom. How do you take your coffee?"

My jaw fell open a little. I quickly closed it when I realized I probably had morning breath and that she'd be able to smell it from across the room with her canine senses.

This was Avery: Sloane the *Rogue's* mom that Raul spoke of with such great esteem and affection. The way he'd described her to me last night made it clear he viewed her as a close friend and that he also held her in extremely high regard as a mother for her unwavering dedication to Sloane. But he'd neglected to mention she was also drop-dead gorgeous. And intimidating as hell.

She had wide-set eyes and high cheekbones, and her skin was a beautiful shade of russet brown with olive undertones. She appeared to be a perfectly gorgeous mix of multiple races, most immediately recognizable of which was African. She was wearing no-nonsense black shorts and a simple tank top that showcased her lean, athletic build. She looked like she'd probably been up for five hours already and had just returned from an important, dangerous Lara Croft-esque mission. Everything about her screamed Alpha female. Even if she hadn't been a were-wolf, I was positive she could've kicked my ass in seconds flat. Instantly, I regretted skipping out on so many sessions at the gym in recent months.

Her eyes on me were friendly, but their depths guarded like Fort Knox. And one of her finely shaped brows had just arched.

Oh. She'd asked me a question. About coffee.

"Ah-mm … cream and sugar?"

"Are you asking or telling me?" She leaned her hip against the bedpost, her brown doe eyes unblinking. "Because that sounded like a question. You want a reputation for being firm and decisive if anyone's going to take you seriously around here. And as the tired saying goes, you only get one shot at making a first impression." She cupped her hand to the side of her mouth and whisper-shouted, "Particularly when ninety-three percent of the guys here are sexist pigs."

I rubbed my eyes, wondering for a moment if I was still asleep. "I'm sorry, I'm just waking up and I don't—"

"Don't apologize. That's even worse. You're digging a hole now. You're liable to tumble down the well of rationalization next if you aren't careful."

What on earth? "I really don't understa—"

"You're our Alpha's mate. You *need* to be taken seriously around here." She crossed her arms over her chest. "Believe me, woman to woman, I wish I could give you more time with this whole adjustment, but there's simply no time. You feel me, Bethy? I can call you Bethy, can't I." She pointed her finger at me. "See what I did there? I just told you. I didn't ask. Feel the difference? Good. Because I'm calling you Bethy."

Holy baby Jesus, she was intense. I nodded. "I take cream and sugar. Please." I could still say please, couldn't I?

"You got it. There's a bathroom down the hallway. Raul left a little overnight bag with some of your stuff he thought you'd need at the foot of the bed. See you downstairs."

"You can't imagine how stoked I am to finally meet you." Avery's face was animated as she sat across from me at her breakfast table, enjoying a huge plate of eggs and bacon and waffles. She'd told me that her mate had built this house himself. The two of them lived here with Sloane, while Raul resided at the main Salvatella mansion a short distance away.

"Thank you," I said once I'd finished chewing the bite of bagel in my mouth. "It's so nice to meet you, too. Raul told me what good friends you two are. How long have you known each other?"

"Seven months."

"Oh."

"When I first met Raul, I couldn't figure him out, you know?"

I nodded, not really sure what she meant, though.

"I couldn't for the life of me get a clear sexual orientation read on him," she continued, prompting me to nearly choke on the next bite I'd taken. "There were moments when I was certain he was gay, but then it didn't quite fit. Now it makes perfect sense that all this time he was simply mated and resisting his mating bond to you." She brought a forkful of eggs and waffle to her mouth.

I tried to tamp down the absurd happiness that bloomed in my chest at Avery thinking Raul was gay. I cleared my throat. "Yeah ... Raul said something similar to me about that. If you don't mind me asking, what does that mean—he resisted his mating bond to me?"

When she'd finished chewing, she said, "It means he was dumb enough to try and do the impossible—go against the mating bond pull and say F you to the hand of fate, spirit ancestor bullshit, and all that jazz. Ballsy move.

But ultimately, stupid." She took a sip of coffee. "I'm still in shock he made it ten years. That's gotta be some kind of mating bond avoidance record. That shit's painful."

"How painful?"

"Well, put it this way, I only lasted a few days." Her face screwed up, and she looked at the ceiling. "No, wait a minute ... not even that long, now that I think of it."

Why had Raul resisted his mating bond to me? He'd claimed on the plane that he'd done it for my own good. For my safety. But what did that really mean? What was so bad about me being with him that he had willingly stood by and allowed me to get engaged to Gregg?

As if reading the direction of my thoughts, Avery offered, "Gabe, the last Alpha, would've killed you." She brandished her fork at me. "Straight up. Probably would've tortured and dismembered you a few times first, too. Just for kicks. Maybe done some kind of ritualistic sacrifice and then made a satchel and some moccasins out of your skin. The guy was a psycho creep."

She leaned forward and whispered, "Between you and me, I think insanity runs deep through the Salvatella bloodlines." She patted me on the wrist with her free hand. "I'll make up a cheat sheet for you of all the ones I've got my eye on as nuckin' futs around here."

Wow. *Process the satchel comment later, Bethany.* "So you knew the last Alpha? Gabe?"

"Unfortunately. Only briefly. Even that was far too long for me. He tried to kill me. Twice. Raul saved me the first time. The second time didn't go as well." Her color darkened with what looked like embarrassment. "I totally ate it and croaked the second time."

"Um ... I'm sorry, but—"

"Ah-ah-ah." She clucked her tongue at me. "Lose the 'sorry,' Madam Alpha."

"Got it, but did you just say Gabe was successful in killing you the second time he tried?"

"Yeah. It was partially my fault, though. I should've seen it coming. Gabie baited me. Wasn't one of my better moments."

Did I want to ask? I settled on nodding and eating my bagel. I'd ask Raul later. "Raul told me you weren't born a werewolf—*erm*—werelock. You are a werelock, right? I can't really tell the difference yet. Is that racist?" I wanted to face-palm. "I mean in the werewolf world sense?"

Her brown eyes glittered with amusement. "Extremely. Yes, I'm a werelock. And no, wasn't born one. I was bitten by a rogue and changed ten years ago."

I nodded and reached for my coffee. Raul had told me as much. He'd told me Avery had also been raped and impregnated by the same rogue werewolf who'd bitten her—Sloane's biological father.

"So, look, I'm going to level with you, Bethy. Your getting claimed by Raul as his mate right now is really bad timing for us as a pack."

My brows went up along with my back. "Well, that's something we all have in common then, because it wasn't on my agenda for the week, either."

"Ooh, I caught a glimmer of fierceness coming from you that time," she commended me with a snicker. "More of that and less apology, 'kay?"

Rolling my eyes, I found myself chuckling along with her. Raul was right. So far I did like Avery. "Care to elaborate on the bad timing?"

"What I mean is you're in a werewolf baptism-by-fire situation here, whether you like it or not." She pushed her plate aside and propped her elbows on the table. "Here's the deal: Gabe was an evil prick, and everyone in this pack is obviously better off without him. But they're still healing from years of his abusive reign. And before that, his brother's abuse. And before that ... well, basically every Salvatella Alpha has been an asshole as I understand it."

She steepled her hands beneath her chin and interlaced her fingers. "As a pack, we're still somewhat divided and volatile. It's crucial right now that Raul remains in power and establishes some measure of stability." Her expression changed suddenly, and she appeared distracted, like she'd gone into her own head. Then, just as abruptly, her expression changed back and she concluded, "So you can't fuck this up for him, okay?"

I was in too much shock at first to respond. Laughing in her face and throwing the c-word at her would've been somewhat gratifying, albeit childish, but I knew it would gain me nothing as far as allies and information.

"Just so we're clear, I didn't ask for this," I set her straight. "And I'm not planning on staying here long enough to fuck up anything for Raul or your pack. I want nothing to do with this. I have a life in San Francisco. I'm finishing my residency, and I have plans in place to start my own practice next year. Do you have any idea how hard I've worked to—"

"I know, I know. Believe me, Bethy, I empathize with you more than you realize. I'm on your side." Her tone was gentle, but firm. "I've been in your shoes. Ten years ago, I was thirty-two years old, engaged to be married, and ready to start a family. I'd finished my Ph.D. in molecular biology at M.I.T., and I was working a job I loved in genetic research. You think I planned on a rogue werewolf crashing my camping weekend, killing my fiancé and my friends, and forever altering the course of my existence as well as my DNA?"

Well, crap, when she framed it that way, she made my night of hot club sex followed by werewolf biting and kidnapping sound like a sexy holiday compared to her own werewolf baptism by fire.

Sometimes perspective was a bitch.

"Life throws us curves, and we've got to be like water and adapt. Like Darwin said, it's not the strongest of the species that survives, or the most intelligent. It's the one that is most adaptable to change. Fighting against the inevitable isn't going to help you with this, and it isn't going to help our pack. You and Raul are mated. Done deal. No backsies or exchanges."

She let me mull on that while she took a sip of coffee. "By the way, Raul just communicated with me a moment ago through our mind link. He'll be here in five."

That explained her distraction before. "Thanks." I was enjoying my time with Avery, but I couldn't deny the excitement I felt knowing Raul was on his way. As crazy as it was, already it felt like it'd been too long since I'd seen him. "So, is that weird? Communicating telepathically?"

"At first. But you get used to it. At least I did. My mate, Alcaeus, isn't a fan. I don't think they practiced that method of communication as much within his former pack. Mike says it's a generational thing—that the younger werelocks are more comfortable embracing it. My mate's old school." She rolled one shoulder, and the goofiest, dreamiest smile broke across her face for just a moment. It was so sweet I felt myself grinning with her.

"To me," she continued, "mind-tapping is a tool like anything else. Helpful at times, other times annoying as fuck. Oh, and the other thing they do a bit differently in this pack is tap emotions—which, normally, is something that I think only occurs between mates." Her brow creased. "Not positive. I'm not exactly the resident expert on 'normal' werelock behavior. In any case, Alcaeus and I have never gotten into the emotional swinging that goes on between our Salvatella pack mates. Frankly," she said, leaning in and whispering conspiratorially, "I wouldn't advise it, given the mostly crazy werewolf pool we're swimming in here."

I nodded absently. Sounded like a whole lotta rampant codependency to me. I decided to change the subject before I started freaking out.

"So, I'm really looking forward to meeting your daughter. Sloane sounds amazing."

Avery beamed with pride. "Thank you. She is amazing."

"It's so sweet how she and Raul have formed such a special, unique connection. Will I get to meet her today?"

She set her coffee mug down. "So, about that. You should know, Sloane's not always very embracing of new people in her life."

"Oh, I understand," I reassured her. "Raul told me."

"Her verbal communication skills have improved by leaps and bounds since Raul has come into her life, but she still struggles with self-expression and often resorts to tantrums and other forms of ... *demonstration* when she has difficulty processing her emotions."

"Really and truly, Avery, you don't have to worry. I would *never* judge your daughter or hold her to some arbitrary standard for proper child behavior and expression."

She started laughing. "Oh, you're so sweet. That's not what I'm worried about." She shook her head. "How to say this? I'm actually relieved that Raul claimed you as his mate now rather than holding out any longer. Because even though Sloane might be upset initially by your arrival on the scene, she's right at that tender age where ... well, you know?" She gestured vaguely with her hand. "If it went on any longer, it'd only become potentially more awkward and difficult for her to understand."

"Not sure I'm following."

"What's your age difference with Raul again?"

"Roughly eight years. Why?"

She nodded. "Perfect. That's what I remembered him telling me. And Raul's estranged father brought him back to Brazil to live with him when Raul was how old?"

"He was a senior in high school. Probably eighteen or close to it?"

"So you were around Sloane's age at that time." She tilted her head at me. "And then you saw him briefly every few years during your teenage years whenever he'd come home to visit? Tell me, what'd you think of Raul back then? What was your predominant lasting impression of him from the age of ten onward?"

I blushed.

She leveled her pointer finger at me. "You follow me?"

"Oh, my. I don't think Raul has any idea Sloane has a crush on him."

"Of course not. He's a guy. Chaos is in complete denial too."

"Chaos?"

"Alcaeus, my mate. He prefers the nickname Chaos."

Huh. "Okay." I nodded, making a mental note.

"It's easier to say and remember, don't you think? Anyway, I hope you won't take it personally if Sloane has a less than positive initial reaction to you."

"No, of course not. I understand."

"So what's on the agenda for today?"

"Well, I know Raul's taking me to see the pack's head werelock doctor. I'm not sure what else he has planned after that."

She scrunched her nose up. "That'd be Rafe. Really hot Afro-Argentine werelock with an enormous chip on his shoulder and a transforming scar running the length of his face through his right eye. Try not to stare at it. It's really hard, I know, 'cause it's kinda mesmerizing in a disturbing way."

"Transforming?"

"Changing. Mutating. It's a curse. It transforms with his mood. The happier Rafe is, the more grotesque his scar becomes. If he laughs, he loses vision in his right eye entirely."

"That's horrible."

"Yeah, so try not to take it personally when he's a dick to you. He's a dick to everyone."

I nodded. "That poor man."

"No, no, don't fall into the trap of feeling sorry for him, either. Because he really is a dick, scar or not. But hey, he can scent a kidney stone inside a person from a town away."

Yuck. "As part of the curse?"

"No, as part of him being a medical genius."

"Oh." Right. "I'm sure that comes in handy." For something.

CHAPTER 26

Bethany

Raul showed up at Avery's front door a few minutes later, giving me butterflies with the way he eyeballed every inch of me in the short, strappy sundress I was wearing—the one he'd chosen from my clothes and had left for me at Avery's.

I asked Avery if I could borrow a sweater or a jacket as Raul and I were heading out the door, but they both dismissed the need for one, claiming it was warm outside.

"I always thought Bariloche was where people came to ski," I commented to Raul as we began to make our way, hand in hand, from Avery's house on the outskirts of the compound to the main Salvatella mansion. "Pretty sure the forecast called for colder weather in San Francisco today than you have here."

Not only was it green and lush everywhere I looked, the sky was a perfect shade of blue, the sun bright, and the temperature a breezy seventy-six degrees. Vibrant lupines and other colorful wildflowers covered the earth like a rolling patchwork quilt.

"February is a summer month here. July and August are for skiing. Gorgeous, right?"

"Um, duh! Utterly breathtaking times ten. It doesn't even seem real to me. Between the Andes Mountains and the stunning crystal-clear blue lake, it looks like a fairy tale. Or a movie set backdrop. What's the name of that enormous lake?"

"Nahuel Huapi."

I made a face. "Like the moonshine drink guy? The one who got his head—"

"Yep. He was named after that lake."

"Nice. You just ruined a perfectly beautiful lake for me. Thanks for that."

He laughed. "Did you want me to lie and invent a fake name for it?"

"Eh, maybe," I said with a playful toss of my hair, re-verting to the role of airhead captive I'd adopted on the plane. "Sometimes truth-bending is arguably the more considerate, humane approach."

We'd walked a few more paces when he stopped, pull-ing me to a halt with him. His eyes were serious, despite the smile on his lips, as he took both my hands in his. "You're joking, I know, but don't you think that sometimes, in certain situations, it *can* be the humane approach? Like Plato's concept of a 'noble lie' for the greater good and all that?"

Was this a trick question? "I thought they discovered that was just a really bad translation of *The Republic*. Didn't they?"

He nodded slowly and we resumed walking.

"Well, since the lake's ruined for you, I guess it won't hurt to tell you that there's also a legend about a giant crea-ture known as Nahuelito who lives in that lake."

"That in no way qualifies as a noble lie, Raul."

He laughed. "Nah, I'm serious. He's our Loch Ness. Ask anyone in my pack about it; they'll tell you."

I gave him a sidelong glance. "You know I'm gonna Google this as soon as I have my freedom and Internet privileges back, right?"

My words had been spoken in teasing, but I immediately wanted to take them back. Because the moment between us was so fun, so carefree, I realized how much I didn't want the fact that I was essentially his hostage to shatter the spell.

Annnd I was ten shades of fucked up in the head for thinking that.

One side of Raul's mouth kicked up. "I'd expect nothing less. I'm not jerking your chain on this, Bethy. It's true. You'll see."

"So is that how you get by surfing here? A Loch Ness monster at the bottom of the lake creates waves for you? How does that lake-surfing compare to Stinson Beach in San Fran or Steamer Lane in Santa Cruz, huh?"

"Yeah, not exactly. Actually, I tend to teleport over to Playa Mariano to surf. If I want to stay close, that is. Sometimes I go to Lima. Or, you know, I might go all the way to Oahu or even Gold Coast or Jeffreys Bay." His face still lit up whenever he talked about surfing, reminding me of the Raul he'd been growing up. "Teleporting does have its perks. Sometimes ... I even go back to Santa Cruz to surf."

"Really? How often have you been back to NoCal to surf?" I pulled my hand from his as I stopped and squatted down on my haunches to inspect a beautiful blue flower. "Oh, wow, is this a wild orchid?"

How often had he gone back to check on me, I really wanted to ask.

"It is. There are wild orchids all over around here." He squatted down next to me, and the simple brush of his bare knee against mine caused my breath to come faster, my belly to tighten and tingle. "This mean you'll stay? I think I can arrange for you to have orchids and Internet access twenty-four-seven."

"But not my freedom?" I'd done it again. My cheeks burned as I met his eyes, and I couldn't understand why. "I—I'm sorr—" I cringed as I realized I'd been half a breath away from apologizing, when I had no reason to be sorry. Something was clearly wrong with me.

Raul's expression mirrored my thoughts. "Why the hell are you apologizing to me?"

Fuck if I knew. "I don't know. Because I like you—I enjoy spending time with you. This is all so weird and fucked up, Raul, and yet I wish so badly that it wasn't. I mean … this is madness what we're doing right now."

His smile was an arrow straight to my heart. "Isn't that the way it's supposed to go? When love is not madness, it is not love."

It took effort to swallow as our eyes held and I tried to act casual. "Who said that? Shakespeare? Johnny Depp?"

Are you saying you love me?

I supposed that in a way he'd already implied as much. Several times. And yet he hadn't made it clear: Was it the mating bond that he'd avoided for a decade driving his desire for me now, or was it genuine desire for me?

Was this love?

"No. Pedro Calderón de la Barca said it."

Fancy. "Never knew you were into Spanish Baroque literature. Did you study world literature in college? I'm guessing you didn't actually go to school for special education, did you?"

"Nah." He ran a hand through his hair and reached out to pluck a long blade of grass. "I've just always read a lot. I never made it to college." He sounded sad—maybe a little embarrassed—to admit it.

I was sure I'd heard Milena and her mom talking about Raul being offered scholarships to a number of colleges back in the day. He'd played and lettered in virtually every sport in high school. Often when I'd hung out over at Milena's house as a kid, he'd be rushing in and out, always headed to some game or practice. I remembered Milena saying that he'd gotten great grades in school, too—complaining that he'd set the bar high for her with his former teachers.

"Didn't you have scholarships? I seem to remember—"

"Yeah. I did." He dropped the blade of grass he'd been twisting between his fingers and stood—apparently set on dropping the subject, too. "To answer your earlier question, Bethy, I haven't been back to NoCal as much as I'd have liked in the past decade." I knew he wasn't talking about surfing anymore.

"Did you really have to stay away?" I squinted against the morning sun as I looked up at him. How desperate had he been to see me? Was resisting the mating bond as painful as Avery said? *Would Gabe really have made a handbag out of me?*

"I did." He frowned down at me. "Why do you ask?"

Why did I ask? "No reason." I stood as well, simultaneously attempting to mask and quell my pointless sense of disappointment.

What answer did I want from him, anyway?

I didn't know. I only knew something was missing. *Something he wasn't sharing with me.*

He cupped the side of my face in his hand before I could turn away. "Sometimes I wondered if you felt some small part of the mating bond pull, too. If it hurt you at all the way it did me."

Was he asking if I'd thought about him in the decade since he'd shown up at my parents' house trying to whisk me away to a surprise party in Argentina for Milena? *Most definitely I had.* Had those thoughts often sparked fantasies and masturbation sessions? *Affirmative.* Had I felt a gnawing ache in my gut and ongoing pain in my chest for more than a decade that I'd simply dismissed as stress when ulcer tests repeatedly came up negative? *Fo' sho.*

But I chose not to share any of those things with him. Because he hadn't outright asked. And I could hold cards to my chest, too, on occasion.

He'd confessed to me last night that the day he'd shown up at my parents' house had been the moment his wolf had first recognized me as his true mate. Yet he was still looking at me now the same way he had then—his soulful brown eyes projecting so much internal conflict. *Beckoning me closer while begging me to keep away.* And I knew in my heart that I was missing something.

"Is there something you wanted to tell me?" I asked.

My heart fluttered in my throat when his lips parted and his gaze dropped to my neck. Slowly, his hand trailed down my face, following the path of his eyes, his fingertips lingering over my new scar.

I knew the moment he closed himself off to me, even before he shook his head and his fingers dropped from my throat to clasp my hand once more.

We began to pass werewolves, both in human and giant wolf form, as we drew nearer to the main estate. They displayed deference to Raul, while feigning courtesy to me. The closer we got, the more there were—including a lineup of big, hulking guard werewolves who looked like they could each easily fit half my torso in their mammoth jaws.

I tried to bear in mind Avery's advice, but I couldn't help but feel a little freaked out about the reality of my situation. Raul held my hand tighter, pulling me in to his side a little closer. But the only pointer he gave me was a whispered, "Meet their eyes. Don't be afraid."

I whispered back out of the side of my mouth, "Can't they smell it on me anyway? Tiago said—"

Raul shushed me and gave my hand a squeeze, and we didn't speak the rest of the way. I was so out of sorts I felt like I might puke by the time we entered a pretty building adjacent to the main estate.

There was a supermodel sitting behind a reception desk. Raul barely nodded at her in greeting, and I had to restrain myself from asking if he'd slept with her as he pulled me down a sterile white hallway. We must've passed seven or eight identical doors with no discernible room numbers or markings on them before Raul stopped in front of one and opened it for me.

The spacious examination room we entered was sterile white, well lit, and sparsely furnished, as one might expect to find in a modern medical facility. But despite its classic utilitarian features, something felt off—and strangely sinister—about the whole space.

And then I saw him—standing in profile, hunched over the scope of an odd-looking piece of machinery in the corner of the room. He wasn't dressed like a doctor. He was dressed like a civilian in jeans and an Iron Maiden concert T-shirt. He was tall, dark, bald, and built. Already I could see why Avery had described him as "really hot" simply based on the way his ass filled out his jeans.

"Rafe, I'd like for you to meet Bethany Garrett. Bethy, this is Rafe, our head—"

"Congratulations," Rafe responded without turning to look at us. "You're mated."

Raul's knuckles cracked at his side, and I heard his exhale. His voice remained calm, though, as he said, "Rafe, you didn't even look at her bites—"

"Don't need to. I smelled you on her from fifty yards away. You're mated. And she's changing in four days."

"Six days," Raul corrected him.

"Four," Rafe insisted. Slowly, he straightened to his full height and turned to face us. And even though I was prepared for the scar, I wasn't prepared for the impact of seeing something so alarmingly grotesque bisecting such an otherwise gorgeous face.

"You mean she'll *start* the initial transformation in four days," Raul proceeded to press. "But she'll be done in—"

"*Four.* She'll be fully shifted in four days. A full-fledged bitch."

Um … bitch?

"That's too soon," Raul argued. "I bit her Friday night."

"You bit her ten times."

"So? That makes a difference in the shifting timeline?"

Rafe shrugged. "Never seen anyone infected that

many times before. But apparently, yes, it does. Because she smells four days away from turning bitch."

"You know what?" I broke in. "Let's drop the bitch label if you don't mind."

"But I didn't infect her every time I bit her," Raul argued with Rafe.

"No? Could've fooled me."

"Just fucking humor me and take a blood sample to see where her cells are in the transformation process."

"Not necessary. It's four days."

"What if you're wrong?"

"Then you have an extra day or two to figure out how to get inside her head and control her shift. If I'm right, and you still don't have this mind block shit sorted out in two days when she starts shifting, then your mate's dead, and so are you."

Talk about a horrendous bedside manner. I blinked at him in disbelief—while trying not to look at the hideous scar running down the midline of his amber-colored eye. "Beg your pardon?" I attempted to insert myself into the conversation again. "Could you repeat that part about the mind block—?"

"It's nothing for you to worry about." Raul squeezed my hand. "I've got this."

"No, nothing for you to worry about, sweetheart," Rafe mocked. "Not until your body starts blowing up from the inside at least."

"Would you shut the hell up? That is not going to happen, and you know it."

"If you die, I'm putting in a bid for Alpha," Rafe announced callously. "So do not disappoint me in this, kid."

My mouth gaped open. "This is the best doctor in the world? The amazing werelock physician that you brought me all this way to see?"

"Aw, did you say that about me, Raul?" Rafe smiled, and the scar running down his face widened—the skin breaking open before my eyes.

Ugh! Jesus, that was freaky.

"That's really fucking touching. If I had feelings or any sense of pride left, I daresay I'd be flattered in this moment. But …" He waved an errant hand. "Let's get on with this, shall we?" Rafe's predatory gaze swung in my direction, and I realized it was the first time the crazy doctor had looked at me other than in his periphery. "I'll need you to take everything off but that soaked-through thong you're wearing and bend over the examination table for me."

No further words—of a pseudo-medical nature or otherwise—were exchanged after that as Raul transformed into a giant black and white wolf and lunged for Rafe's throat.

I didn't get to see more than the initial attack, though, because Raul poofed me back to the waiting room area, and I found myself standing next to the supermodel receptionist's desk as crashing and growling ensued inside the examination room.

Smiling, I extended my hand and introduced myself.

And then I held out all of fifteen seconds before asking Yamila Diaz's doppelganger if she'd ever slept with my mate.

CHAPTER 27

Raul

THE MEETING WITH RAFE HAD BEEN A COMPLETE disaster. I needed to talk to Alcaeus about Bethy's emotional block, and Mike was blowing my head up wanting to discuss some development related to the seer.

I decided to drop Bethany off with Wyatt, who'd returned from Puerto Iguazú yesterday, while I handled business with Alcaeus and Mike.

Wyatt was the quintessential "good guy" type. Born with a golden spoon and having only recently been turned, Wyatt was the most civilized werewolf within my entire pack—which was exactly what Bethy needed after her experience with Rafe and following the frightened reactions I'd sensed from her upon seeing the guards surrounding the mansion on our walk over.

But I quickly remembered that Wyatt's upbringing and ingrained sense of decorum also backfired on me sometimes, when after his initial introduction to Bethany, he told her right in front of me, "I'd like to state for the record that I in no way support or condone your present abduction predicament. On behalf of our pack, please allow me to offer my sincerest apologies for any undue stress and in-convenience this has put on you."

"Oh, my gosh, *thank you*." Bethany's eyes warmed on him as she made an "aw" expression, her fingers flying to her lips. "You're the first person in this pack to even ac-knowledge that I've been kidnapped." Her eyes slanted at me. "Others have tried to dismiss it as a 'rescue mission.' Even a vacation."

"*What the fuck, man?*" I snapped inside Wyatt's head, fighting not to roll my eyes in front of Bethy. It was a good reminder that I needed to put a more thorough gag order on Wyatt later to doubly prevent him from meandering into forbidden talking points with Bethany.

I pulled Bethy in for a quick embrace, telling her I'd be back as soon as possible. She purposely turned her cheek to me when I went in to give her a peck on the lips.

She'd become standoffish following our visit with Rafe after I'd told her that I had some business to take care of that would require leaving her with my friend Wyatt for about half an hour. She'd responded with a surly, "You know what? I have business to take care of right now, too—*in San Francisco at my hospital job.*"

Dismissing the ache I felt in my chest at her distress, and ignoring my wolf's demands to stay and comfort her, I told myself I would make it up to Bethy later as I forced myself to turn away, rushing off in search of Alcaeus.

To my annoyance, I got waylaid by nine of my Betas, one after the other. Meanwhile, Mike kept tapping my head, insisting I meet him down in the catacombs beneath the mansion—the underground Salvatella vaults and maze of tunnels that stretched the length of the property and beyond. It was where our pack's dead bodies were buried, both literally and figuratively. But predominantly, it served as Mike's team's surveillance lair.

I knew Mike wasn't happy that I'd decided last night after my confrontation with Kai to press forward and escalate things by threatening the seer's life in exchange for Bethany's emotional shield being lifted. But it couldn't be helped. If Rafe was right and I only had two days before Bethany started shifting, I couldn't afford to waste any time.

As I caught up with Mike in one of the eerie underground corridors, I decided to head him off by getting straight to the point before he attempted to plead some long-winded case to me about the seer.

"Look, Mike, I get it. You have a hard-on for the seer. Don't worry. Clearly Kai does too. He'll get Remy to lift the shield on Bethany for us, and we won't have to carry through on our threat to kill the girl." I clapped him on the shoulder. "It'll all work out. No harm, no foul, right?"

Emotions swirled to life in Mike's eyes, the gold color of his wolf flashing through the grey for an instant, before closing off again. "Right," he said tightly. "Except for a little poisoning that could possibly lead to permanent brain damage and paralysis. Sure." He exhaled. "But that's only part of what I wanted to talk to you about."

Jesus, he was being dramatic. "C'mon, we can repair any damage to her. Rafe said he'd come up with a poison spell that's fully reversible. She'll be fine. And besides, the Reinosos are going to cave in an instant and unblock Bethany; you know it. You're stressing over a non-issue."

He held his hand up. "Raul, we need to talk about the vision I saw in Lauren's dream. The one where you and Kai were fighting in wolf form."

"You mean the one from that time when you *'accidentally'* made out with her?"

Ignoring my razzing, he said, "After your confrontation with Kai on campus, I went back late last night to check on Lauren." His jaw tightened when I gave him a raised brow. "Check on her *mind*," he justified. "To make sure she didn't remember anything from your encounter with her."

Right. "Of course," I played along, rubbing the back of my neck and nodding for him to continue.

"That is," he said in an embittered tone, "once Kai had finished checking on her by railing her like an animal in the library."

"Are you setting me up for an accidental sex story?" I jerked my thumb over my shoulder. "Because I left Bethy with Wyatt twenty minutes ago and—"

"She had the same dream again last night." He shifted on his feet, glancing down the corridor behind me. "And … well, I have a bad feeling about us going this course with the seer and antagonizing Kai."

"Uh-huh …" Riiight. I folded my arms across my chest. "Go on. I'm listening." *Humoring.*

"I know what you're thinking. And yes, maybe my emotions are a bit compromised on this mission where Lauren is concerned." He lowered his volume. "But there were two white wolves in her dream last night." He paused, his eyes on me, awaiting my reaction—as if he'd just dropped some major bomb on me that required settling, when all I could think about was what stupid werewolf and pack-life things Wyatt might be blabbing to Bethy right now that I hadn't wanted her to worry about yet.

I needed to get back to them.

"Wow, that's interesting. Can't wait to hear all about it. Later. I gotta get back to Bethany." I pivoted on my heel and had taken three strides down the darkened hallway when Mike's voice halted me.

"You don't win the fight, Raul."

I looked back over my shoulder at him.

"The one with Kai," he said. As if it needed clarifying. "I saw you go down in her vision. I didn't see you get back up."

"You're grasping, Mike. Kai's never been much of a fighter."

"Not since you've known him, he hasn't. Not for the past few centuries. But he's changed recently. The stress of losing his friendship with Alcaeus was just the start. His behavior with the seer goes against every tenet he's upheld since abandoning the feral arctic beast nature of his early self."

I shook my head, scrubbing a hand over my jaw. "Mike, you told me yourself that her abilities were novice. That she was confused. That there was too much fear in her heart for her to be an effective seer."

"I know."

"You told me that because you were afraid I would order her killed to protect Sloane if Lauren proved to be a valuable seer and a threat."

He rubbed his temple. "I know I did."

At least he wasn't denying it.

I turned and stalked back over to him. "And now you're hoping to convince me she's a valuable seer because you don't want her harmed in our plan to trade her for access to Bethy's mind."

He nodded. "I know it looks that way. And it is in part. But it's more complicated. This isn't simply about my protective instincts for Lauren anymore. It's about you. It's about making a more prudent, strategic move where Kai is concerned."

I bit the insides of my cheeks. Again, I was glad he at least wasn't denying that his motives were compromised where the seer was concerned. But he was doing that thing where he dithered … knowing I wouldn't like what he had to say.

"What are you getting at, Mike?"

"I don't think we should incite Kai's wrath by harming the seer. Whatever his twisted fascination with her is about, it's serious."

"Which is to our advantage where Bethy's mind block is concerned."

"Yes. *Maybe*. Kai has changed recently. I think these visions might mean something. The two white wolves in Lauren's dream—what if they represent two opposing sides of Kai? After Kai's white wolf takes you down, a second white wolf shows up and starts tearing apart the first one. Killing it—*killing Kai*. And the first white wolf doesn't even fight back. What if the vision represents Kai's feral nature completely overtaking him?"

"What if it just means there are two white wolves?" Avery's voice startled us both as she teleported into the corridor. "And that I'm about to become BFFs with whoever this second white wolf is?"

Jesus, that girl was getting good at teleporting without a trace. I was torn between being impressed and pissed at her.

"What?" she balked when both Mike and I glared at her.

"Not cool, Avery," Mike said.

"Hey, you're the guy who is supposed to have eyes everywhere, Mike. I'm just keeping you on your toes."

"How very thoughtful."

"I know Chaos told me all this before, but remind me again. What's the big deal with the white werewolf legend? How do we know for sure that Kai is the only white werewolf left in existence?"

"No one has encountered a white werewolf other than Kai in over four centuries," Mike told her. "I think it's safe to say Kai's the only one left."

"There's an old Norse legend about a werewolf bringing about the end of the world," I supplied. "You know—typical prophecy paranoia-sparking-type bullshit. Nordic werewolves were persecuted to the point of extinction as a result—particularly the white arctic werewolf."

"White werewolves had all been brutally annihilated across the globe by the beginning of the seventeenth century," Mike filled in. "All except for Kai, that is."

"Yay for us," Avery muttered.

"Look, obviously, Lauren's vision wasn't crystal clear," Mike conceded to me. "She was viewing the wolves from a distance. There were a lot of fragmented pieces to the dream, and then Lauren's own emotions became involved when the first white wolf went down. But she seemed to identify both white wolves as being parts of Kai: *his past and present.* I think the second white wolf represented his past come back to haunt him—Kai's original, true feral nature before Alcaeus's father rehabilitated him. And I'm sorry, but there was no mistaking your wolf going down."

I knew and trusted Mike well enough to believe he was telling me the honest truth about the vision as he saw it. That didn't mean his judgment hadn't been clouded by his own fear for me, though, or by his feelings for the seer.

But when all was said and done, I had enough history with Mike to know he would always have my back. What's more, Mike was a brilliant strategist and a born leader.

"What are you proposing as an alternative?" I asked.

"I say we start by fighting fire with fire. We get inside Lauren's head and fix it so that she recovers all of the memories that Kai has suppressed. We let her recall every single creepy stalker mind-raping episode Kai ever pulled with her. Then we block Kai out—erect a mind shield he can't penetrate."

It wasn't unreasonable.

"I vote hell yes." Avery raised her hand. "Lauren getting poisoned just hurts Lauren. Lauren realizing that Kai's a perv creeper who's been playing God inside her head—*now that* hurts Kai more where it counts."

"Okay," I agreed. "But what sort of mind shield do you think you can create that Kai won't be able to penetrate?"

Mike smirked. "So glad you asked. Why an emotional shield, of course. While Kai's been busy playing sadistic sex games with the seer, I've been busy actually getting to *know her.*"

"And you don't sound the least bit bitter about being friend-zoned, either," Avery deadpanned.

Trust Avery to say out loud what she and I were both thinking.

"All right," I said. "I'm in. But we have to move quickly. It needs to be done by tonight. Rafe says Bethany is going to start shifting in just two days."

"Perfect," Mike said. "Because I already took care of it last night."

He gave me a cheeky grin and teleported out before I could throw a blast at him, the motherfucker.

CHAPTER 28

Raul

"**S**O, YOU TAKE ME TO YOUR ESTEEMED PACK DOCTOR," Bethany proceeded to grumble at me, "who, by the way, is a complete asshat. Without conducting a single viable medical test, he determines—*by sniffing me*—that I'm going to start blowing apart from the inside in two days' time unless you can figure out some 'mind block shit.' *Then,* with no further discussion about my impending blow-apart-and-die-shifting prognosis, you drop me off with Wyatt: a perfectly lovely gentleman whom I very much enjoyed speaking with. However … *surprise!* Wyatt wasn't allowed to tell me anything about the shifting process either. Go figure.

"But you know what Wyatt did tell me that was interesting? He told me he has a 'true mate' who is part of a rival Brazilian werewolf pack."

Christ. Fucking Wyatt!

"Wyatt told me he basically just decided he didn't want to be with his mate because she's an untrustworthy, conniving, murderous bitch. And so … *he's not. With her.* End of story. Imagine that? He didn't even have to take her head off or anything to accomplish it."

When I'd gone back to retrieve Bethany from the drawing room I'd left her in with Wyatt, her scent had indicated she was more distressed than ever. And she'd looked utterly despondent. But the moment she'd spied me walking toward her, she'd simply looked *pissed.*

Clearly, she was. Because she'd started venting to me immediately, and she'd refused to be put off when I'd tried to tell her we would talk about things later.

I hadn't wanted to risk an altercation with Bethany where we'd be overheard by too many members of my pack, so I was speed-walking us as discreetly as possible the long way through the outdoor gardens, heading to a spot where Avery had agreed she and Sloane would meet up with us.

"Apparently, they've just been living out their separate lives with minimal ill effects for seven months now. Care to explain to me how that works? Because it kinda contradicts everything that you, Avery, and Tiago have told me about true mates."

"Honey, Wyatt's situation is unique—"

"Oh, unique like our situation is unique in that you were able to go *ten long years* resisting a mating bond pull to me? Must've been hard for you, I bet, with all the supermodel werewolves crawling all over this place. And by hard, yeah, that's a double-entendre ref to your dick."

Wait a minute. I pulled her to a stop. Wrapping an arm around her waist, I teleported us to a private alcove in the garden closer to where we'd be meeting up with Avery.

"Are you jealous?"

"You know, a pre-*poof* warning, or maybe a poofing safeword, would be nice, Raul."

"Answer my question, please." I tilted her chin up in an effort to get her to look me in the eye. She refused, looking everywhere but my eyes. I couldn't believe this. "Are you seriously feeling insecure about the fact that I waited so long to claim you? Is that what this is about?"

Yanking my fingers from her face, she took a step back, her blue eyes meeting my steady gaze.

"It's not exactly flattering, Raul, to know that you were able to resist for a damn decade something that other werewolves can't withstand for mere days. Hours even. Except for Wyatt, that is. And in *his* case, his 'true mate' was plotting to kill Avery and Sloane—even though she knew that Avery was one of Wyatt's closest lifelong friends. Can you fucking believe that? So yeah … apparently it's me and some murderous cuntbag who are holding down the exclusive minority title for the most ardently dodged werewolf mates ever."

"Dodge you?" I didn't know whether to kiss her or shake her. "Have you lost your mind?"

She paused a moment, as if considering it. "*Yes,* actually. I think I have. And no thanks to you." She pursed her lips and made a study of the ground between our feet. "I just … don't know why I'm here. You brought me here against my will. You said it was because you couldn't bear to be without me a moment longer. But all you've done since is leave me with strangers." Her narrowed eyes lifted. "And you're so closed off to me. There are important things you aren't telling me right now that I know *involve* me. Do you have any idea how fucked up that is? I'm a grown woman, Raul. It's not right. It's not normal to keep people you supposedly care about in the dark while making critical life decisions for them—like how to prevent them from blowing apart in the next forty-eight hours."

"Raul!" I heard Sloane call out to me.

I turned to find Avery and Sloane swiftly approaching us. Sloane's timid smile turned to stone as her gaze swept over Bethany, while Avery grinned and waved at us in greeting.

Bethany gasped. "Oh, my gosh, she's beautiful, Raul."

She stepped from the alcove and rushed right up to Sloane. Every muscle in my body jerked forward in reaction, and I had to hold myself back from stopping her.

Bending at the waist, she crouched down to Sloane's eye level. "Wow," she gushed. "Your eyes! I've never seen eyes that color before." Bethy turned to me, then looked at Avery, her own eyes wide with awe and excitement. "Avery, your daughter is positively breathtaking. What a little stunner she is."

"Sloane, this is Bethany," I introduced, unable to stop myself from stepping forward and hovering in between the two of them. "Bethany, this is my friend Sloane—the amazingly talented young lady I was telling you about."

"Hi, Sloane." Bethany beamed at her. "It's so good to meet you." She offered Sloane her hand.

Sloane didn't take it. Her expression had gone blank *(on the surface)* as she stared back at my innocent, unsuspecting mate. Beneath the surface, a mutiny was brewing. I could sense it. Her tone was flat as she looked up at me and asked matter-of-factly, "Where'd you find her? Can you send her back there now?"

I faked a chuckle, my eyes seeking Avery for assistance. Avery forced a laugh in return, looking distracted. This reassured me somewhat because it was a good bet she was telepathically calling in for backup: Alcaeus.

"Bethany is visiting from California," I told Sloane. "She and I grew up in the same town together."

"We knew each other when we were kids," Bethany inserted with a warm smile at Sloane, withdrawing her outstretched hand. "Isn't that cool? I knew Raul when I was your age."

Sloane's amethyst eyes flared, spearing me with a look of betrayal. "You played *Frozen* with her?" Her little chin wobbled.

Ah, shit.

"*No*," I rushed to assure her. "Never. Bethy and I *never* played Frozen together. I promise."

"*Bethy?*" Sloane repeated on a breath, her dismayed eyes beginning to glow.

"Omigosh, *Frozen*—of course!" Bethany exclaimed. "I knew I recognized your beautiful blue gown from somewhere. I love that movie. And Queen Elsa is my absolute favorite. You make a wonderful Queen Elsa, Sloa—"

"It's *Princess* Elsa," Sloane corrected her, her expression cold.

"Ah ... okay. But by the end of the movie she's a queen, right?" Bethany looked to me and Avery for confirmation.

Avery gave her a smile. "Yeah, we're going with the princess designation lately. We think it's cooler and fits Sloane better."

"Elsa becomes queen after her parents die in the film," Alcaeus's booming bass carried through the garden courtyard as he entered it. "Sloane still has both of her parents," he pointed out with a goofy grin and a wink in Avery and Sloane's direction, his long strides bringing him to his mate's side. "So we decided *Princess* Elsa fit Sloane better."

Alcaeus had decided that. All on his own. Pretty sure he was afraid the film might give Sloane ideas about killing him at some point.

Bethany straightened and turned from Sloane to face Alcaeus at his approach. The welcoming smile on her lips abruptly faded when she saw him, though, her jaw going slack, her eyes crinkling with confusion and then widening with horror as a bloodcurdling scream climbed up her throat.

Birds shrieked and scattered from the treetops, and every werewolf within a three-mile radius probably cringed.

Too late, Bethy slapped her hand over her mouth.

"Wow, I am so, *so* sorry." She tossed her head from side to side, giggling strangely and a little too hard as she tried to regain her composure amid her embarrassment. "I—I don't know what came over me. It's just that your face"—she flapped her hands at Alcaeus—"it's … oh, crap, that came out so wrong." Her eyes widened in apology at Avery next for using crass language in front of her child.

Avery gave her a stern look and shook her head. But she clearly wasn't upset about Bethany's reaction to Alcaeus or about her language in front of Sloane, because she scolded, "What did I tell you about apologizing, Bethy?"

Meanwhile, Sloane's expression had gone from devastated to quietly delighted as she watched Bethany stumble through managing her mortification.

Bethany's eyes cut to me next, shining with profound apology and confusion. She looked completely rattled. And still terrified. *Of Alcaeus,* of all incomprehensible things.

"You must think I'm crazy," she said to Avery. "What an introduction, right?" she attempted to joke to Alcaeus, who looked at her strangely a moment before recovering and giving her a practiced smile.

"Nah," he dismissed. "I get that reaction all the time."

Avery couldn't contain a snort behind her hand as she elbowed Alcaeus in the ribs.

And I couldn't contain an eye-roll. I'd never understood what Avery saw in that old dork. But she was constantly finding his tired antics adorable. Hilarious even.

"You just remind me of … someone." Bethany fluttered her hand and shook her head, still studying Alcaeus. *Still looking terrified of him.* "Or … not." She tilted her head to the side. "We haven't met before." She squinted one eye. "Have we?"

"Mm." Alcaeus pretended to consider it. "Possibly." Not a lie. He gave her a cheeseball grin and shrugged it off. "People tell me I have one of those faces."

"You mean like a male model?" Bethy proposed. "Yeah, you know what?" She nodded in agreement. "I was just thinking maybe that was it. That you remind me of a male model I've seen in magazines or billboard ads before."

Avery snorted again, and I realized she was snickering at me this time—at my jaw that had just unhinged.

Bethany had to be fucking joking.

"Well, it's true. I do get asked if I model quite a bit, as a matter of fact," Alcaeus said with a self-satisfied grin while tugging sheepishly on the back of his neck—*feigning modesty he had never in his lifetime possessed.*

Of all the ridiculous—

"What's a male model?" Sloane piped up to ask.

"It's a guy who can't get a real job," I told her, "so he dresses up in different outfits all day like a Ken doll and posts an embarrassing amount of selfies online."

"Raul," Bethany chastised with an indignant laugh, punching me in the arm. "Don't tell her that. Sloane, that isn't true at all. It's a perfectly respectable career for a man, the same way it is for a woman."

"Could I be a model when I grow up?"

"No," Alcaeus and I answered in unison.

At least we agreed on that.

"Wow." Bethany shook her head at us both. "Protective much? Limiting much? Sloane can be anything she wants to be when she grows up. And she's definitely gorgeous enough to be a model." She bent at the waist and directed her words at Sloane. "I mean that. You are positively the most beautiful little girl I've ever seen. And I hope we get to spend—"

Kitsune's excited yapping filled the courtyard as he bounded over to Sloane, who turned away from Bethy mid-conversation and knelt to gather the Akita in her slender arms.

"Good boy," Sloane told him, hugging the orange furball close and rubbing her cheek against the top of his head.

"How did ..." Bethany looked at once elated and confused. "That's my—"

"Kitsune," Sloane said. "My new puppy."

I glared at Stephen, who had entered the courtyard a few paces behind the mutt. *"You gave Bethany's dog to Sloane?"* I barked inside his head.

"Sloane will take better care of him," he had the nerve to respond telepathically. *"Hopefully."* He appended. *"It'll be a good test for her."*

Closing my eyes, I raked my fingers back and forth across the top of my scalp, grasping for composure as I scented Bethy's mounting confusion and anxiety. By "test," Stephen meant a test to see if Sloane would kill the puppy. *Bethany's puppy.*

My mate was distressed enough already. She didn't need this on top of everything else.

"Sloane," I said, kneeling at her side and smiling into her violet eyes. "I think there's been a misunderstanding. Kitsune is actually Bethany's puppy. We brought him here for Bethy." She stared blankly at me. "But I'd love to get you your own pet. How about I get you another Akita wolf puppy?"

Her eyes blinked once. Twice. "No. I'm keeping this one."

"For real, Stephen?" Avery admonished. "That's so low rent. Who gives away another person's dog?"

"Bethany only got him a week ago," Stephen argued in his defense. "She hasn't even potty-trained him yet. Or attempted *any* form of training of him," he said under his breath.

"Quit judging her," I snapped, straightening upright. "Bethany works crazy long hours at the hospital."

"That's evident. Her dog ran straight to Sloane just now while ignoring her," Stephen pointed out like it was the final damning evidence of Bethy's failure as a pet owner. "We all saw it."

I was on the verge of flattening him as I sensed Bethany's embarrassment.

"Kitsune is *my* puppy," Sloane announced quietly to no one in particular. "I'm keeping him."

Alcaeus and Avery were the next ones to kneel down to talk to Sloane at eye level. They were trying to explain to her that she couldn't just keep someone else's pet, when Bethy jumped in with a shaky smile and offered sweetly, "You know what? We can *share* ownership of Kitsune while I'm here. How about that, Sloane?"

Sloane never uttered a word in response. But ten seconds later, the hem of Bethy's sundress inexplicably burst into flames.

"What the hell happened back there?" I demanded of Alcaeus.

After we'd put Bethy's dress fire out, Avery had teleported her to my bedroom in the mansion for a change of clothes, and I'd sent Stephen off with Sloane to play with Kitsune in the gardens, affording me space to talk with Alcaeus in private at last.

"Sharing is a difficult concept for an only child to—"

"Not that." *Idiot.* "I'm talking about Bethany's reaction to you."

"Oh, yeah, that was a good sign. Seeing me must've triggered something for Bethany in her subconscious. I'd bet money her mind recalls everything that happened ten years ago the moment her emotional shield comes down."

He gave me a ridiculous grin and whacked me harder than necessary on the back. "Don't worry, I'm sure you didn't do anything that you now regret—you know, during the time in which you helped psychopathic werelocks kidnap your unsuspecting mate and hold her life for ransom."

"Nah." I gave him my best imitation of his own exaggerated, mocking grin in return, whacking him so hard on the back his upper body lurched forward slightly. "Nothing too memorable." I sniffed. "Nothing nearly as bad as what she'll remember of you, anyhow."

"Right?" He laughed. "It's a damn good thing I'm not her mate, isn't it? How long was it that you kidnapped her for again?"

Forty-six hours. I'd had forty-six wonderful, terrifying stolen hours in Argentina and Brazil with Bethany a decade ago.

"She wasn't kidnapped, Alcaeus," I reminded him.

Technically, Bethany had come willingly with me, Gabe, and Nuriel to Argentina. We'd taken her to the Salvatella compound in Puerto Iguazú, and that was where Bethy and I had stayed up all night talking and connecting. At the time, I'd made Gabe think I was doing it to help him figure out Bethany's emotional shield.

That was the night when she'd confided in me about her parents' relationship. And I had confided in her the truth about Miles and me being full-blooded siblings rather than half—as Bethy had always known us to be growing up. I'd told her about Aunt Cely being my aunt and not my real mother, which had prompted Bethy to ask me questions about Mom and how she'd died. And I'd somehow ended up word-vomiting to her like there was no tomorrow, confessing things to Bethy about my mom and my childhood that I had never shared with anyone before. And hadn't since.

But then we'd taken Bethy to the Reinoso compound in São Paulo for the "surprise party" for Miles that she'd been led to believe was the reason for her trip abroad, and everything had quickly gone to hell. She'd discovered in brutal fashion that we were all killer monsters—*and that I was a liar who had set out to kidnap her.*

Alcaeus and I had been on opposite sides back then, and he'd lost his shit and had gone on a massive killing spree that day—right in front of Bethany. In fact, it had taken three of the most powerful werelocks in existence just to stop Alcaeus from killing me.

It seemed entirely plausible that seeing Alcaeus again had triggered dormant, suppressed memories in Bethy of the gruesome dining hall confrontation between the Reinoso and the Salvatella packs that she'd witnessed years ago.

"Oh, that's right," Alcaeus said. "I forgot. You guys *charmed* Bethany into going to Argentina. But you *compelled* her mom in order to get her to go along with it. I do remember that. Because Alex had Remy go back and alter Bethany's parents' memories for the time period that Bethany was away. And you *would've* compelled Bethany if she hadn't had a shield already," he reminded me. "These'll be fun stories to tell your kids and grandkids someday."

I gave Alcaeus a hard look, unwilling to dignify his remark with a reply. Instead, I asked, "How much do you know about the emotional shield Remy placed on Bethy?"

"Well, I know that in order for Remy to have placed such a solid emotional shield, Bethany had to have trusted him. She had to have opened up to him quite a bit and shared things that were very personal to her—stuff she keeps close to the vest." He smiled and added, "Private feelings and memories she doesn't share with just anyone." *Rubbing the salt in my wound.*

"I think I understand the basic concept of an emotional shield," I said flatly. And I didn't appreciate the reminder that my mate had apparently shared more with Remy than she had with me.

Alcaeus continued, "Remy does this emotional mapping thing where he takes the most poignant, private memories and the feelings attached to them, and he weaves them into the mind shield so that they become locks essentially." His face twisted. "Or maybe trigger points. I don't really know the full mechanics involved."

He was no help at all. "But it's usually just one key, central memory that connects it all, right? Locking it together?"

"In theory." He shrugged.

"Theory? We're way past fucking theory at this point, Alcaeus. You wanna try a little harder to help me with this? Bethy could start the transformation the day after tomorrow, according to Rafe."

"That's a day or two too soon."

"Tell me about it. That's what I told him."

"Although, you did bite her a dozen times."

"It was *ten*."

He chuckled. "Guess that leaves you no choice but to do something completely radical—like communicate with your mate and find out what her feelings are on things."

"You think I haven't tried? Could you stop assuming I'm your brother Alex for once and take this seriously? My mate's life is on the line."

"Raul, we can place one phone call to Alex and Milena to fix this."

Not an option. "There's no fucking way they'll willingly lift Bethy's shield."

"Of course not. And they'll demand that you turn Bethany over to them, too. But at least she'll be safe because Remy can allow any one of them access to control her shift. You're making this a life-or-death situation it doesn't need to be simply because your ego can't handle the thought of turning Bethany over to your sister—Bethany's best friend," he emphasized. "When you know Milena would guard Bethany's life with her own.

"Given all the bad shit Bethany's going to remember about you shortly, it might be in your best interest to turn her over to them. At the very least you could feign giving her some semblance of a choice in your mating bond connection that you already took away from her."

What a crock coming from a guy who had waited all of about a minute after meeting his true mate, Avery, to get his dick in her—in a public restroom, no less. For someone with so little self-restraint, he sure didn't give me any credit or sympathy for the pain I'd suffered for my mate situation. "I stayed away for ten years to give Bethy a choice!" I reminded him—and everyone else within earshot in the gardens.

He cast a raised know-it-all brow. "And your wolf bit her for every year he missed out on."

CHAPTER 29

Bethany

I NEEDED ANSWERS. *REAL* ANSWERS FROM SOMEBODY who wouldn't sugarcoat things. Straight answers from someone who wasn't completely loyal to or controlled by Raul.

There was only one werelock I'd met in the Salvatella pack who fit the bill. The downside was he was a giant dickbag.

And the bigger hurdle that remained was how to orchestrate a private conversation with Rafe.

I knew Raul didn't want me seeing the Salvatella pack's head werelock doctor without him present. He'd made that much clear—and frankly, who could blame him after my meeting with Rafe yesterday?

Sneaking over to the medical building to confront Rafe wasn't a realistic possibility. I was free to roam the mansion, but there were guards everywhere, and I was constantly being watched it seemed. I needed a werelock who had a reasonably high-standing position within the pack to help me. Someone who could smuggle me past the many guards and get me into Rafe's building. But who, among the Salvatella werelocks I'd met, held enough authority to help me while being disloyal and unscrupulous enough to take the risk?

I considered my options as I strolled through the creepy gallery of statues in the west wing of the main mansion. Even if I didn't get a single answer out of Rafe, the visit would be worth it if only to take refuge within the sterile white walls of the medical building for a few stolen moments.

While the exterior architecture of the five-story, palatial Salvatella estate was reflective of neo-gothic elegance, the interior was an epic shitshow of avant-garde fails. It was as if Versace and Liberace had taken turns decorating rooms, and then Picasso's lesser-known, *lesser-talented,* bastard stepbrother had followed them vomiting random kitsch throughout. To make matters worse, everywhere I turned it seemed a flash of gilding was blinding me in the eye. They'd seriously gone to town with the gold leafing and gold accents in the place. In the words of my Granny Jean: *Shit was basic.*

Anyone would be anxious and on edge surrounded by such monstrous décor—*before* factoring in the actual monsters the place was inhabited by.

I was staring at an ostentatious marble bust of the last Alpha, Gabriel Salvatella, when Jorge came up from behind and startled me, asking in a flirtatious tone what I was doing all by myself in the gallery. My first instinct was to try and flee. My second was to scream as he came to stand uncomfortably close to me. But when a look of admiration came over Jorge's features as he stared at the statue before us and he commented on what a great leader Alpha Gabe had been, I knew I'd found my man.

Going up on tiptoe to whisper in his ear, I told Jorge I feared I was on the verge of experiencing explosive gastrointestinal distress, and had come to the mostly empty gallery hoping to let out a little pressure where it would offend less werewolves. Keeping in mind what Tiago had told me about werewolves being able to scent lies, I tried to relay it with as much conviction and sprinklings of truth as possible. I mean, I *was* sick to my stomach over the décor in the mansion, not to mention my entire situation. So, not a total lie, right?

Jorge recoiled immediately, and I asked him sweetly if he would mind discreetly escorting me to see Doctor Rafe, saying I was too distressed over my situation to ask Raul, and that I didn't know the guard werewolves well enough to admit to any of them that I felt on the brink of shitting my pants.

Jorge smuggled me through a few shortcuts within the walls—which added a new layer of creepiness to the mansion. I made a mental note that this most likely meant Jorge couldn't teleport. Raul had evaded the question when I'd asked him how many of the werelocks besides him could poof. So far I only knew of Avery and Mike having the ability.

Jorge dropped me like a dirty bomb as soon as we were inside the medical building, claiming he was late for some meeting. The supermodel receptionist was nowhere to be found, so I wandered down the white hallway I'd gone down with Raul before, once again passing multiple identical doors with no discernible room numbers or markings.

As I got farther down the hall, I heard a woman moaning. Followed by a man grunting. *Damn my rotten luck.*

The next door I came to was ajar. And the much-revered quack of a werelock doctor was inside the examination room fucking his own receptionist—*Yamila Diaz's doppelganger*—within an inch of her life.

Wow.

Like, holy shit, wow.

I froze, my eyes locked on the scene in front of me. I couldn't have stood there for more than six seconds. But six seconds was plenty of time to see things I'd never be able to un-see.

And I didn't just mean the size of Rafe's dick.

I meant the way her breath escaped her each time he rammed deep—as if he filled her so completely there wasn't room left for air in her lungs. The way her clawed fingernails dug into the examination table, the way her ass jiggled each time his muscled thighs smacked up against the backs of hers. How big his hands looked encircling her tiny waist. And how much raw emotion—how much profound bliss—her orgasmic face conveyed even when half of it was covered by a blindfold.

And Rafe's wasn't. Partially covered, that is. His face was on full display, his scar in full bloom—so much so that he was almost unrecognizable from the werelock I'd met yesterday.

When his head snapped in my direction, I ran.

I didn't get farther than the next examination room door before I found myself *blown* inside of it onto my ass, the door shutting and a lock magically clicking in place behind me.

The noises got louder from the room on the opposite side of the wall. Rafe's grunt's got angrier. The sound of flesh slapping against flesh came faster. Harder.

She started begging in Spanish.

He started swearing in Spanish—cursing her tight pussy and promising it would be the last time he fucked it.

I felt torn between rolling my eyes and touching myself as I sat on the hard cold floor—a captive interloper.

She wailed as she came.

But then he kept on going. *And going.*

Oh, seriously? How long was I going to be stuck in here? I got up and tested the door. Yep. No dice. It locked from the outside. *Probably the only way Rafe kept any patients.*

Several minutes and successive squealing orgasms later, Rafe finally shouted his own release. Two minutes later, he swung the door open to the room I was in to find me waiting, my arms crossed over my chest and the most fearless expression I could manage on my face.

He was dressed. *Thank God for small favors.* And his scar was back to looking normal-*ish*. He tilted his chin and sniffed the air as he sauntered in. "Shall I get you a change of thong?"

"What?"

"Your underwear. Is soaked through. Again, I might add."

Oh, my God.

I felt my skin betraying me, my face flushing.

His upper lip twitched like it was having an epileptic fit trying to restrain the humor he so desperately wanted to express. "Heard about you being an exhibitionist. Seems you're a voyeur as well."

"I was *not* watching you," I objected. "It's hardly my fault that I walked in on you ... you—"

"Fucking." He smiled, enjoying my discomfort. The scar running down his face split open. "You're here against Raul's orders and without an appointment, so I'd say it's entirely your fault."

I tried not to react. "Look, I came to talk to you as a medical professional. Obviously, I didn't expect to walk in on you. Where I practice medicine, doctors don't copulate with their staff in examination rooms."

"She is my patient first and foremost."

"Great." I rolled disgusted eyes. "Where I practice medicine, doctors *definitely* don't copulate with their patients—in exam rooms or elsewhere."

"Shame." He canted his head. "What if it's the only cure for what ails them?"

"This was clearly a mistake." I stepped forward.

He moved to block my path, entering my personal space. "Not at all. I was hoping you'd be back for a more thorough examination. You know, I regret I didn't get to watch Raul fuck and mark you. I think I would've enjoyed it. Very much."

I slapped him hard across the face.

Annnd now things were really uncomfortable.

And I might've broken some bones in my hand.

I sucked in a desperate breath, telling myself it would be worse if I backed down now, as I shook my poor hand out and scolded, "Your bedside manner is atrocious. It's unacceptable."

Smirking, he reached down and adjusted the bulge

in his pants. "Honesty's not part of your modern-day Hippocratic oath where you practice?"

My eyes sought refuge on the ceiling, wanting to escape his penetrating amber gaze, his transforming scar, and the sizeable erection now pushing out against the fly of his jeans.

This had been a *huge* mistake.

"Let me see your hand."

"Uh—yeah, I don't think so." Now was probably the right time to start screaming for help.

"I'm not asking. Give me your hand."

My eyes snapped from the ceiling to his. "I am not going to give you a handjob, you psycho!"

He tucked his lips between his teeth and brought his fist up to cover his mouth, his shoulders shaking as his scar shifted and widened, the skin breaking apart once more. "Bethany, please," he implored from behind his closed fist, his deep voice thick with suppressed amusement. "You have to stop making me laugh so much. I don't want to traumatize you."

Ha! Could've fooled me. "If you don't step aside and let me leave, I'll—"

"Give me your hand so I can heal it." He dropped his fist from his mouth as he regained his composure. "You have a hairline fracture in your second and third metacarpals." He held his hand out, palm up. "There's still a doctor behind the monster."

I wasn't so sure. But I swallowed the lump of nerves in my throat and gave him my hand.

"I could use my saliva for this, but I'm guessing you'd be more comfortable with an injection."

I huffed. "You guessed right."

"Did you mean what you said before? About wanting to take Raul's place as Alpha?"

"No. I didn't." Rafe's fingers were gentle as they palpated the fine bones in my hand, testing the results of the magical serum he'd injected only moments ago. Already, my hand felt completely healed. "Everyone knows Mike would succeed Raul as Alpha. There. Good as new."

"Mike?"

He nodded, releasing my hand. "And I would back Mike as Alpha. If not for Raul's Joaquin blood inheritance and his strong alliance with the *Rogue*, Mike would be our Alpha now."

"Really? Why not Alcaeus? I thought Alcaeus was second in command."

Rafe barked out a laugh—a great *guffaw* would be more accurate—and the scar that ran through the midline of his right eye tore clean open. As I watched in fascinated horror, wondering what in the heck had been so funny about my Alcaeus remark, the white of his right eye turned blood red, then grey, and the iris turned a milky marbled black. "Fuck. Now see what you've done?" he said, still laughing. "You've gone and blinded me."

"The last Alpha … did he do that to you?"

The brow over his good eye shot up. He ceased chuckling. "For real? You're going to address the elephant in the room? During our second encounter, no less?"

I paused for a beat before committing. "Yeah. I am. Am I the first to ask about it so soon after meeting you?"

"No. Avery asked within seconds of meeting me. I think her exact words were: 'What the fuck is going on with your face?' "

I giggled, then immediately slapped my healed hand over my mouth. "I'm sorry. I don't mean to laugh."

"By all means, do. Someone should get a good laugh about it. Yes. Gabe and his brother Nuriel cast this spell on me."

"Why? Just to be cruel?"

He leaned against the steel laboratory table behind him. "Their younger brother was killed on my watch."

"Gasoline drink—I mean the werelock you named the drink after? Nahuel's Blunder?"

"Same."

"How was his death your fault?"

"It wasn't. But I made the mistake of blaming myself for it, and they scented the guilt on me when I came back delivering burnt pieces of his remains."

Damn. Burnt, too? That had been one pissed off mate.

I knew it was probably terrible to ask it, and yet I did. "Can it ever be reversed? Your curse?"

"They *said* that it could—Gabe and Nuriel, that is. But I don't know if it actually can." A faraway look clouded his eyes, which had returned to their normal amber shade. I didn't have to ask to know he'd spent the past sixty-some odd years trying to figure out how to reverse the curse. "I've come to think that was part of their torture plan all along: to dangle false hope in front of me. Keep me searching. Reaching for something I could never reclaim."

"I can't get over what monsters those Salvatella brothers were."

"Gabe and Nuriel were no worse than their predecessors. Just different. And Nahuel, the youngest brother, wasn't a bad person. Once upon a time, many of us, myself included, harbored high hopes for him."

It was my turn to laugh—without humor. Silly me for forgetting for a hot second that Rafe was anything but a lunatic. "The brother who slaughtered his own mate's parents? You think he was a good person?"

"I didn't say he was a good person, Bethany. I said he wasn't a bad person. There's a distinction. As there are degrees. These mountains are full of monsters far worse than Nahuel. Some worse than even Gabe and Nuriel."

"Don't tell me: There's a rival evil werelock camp on the other side of the lake? Let me know when the annual softball game face-off is."

He smiled, flashing white teeth. This time, when his scar shifted, and the skin broke apart, I barely noticed it. I was beginning to get used to it as part of his normal facial expressions.

"It's the truth."

"What are you talking about? You can't mean Nahuelito the Loch Ness," I told him wryly, "'cause I know that dude lives in the lake."

"No. I'm referring to the thousands of Nazis who established residence here to escape persecution after World War II. Bariloche is known as the Third Reich Capital in Exile for a reason. Many of them continued their legacy here."

A chill ran through me. Because I knew he wasn't joking. I couldn't recall if I'd learned it in school or elsewhere, but I did remember reading about Nazis fleeing Germany for South America. The exact locations they'd fled to in South America just hadn't stayed with me.

I felt a little sick now for having ever thought Bariloche

was a beautiful place. And I was suddenly more homesick than ever for San Francisco.

"Make no mistake, Gabe got some things right," Rafe said. "As did his brother before him. Prior to their reign there was nothing but constant infighting and defection. It was eroding and destroying our pack. Their first order of business was to put a stop to all that."

My thoughts went to Mike and what he had shared with me on the plane. "By killing defectors while their children watched?"

"Yes. For starters. You see, shared pain has a way of bonding individuals in a manner that few things can. The Salvatella pack is unique from others in that we don't just tap each other's minds; we often tap each other's emotions—both past and present. Gabe encouraged this practice. Preached it. Enforced it. And through this twisted dysfunction, he *did* succeed in unifying us as a pack once again. While paralyzing us as individuals. Breaking us as humans, and molding us back together as codependent brothers.

"He did it so that the horror Mike experienced as a boy seeing his mother tortured, raped, and killed could be my torture forever as well. So that it could be Tiago's and Stephen's and Raul's. Never in the same manner that it will always be for Mike, of course, but enough that it sticks. Cementing us through our collective torment and grief."

Disturbing as it was, it made sense from a psychological standpoint. I was all too familiar with the manner in which shared pain and grief could strongly bond individuals. Even when it was unhealthy. *Especially when it was unhealthy.* It was the glue that had sustained my parents' marriage.

"Just like the ongoing pain and humiliation of my facial curse is felt by my pack brothers and sisters," Rafe relayed. "Even if only for fleeting moments from time to time, it's enough. Because we're already pack creatures, Bethany. Co-dependent behavior is written in our werewolf DNA. Gabe merely magnified something we were already cursed with by nature. It was a tool to help him spread fear. A way for him to keep us under his control, constantly trauma-tized and on edge, waiting for the next axe to drop. And believe me, someone was constantly either getting tortured or reliving torture around here."

He smiled—a smile so cynical it wasn't rightfully a smile at all. The fact that his scar didn't alter a hair proved it. "He maintained that it was for healing—to promote a uni-versal consciousness and strong sense of empathy within the pack." A muscle tightened in his jaw. "Gabe only ever had noble intentions."

He straightened, pushing off the laboratory table be-hind him. "And now you understand why Sloane's well-be-ing and safety mean everything to our pack."

Huh? Had I missed a key segue somewhere? "No. I don't follow. How does Sloane fit into all this?"

"Sloane is the prophesied *Rogue* who will beget all rogues. The firstborn of a new and errant breed of werewolf species. Some interpret the prophecy to mean that she will literally give birth to the new breed of werewolf species."

"But you don't think so?"

"No. I think her impact on our world has already be-gun. Her mere presence is already altering us as a species. Look at what happened with you and Raul. It's inconceiv-able that anyone would be able to forgo a mating bond pull for so long."

"You know what? It'd be great if everyone could stop rubbing it in. I get it—I'm easy to resist." *For ten fucking years.*

"It wasn't you, Bethany. It was Sloane's influence. The same thing is happening with Wyatt. He's been separated from his mate for seven months now. That isn't normal."

"What are you saying?"

"When Avery first became a werewolf, she had the same drive we all do to belong to a pack. But once Sloane was born, that drive fell away. This is only the beginning. Sloane hasn't even shifted yet." He raised his chin. "That little girl is our deliverer. Our savior. And she's going to be an early shifter, too. Mark my words."

Wow. "Don't you think you *might* be putting a lot of inappropriate pressure and responsibility on a not-even ten-year-old girl? She's a kid. Not a savior."

He shook his head minutely. "Every day, she brings us closer to claiming our freedom simply by breathing, Bethany. By *existing*. Don't you see? She's already begun giving us a choice in mating. She's ultimately going to give us our free will as a species at long last."

Why did this feel so upsetting to me? This was good news. *Wasn't it?*

If what Rafe said was true, it meant that despite my ten mating bite marks, Raul and I might be able to gain freedom from one another.

Go our separate ways.

Through Sloane breathing.

"Avery said she barely made it a day or so resisting her mating bond to Alcaeus," I pointed out. Why was I so set on arguing this? "And Avery's Sloane's mom. Why didn't she have a choice?"

The brow over Rafe's good eye shot up. "Have you seen those two fools together?"

I sighed. Yeah, I had. Avery and Alcaeus were hopelessly in love. It was impossible to miss. There was more than just a mating bond binding them.

"But werewolves live in packs to prevent their exposure. You're suggesting that as Sloane's influence spreads, werewolves everywhere will simply abandon pack existence and go out into the world, assimilating into human society? No offense, but not all of you represent your species very well." *And that was an absurdly generous understatement.* "Pretty sure humans still grossly outnumber werewolves across the planet, right? Aren't you afraid of human mass hysteria? Your entire Liberace estate could be nuked overnight. The world could be turned upside down in a week if werewolves started coming out of hiding in droves. You're advocating chaos."

"No. I'm advocating Darwinism."

CHAPTER 30

Bethany

I'D TRICKED JORGE INTO SMUGGLING ME OVER TO SEE Rafe under the guise of needing medical assistance for digestive distress. So it was probably only fitting that by the time I'd left Rafe's office, I was shitting my proverbial pants over the disturbing information I'd gleaned from the wacky doctor.

Before I'd left, I had pressed Rafe about the strange "mind block shit" comment he'd made to Raul during our meeting with him the day prior. Rafe explained that most humans couldn't survive the initial shift into a werewolf without magical assistance from a werelock. To do so, the attending werelock needed to be able to control bodily functions and processes related to the initial shift by redirecting commands through the brain and central nervous system.

Which meant they needed access to the shifting human's mind.

And according to Rafe, my mind had been blocked at some point by an "enemy" werelock.

The notion that an unidentified "enemy" supernatural creeper had been inside my head before to set up some sort of deflector shield around my brain was disturbing enough. When Rafe reconfirmed his prognosis that, unless said shield was lifted, I was definitely going to die an excruciatingly painful blow-apart-from-the-inside death during my initial werewolf transformation, it was just the sort of over-the-top kind of terrifying news that made a person recently subjected to too much gilding and candelabras crack and start to fall apart.

My brain was set somewhere between autopilot and comatose as the werewolf guard Rafe had secured for me led me back over to the main mansion.

If what Rafe had said was true, that meant Raul had lied to me on the plane when he'd said he hadn't accessed my mind out of respect for my privacy.

I was feeling more insecure than ever about where I stood with my supposed "true mate." Raul had become increasingly withdrawn from me in the day and a half that I'd been at the Bariloche estate.

I didn't know what was real or what to believe anymore. I just knew I needed to escape this Liberace house of horrors and get back to my life in San Francisco.

And that was why, when I was dropped off with Wyatt yet again, I found myself pickpocketing his phone and then stealing away to a hallway bathroom in the mansion.

Locking the door to the gaudy golden bathroom I'd found myself in, I wasted no time in dialing one of the few numbers I still knew by heart: Milena's.

I lowered the volume on the receiver and cupped it tightly against my ear. I held my breath as it began to ring. Once. Twice.

By the third ring my heart sank as it occurred to me there was no way Milena would pick up. Even if I was lucky enough to catch her when she was available and with her phone in hand, she wouldn't recognize Wyatt's number and would let the call go to voicemail. What should I say in a message? Did I dare leave one?

Then a miracle happened: The ringing stopped and the line picked up.

"Who the fuck is this?" Alex's stern voice demanded.

I nearly cried tears of relief as I whispered back, "Alex, it's me, Bethy."

My voice cracked slightly on the last two syllables. I knew Alex heard it, because his whole demeanor shifted to high-alert, protective big-brother mode, and God, did I appreciate him for that quality in this moment.

"Bethany? What's wrong? Where are you? Whose phone is this?"

"I didn't want to call and upset Milena in her current condition, but things have gotten—"

"Where are you, Bethy? I need a location."

"Um … South America. In Arg"—an involuntary sniffle-shudder escaped me—"Argentina."

The line went quiet. "Who are you with?"

I hesitated for a moment before answering, knowing that I was about to ignite the mother of all sibling rows. "Um … I'm with Raul."

The line went quiet a second time. When he spoke again, Alex's voice was strangely calm and devoid of emotion, his words delivered slowly and carefully as he asked, "Has he hurt you?"

Four simple words. But such a loaded question.

"N-no. I mean … not … really … on purpose," I faltered. I'd been about to say, "not physically," but then I realized that would've been a lie. He'd bitten me multiple times. He'd marked me and infected me with werewolf venom. And he had drugged me in order to kidnap me. "I mean … not out of … malicious intent …" I winced as I realized how bad that sounded.

"He kidnapped me, Alex," I finally blurted. There was no sugarcoating it. "He almost killed Gregg. When I flipped out over it, he drugged me. And he kidnapped me."

"He's a dead man."

"*No.* No, I don't want that. It's not like that, Alex. He didn't mean to hurt me; things just … got out of hand." Christ, I sounded like a traumatized battered woman undergoing the intake process at a shelter. "Never mind that last part. I just need to get back to San Francisco. I can't miss any more hospital shifts. I need you to call the American embassy in South America for me, okay? I mean—*Argentina.*" I shook my head at the ceiling, feeling like an idiot. "The American embassy in Argentin—"

"Bethy, I know you're scared. The situation with Raul must be bad or you wouldn't have called Milena. But I need you to trust me and put Raul on the phone so I can speak with him."

"No, no, can't do that. That's not a good idea."

"It is, Bethany. Please trust me. I give you my word it'll be okay."

"You don't understand, Alex. Raul's not exactly … himself anymore." Oh, crap, here goes. "So … I'm guessing there's a small chance that you and Milena might possibly know this already about him and that's why she's been es-tranged from him for the past decade … but Raul's a … a werewolf."

I waited for a reaction. "Are you there? I'm not crazy, Alex. I know what I'm saying sounds crazy—"

"Bethany …" He sighed. "I know. I know Raul's a were-wolf. It's okay."

It's okay?

What the hell did that mean?

"Um … it's not that okay," I refuted, my hysteria sky-rocketing. "Because he's more than just a regular werewolf, Alex. He's a *werelock*. Which means he has super-cool powers and can poof places. And not only that, he's the head of a big pack of werewolves and werelocks. It's like some kind of supernatural shapeshifting crime syndicate."

I was babbling. Unraveling. Did Alex not believe me? Why would he say that he knew Raul was a werewolf like it was no big deal?

"And Raul's also a manny for this prodigy werelock girl with purple eyes. And she tried to set me on fire yesterday, Alex. I mean *literally* on fire. She didn't even need a match, either, because she's like that little girl from *Firestarter* and can do it with her thoughts. Raul keeps telling me she's harmless, but I actually think she's plotting to kill me. I can't explain it … it's just this look she gives me and this feeling I get when—"

"Bethany, listen to me. Everything's going to be okay, I promise. But the American embassy can't help you with this. I need you to put Raul on the phone. Now. Please."

"No!" I whisper-shouted before checking my volume. "Didn't you hear anything I just said? This is not a joke. Everyone here turns into a giant monster wolf, Alex. I snatched a phone and I'm hiding in a bathroom. Raul doesn't know I'm making this call, and I don't think he'll be happy with me if—"

"Bethy, open the door." Raul's voice made me jump.

Shit! I froze in place as he jiggled the knob. My heart galloped.

"Baby, it's okay. Please don't be scared. Just open the door. We need to talk."

"In a minute," I called back. I raced to the toilet and flushed it, before whispering into the phone, "I gotta go."

"Bethany, do *not* hang up. He can still hear me," Alex insisted, raising his volume to compete with the rushing water. "Even through the door. Through the phone line. And with the toilet flushing," he stressed. "He has supernatural canine senses, honey."

Oh, God. I immediately felt sick. Alex knew way too much and was way too calm about all this werewolf business.

"He's telling the truth," Raul confirmed from the other side of the door. "Please let me in. I want to talk to Alex, too."

I was suddenly dizzy—so lightheaded I feared I'd actually faint—as I stood frozen in place in the Versace bathroom, holding Wyatt's phone to my ear and staring numbly at the closed door, wondering how long Raul would give me to open it before he simply poofed through.

Breathe, Bethany. Just breathe.

"Bethy?" Raul rapped lightly on the door with his knuckle. "You okay?"

"Bethany?" Alex's voice was familiar and reassuring in my ear, but there was a tone of resignation to it that raised the fine hairs on the back of my neck. "I have a confession." I closed my eyes. My free hand reached out blindly, my palm flattening against the marble countertop to steady myself as Alex spoke the words I'd known in my gut he was about to say. "I'm a werelock too."

I nodded in reply—as if Alex could see me.

I reminded myself that I was a doctor. I'd never fainted before. I wouldn't start now.

I'd held it together so well up to this point, despite everything that'd happened.

In the moment, I couldn't process why Alex's revelation was the one to push me past my breaking point at last.

"And Raul's not going to harm another hair on your head," Alex told me through the phone with certainty. "Because he knows that I will kill him. Painfully."

Bile rose up in my throat.

They were all killers. *Killer werelocks.*

So where did that leave Milena?

Where did it leave me?

"I'm not a fainter," I heard myself say thinly in reply as everything began to spin inside my head. "I've never fainted before … not even in medical school …"

I heard Alex's voice through the phone calling out for Raul—which struck me as odd—right before my equilibrium tilted and the phone slipped from my fingers. It connected with the stone floor with a hard clatter. Absently, I wondered if I'd broken it.

I swayed on my feet, the fingers of my other hand losing their grip on the countertop. Fleetingly, I wondered if I'd break too as I felt myself going down.

"Easy, baby." Raul's voice floated above my head as he caught my dead weight in his arms and hefted me off my feet. "I've got you. Everything's going to be okay."

CHAPTER 31

Raul

ALEX WAS STILL TALKING AT ME FROM THE OTHER END OF the line that had begun to crackle, demanding to know if Bethany was all right in between making threats to castrate and kill me.

"I'll call you back," I barked at the phone on the floor, shifting Bethany's weight so that she was cradled to my chest and supported with one arm, leaving my other hand free as I checked her pulse.

Her heartbeat sounded fine. Her pulse was normal too. I stroked her pale cheek and brushed my lips across her forehead, murmuring, "It's okay. Everything's okay. I'm so sorry." *I love you.*

An awful pain burned in my throat, then lodged in my chest like a cold, heavy stone as I looked at her. The scent of her distress was so thick in the bathroom. The scent of her fear, too.

I'd done it already. I'd pushed her away. I'd made her hate me. *She didn't trust me: her own true mate.* I should've known I'd never get this right with her.

She'd reached out to Miles and Alex for help. *For help*

getting away from me.

And I had no one to blame but myself. What the hell had I been doing for the past two days since I'd brought her here? I should've been spending all my time with her—making her feel welcome, making her feel loved.

What was wrong with me? How did I always fuck up the relationships that mattered most?

"This is the last line you'll ever cross with Milena, do you hear me?" Alex's muffled voice raged from the bathroom floor. "We agreed Bethany was off-limits. What the fuck are you thinking? Put Alcaeus on the line!"

I kicked the phone toward Wyatt, who was pacing outside the doorway—feeling guilty, no doubt—and told him, "End the call, Wyatt."

"Right." He nervously bobbed his head and dove to the floor to retrieve the phone that he'd been careless enough to allow Bethy to get a hold of.

"Do *not* hang up on me, Wyatt," Alex ordered through the line. "Your entire pack is in danger if Bethany isn't turned over immediately. If any member of your pack harms Bethy in *any* way, you will *all* be held accountable. Am I making myself clear? Now get Alcaeus! I want to speak with an adult."

"I'm the Alpha of this pack, Alex. You'll speak to me and no one else."

"Alpha," he mocked. "You conniving, power-grabbing shit. I watched you use my sister Lessa to gain a foothold within my pack. I watched you use your own sister to gain entry to the Salvatella pack. Seven months ago, I watched you use a little girl to overthrow Gabe and steal control of his pack. I don't know what your game is this time—what you hope to get out of Milena by using Bethany—but it's

not going to go in your favor on my watch, I guarantee you that. You will turn Bethany over to me now. And if I find so much as a scratch—"

"I marked her, Alex." My words came out sounding as cold and heavy as they felt in my heart in that moment— weighted with self-loathing and regret. "More than once. And she's been infected with werewolf venom. She's got less than a day before the shift starts."

The line went dead. I suspected Alex had probably crushed the phone he'd held in his hand.

I teleported Bethy upstairs to my room and put her into bed. Then I went to talk with Mike and Avery. It was time to poison Lauren, the seer.

"I'm sorry," I told Mike. I meant it. "You know I wouldn't do this unless I thought we had to."

He nodded and mumbled that he understood, which only made me feel worse. Mike had been in such a great mood ever since he'd blocked Kai from the seer's mind late Saturday night. Once he'd fixed it so that Lauren had re-covered all of the memories of Kai's creepy exploits in her head for the last several months, he and Avery had been in the catacombs glued to the hidden surveillance camera feed on Lauren. Watching footage of Lauren repeatedly reject Kai and refuse to see him for the past twenty-four hours had become their new favorite reality TV.

But it had done nothing to help us with Bethy's mind block thus far. Mike and Avery had made sure Kai knew ex-actly who was responsible for giving Lauren her memories back and blocking Kai from accessing her mind. And they'd made certain Kai knew what our demands were as they related to Bethy's emotional shield. But based on the surveillance in place on the Reinoso pack, Kai hadn't told Alex or Miles about any of it yet. He hadn't even reached out to Remy.

He was too busy wallowing in his own embarrassment and guilt, and probably telling himself this development was for the best with his coed obsession. Clearly, the danger to Lauren needed to be far greater before Kai would be moved to take any action that might draw Miles's attention to what he'd really been up to with the seer.

Mike and Avery had already teleported to Washington to carry out plan B when Alex called my phone.

"Congratulations, Raul," he greeted the moment I picked up, sounding a lot calmer than he'd been twenty minutes ago. "What a victory this is for you. So, what—now I can't kill you without risking Bethany's life? That your angle with this? Here's a newsflash: you were already off-limits!"

I jerked the phone away from my ear as Alex proceeded to shout through the receiver. *Not so much calmer after all.*

"The moment I laid eyes on your sister, I knew I could never kill you. Swallowed that bitter pill with plenty of good pinot a long ass time ago, I assure you. So you've ruined Bethany's life and mated yourself to a woman you don't love for no reason."

"That's not what this was about, Alex. This had nothing to do with you, and nothing to do with Miles."

"No?" He laughed. "You mark your sister's best friend, and it's got nothing to do with her?"

"This is between me and Bethy. And I do love her, Alex. I'm keeping her."

"She's a *person,* Raul. You can't just keep her because you want to."

"Oh, that's rich." Fucking hypocrite. "You mean like how you kept my little sister?"

"I didn't keep Milena, Raul. She *chose* me."

"You stole her. You brainwashed her against me."

"Well, it's obviously more convenient for you to believe that."

"Conveniently *true.*"

"You lost your sister because you lied to her. You betrayed her trust and behaved like an asshole to her. You used her for your own gain and then expected her to be happy about it—like you'd done her a favor."

"That is not what happened."

"It's exactly what happened."

"You have no right to talk. You held Miles hostage."

"And you're holding Bethany hostage—*for the second time.* Don't take your bitterness over losing your sister out on Bethany."

"For the last time, this has nothing to do with my sister, Alex. It's between me and Bethy."

Just like every conversation I'd ever had with Alex, this one was going nowhere. So I cut to the chase and told him we'd blocked Lauren Novak's mind and had just poisoned her with a moderated synthetic nerve agent formulation that would kill the seer within approximately eighteen hours. Not a lie—Avery had tapped my mind moments ago to let me know the deed was done.

I gave Alex the ultimatum that the seer would die unless Bethy's emotional shield was lifted in the next fourteen hours.

He was silent. Then he started muttering to himself in Portuguese about what an imbecile I was and how much better Bethy deserved.

I didn't dispute the latter.

"Are you really this much of an idiot? *Still*? After all this time? I can have Remy grant me access to Bethy's mind right now, Raul. I'll control her shift just fine from here if I have to. Thanks for the heads-up on her shifting timetable, by the way. Now I know. I'll be sure to clear my schedule for tomorrow." He made an annoyed grunting sound. "Seriously, put Al on the phone already. I'm losing IQ points."

He was bluffing. "Really? You don't care if I kill an innocent girl?"

"What's her life to me compared to Bethany's? My God, it's like you didn't even think this through," he complained.

"That's your final answer, Alex? You don't care if we kill the seer?"

"No. Why should I? Is that it? The only bargaining chip you were able to produce on short notice?" He laughed. "By all means, kill her. You think I'd trade Bethany's life for Kai's little college fling?"

"Fling?" I was starting to second-guess whether or not he was bluffing.

"As if I'm having some kind of 'aw' moment over Kai finally getting his dick wet after his century-long idiocy-induced bout of celibacy? Kill the girl. Kai will get over it. I'm sure there'll be others now that he's finally come to his senses and rediscovered he's not actually a eunuch."

"But she's the *seer*," I stressed.

"Sure, as much as I'm a seer and you're a seer and the woman with a crystal ball reading palms down at the street corner is a seer."

Wait—did he not know? Downplaying the seer's importance to me and to Mike was one thing, but had Kai hidden the fact from his own pack that his little coed was more than a fling—that she was potentially the next great seer the werewolf world had been searching for?

Fuck it. I was getting nowhere with Alex, and I had a sense he was determined to keep Miles out of this situation right now. I needed to make certain that word got back to Miles quickly about Bethy's present situation and about Kai's "fling"—an alleged seer—being poisoned.

Curtly ending my call with Alex, I told Stephen to get a message directly to Remy and then to Alex's sister Lessa. I'd spent eight miserable years as a human servant to the Reinoso pack. I knew that the fastest way to escalate anything within their hierarchy was to instigate a fight between Alex and his siblings. With that in motion, I went to check on Bethany.

CHAPTER 32

Raul

S HE WAS AWAKE, SITTING UPRIGHT WITH HER LEGS OVER
the edge of the bed.

The moment our eyes met, I knew something was different.

No, not something. Everything.

Her eyes were puffy; they looked more teal than blue. She'd been crying since waking up.

But the differences went well beyond that. *She'd changed.*

She knew.

It wasn't only the recent revelation about Alex being a werelock that I saw written on her face. Somehow I got the sense that she'd remembered *everything* she had once known and had forgotten about our world.

Everything she had once known about me. *About us.*

For some reason, the Reinosos must've lifted the shield already. And either they'd purposely given Bethany back all of her memories from a decade ago or, as Alcaeus had predicted, all of Bethany's blocked memories had simply returned on their own now that the shield was removed.

At first, I thought maybe I was projecting. Imagining it. It seemed utterly inconceivable that the Reinosos would have caved so soon based on my last conversation with Alex.

I could've simply tried to tap Bethy's mind to check for certain that the shield was gone, but I'd never been more terrified to probe a mind before.

I found that I didn't want to do it.

Couldn't bear to look. Didn't want to see what I feared most I would find: Disgust and anger. *For me.* Disappointment. *In me.*

Worst of all: Pain. *Hers*—caused by me.

She hadn't spoken a word since I'd entered the room. Hadn't moved.

I needed to say something. "I—I didn't know how to tell you." I paused. Waited for better words to come.

They didn't.

"I'm sorry. What happened ten years ago … the thing is … Miles … Alex … my sister's pack … I asked them to—to lift …"

I couldn't even string together a damn coherent sentence to salvage the love of my life. Each progressive word tasted more grossly inadequate and idiotic on my tongue.

I should just stop.

I'd already lost her. It was too late. The signs had been there before this. She'd tried to tell me for the past two days how unhappy she was—while I'd been busy shutting her out. While I'd been too preoccupied steeling myself against the inevitable loss of her to do something constructive that might actually prevent her from slipping away—*like communicate.*

"I've been so terrified you'd hate me … once you knew. That I'd … lose you …"

My voice came out wooden, sounding all wrong. Sounding false and unfeeling. And the burn was I'd never been so earnest, so sincerely present, invested, and desperate to bare my heart before.

Why couldn't I do this right?

She didn't say anything. Didn't move or emote. But a fresh tear slid down her cheek.

Say something to her.

Something good.

Something meaningful.

But I could think of nothing inspiring or even remotely intelligent to express. The stakes were too high. My likelihood of failure too great.

Tears slid down both Bethy's cheeks, catching the light from the gilded chandelier above.

Yet I remained an idiot.

I said the word "sorry" a few more times.

I asked if she hated me. She didn't reply.

Panic gripped me, and I did something I hadn't done since I'd been a kid.

I prayed. Not to God or to Jesus like I'd been taught to do in Bible school. But to my mom—that she'd help me find the right words to say.

Mom had loved words. She'd loved to read and share her favorite quotes from poems and literature with me. She'd been so good with her words. They had flowed from her, forever eloquent and ringing clear as a bell with their truth. Even as she'd been dying, she'd said such beautiful things. Meaningful things. *Convincing things* as she'd persuaded the paramedics to save my unborn sister's life over her own.

And I'd stood there the whole time watching. Listening.

Blubbering. Feeling impotent. Desperate to be able to do something to save her, while knowing I'd already failed.

Because I'd paused my video game too late. I should've gone to check on her when I'd heard the dish crash—the moment I'd caught the weakness in her voice. If I'd dialed 9-1-1 sooner, the paramedics might've come faster. They might've been able to save her.

But I'd been a fuck-up even at age eight.

My vision had begun to go hazy, so at first I wondered if I was seeing things when Bethy's slender forearm lifted from her lap and her hand extended—her palm open and beckoning to me. *Reaching out for me.*

Then she spoke. And I knew at once for certain Bethy remembered absolutely everything that had happened between us ten years ago when she repeated the words I'd never shared with another soul but her before. They were the last words my mom had spoken to me before she'd died—after I'd finished begging Mom through my tears not to leave me, then stammered nothing but nonsense at her because I was in too much shock to know what to say.

"I know, Raul. I know. Remember, the small truth has words that are clear; the great truth has great silence."

Bethy sniffled, her trembling lips forming a smile. "I saw that Rabindranath Tagore quote on a refrigerator magnet at the co-op market four years ago. It was written in fancy script over some cliché image—a sunset, maybe a field of flowers. I started bawling my eyes out right there in the checkout line, and I couldn't for the life of me understand why."

She gave a startled giggle, and more tears fell, as I teleported straight in front of her.

Taking her outstretched hand in both of mine, I knelt

at her feet. I felt a smile erupt on my face as my eyes watered too. Because the whole world was mad. And madly beautiful. There were people selling *Stray Birds* verses on cheesy fridge magnets. And Bethany Garrett got me. *Loved me*—for the sum-total fuck-up I was.

"I love you," I told her. "So crazy fucking much, I don't know what to do with it. And I'm so afraid that I won't know how to love you the way you want me to. I remember what you told me ten years ago about your parents' marriage—about growing up feeling like you were caught in the middle of a crazy dysfunctional unrequited love story. I've already messed up so much with you. I'll probably fuck up a lot more still. And I can't handle the thought of making you unhappy—of watching you grow to quietly despise me—"

"We're not my parents, Raul. What we have—*our* love story—is so much more dysfunctional already." She laughed and wiped at her tears. "And I want all of it. But right now, I just need to feel every hard inch of your fucking crazy coming inside me. Because I don't want to waste anymore time living without you."

'Nuff said.

We melted together, her soft parts meeting my hard aching ones, her mouth fusing with mine. I swore I could taste every emotion she felt for me in her kiss. And each emotion felt like a truth I hadn't earned, a gift I didn't deserve to keep.

But I accepted them anyway—consumed everything she gave me like a starving man as I vanished our clothing and shoved every inch of my crazy deep inside her. Because I could no longer breathe without Bethany. Didn't want to try.

Over and over, I drove into her. Losing myself, while finding all the parts of me that had always been missing.

I drank in her every moan, her each shuddered breath, reveling in her body's responses. And as I felt her wet, welcoming heat squeezing around me, pulling me in deeper with each heady thrust, I let the mistakes of my past go for just a moment. I set my outdated fears aside.

For the first time ever, I let everything go inside of a woman—*my woman.*

Mom—*and Tagore*—were right. There were certain truths that words could never do justice. Emotions no language could encompass.

Sometimes the greatest truths could only be conveyed in silence.

Or to the music of Bethy's breathy I-need-to-come noises, and the sound of flesh smacking against flesh.

CHAPTER 33

Raul

"Yeah, yeah, Mom. I know the Nazis settled here."
Bethy was naked, pacing back and forth across the
floor at the foot of our bed, talking on the phone. "Yes, I
have the American embassy on speed dial." She gave me
an apologetic look as Marlee continued yapping in her ear.

I grinned lazily back at her, engrossed in enjoying the
view from where I lay stretched out on my side across the
bed, propped up on my elbow, watching the sway of her
hips and the jiggle of her bumper as she moved.

I was coming in that ass of hers next. My balls tightened at the thought of it.

"Well, I'm sure it looks that way, but I'm not the re-
bounder type, Mom. You know that." She rolled her eyes
and made a wrap-it-up gesture as she proceeded to pace
closer to the windows.

It was dusk outside, and our bedroom was well lit. I
shook my head. *Definitely an exhibitionist.* She was going
to be the death of me with that shit. I didn't share. So I
didn't particularly like the idea of anyone else even looking
at what was mine.

But Bethy clearly enjoyed the thrill, despite her being somewhat in denial still about those preferences. I knew we'd have to establish some ground rules in order to make it work for us both. Maybe do what we'd done in the club the other night—where my men had surrounded us and shielded her from view. I'd probably start with fucking her in the garden maze tonight—giving her the excitement of *potentially* being watched.

Or … I could start by fucking her right now in front of the windows. *While she talked to her mom on the phone.*

I got up from the bed and stalked over to her.

"Yes, I realize the suddenness of it all must seem a bit unbelievable to you and Dad, but I need to spend some time with Raul here at his home. I'll be back in a week to square things away with the hospital, and we can talk in person then, okay?"

Bethy gave me a stern look and shook her head at me the moment she caught sight of my approach—and the size of my erection pointed straight at her.

It was hard not to laugh. *Fuck, she was fun.* She was giving off a serious schoolteacher vibe with her expression.

"Mom, I really have to get going now." She glared at me again, while backing up toward the window—exactly where I wanted her.

In one supernaturally fast move, I had her lush body pinned against the pane. Marlee's voice was still prattling away in Bethy's ear as I spun her around so that her back was to my front and her naked front was on full display in the curtainless, giant arched window of my bedroom that overlooked a courtyard in the garden below.

Bethy didn't need to know there was a longstanding spell in place on all of the windows in my room that worked better than any tinted glass to prevent anyone from seeing in.

What would be the fun in telling her that?

She squirmed frantically against me as I pushed her legs wider apart with my own, pressing my cock between her ass cheeks as my hand skated down her abdomen, between her thighs, to palm her sex.

Soaking wet.

Yep. Complete exhibitionist.

Pinching her nipple with my other hand, I dragged my fingers through her folds before sinking several inside.

She began giving breathy, one-word answers into the phone, and otherwise letting her mom do all the talking, as my thumb joined in to work her clit.

Her squirming only got me more aroused as her ass pressed and rolled up against my dick. And somewhere amid her silent squirms of protest, she began shamelessly riding my hand.

My whole palm was soaked, but she was still holding back, so I reached out to Tiago through our mind link and told him to send a dozen or more werewolf guards—both male and female—out to the courtyard. *And have them stare up at my bedroom window.*

Because Bethy was my mate, and I would do whatever it took to make her happy. And just because I could. *Sometimes it was good to be king.*

Lining up my cock with her dripping entrance, I told her to hang up the call and brace her hands against the glass.

She did. She straight-up hung up on her mom before dropping the device. It clanked to the marble floor—the second phone she'd broken in less than twenty-four hours.

Slipping my right forearm under her right thigh, I raised her knee up and out, spreading her open wide for the whole courtyard to *not* see as I shoved into her ready center from behind.

She went up on tiptoe, balanced precariously on one shaky leg and supported by her sweaty palms against the glass as I began to fuck her, slow and deep.

At first, her eyes were riveted on our reflection in the pane as she watched my dick glide in and out, disappearing between her spread pink folds.

My free hand alternated between pinching her nipples and rubbing her exposed clit.

Then I had Tiago illuminate the garden area, drawing her attention there as the first several guards entered the courtyard below and looked right up at us. She started desperately pushing back against the glass, trying to get away from view—which only served to press her ass into my groin and push my dick deeper inside her.

She might've been fooling herself, but she didn't fool me. Because her pussy began gushing and fluttering like mad the moment she thought we had an audience.

Fuck, the things I was going to do to her once she was a werewolf and went into heat. Then it occurred to me the things I could do to her now that I had access to her mind at last.

Ask permission.

I waited until she was on the brink of her first orgasm—knowing she'd say yes to anything. "Baby?" I licked the bite on her shoulder as she began making incoherent sounds. "Would it be okay if I entered your mind now to make sure everything's feeling good for you?"

I took the next little squeak she made as a yes, and

carefully, gently slipped inside just as she was going over the cliff. And oh, fuck me, I nearly shot my load prematurely, it was so beautiful inside Bethy's orgasmic mind.

Feeling what she was feeling and hearing her disjointed, dirty thoughts in her highly aroused state was the ultimate turn-on—the most exhilarating sensation I'd ever known. I had to count to five and calm my shit to stop myself from running wild like a kid in a candy store triggering every single nerve bundle in each of her erogenous zones all at once.

Subtle and gentle, I reminded myself.

The gentle approach was best for her first time having me in her head. *And her ass—which was where I was going next.*

I started by causing her to feel a steady, light pulse against her G-spot, and then I added a sucking sensation on her clit. Her leg gave out and she released a gasp of alarm the moment I added the less subtle sensation of phantom mouths latching on and sucking her hard nipples.

"Raul?"

"You're okay." My arm tightened around her midsection, taking all of her weight. "You're safe." I nuzzled the shell of her ear. "It's just me. It's not real. It only *feels* real because I'm inside your head directing messages throughout your body—causing it to believe it's experiencing certain things."

"You're in my head?" The question came out breathless. She sounded surprised. Dazed.

"Yeah. Remember? You gave me permission." I sent a wave of calm through her system as I said it, helping her to relax. "You like that?"

She moaned and nodded. Her head lolled back against my shoulder. Her hands slipped from the glass pane.

"Good." I kissed her cheek. "Just relax and feel good for me. If you don't like something, let me know, and I'll stop."

Slowly, I began to arouse the nerves throughout her anus next, building anticipation. Getting her used to the sensation. Stimulating her desire to feel more of me there.

Then I worked two slick phantom fingers inside her asshole, twisting and scissoring them, preparing her to take me as I continued to slowly fuck her.

I watched her reflection in the glass as her eyes rolled back—as the sensations began to overwhelm her, making her body tighten and coil with need. My own eyes had shifted; my fangs were extended and salivating with the need to pierce her flesh.

Her arms reached up over her head to wrap around my neck; her fingers gripped and pulled my hair.

She was so ready to come, but I was in her head and able to delay her orgasms now, thank God. Otherwise I would've spilled inside her a long time ago.

"Keep looking out the window, baby," I told her.

More guards had arrived in the courtyard. I'd requested that Tiago grab a few mated couples, too—and preferably any females who were in heat who felt like putting on a show. One of the couples was already going at it. *Bethy's exhibitionist tendencies weren't entirely novel within a werewolf pack.*

She started coming apart again when she saw the crowd gathered below staring up at our window. But I stopped her orgasm and simply held her there—leaving her dangling over the precipice, her inner walls throbbing and pulsating with need around my painful erection. I told her she'd get to come once she took my whole cock in her ass—*because #relationshipgoals.*

Then I waited until she was a shaking, babbling, desperate-to-come wreck before I finally pulled out of her drenched pussy and went for her smaller hole.

Raising her bent leg higher, I nudged her upper body forward and pulled her hips up and back. I told her to brace her hands against the window again as the head of my wet cock sought her tighter entrance.

I reminded her to breathe and push out as I pressed forward.

Phantom mouths and hands alternately rubbed, sucked, and gave her clit light slaps as the head of my cock slowly breached her ring of muscle. Phantom fingers filled and fucked her pretty cunt.

"You okay?" I forced myself to pause and check, even though I was sure that she was, based on the thoughts and sensations I was privy to in her head. *And based on the noises she was making that were driving me insane.* She moan-babbled in reply, and I kept going, pushing farther inside.

My hand ran soothingly up and down her spine. I paused several more times to allow her body to adjust—to wait for the pleasure receptors within her to catch up and override any discomfort she was experiencing.

Meanwhile, I was barely keeping it together as I watched my dick slowly sink to the hilt inside her. As soon as I was balls-deep in her ass, I knew I wasn't going to last much longer. And neither was she.

The moment I stopped holding back her orgasm, she went off like a rocket, her mouth falling open in a silent scream, her ass clenching around me, her pussy exploding against my palm as I cupped it, then slapped it one final time.

Fuck me, her ass was so incredibly tight and hot as her walls convulsed around me and her orgasm choked my cock. A growl rolled up my chest.

Gentle! Be gentle, I reminded my inner beast as my body went rigid, my movements becoming hard and jerky as I withdrew barely an inch before shoving back into her. Once. *Twice.*

I was just about to blow when suddenly I heard a vaguely familiar male voice speaking inside of Bethany's head.

"Bethany? Can you hear me?"

What in holy—?

"This is Remy Bertrand, Milena's brother-in-law. You may not remember me, but ten years ago—"

"What the fuck, man?" I shouted back at him. *"Get out of here!"*

"Raul?" Remy sounded genuinely surprised. *"Wait. How're you in Beth—Oh!"*

"Omigod, what's happening?" Bethany asked aloud, freaking out as her orgasm waned and she became lucid enough to realize I was arguing inside her head—with another guy!

"Well, this is a little awkward." Remy's voice was amused. *"I'll just … have Alex call you."*

"That anal orgasm was intense," Bethy confessed, her voice quiet despite the echo in the large bathroom. Her blue eyes were still a little dazed, her cheeks a freshly scrubbed pink. "Way more earth-shattering than the clinical studies and dirty *Cosmo* articles I read ever made it out to be." She was sitting on the edge of our bathroom's sunken tub, my bathrobe dwarfing her frame as I towel-dried her hair. "But I think having two werelocks in my head is an exhibitionist hard limit for me."

I nodded and forced a placid expression. I wasn't sure I pulled it off, considering my jaw was clenched so tightly it felt like I might crack teeth. "It's an absolute hard limit for me," I told her stiffly. "And it will never happen again."

Because I was going to invent the most complicated, most powerful mind shield of all time to place on Bethany.

Following the epically awkward *Remy interruptus,* I'd settled Bethy into a warm bath to relax her. And then I'd dialed Alex. After laying into him about Remy's intrusion, I'd discovered that the Reinosos had never lifted the mind block on Bethy.

Once word had finally reached Miles through Alex's siblings about Bethany's situation and about Kai's coed being poisoned, my sister had promptly ordered Remy to lift the emotional shield on my mate. So Remy had entered Bethany's mind to check on her and carry out Miles's command.

Except the emotional shield had already been lifted on its own, and Bethany's blocked memories recovered as well. The question remained: How? What had triggered it?

"Honey, I need you to tell me what happened when you first woke up after your fainting spell. What were you thinking about when your memories resurfaced?"

"Well, I'd just had a really vivid dream about my baby brother, and as I woke up, I was still thinking about him. And then all of a sudden I started to rememb—"

"What?" The towel stilled in my hands against her scalp. "You have a brother?" *Since when?*

She nodded. "Yeah. *Had.*" Her eyes watered as she gave me a soft smile. "Evan only lived to be thirteen months old."

"I—I'm sorry," I sputtered. *How in the world had I not known this?* I let the towel fall around her shoulders. I straightened and backed up a step, floored.

How was it possible that I hadn't known Bethy had a sibling? A baby brother who had died? I ran a shaky hand through my hair. I was such an insensitive asshole.

And an idiot. Evan had been the key to her emotional shield all along. It should've been so obvious, and yet, I'd never heard about him before.

"Fuck, I—I should've known that already. I don't know how I didn't know."

"Raul, stop." She shook her head, her gaze on me nothing but kind. "Don't beat yourself up. Not for this. There's no way you could've known. I think I only mentioned Evan to Milena maybe once when we were little—twice our whole friendship at most. He died before I turned four—before Milena and I met in kindergarten."

She rolled one shoulder, looking small and vulnerable wrapped up in my giant bathrobe. "I guess I've made it a habit for most of my life not to talk about him much. Close friends like Kylie and Jessie don't know I ever had a brother. Maybe it's weird of me, but I have such precious few memories of my baby brother, I've never liked sharing them. I always wanted them to remain mine alone."

I sat next to her on the side of the tub, taking her hand in mine. "Not weird at all. I get that." Boy, did I get that.

"For years, I blamed myself for Evan's death, even

though I knew it had absolutely nothing to do with me. Because that's what kids do: blame themselves for bad things that happen, and for the things that upset the adults around them."

I linked our fingers and brought her hand to my lips as she continued.

"My parents weren't the same after Evan died. They fought a lot at first. Then they'd go weeks at a time barely speaking. I blamed myself for that, too. Then at some point it was like my Mom stopped loving my Dad—like she couldn't move past the loss of Evan and was mad that my Dad had." Her forehead creased. "Or rather, she couldn't accept that my Dad had processed his loss in a manner that was different from how she had.

"Anyway, it made me feel as if nothing I did would ever be enough—not enough to fill the void Evan left behind, you know? Not enough to make them happy again. Certainly not enough to make them love each other the way I'd thought they once had.

"They talked about divorce a lot. *Threatened* divorce a lot to one another, I should say," she clarified. "It got pretty intense sometimes. To the point that I starting wishing they'd just get divorced and get it over with. I always felt like they only stayed together after Evan's death because of me." Her throaty chuckle was dry. "But then they stayed together after I went to college and moved out."

She pinched the bridge of her nose, shutting her eyes and shaking her head. "And I finally realized they were locked in their own dysfunction that had nothing to do with me."

"I'm sorry." I stared down at our joined hands in my lap. "I can't even imagine."

"There's nothing to be sorry about." She leaned in and laid her head against my shoulder. "And I have a feeling you *can* imagine—that you can relate all too well, actually."

She tilted her chin back, looking up at me from the side of my shoulder. "Remember how I told you I had an emotional reaction to seeing that Tagore magnet at the grocery store? A similar thing happened when I was studying obstetrics and learned about amniotic fluid embolism—the rare condition your mom suffered in childbirth."

My heart began to beat faster. I was grateful Bethy couldn't hear it as I averted my gaze.

"I got so emotional reading about it," she continued, "so frustrated learning how impossible a condition it is to diagnose and treat with any success. It felt so deeply personal to me for some reason, and I couldn't understand why."

"I'm sorry. I shouldn't have told—"

"There are no signs, Raul." She raised her head from my shoulder and pulled back to look at me. Reluctantly, I met her eyes. "There are virtually no formal studies on the condition because it can't be prediagnosed, and when it happens, it hits so fast that by the time there are any symptoms, it's almost always too late."

As she proceeded, her tone became purposely clinical. Detached. There was even a hint of that schoolteacher vibe again. It was something I would later look back on and remember as a moment in which I fell even more in love with my mate and future wife, as Bethany spoke like she was merely stating medical facts rather than attempting to exonerate and free me from some of the worst demons of my life.

"Once amniotic fluid enters the mom's bloodstream, it

sets off an anaphylactic reaction, usually leading to rapid multisystem organ failure and cardiovascular collapse. Both the delivering mom and the baby have only a twenty percent chance of survival when they receive the right immediate emergency medical attention at a hospital.

"Paramedics couldn't have saved your mom, Raul. They didn't have the tools or the skills—much less the ability to properly diagnose what was happening. Your mom made the right call—the *only* call left at that point. If she'd let them waste time taking her to the hospital, neither she nor Milena would've survived. It was a miracle Milena survived anyhow, and the only reason she did was because your mom was already in the final stages of labor by the time the paramedics arrived."

I wanted nothing more in that moment than to pull Bethy into my arms, kiss her senseless, and eat her out on the golden tile floor until she cried for mercy.

Unfortunately, Alex and Miles were teleporting in to meet with us in the next twenty minutes.

CHAPTER 34

Raul

IT WASN'T THE FURY IN HER GLOWING GREEN EYES THAT knocked the wind out of me, robbing me of my rehearsed tirade. I was used to that look from my sister, and it hadn't been that long since our last confrontation over half a year ago. I'd long lived to rile Miles up, and in truth, I preferred her green wolf eyes. I looked forward to seeing them the same way that I looked forward to provoking disapproving Aunt Cely faces from her.

What was throwing me so far off balance now that my throat tightened and my eyes burned as I stood facing her alone in the large receiving room was the way that her skin was glowing and how much her cheeks had filled out since the last time I'd seen her.

And the way her normally flat stomach was now distended.

She really was pregnant. It'd been crushing enough to hear the news from Bethany's mom, but seeing it was something else entirely.

Painful as it was to look at her, I couldn't stop myself from staring. Nor did I bother to mask my horror at the uncanny, unwelcome resemblance she bore to some of the last memories I had of my mother. It was like staring down my darkest nightmare.

Miles was twenty-eight now—the same age Mom had been when she'd been pregnant with her. *The same age Mom had been when she'd died giving birth to her.*

Aunt Cely had once asked me if I resented her because she looked so much like my mother. It was a fair assumption since Cely was Mom's twin sister. But I'd had eight years with them both prior to Mom's passing. Aunt Cely would always look like Aunt Cely to me. Even in my earliest childhood memories, Mom and Cely hadn't looked that much alike, and I'd never understood how people could confuse them.

My reasons for resenting my Aunt Cely ran far deeper than the shallow emotions she'd preferred to assume about me. And yet, she hadn't been so far off the mark. Because the miniature version of Mom running around our house was the one I had often resented growing up: the kid sister who had followed after me everywhere—looking up at me with Mom's bright blue eyes like I hung the moon and stars. *(As Cely would've put it.)*

She wasn't looking at me that way now, though. Hadn't in years.

I'd alternately loved and hated my little sister for her ability to make Mom's faces. It was always better when she made Aunt Cely's faces. Better still when the fiery green eyes of her wolf replaced Mom's loving blue ones altogether, as they had now.

I saw my sister's mouth moving, but her words didn't register. It wasn't until I was halfway across the room flat on my back that it occurred to me I should try to defend myself.

It felt like a boulder had been hurtled at me, knocking the breath from my lungs and causing my vision to go black as pain radiated all along my right side.

"What the hell is it you want from me, Raul?" she hissed down at me.

Dang. She moved quickly for someone who couldn't teleport.

I braced myself for the next blow. But as I did, it occurred to me the worst blow had already been dealt, and I'd survived it. Bethany had remembered everything—and she'd forgiven me. *Bethy loved me.* And I was riding so high on that victory, there wasn't a whole lot else I could be bothered to give a fuck about right now. Not even the fact that I was about to get my ass handed to me by the spitting image of my late mother.

"When will you stop?" Miles demanded from above me. "When will it be enough to satisfy whatever you're so angry at me for? When you've harmed every single person I love? How many more times can you betray my trust?"

My little sister smelled pissed—royally so. Like the rising swell of a storm that was long overdue, the pungent scent of ozone hit my nostrils, and a mounting electrical charge pulsed through the air: a warning of what was to come.

She wouldn't actually throw a blast that could kill me, though—if for no other reason than the fact that I was mated to Bethany now. *Ironic.* Since it was also the reason she'd come to kick my ass.

I cracked one eye open, my gaze meeting Miles's spitfire green eyes above, and I tsked. "Classic Miles. So typical of you to assume this is all about you."

"Like hell it's *not!* Bethy is *my* best friend, Raul. From the time I was four she and I have been—what the fuck is so funny?"

I'd started cracking up at her possessive "*my* best friend" declaration for some reason, and I couldn't stop. When I didn't answer her, and I proceeded to dissolve into great body-quaking guffaws on the marble floor, she did strike me with lightning.

It only made the whole thing funnier somehow, further escalating the crumpled state of hilarity I was swimming in as I told her in between fits of laughter, "Do your worst, little sis."

She blasted me multiple times, doing more damage to the marble floor, walls, and furniture than she did me. *Just as well—Bethy hated everything about how Gabe and Nuriel had decorated the place.*

Eventually, though, beneath the smell of my sister's self-made storm and of her trademark self-righteous fury and indignation, I began to scent her frustration. Her disappointment. *Her hurt.*

And I stopped laughing. Because this situation between us had never been funny. Despite all the bad blood in our recent history, she was still my sister.

The blasts stopped.

I heaved a sigh and waited, my arm flung over my face on the floor.

Her breathing had gone ragged. I smelled the salt of fresh tears in the air.

"Why, Raul? What did I ever do to you to make you resent me so much?"

Nothing. Absolutely nothing. *And everything.*

"You didn't … you didn't do anything, Miles. I don't—"

"I deserve an answer, Raul! Without the layer of

bullshit. What did I do to make you hate me the way you do?"

There was no earth-shatteringly brilliant answer to that question. So I gave her the only truth I had: "Loving you got too complicated."

Too hard.

Too painful.

It was a truth I'd come to grips with long ago. I'd lost a part of myself the day I'd realized it—the day I'd made the choice to go against every single longstanding marching order of Mateus and Cely once and for all. But I'd also recovered myself that day.

I sat up to face Mom's blue eyes set in an Aunt Cely expression. I didn't bother getting up off the ground. What would be the point? She was likely to blast me many more times before this conversation was through.

"I've never hated you, Miles. I just … gave up on loving you." As I said it, I realized for the first time how much worse that truth was.

"Loving you required too many concessions. Too many sacrifices, and far too many fucking lies." Lies I'd never been able to stomach, and over time, could no longer force myself to swallow.

"Loving you came with too many rules and boundaries that I never got to set. And it came with sacrificing myself—suppressing who and what I was." I felt the old rage and resentment I reserved for Mateus alone rearing its ugly head in me.

"And for what, Miles? So we could be apart? So you could stay hidden? So that our lives could be ruled by fear? So that I could spend my life as an indentured servant to the Reinoso pack? So that the Salvatella assholes who'd slaughtered our ancestors could continue to subjugate us?

"What the fuck kind of life would that have been? It's too high a price to pay for safety if you have to keep your nose down, your dreams dead, and look over your shoulder forevermore. That's not living."

"They were trying to protect us—"

"They were wrong." I got to my feet. "More importantly, *none* of the things that Mateus and Cely set in motion for us were things Mom would've wanted."

"What about what I wanted? You lied to me, Raul. You made choices for me—completely reckless decisions on my behalf that put my very life at risk without even once thinking to ask!"

"I know. I *know* I made choices for you. I know I wasn't completely honest with you."

"Completely?"

"Miles, our whole childhood together—the entire foundation of our relationship—was one fat lie on top of another. From the day you were born, I was made to lie to you, to lie about you, to lie about myself and our family."

"And you could've stopped lying to me at any time after both Aunt Cely and Mateus were gone."

She was right. I could have. There'd been limitations placed on me at the time as a newly transitioned werelock that had made communicating honestly with Miles difficult to nearly impossible at times—between Maribel in my head helping me and Gabe constantly up my business trying to mind-rape my thoughts and emotions. But in hindsight, I could've approached things differently with my sister. *I could've at least tried.*

"You're right," I admitted. "I'm sorry." I focused on her

hands that had settled over her pregnant belly, noticing for the first time how much they also resembled Mom's. "I guess I didn't see that I was doing to you the same thing Mateus and Cely did to us—pressing forward with whatever I thought was best, without consulting you."

A heavy sigh left her. "Thank you for acknowledging that."

The silence that stretched between us felt like an ocean we'd never bridge; a past we'd never reconcile.

Miles turned away from me, and for a moment, I thought she intended to leave. But then she crossed to an oversized white leather wingback chair and sank into it, facing me.

"Tell me, Raul, why did you hate"—she stopped short, and with a swallow of acceptance, offered the first concession—"our Aunt Cely so much?"

Coming from Miles, this was a major olive branch—despite the true identity of the woman she knew as her mother being a foregone conclusion and an indisputable fact we both knew I would never let her deny.

Miles had learned soon after Aunt Cely's death that the woman who had raised her was in fact her aunt and not her mother, and yet she'd stubbornly insisted upon continuing to refer to Aunt Cely as our mother to everyone. *Including me.* She'd even had the gall to get pissy with me every time I'd insistently—*correctly*—referred to her as Aunt Cely.

While I could see that from her perspective, Aunt Cely would always be her mother, Miles's staunch, misplaced loyalty to Aunt Cely was to me a dishonor to her real mother's memory, and to the ultimate sacrifice Mom had made for her.

"I didn't hate Aunt Cely." But I'd sure resented the fuck

out of her for most of my life. Maybe not as much as I had Mateus, but it was always a close tie between those two.

Where to start?

"It bothered me that Aunt Cely talked tough but ultimately always caved and went along with Mateus's wishes for us. And yeah, I resented her for making me call her Mom and for forcing me to lie to you and to everyone else about who we were as a family."

"Mateus never gave anyone a choice, Raul. Bulldozing was his specialty. You of all people should know."

I held my hand up. "You asked, Miles. Let me finish. It bothered me that Cely never understood Mom—her own twin. I get that Cely was insecure and couldn't let go of her jealousy over Mom being the favored twin who she felt that the world had handed everything to. But I saw how she tainted your view of Mom with the stories she told you of her: of the tragically deceased twin sister of hers who you were raised to know of only as your late Aunt Kamella— the flighty fuck-up twin who made all the wrong choices in life and couldn't be saved from herself." *Essentially, the female version of me in Cely's mind.*

"That's not true," she denied.

"It is, and you know it." I walked over and sat on the edge of the marble coffee table in front of Miles's chair. "I get that Cely was bitter that she'd been born barren and then was left holding the bag raising her twin's two kids— one of whom gave her grief and discipline issues at every turn. I can understand her wanting to sway your loyalty and affection, knowing that she would never have mine. But she judged Mom too harshly, blamed her too readily.

"I know it couldn't have been easy for Cely, and that she probably did her best. But I hated how she did everything in her power to preach and instill in you the exact opposite of everything Mom stood for—the opposite of everything Mom would've wanted for you. She parented us through fear, the same way Mateus did."

Miles made a noise that was somewhere between a groan and a huff as she closed her eyes and rubbed her temple. "Look around you, Raul. How can you continue to blame Aunt Cely for wanting to protect us from this world? For trying to instill a level of caution and pragmatism in us that clearly didn't exist for her twin sister, given the choices Mom made in her relationship with Mateus?"

"Because I knew them both, Miles!" It came out harsh, and I shook my head at the ceiling. "I didn't mean it like it was your fault. Just that I'm sorry you never knew Mom. And it frustrates me that the version of Mom Aunt Cely raised you to know of was so one-sided. So negative." I leaned forward, resting my elbows on my knees as I looked at Miles and confessed, "You look exactly like Mom, by the way. Especially now."

Funny thing was, as I stared into her blue eyes and said it, I saw more Aunt Cely there than ever before.

"Mom loved with all her heart. She was full of passion and light. She believed in miracles. She didn't believe in lies. And she didn't believe in bowing to fear. She always said that lies divided people, that fear was the only thing that could destroy a life. I did what Mom would've wanted for us, Miles."

She'd begun shaking her head at me. I knew she was closing off, but I pressed forward nonetheless as I said, "I brought us out of hiding. I claimed the blood inheritance that was rightfully ours. You can shake your head and disagree with me on this until your dying days, Miles, but *I.*

Fucking. Freed us. And you'll never understand what that really means—because before I did what I did, you only knew the lie. You weren't the one forced to dishonor your mom's memory and lie to your little sister. You weren't the one shipped off to Brazil your senior year, forced to give up all your dreams to go be some werelock pack's lowly whipping boy."

I straightened my back and stood, resigned that she was never going to see my side in this as I crossed to the enormous leopard-print leather couch she'd marred with a lightning blast earlier and plopped down on it. This conversation was a lost cause. I had to focus on Bethy.

"I can't take back what I did," I said with a heavy exhale. "I am sorry I lied to you and hurt you. But none of that has anything to do with the way I feel about Bethany or my mate connection to her. I don't want her to feel punished for the bad blood between us. It's bound to be a tough transition for her—being thrust into our world—and I'd like to make it as gentle as possible."

"Wow." Miles's hand lifted from her belly and fell to her knee with a smack. "This from the man who bit Bethy ten times, almost killed her fiancé in front of her, drugged and kidnapped her, brought her here to the ultimate palace of evil, and let the *Rogue* set her on fire the other day."

Typical Miles to only keep a running tab of the negative stuff.

She continued, "I'll sure do my best not to 'punish her' for our bad blood, so that you may proceed with your *gentle* transition plan."

"Thank you. Glad to hear that. Because I didn't appreciate the way you punished her for choosing to have her memories of our world erased."

"Excuse me?"

"Gregg," I spat. "How could you not tell her about him when you knew?"

She shook her head, her eyes narrowing. "Raul, I've never liked Gregg any more than you do, but there's no way I would have known about his cheating if Alex hadn't been reading his mind. More importantly, you can't just fix things for people when they haven't asked you to—*pressing forward with whatever you think is best.*" She repeated my words back to me. "I guess if it were up to you, you would have just killed Gregg without consulting her, or maybe erased his mind of her memory and shipped him off to Siberia."

I shifted uncomfortably in my seat. She had a point—although erasing his mind and teleporting him to an Amazonian jungle was closer to my style.

"Raul, you told me once that you and I were simply victims of shitty circumstance. You were right. As children, we were. But we're not victims of circumstance now. Our relationship today is the result of the choices you and I have both made as adults. We can't blame Mateus or Aunt Cely anymore. From here on out, we both need to take responsibility for the choices we make. For the sides we choose."

I had to stop my eyes from rolling out of reflex. *Here it comes.*

"I'll never side with Maribel, Raul. I'll never endorse a world where she is allowed to reign as the *Rogue.*"

"She isn't Maribel anymore. She's Sloane."

"She is the *same soul.* I know you and Alcaeus see her as a new being deserving of a second chance—a cute little girl trying her best not to succumb to the living embodiment of the bloodthirsty dark spirits within her. But it doesn't matter what you or Alcaeus or anyone else who's been charmed by her thinks." Her eyes flashed green. "I know. *I* lived with the black heart of Joaquin's blood curse before Maribel came along from the ether—murdering Lupe, Kaleb, and countless other innocents in order to rip it from me.

"*I* was the one who lived with those voices. I have felt their wrath and tasted their thirst for revenge. As twisted, dark, and crazy as Maribel was, she never meant to be reborn as an altered being attached to that black curse. Because even *she* knew she couldn't handle it, Raul! She told us both as much. And wishing and hoping and believing in miracles won't change what we're up against with this."

We'd circled the battleground and arrived at the anticipated impasse. Mike was tapping my mind, and Bethany had been left with Alex under minimal supervision too long for my comfort. I needed to get back to my mate.

"*We're* not up against anything, Miles," I told her flatly as I got to my feet. "Because this isn't your problem anymore. It's *Sloane's*," I reminded her through gritted teeth. "And whether you want to admit it or not, she did you a favor by taking the faulty heart of the curse off your hands."

She opened her mouth to protest, but I cut her off.

"You scoff at believing in miracles. So tell me, Sis, what great *logic* makes you think that killing Maribel as Sloane will yield any different result than it did the last time Maribel died? You really think it'll solve anything? That somehow the blood curse will magically go away this time and not return?

"Don't you get it? If Maribel wasn't powerful enough to drag it to the other side and keep it there, then *no one can.* Sloane isn't the problem. She's our only answer."

CHAPTER 35

Bethany

"**Y**OU'RE HAVING A BOY. JUST ADMIT IT." I'D BEEN DYING to know the sex of Milena and Alex's baby for months now, but they'd been tight-lipped about it. "I can totally tell from the way you're carrying and how much your skin is glowing."

The smile that broke out on my best friend's face put every single chandelier and candelabrum in the ostentatious receiving room we were in to shame. "Yes," Milena admitted at last. "I am."

I started bouncing up and down on the balls of my feet, clapping my hands and squealing with irrepressible glee. It felt like we were teenagers back in high school again when Milena's cheeks grew pink and she started cracking up and rolling her eyes at me.

Growing up, Milena had always been super-shy, easily embarrassed, and often overwhelmed by her emotions—which ran deep and flowed close to the surface. She blushed at least ninety-seven times a day, and her tear ducts operated on a hair trigger. *No joke*—I'd seen her blush from the look a cat had given her once, and cry at the sight of Fiji bottled water.

"I am shopping for adorable, preppy little boy outfits *immediately*, and there's absolutely no supernatural force in the universe that can stop me," I announced, taking her by the hand and leading her over to a perfectly hideous-looking diamond-encrusted red settee.

"How do you know he'll be the preppy type?" she asked as we sat down next to one another on the gaudy monstrosity.

"Duh! He's Alex's son. And you are going to need so much help with him, because he's destined to be off-the-charts adorable."

"I know," she agreed—grinning, blushing, and getting teary-eyed all at once in the next blink. But then her expression sobered and her smile slipped. "Are you sure you're okay with everything?" When I nodded, she added, "Being with Raul—you're sure that's what you really want?"

"Positive. Don't worry about me. Everything's going to be fine."

Her emotive blue eyes said she didn't believe it. "Bethy, this place"—she glanced around the room—"gives me the willies."

"Oh, trust me, I'm planning to redecorate the whole estate."

"Well, that'd be a good start." The smile she gave me looked more like a wince. "But I was referring more to the energy of the place."

I nodded. "I know, Milena. I feel it, too. But it's not all coming from the Salvatella pack. There's a Loch Ness Monster living in the lake and the hills are alive with Nazis, *so*"—I shrugged—"I'll probably have to burn a lot of sage around here for a while."

In truth, I was pretty sure the Salvatella estate had been

built over a Hellmouth like the one in Sunnydale on *Buffy the Vampire Slayer.*

"Bethy, it's just … the whole Salvatella pack. They're kind of a motley crew with a really disturbing history of violence. I don't trust them."

That made two of us. "You don't trust Raul either. Do you?"

She barely hesitated before shaking her head. "Don't misunderstand me, I think my brother's heart is in the right place where you're concerned. I think his intentions are in the right place where Sloane is concerned, too. I just worry he's in over his head. I guess what I'm saying is I don't always trust Raul to make the right decisions for himself. And now I worry that his decisions might put you in danger, too."

"I'll be okay, here. Really. They're not all bad guys." In my head, I counted Wyatt and Tiago.

She lowered her voice a fraction as she asked, "And you've met Michael Salvatella?"

"You mean Mike?" I'd never actually caught my *step-cuz's* full name before, but it made sense that it could be Salvatella. Mike had told me on the plane that his mom and Gabe Salvatella had been first cousins. And Raul had said something in passing about how he and Mike had initially bonded over their shared experience of having single moms who they had lost early in their childhoods. Growing up, Raul had always gone by his mom's surname, too, rather than his estranged father.

She nodded slightly, her eyes reflecting concern. "Be cautious of him, okay? He's more powerful than he seems."

Her anxiety was starting to make me nervous. "Milena, really." I gave her arm a playful punch. "I got this. I mean

I may not be a badass Alpha and Goddess of Thunder like you are, but you know that in a pinch I can still throw down and cut a bitch." *Sorta-maybe—even though I had never.*

"I don't doubt that," she professed with a smile. "But promise me one thing?"

"Uh-uh," I denied her with an exaggerated groan, trying to keep things light. "If it involves poopy baby diapers, the answer is no. That's Alex's job."

"Bethany, I'm serious." She giggled. "Please promise me that if things change—if it ever gets weird for you here—that you'll consider talking to Raul about the two of you joining the Reinoso pack. I want you to know that you and Raul are *always* welcome with us."

"I appreciate it," I told her. "Believe me, I would love it if we could all be part of the same pack one day." But that wasn't likely to happen anytime soon, given what Raul had told me about Milena's rigid position where Sloane was concerned. The fact that Alcaeus had left his own family's pack over their ardent position against Sloane was as strong an indication as any as to how divisive the *Rogue* issue really was.

And as Rafe had said, this was only the beginning.

I decided to steer the conversation away from the conflict between Milena and Raul and their respective packs. As Raul's mate and Milena's best friend, I knew I was destined to feel caught in the middle between them forevermore, of course, but I was going to do my damnedest to keep the triangulation dysfunction to a minimum.

"Milena, I owe you an apology for the way that I abandoned you ten years ago when you needed me most. You know—choosing to have my memories erased after the crazy fallout in the Reinoso dining hall. I was just so shell-shocked and confused about everything." Including my feelings for Raul at the time and what to do with them. "But looking back, I feel like the worst friend ever for leaving you to deal with everything all on your own."

"Stop." Milena made a dismissive hand gesture and dabbed at her teary eyes. "Give yourself a break. You witnessed a machete skewer my heart and saw a guy catch fire from the inside and melt like a candle. And that was all *before* Alcaeus's mad killing spree. You were traumatized—rightfully so."

My eyes misted, and I went in for a hug as she said, "You made the right choice in opting to forget that whole awful episode." Her slender arms squeezed around my shoulders. "Besides, it was always safer for you not to know about our world."

She pulled back to face me. "If I'm honest, Bethy, there've been times when I've been jealous that you were able to forget all of this. That you were able to go back to your blissfully werewolf-ignorant life, attend college, and do normal late-teen and early-twenties stuff that I knew I'd never get to do." Her smile was sad. Apologetic. "I guess it was hard at times not to resent you a little for that. But I always understood it. And I'm sure that had our roles been reversed, and I'd been the one in your shoes, I'd have chosen to forget about werewolves and werelocks, too."

I sniffled and bit back a smile as I looked at her, seeing for the first time how much she'd changed. Also, how much my best friend was still the same.

"You're still the worst liar ever," I told her. "Never in a million years will I be convinced that you would have chickened out and done the same—that you'd have asked to have your memories erased. But it's sweet of you to say that to make me feel better."

"No, I mean it, Bethy. I do understand. And *I* want to apologize for distancing myself from you these past ten years. I didn't do it out of retaliation or to hurt you. It's just that there were so many things I couldn't talk to you about. So many secrets I had to keep from you. It just became impossibly complicated to remain close to you when there were so many lies and I—" She stopped short, her forehead crumpling.

"What's wrong? Oh, is there someone talking in your head right now?"

"What?" She looked troubled as her suddenly glassy eyes refocused on me. "In my head? *Oh.* No," she said with a chuckle as tears spilled down her cheeks. She wiped them away and mumbled something about pregnancy hormones making her cry more than usual. "You know I'm not much of a crier."

I stifled a laugh and nodded good-naturedly. People who cried the most never thought they were criers.

"I was just saying, I'm sorry, Bethany. I guess I never realized how the lies between us could divide us—how they would complicate our friendship." Her smile was uneasy.

"Milena, it's okay." I reached out and squeezed her hand. "C'mon, you know I've never been one to hold a grudge. And I understand where you were coming from. So … can we move on now to talking about baby clothes, nursery décor, and how werelocks give birth?"

"Yes," she agreed, her expression brightening. Then her nose wrinkled. "But we should probably go check on Alex and Raul first."

When Milena and I joined Raul and Alex in the study, we were pleasantly surprised to find they hadn't torn one another apart—at least not physically. The conversation of the room quickly turned to my impending transformation, and Milena suggested to Raul that she should be the one to guide my initial shift tomorrow. She had proposed as much to me in passing when we'd chatted separately.

Within seconds, she and Raul were arguing. Alex and I shared a knowing look.

While Raul and Milena had been talking earlier, Alex had educated me about the initial transformation process. He'd also explained to me that even though I'd been bitten by a werelock, Raul's bite would only turn me into a common werewolf.

Werelocks were born from other werelocks—or rather, at least one birth parent had to possess werelock DNA in order to pass it to their offspring. However, there were a few known exceptions, such as Raul and Milena inheriting werelock power through a revenge blood curse that a former Salvatella Alpha named Joaquin had created a century and a half ago, and Avery gaining her werelock status through Sloane sucking the werelock power—and life— from Gabe and transferring it to Avery.

The latter was *highly* irregular, and had caused Sloane to be greatly feared throughout the werelock world, according to Alex. Sloane was also her own anomaly in that neither of her birth parents had been werelocks at the time of her conception. In her case, as the prophesied *Rogue,* she'd apparently carried her massive power into this world with her at birth.

But aside from those rare deviations, if a werelock mated with a common werewolf—or with a human who was subsequently turned—the werelock in the pair could share power with his or her mate in order to provide the mate additional protection. However, the mate on the receiving end would never become an actual werelock.

This explained Mike's cryptic comment on the plane about me changing things, and Avery's expressed concern that I might jeopardize Raul's newly gained status as Alpha—and in doing so disrupt the fragile stability the Salvatella pack had only recently attained. It explained why I'd sensed the guys on the plane regarding me as a threat.

I *was* a threat in that I was bound to weaken Raul as a werelock as a result of him sharing his powers with me. But Alex maintained that there was no alternative, because neither was it an option for Raul *not* to share his powers with me. Doing so would only put us both at greater risk.

"I've given this a lot of thought," I said, interrupting the bickering between Raul and Milena. "And I've decided that I don't want either one of you controlling my shift tomorrow."

Raul and Milena both frowned as if they couldn't have heard me right.

"Bethany, don't be silly; one of us *has* to control your shift," Milena said. "Trust me, it's for the best."

"Absolutely," Raul chimed in. "We're not letting you shift unassisted, honey. That's never been an option."

"Slow your roll, Alpha," I told him. "I never said I was choosing the blowing-up-from-the-inside-without-anesthesia option. But it's not an option for me to be one more thing for the two of you to fight or resent one another over."

"That's not going to happen here," Milena denied.

Raul muttered a variation of the same.

"Damn straight it's not," I announced. "Because I'm choosing Alex to control my shift."

"What?" Raul balked, delivering a whole-body reaction of abject disgust. "Are—are you kidding?"

Milena looked equally affronted and baffled.

Despite my best efforts, it was impossible not to giggle as I turned to a clearly self-satisfied-looking Alex and asked, "As long as that's okay with you, of course?"

"This is not happening," Raul grumbled next to me, dropping his head in his hands.

"*Me?*" Alex's hand flew to his heart in an exaggerated display of surprise and modesty. We'd already privately discussed it, and he'd agreed to control my shift. "Why, Bethy, of course. I'd be honored to assist you." His eyes flitted from my dumbfounded mate to his, taking delight in their reactions, before focusing on me again. "You've always been like a little sister to me."

Raul groaned. "I'm gonna fucking puke."

Once the pouting over Alex guiding my initial transformation settled down, Milena revealed *(tattled)* that Raul had recently poisoned an innocent college student named Lauren Novak—the purported seer that the guys had been talking about on the plane—in order to coerce the Reinosos into lifting my mind shield. Milena also relayed that fortunately, Mike and Rafe had delivered an antidote as soon as my shield was down, and that Lauren had recovered fine.

Honest to goodness, I almost smacked Raul on the back of his head out of reflex, as I demanded, "Why on earth didn't you just call your sister?" These two were going to make me crazy.

"Right?" Alex provoked. "I couldn't believe he was willing to resort to such unnecessary violence like that."

"Oh, of all the fucking—" Raul's exasperated outcry was cut short by Milena's much louder one as she laid into her husband for apparently responding to Raul's threat by telling him to go ahead and kill the seer.

It would take a long time—if ever—for me to wrap my head around the level of violence with which my new werewolf world operated.

The conversation then turned to the subject of the Reinoso pack's head doctor, Kai, and his outrage over Raul's poisoning of Lauren. Now that I had my memories back, I recalled meeting Kai briefly in passing ten years ago. Apparently, he had been involved with Lauren recently in what I gathered was a romantic sense. But the exact nature of their relationship and the manner in which Kai had been engaging with the seer seemed to be an uncomfortable matter for Milena to reconcile, because she immediately shut both Raul and Alex down when they tried to tattle to me about the details.

"He has not been himself lately," she stubbornly maintained in the doctor's defense. To me, she said, "We've stationed Kai in Nepal for the time being, and I've forbidden him from contacting Lauren in any way for now—at least not until I can figure out what's been going on with him."

"Yeah," Alex chimed in. "He's also dead set on killing Raul right now, by the way. So Milena put an order on Kai forbidding him from retaliating against her brother." He shook his head at Raul and lamented, "I was rather looking forward to seeing that fight."

The hour was late by the time Milena and Alex departed. It was agreed that they would be back tomorrow so that Alex could control my shift, and so that Milena might have a word with Alcaeus—if he was willing to speak with her.

"God, I thought they'd never leave," Raul complained once they had teleported out. "Now then, where were we?"

I flattened my palms against his chest, holding him off when he pressed himself closer. "I believe I was about to lay into you for poisoning an innocent college student."

"Oh, right." He had the good sense to look contrite. "About that …"

"Was that really necessary?"

"Apparently not, since you managed to unblock yourself—with the help of Alcaeus's traumatizing presence triggering you, that is. But at the time, yes, I did think it was necessary to use the seer as a bargaining chip."

"Her name is Lauren. She's a person first and foremost, possibly a seer second, and never again a bargaining chip, do you understand? Just like Sloane is a child and a person first, not simply the *Rogue*."

"Yes, dear." He hugged me closer, one hand sliding from my waist to my ass. "You're absolutely right."

"It's not sexy when you patronize me, Raul."

He sucked my earlobe between his teeth. "What if we're both naked when I'm doing it?" My clothes vanished. His did too. "Does that help?"

I sighed and held back a giggle. "That's even worse."

"Really?" He kissed the mark on my neck. I felt his smile there. "I'll make it better." His tongue licked over my love-bite scar. "Promise."

"All you think about is sex," I protested. *Weakly.*

"Yes, but you love how badly I want you." He squeezed my naked ass, his fingers dipping lower between the cleft to the juncture of my thighs where I was already wet.

He wasn't wrong. I didn't hate it.

"I need to be inside you, Bethy," he stated like it was his right—and a physiological imperative.

"Here? In the study?" I pretended to object as he growled and raised me off the ground. "But what if someone walks in on us?"

My legs locked around his waist as he fitted himself at my entrance. His lips curved into a smile as they brushed mine. "Don't worry, love. If that happens, I won't stop."

EPILOGUE

Bethany

KITSUNE TUCKED TAIL AND RAN THE MOMENT I SHIFTED. I didn't like the idea of scaring the pup, but at the same time, his reaction was mildly gratifying. At this point, Kitsune was probably the only member of the Salvatella pack who was intimidated by me in my wolf form.

Overall, my transformation into a scary Halloween monster a week ago hadn't been as awful as I'd feared. I mean sure, technically I turned into a big hairy dog now— typically several times a day. But all things considered, I think I kinda rocked the whole killer werewolf look. My fur was a light sandy-brown shade in my wolf form, and my eyes were amber-gold.

Raul repeatedly assured me that I was a sexy bitch— both in my human and in my animal form.

He had shared a portion of his werelock powers with me a few days after my initial transition. It was decided beforehand that Mike would be prepared to step in and take over as Alpha should Raul's powers weaken significantly. But to everyone's surprise and relief, Raul's powers didn't diminish at all after sharing what he had with me.

Rafe attributed the phenomenon to Sloane. I didn't quite follow how he'd arrived at that correlation, but I was thankful for whatever had caused it.

It seemed that others shared Rafe's theory, however, because as word spread that Raul was still Alpha of the Salvatella pack even after being mated to a common werewolf, it spawned a bit more fear and suspicion within the werelock world about Sloane—the *Rogue* werelock and embodiment of a dark curse—who had previously demonstrated the ability to seize and redistribute power at whim when she'd pulled powers from Gabe to give to Avery.

"Okay, that was good," Raul coached me. "But try doing it a little faster next time."

He had teleported Sloane, Kitsune, and me to Big Basin. It was early morning, and we'd stopped at a secluded spot along the trail so that I could practice my shifting.

I'd felt a little self-conscious practicing it at the Bariloche compound where so many experienced werelocks and werewolves could see me. So Raul had suggested I might be more comfortable doing it here, on my home turf in NoCal, until I gained more confidence with the process.

Sloane, who herself had never even shifted before, kept dropping quiet, stoic commentary about how I needed to be faster at it, more graceful. She kept mumbling to herself about how she could do it so much better than I could.

But despite her criticism, she seemed to be warming up to me—at least a little bit, I thought. Possibly she was simply resigned to tolerating me, though, since Mike and Rafe had straight-out told her that my death would trigger Raul's death now. Basically, they'd explained to her that she couldn't kill me without losing her favorite manny in the process.

I'd just shifted for the tenth time in a row, and Raul was giving me pointers inside my head, when suddenly he stopped talking mid-critique, his words in my mind trailing off with a quiet, *"Ah, shit."*

I turned my muzzle in the direction of Raul's troubled gaze and spied a tall, well-muscled, naked man standing thirty feet away from us up the trail. His hair was brown—although it was tough to say whether that was simply from all the mud that was caked in it. His body was smudged and streaked with mud as well, and he had leaf litter sticking to him in random places.

He looked familiar, but I couldn't place where I'd seen him before. At first glance, he reminded me of the British male supermodel, David Gandy—*if Gandy had been a dirty, feral-looking homeless man flashing people on nature trails.* And also a werelock.

The werelock's eyes, which glowed a cold, killer-blue shade, were pinned squarely on my mate, when suddenly it hit me where I'd seen him before.

"Isn't that the Reinoso pack doctor? Kai?" I telepathically asked Raul, who was still inside my head.

"Stay with Sloane," Raul ordered inside my mind, just as the homeless-looking David Gandy doppelganger burst into a giant white wolf.

THE END
(Until sexy werelocks throw down again in Seer.)

SEER

A Werelock Evolution Series Duet

I gave him my best resting bitch face, wondering how much longer I should humor this humiliation before getting up to find Abbie.

Annnd … more awkward silence.

"What's your major?" he finally shouted across the small table at me.

"Sociology," I shouted back. This earned me another frown. "What?"

He shook his head, mouthing what looked like, "Nothing." Then he glanced away, drumming his fingers against the tabletop. He seemed disappointed. Or … annoyed.

"What?" I repeated, eliciting a shrug as he returned his attention to me.

"That's a fairly worthless major, don't you think?" he announced in a voice loud enough to carry.

Assuming he was razzing me, I busted out laughing. Until I realized that he wasn't smiling or laughing along with me—he was serious. *Seriously insulting my choice of a major.* My expression straightened along with my spine.

Superiority complex. *Check.* Douchebag. *Check.*

"What was your major?" I countered. "Back in the olden days when you went to school?"

"Medicine," he answered, stone-faced. "I'm a physician."

Hot as hell. *Check.* No sense of humor. *Triple check. And fail.*

"Well, congratulations to you," I said, saluting him with my shot glass, "on your worthy choice of major and profession." Upon downing the cheap liquid courage, I set the empty glass onto the table, smiled, and slowly, very sensuously licked my lips. "So nice to have met you. *Doctor.*"

I dropped the word "doctor" like I was saying "asshole." I could only hope his humor-impaired intelligence was superior enough to catch the distinction.

I'd already sashayed my heart-shaped hiney halfway back to the bar in search of Abbie when I felt someone take hold of my elbow and steer me in a different direction. I didn't have to look to know that it was him—my hot campus stalker-slash-doctor who thought I had a dumb major.

"Dude, what is your problem?" I grumbled, allowing him to guide me through the throng of dancing bodies toward the rear of the crowded club.

He couldn't have heard me anyway, it was so damned noisy, so I proceeded to bitch aloud for my own gratification, "You're the one with less than zero social skills who's been following me around, spying from the shadows and leering at me like some hot, older James Bond on a foreign affairs mission to fuck my brains out. Well, trust me, Dr. I'm-too-good-for-the-dumb-college-girl-I'm-stalking, you could stand to take a course or two in the social sciences."

Bond barked something at the two bouncers blocking the rear exit as we approached, and oddly, they stepped aside. "Close the door and allow no one to come out this way after us, understand?" Dr. Bossypants further decreed as he led me through the back door and into the dark alley behind the club.

"My problem"—he rounded on me once the metal back door had shut with a heavy thud, silencing the noise of the club—"is that you insist upon wearing clothing that is too short and too tight."

"Oh … Em … Gee." I jerked my elbow from his grasp. "You did *not* just say that to me."

"My problem," he continued, stepping right up into my personal space, "is that your ass in that pencil skirt makes me want to drop to my knees and thank God for finally creating a perfection worth sinking my teeth into."

Uh … *wha—?*

I backed up a step, reclaiming my personal space and praying that my eroding equilibrium would follow suit. He stepped closer, stealing it right back.

"My problem is that just looking at your face gets me hard. So hard I'm afraid I'll come in my pants like a horny teenager if I stare for too long."

Oh.

Wow.

"My problem," he told me in a matter-of-fact tone of voice as he proceeded to back me up into the brick wall of the building we'd just exited, "is that none of this should even be happening. I never should've noticed you or your luscious round ass and angel face and perfectly formed tits"—he slammed his fist against the brick wall behind me—"with the perfectly diabolical nipples that are constantly, *constantly* fucking hard, in the first place."

"Did you just call my nipples … diabolical?" I asked in a strange, breathy voice that came out as sultry as the molten inferno his words had ignited in my sex.

"Yes." He reached for the buckle of his pants.

My eyes tracked the movement and saw that he was so not kidding about the "hard" part of his rant. No part of him was touching me, but he was standing so close, I swore

I could feel the heat emanating off of that big cock—warming the butterflies scattering in my lower belly through the fabric of my high-waisted skirt.

"My problem … is that I'm about to fuck you in a dirty alley, unless you set a clear boundary right now and tell me to stop."

My clit began throbbing so rapidly at his ultimatum that I was certain had there been more light in the alleyway, its fluttering would've actually been visible against the front of my tight skirt.

"Fuck no, I am not stopping this!" I blurted.

I saw his eyes momentarily widen and his lips part in the dim light of the alley.

"Fine, then. But understand that I am not calling you tomorrow," he warned, abandoning his belt to reach for the hem of my skirt.

"Damn straight you aren't." I gasped as he pulled the hem of my skirt clear to my waist and simultaneously spun me around to face the brick wall. "Because I'm not giving you my number."

I yelped when his palm connected sharply with my now-exposed thong-clad ass. "Brat. You would give me your number, and you know it," he scolded in my ear, squeezing my smarting ass cheek in his hand.

I meant to groan an "Oww," but somehow it came out as "Ohh" instead. This seemed to irritate him further, because it earned my other cheek a smack.

"Cut it out or I'm gonna come in this alley before you even get that hulking cock of yours inside me," I complained.

That did it.

My panties were shredded straight off of me, and his

hands were suddenly groping me everywhere at once, so fast it made my already-dizzy-with-lust head spin. I made a noise that sounded something like a cat getting strangled when both of his hands attacked my soaking core—his fingers scrambling to penetrate me like they were starving to get inside.

"You're going to feel me for days," he threatened, pressing his naked, hard length up against my ass as he thrust several fingers inside me.

"Bring it," I managed to rasp.

AVAILABLE NOW

THANK YOU, dear readers!

Thank you for reading *Just Like Animals (Werelock Evolution, Book 5)*. If you enjoyed reading this story, I hope that you will consider leaving a few words in a review to help other readers discover it. Every review is very much appreciated.

If you'd like to check out other books that I've written, please feel free to visit my website at www.hettieivers.com, sign up for my Newsletter, friend me on Facebook, or join my Facebook Reader Group to keep in touch.

Warmest Regards,
Hettie

ACKNOWLEDGEMENTS

To my awesome professional editor big sis, thank you for taking time out from reviewing and editing critical life-saving medical publications in order to point out *(with a Jerry Seinfeld inflection),* "Now we need something *here,*" each time it was required this Werelock Evolution installment.

To my amazing husband, thank you for always being so supportive of my writing hobby, for beta-reading chapters on demand, and for making me laugh myself silly with your portrayals of my werelock characters. I will take your recommendation to write a *Vamplock* series under serious consideration.

To my awesome friends Lauren, Sheena, and Erin: Thank you for being early readers/beta testers/bouncers-of-ideas at various points in this process for me. I am so thankful for your honest feedback and your kind encouragement for this story!

Thank you to Lauren for urging me to lose my literary anal cherry with this book. *#RemyInterruptus*

A special thanks to Sheena for tirelessly spreading my name, banners, and covers all over Facebook on a daily basis. I don't know what I did to deserve your support, but you're beyond amazing, and I really appreciate you!

To my longtime SOAM readers and all of the fabulous ladies in my reader group, thank you for your ongoing friendship and support, and for the countless hours of fun, laughter, and fantastic female camaraderie.

Have you read Alex and Milena's enemies-to-lovers tale?
***Werelock Evolution: The Complete Trilogy* is the story that started it all.**

Werelock Evolution: The Complete Trilogy

He's a spoiled Alpha used to getting whatever he wants. She's a stubborn eighteen-year-old determined to disappoint him.

Finding love at first sight with your fated soul mate sounds so romantic. *Unless*, of course, that "mate" happens to be your brother's sworn enemy and the overbearing Alpha werewolf-warlock who has taken you hostage.

Things get complicated in this twisty enemies-to-lovers trilogy about an American girl who stumbles upon forbidding paranormal circumstances when she travels to Brazil and finds herself at the center of a blood feud between rival South American werewolf packs.

The task of taming a formidable, drop-dead sexy werelock has never been so hard. And so hot.

Excerpt from SLIP OF FATE
(Werelock Evolution, Book 1)

I wasn't sure what I'd expected to find when we approached the foyer, but the scene we came upon was far worse than any I could've envisioned.

There were more people gathered in the semi-cylindrical receiving area than before. We entered the open room, and Alessandra deposited me on my feet in time to see Felix suspended by his throat against a wall, his feet dangling at least a foot off the ground, his broken arms hanging uselessly at his sides.

A tall, dark-haired, formidable man in a tuxedo was holding him up by the neck with just one hand. Felix's eyes bugged out in horror and his face went from red to purple to blue while the cruel man, whose face was turned from me, proceeded to mercilessly crush his windpipe.

My first instinct was to scream at the faceless, heartless man to stop and let him go, but the words died in my throat and ice coursed through my veins as he leaned in closer to my dying abductor and rasped, "No deal, Felix. I've no need of Raul's worthless sister. Not as bait, as a trade for your son, or otherwise."

He spoke in a forbidding, deep whisper, presumably meant for Felix's dying ears, yet the words were clearly heard by everyone in the otherwise silent hall as they resonated off the stone walls.

"Raul's dead," he hissed. "I saw to it myself days ago. And thanks to you, his sister will be dead soon, too."

Time and space ceased to exist as I sought to reconcile the meaning of his words. Raul was dead?

"So you've wasted your time," he sneered, "forfeited four lives, and shortened your son's allotted time left by coming here and interrupting my dinner."

He'd died just days ago?

Raul was dead?

I'd never borne witness to much violence in my lifetime, let alone seen a man murdered right before my eyes, and yet I barely registered the visual of Felix's eyes rolling back and becoming lifeless as the final vestiges of his very being were squeezed from him.

I don't know how long I stood stock still, my own eyes wide and glazed over with terror, before the dark-haired devil whom I knew had to be the infamous Alex turned away from his fresh kill to visibly sniff in my direction like some depraved, wild animal honing in on his next unfortunate prey.

As his cold, dark eyes alighted upon me, they widened perceptibly. Felix's dead body was dropped like a sack of trash a millisecond later as the dinner party host I'd so erroneously assumed would be civilized turned his imposing frame in my direction.

He was darkly handsome like Alcaeus, with facial features that more closely resembled Remy's, but with none of the playfulness or boyishness of either of the two men. And his eyes were unlike any of his siblings'. They were a deep, dark shade of brown. His jet-black hair was cropped short, and he was expertly groomed and outfitted as if he'd stepped off the pages of *GQ*.

On the surface, he appeared the perfect male specimen. I was certain many of the girls I'd gone to school with would've fallen all over themselves just to gain a moment of his attention. But beneath his polished veneer, I knew he was just a monster. A brute who had murdered my brother. And never before in my life had I wished more horrific, fatal harm upon another human being as I now fervently hoped to befall him.

As he breathed deeply in and out, audibly inhaling as if to suggest he could actually smell me from across the foyer, he seemed to regard me much like Alessandra first had—as if he was encountering an apparition.

Then his eyes widened further, and I could've sworn the most unfathomable expression of pure elation and inconceivable rapture transformed his confused, horrified features for the briefest of moments.

Strangely, it reminded me of the expression on the face of this lost little boy I'd helped once at the mall—his look upon laying eyes on his mother when they were at last reunited. It was an odd amalgamation of unmitigated joy mixed with relief juxtaposed against the profound terror of realizing one's own supreme vulnerability for the very first time. The face of one who'd just been saved but would never be the same again for that rescue.

Only in this case, the man before me still appeared hopelessly lost. And judging from the way his expression swiftly morphed into that of unadulterated rage, I wasn't sure he'd wanted to be found at all—much less saved.

"Fuck," Alessandra swore under her breath at my side.

Fuck was right. I was sure if eyes could spit fire, Alex's would have charred me alive already.

And then they did. Either I was going completely mad or his irises had turned a bright golden yellow color as they glowered wildly at me.

Alessandra whisper-swore again as every single pair of eyes in the room seemed to fixate upon me in marked disbelief.

Alex's lips pulled back into a snarl, and a deep, unearthly growl vibrated up from his chest and ricocheted off the walls.

"No," he ground out in a low, deathly grim rumble that sounded more animal than human. "Not mine!"

I hadn't a clue what he'd meant by that proclamation, but I was pretty sure any small chance I'd had of surviving the night had just evaporated.

"This ... can't be happening," Alessandra stammered cryptically. "You're ... human ... you're Raul's sister ... "

"Fuck me sideways!" I heard Alcaeus's voice buoyantly exclaim. "No wonder she smells so good and I feel so protective."

My eyes darted to where Alcaeus stood a few feet from Alex. He was grinning from ear to ear like a man who'd just won the lottery. Earlier he'd wanted to save me from Alex. And now, right as I was about to be murdered in cold blood, he looked ready to celebrate.

"Well, isn't this just a juicy slice of poetic justice?" He chuckled, slapping a thoroughly unamused Alex on the back.

"Alex, please meet Raul's little sister and my new best friend, Milena," Alcaeus introduced with a flourish.

"She's injured," he added happily to the otherwise silent, tension-saturated room. "Head trauma," he informed the incensed-looking Alex with glee. "You might want to get right on that, in fact, because Remy and I weren't able to get her to cooperate long enough to heal it."

"Alcaeus, please stop?" Remy's distressed voice implored. He was standing on the other side of the room. He didn't seem to find the situation as funny as Alcaeus did. "This is not the time to antagonize him. Think of Milena."

My eyes darted back and forth across the room from Remy to Alcaeus to Alex. Remy was right. Whatever Alcaeus was doing seemed to be exacerbating the situation and escalating Alex's level of ire. His face was flushed and he'd begun growling at the mention of Remy and Alcaeus's failed attempt to heal my head injury. But Alcaeus waved off Remy's warning.

"I mean, sure," Alcaeus broadcast to the room as he absorbed Alex's every strained reaction with relish, "she enjoyed me licking her inner thighs all right, and she most definitely enjoyed Remy kissing her," he said with a mischievous wink in Remy's direction, "but in general she doesn't much care for warlocks creeping around inside her head. Isn't that right, my dear?" He looked to me for confirmation.

I shook my head in bewilderment. Alessandra was now swearing like a sailor next to me. Alex hadn't ceased growling; his unearthly yellow eyes raked over me as he fisted his hair and his whole body shook with barely suppressed fury—the personification of a geyser ready to blow.

"Alex, please?" Remy beseeched, "I beg you, please don't hurt her. None of this is her fault. Take your anger out on me."

Alcaeus snorted. "He's not going to hurt her. He might be a stubborn, bitter asshole, but he's never been stupid."

I didn't know what the deuce was happening or what they were talking about. All I knew was that Alex had begun cursing a blue streak and yanking at his tie until he'd torn it to shreds in frustration from his neck. He'd just managed to shrug out of his fancy tuxedo jacket when suddenly with an angry roar he burst from his own skin before my very eyes!

Buttons went flying and expensive-looking fabric was torn to shreds as an enormous, viciously snarling black and grey wolf took the place of the enraged man faster than I could blink.

Werewolf!

Almost all the other occupants in the room parted and backed away, bowing their heads in deference to the beast and affording him greater space as with hackles raised he took his first horrifying step forward in my direction.

My mouth fell open and I instinctively took a miniscule step backward. Alessandra's hand shot out and captured my wrist.

"No! Don't move," she warned.

The beast increased his growling and snarling the moment she grabbed me, prompting Alessandra to swear and release my wrist.

"Don't make any sudden movement," she cautioned, speaking slowly and clearly, her voice never rising above a whisper as she began to sidestep away from me.

"And no matter what, do … not … run," she stressed. "When he comes at you, don't panic, okay? Please, *please,* listen to me, Milena?" she appealed. "Alex won't hurt you; just let him scent you."

She didn't want me to run from him? *Wouldn't hurt me?*

He'd just announced to the whole room that I was dead meat next!

Not only had he freely claimed credit for the murder of the only family member I had left, but I'd just witnessed him crush a man's throat with his bare hand after heartlessly denying Felix's dying request to spare his son's life.

What's more, now that the room had cleared, I noted that Felix's compadres seemed to have suffered even worse fates, as their bodies lay lifeless on the marble floor, their chests torn open and their un-beating, bloody hearts strewn thoughtlessly beside them.

And now, when Alex was snarling at me in his true monster nature form—that of a vicious, oversized, supernatural killer dog—Alessandra expected I wouldn't run? If she thought I was going to stick around and let some cross between Cujo and Hannibal Lecter get close enough to sniff and lick my hand, she was out of her goddamned mind.

I didn't run. I pivoted on my heel and flew!

ABOUT THE AUTHOR

Hettie Ivers is an accidental romance author who likes to escape the stress of her workweek with a good dirty book—preferably one that's also funny. Her current career does not allow much time for creative smut writing, but she loves to write after hours and on weekends and strives to publish one to two books per year, as life permits.

To learn more about Hettie and the books she has written, please feel free to visit her website at www.hettieivers.com, sign up for her Newsletter, friend her on Facebook, or join her Facebook Group to keep in touch.

Please feel free to follow/connect with Hettie via any of these platforms as well:

Website: www.hettieivers.com

Amazon: www.amazon.com/author/hettieivers

Goodreads: www.goodreads.com/author/show/15044336. Hettie_Ivers

BookBub: www.bookbub.com/authors/hettie-ivers

Facebook Page: www.facebook.com/hettieivers

Facebook Group: bit.ly/HettieIversReaders

Instagram: www.instagram.com/hettieivers

Twitter: www.twitter.com/hettie_ivers

OTHER BOOKS

34249116R00217

Made in the USA
San Bernardino, CA
02 May 2019